Book Level ___

AR Points ___ 9b1

LEOPARDSTAR'S
HONOR

SUPER EDITIONS

WARRIORS
SUPER EDITION

LEOPARDSTAR'S HONOR

ERIN HUNTER

HARPER
An Imprint of HarperCollinsPublishers

Library of Congress Cataloging-in-Publication Data

Names: Hunter, Erin, author.
Title: Leopardstar's honor / Erin Hunter.
Description: First edition. | New York : Harper, an imprint of
   HarperCollins Publishers, [2021] | Series: Warriors super edition
   ; [14] | Audience: Ages 8-12. | Audience: Grades 4-6. | Summary:
   Leopardstar knows her destiny is to save RiverClan from destruction,
   so as the rise of ThunderClan deputy Tigerstar shatters peace among
   the clans, Leopardstar must decide what kind of leader she will be.
Identifiers: LCCN 2021024291 | ISBN 978-0-06-296306-2
   (hardcover) | ISBN 978-0-06-296307-9 (library binding)
Subjects: CYAC: Cats—Fiction. | Adventure and adventurers—Fiction.
   | Fantasy.
Classification: LCC PZ7.H916625 Lg 2021 | DDC [Fic]—dc23
LC record available at https://lccn.loc.gov/2021024291

21 22 23 24 25   PC/LSCH   10 9 8 7 6 5 4 3 2 1
❖
First Edition

Special thanks to Kate Cary

ALLEGIANCES

RIVERCLAN

LEADER   HAILSTAR—thick-pelted gray tom

DEPUTY   SHELLHEART—dappled gray tom

MEDICINE CAT   BRAMBLEBERRY—pretty white she-cat with black-spotted fur, blue eyes, and a strikingly pink nose

WARRIORS   (toms, and she-cats without kits)

RIPPLECLAW—black-and-silver tabby tom

TIMBERFUR—brown tom

MUDFUR—long-haired light brown tom

OWLFUR—brown-and-white tom

CEDARPELT—brown tabby tom, stout and short-tailed

LILYSTEM—gray she-cat

PIKETOOTH—skinny brown tabby tom with a narrow face and protruding canine teeth

SOFTWING—small, lithe, white she-cat with tabby patches

RAINFLOWER—pale gray she-cat

FALLOWTAIL—light brown she-cat with blue eyes and soft fur

CROOKEDJAW—huge light-colored tabby with a twisted jaw

OAKHEART—reddish-brown tom with amber eyes

GRAYPOOL—dark gray she-cat with yellow eyes

BEETLENOSE—tom with crow-black fur

WILLOWBREEZE—pale gray tabby she-cat with amber eyes

VOLECLAW—gray tom

PETALDUST—tortoiseshell she-cat

WHITEFANG—white tom with brown paws

ECHOMIST—long-haired gray she-cat, fur tipped with white to give her a soft, cloudy appearance

MUDTHORN—brown tom with black ears

GRASSWHISKER—brown tabby she-cat

QUEENS   (she-cats expecting or nursing kits)

OTTERSPLASH—white-and-pale-ginger she-cat (mother to Sedgekit, a brown tabby she-kit, Loudkit, a dark brown tom, and Reedkit, a pale gray tabby tom)

LAKESHINE—pretty, long-haired, gray-and-white she-cat (mother to Sunkit, a pale gray she-kit, and Frogkit, a dark gray tom)

SHIMMERPELT—night-black she-cat with glossy pelt (mother to Skykit, a pale brown tabby she-kit, and Blackkit, a black tom; fostering Leopardkit, an unusually spotted golden tabby she-kit)

ELDERS   (former warriors and queens, now retired)

TROUTCLAW—gray tabby tom

TANGLEWHISKER—long-haired tabby tom with a thick, knotted pelt

BIRDSONG—tabby-and-white she-cat with ginger patches around her muzzle, flecked with gray

THUNDERCLAN

LEADER   PINESTAR—red-brown tom with green eyes

DEPUTY   SUNFALL—bright ginger tom with yellow eyes

MEDICINE CAT   GOOSEFEATHER—speckled gray tom with pale blue eyes
APPRENTICE, FEATHERWHISKER

WARRIORS   MOUSEFUR—small brown she-cat

PATCHPELT—small black and white tom

RUNNINGWIND—light brown tabby tom

WHITESTORM—white tom

WILLOWPELT—silver she-cat

STORMTAIL—blue-gray tom with blue eyes

ADDERFANG—mottled brown tabby tom with yellow eyes
APPRENTICE, THISTLEPAW

TAWNYSPOTS—light gray tabby tom with amber eyes
APPRENTICE, ROSEPAW

SPARROWPELT—big, dark brown tabby tom with yellow eyes

SMALLEAR—gray tom with very small ears and amber eyes
APPRENTICE, SWEETPAW

WHITE-EYE—pale gray she-cat

THRUSHPELT—sandy-gray tom with white flash on his chest and green eyes

PATCHPELT—small black-and-white tom with amber eyes

BLUEFUR—thick-furred blue-gray she-cat with blue eyes

FUZZYPELT—black tom with fur that stands on end and yellow eyes

WINDFLIGHT—gray tabby tom with pale green eyes

DAPPLETAIL— tortoiseshell-and-white she-cat with amber eyes
APPRENTICE, GOLDENPAW

SPECKLETAIL—pale tabby she-cat with amber eyes

SWIFTBREEZE—tabby-and-white she-cat with yellow eyes
APPRENTICE, LIONPAW

POPPYDAWN—long-haired, dark red she-cat with a bushy tail and amber eyes

QUEENS

LEOPARDFOOT—black she-cat with green eyes (mother to Nightkit, a black she-cat; Mistkit, a gray she-cat; and Tigerkit, a dark brown tabby tom)

SNOWFUR—white she-cat with blue eyes (mother to Whitekit, a white tom)

ROBINWING—small, brown she-cat with a ginger patch on her chest and amber eyes (mother to Brindlekit, a pale gray tabby she-kit, and Frostkit, a white she-kit with blue eyes)

ELDERS

WEEDWHISKER—pale orange tom with yellow eyes

MUMBLEFOOT—brown tom, slightly clumsy, with amber eyes

LARKSONG—tortoiseshell she-cat with pale green eyes

STONEPELT—gray tom

SHADOWCLAN

LEADER **CEDARSTAR**—very dark gray tom with a white belly

DEPUTY **RAGGEDPELT**—large dark brown tabby tom

MEDICINE CAT **SAGEWHISKER**—white she-cat with long whiskers

    APPRENTICE, YELLOWFANG

WARRIORS **FOXHEART**—bright ginger she-cat

    CROWTAIL—black tabby she-cat

    DEERLEAP—gray tabby she-cat with white legs

    WOLFSTEP—tom with a torn ear

    MUDCLAW—gray tom with brown legs

    LIZARDSTRIPE—pale brown tabby she-cat with yellow eyes

    TOADSKIP—dark brown tabby tom with white splashes and white legs

    SCORCHWIND—ginger tabby tom

    AMBERLEAF—dark ginger she-cat with brown legs and ears

    FINCHFLIGHT—black-and-white tom

    NUTWHISKER—brown tom with amber eyes

    ROWANBERRY—cream-and-brown she-cat with amber eyes

    NEWTSPECK—black-and-ginger tabby she-cat

    ASHHEART—pale gray she-cat with blue eyes

    FROGTAIL—dark gray tom

    MOUSEWING—black tom with long, thick fur

    BOULDER—skinny gray tom

BRACKENFOOT—pale ginger tom with dark ginger legs

ARCHEYE—gray tabby tom with black stripes and thick stripe over eye

HOLLYFLOWER—dark-gray-and-white she-cat

FEATHERSTORM—brown tabby she-cat

POOLCLOUD—gray-and-white she-cat

QUEENS

NETTLESPOT—white she-cat with ginger flecks (mother to Cloudkit, a white tom)

ELDERS

LITTLEBIRD—small ginger tabby she-cat

LIZARDFANG—light brown tabby tom with one hooked tooth

STONETOOTH—gray tabby tom with long teeth

WINDCLAN

LEADER

HEATHERSTAR—pinkish-gray she-cat with blue eyes

DEPUTY

REEDFEATHER—light brown tabby tom

MEDICINE CAT

HAWKHEART—dark brown tom with yellow eyes

APPRENTICE, BARKFACE

WARRIORS

DAWNSTRIPE—pale gold tabby with creamy stripes

TALLTAIL—large black-and-white tom with amber eyes

APPRENTICE, DEADPAW

REDCLAW—dark ginger tom

SHREWCLAW— dark brown tom with yellow eyes

WOOLYTAIL—gray-and-white tom with bright yellow eyes

STAGLEAP—dark brown tom with amber eyes
APPRENTICE, SORRELPAW

HICKORYNOSE—brown tom
APPRENTICE, FLYPAW

APPLEDAWN—pale cream she-cat

MEADOWSLIP—gray she-cat

MISTMOUSE—light brown tabby she-cat
APPRENTICE, BRISTLEPAW

HAREFLIGHT—light brown tom
APPRENTICE, WRENPAW

DOESPRING—light brown she-cat
APPRENTICE, PIGEONPAW

LARKSPLASH—tortoiseshell-and-white she-cat

ASPENFALL—gray-and-white tom

PLUMCLAW—dark gray she-cat
APPRENTICE, RABBITPAW

PALEBIRD—black-and-white she-cat

RYESTALK—gray tabby she-cat

ELDERS

WHITEBERRY—small pure-white tom

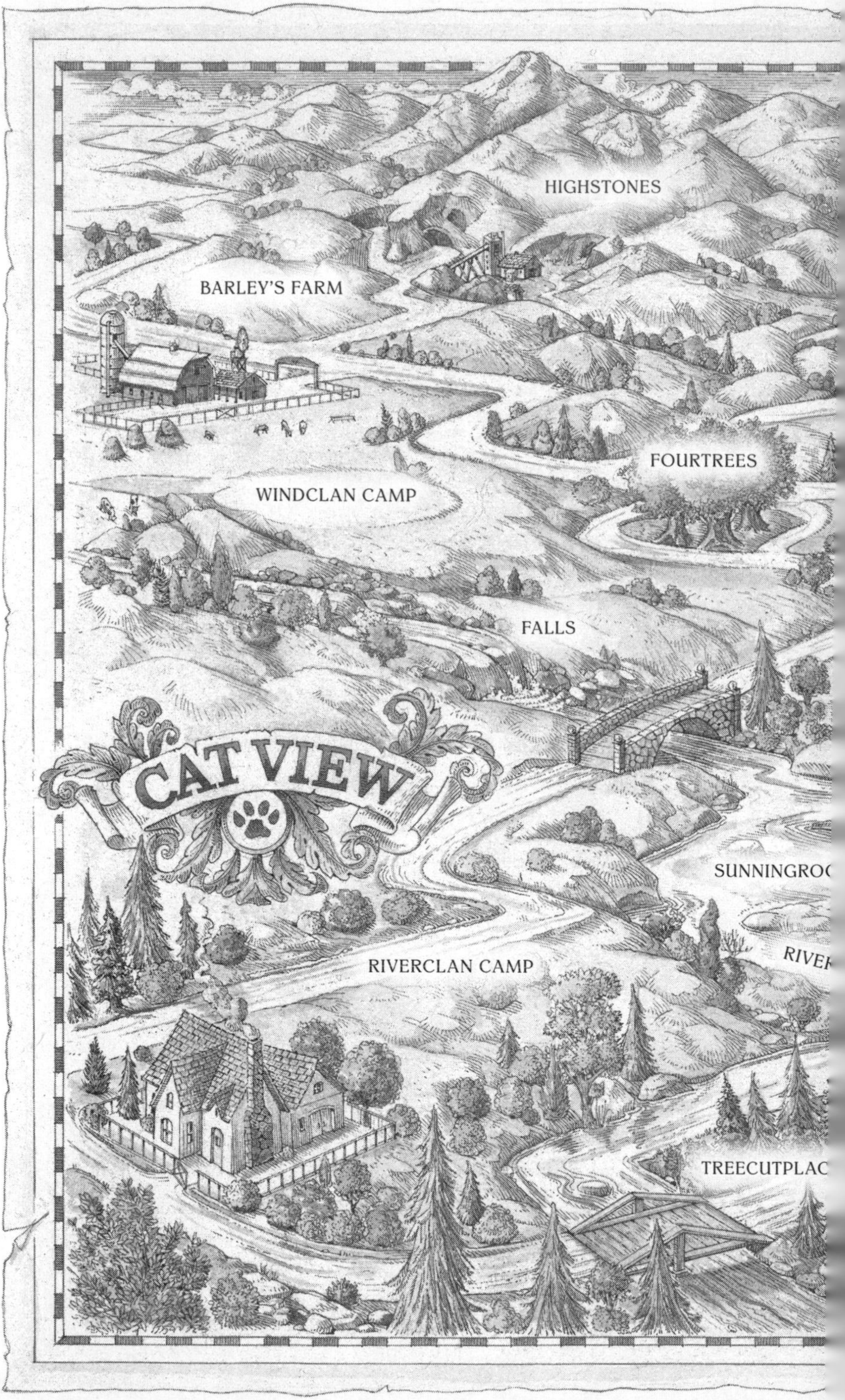

CAT VIEW

HIGHSTONES

BARLEY'S FARM

FOURTREES

WINDCLAN CAMP

FALLS

SUNNINGROC

RIVER

RIVERCLAN CAMP

TREECUTPLAC

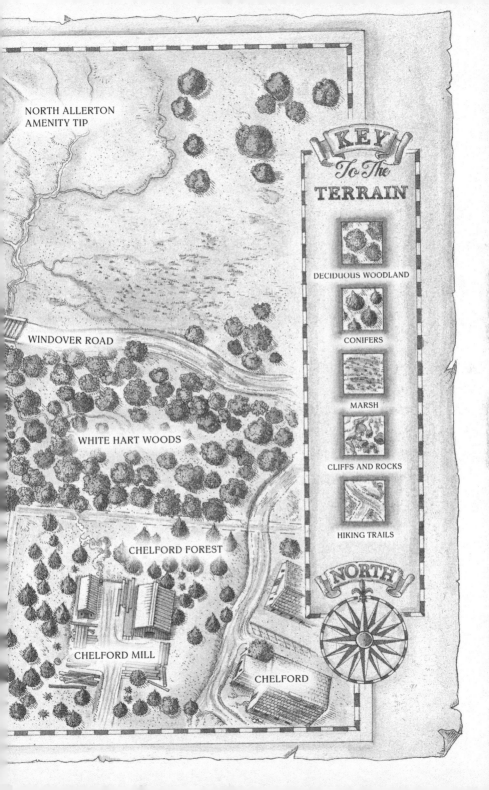

PROLOGUE

❧

The Bonehill glowed beneath the moon. The heaped carcasses, stripped of flesh, reflected its clean, white light. For them, the worst was over now. Leopardstar pressed back a shiver; the leaf-bare chill reminded her of her own bones jutting beneath her pelt. It felt like it had been a long time since the prey-rich moons of greenleaf.

She dared not lift her gaze to Silverpelt. Nor did she risk catching any of her Clanmates' eyes. They had no choice but to watch. RiverClan was part of TigerClan now, and outnumbered in this clearing by former ShadowClan cats. Leopardstar had made a deal with the fierce tom. They must follow Tigerstar's rules.

Stonefur stood in front of the dark warrior while Featherpaw and Stormpaw huddled behind him, their eyes wide with fear. The apprentices had been imprisoned by Tigerstar for being the kits of a ThunderClan tom and a RiverClan queen. As Stonefur flattened his ears against his head, Tigerstar narrowed his eyes to slits.

"I will give you a chance to show your loyalty to Tiger-Clan," the dark warrior told him. "Kill these two half-Clan apprentices."

Leopardstar's blood ran cold. Surely, Tigerstar only meant to banish them! How could he order a warrior to kill his own Clanmates? And they were so young! It made no sense. Stonefur was half-Clan too. Leopardstar felt dread rising in her chest and throat like hot, scalding bile. Was this really what StarClan wanted? Was this the only way for the Clans to become strong?

Stonefur was battered and starved from his confinement, but as he turned his gaze to Leoparstar, his eyes seemed to bore right through her. "I take orders from *you*," he growled darkly. "You must know this is wrong. What do you want me to do?"

For a moment, Leopardstar could only stare at her deputy. *What do you want me to do?* What could she say? She risked a glance at Tigerstar, and was chilled by the hatred in his eyes. Not only for Stonefur, but for her. *If I say no,* she wondered, *how much longer will I be alive to protect my Clan?*

"These are difficult times," she replied finally, struggling to keep her voice steady. *What would Tigerstar say?* She felt sick. "As we fight for survival we must be able to count on every one of our Clanmates. There is no room for divided loyalties. Do as Tigerstar tells you." *StarClan, forgive me.*

Stonefur held her gaze for a moment, and she could see that something had changed inside him. Whereas he had turned to her with hope, he now looked deeply disappointed. He took in a deep breath and turned to face the apprentices, who cowered in fear.

After what seemed like an eternity, Stormfur gave a tiny nod at the apprentices and turned back to look at the TigerClan leader. "You'll have to kill me first, Tigerstar."

Leopardstar clenched her teeth to keep from wailing in despair. *Stonefur . . . don't do this!*

Tigerstar glared at the blue-gray tom, his tail twitching with menace. He signaled to his accomplice Darkstripe. "Kill him."

Leopardstar's breath caught in her throat. She had to stop this. But she hesitated. If she did, she would seem weak. They'd be back where they'd started, at the mercy of the river and the forest and the other Clans. She had no choice but to follow through. And yet the words ached to be spoken. *Stop! Stop this now!* She pressed them back. She could not back down.

She tried not to flinch, horror shrilling though every hair on her pelt, as Darkstripe leaped at Stonefur. Though battered and exhausted, Stonefur managed to haul his attacker to the ground and dig his claws into the warrior's throat. Pride seemed to move deep inside her as she watched her deputy fight fiercely against the cruel tabby.

Kill him! Leopardstar found herself willing Stonefur on. Then she froze. She couldn't think like that! This *had* to happen. The half-Clan cats must die. Once this was over, Tigerstar's vision for a single Clan that united all the warriors of the forest could prevail. It was the only way RiverClan could survive the floods and fires that had battered them like whirling claws, over and over again, keeping them hungry in leaf-bare, and the Twoleg incursions that made them vulnerable every greenleaf. This was the only way forward. It was the choice she had made when she'd agreed RiverClan and ShadowClan should join together to become TigerClan.

Every instinct within her was trying to pull her gaze away from the fight, but she told herself that the least she owed her deputy was to watch the sacrifice he was making, for the good of RiverClan.

"Finish it." Tigerstar flicked his ears at Blackfoot, and his deputy shot forward and dragged Stonefur off Darkstripe. Together the vicious warriors turned on the RiverClan deputy, and as Darkstripe held him down, Blackfoot scored his claws across Stonefur's throat.

Stonefur struggled, then fell still, his blood staining the ground.

Around the clearing, Tigerstar's warriors yowled jubilantly. Leopardstar's Clanmates eyed each other fearfully before joining in, their calls barely audible at first, but soon rising to match the others. Only Featherpaw and Stormpaw remained silent. Leopardstar was aware of Featherpaw's horrified gaze lifting from Stonefur's body and fixing on her like a judgment. She could not meet it, but looked across the clearing at the heavy bulrushes swaying darkly beneath the moon.

She hardly heard Tigerstar announcing that Featherpaw and Stormpaw would not die today but would return to their prison, and she stood stiff and silent as TigerClan melted away, heading back to the camp. Only when the clearing had emptied did her numbness begin to ease. In its place, doubt crawled beneath her pelt. The scent of Stonefur's blood flooded her mouth, bathing her tongue with its sour tang. She padded reluctantly forward and stopped beside his body.

Mudfur had asked her whether joining TigerClan was the right thing to do. There had always been four Clans in the forest. Why should that change? She'd told him they needed to be stronger—to be the *strongest*—and he'd shaken his head in disappointment. *There are things more important than being strong.* His words rang in her head as she leaned down and touched her nose to Stonefur's cold and matted pelt.

How did I get here? She hadn't always been this heartless. Even a few moons ago, she would have defended Stonefur with her life. The thought pricked her heart like a thorn. Every choice she'd made in her life had brought her closer to this moment. Had she led RiverClan along the wrong path?

Leopardstar lifted her head. She couldn't lose her nerve now. Mudfur was old; he'd been a warrior under Crookedstar, and then a medicine cat. He'd been born in a different time, when all RiverClan had to do was dip a paw into the river to scoop out a fish. He didn't understand that the forest had changed, that life was harder—that there were now only difficult choices to be made.

Leopardstar squared her shoulders against the cold as clouds began to trail across Silverpelt. TigerClan would make her warriors strong. They would never again have to give up territory. They would never again go to their nests with empty bellies. Other cats would fear them. If her Clanmates couldn't be strong enough to face the future she had planned, she would have to be strong *for* them. It was the only way to keep them safe.

CHAPTER 1

❧

Leopardkit jumped to her paws. "Let's play hide-and-seek!"

She looked around eagerly at her denmates. They'd been lying around for ages. Frogkit, Sunkit, and Loudkit had been drowsing in the bright greenleaf sunshine after sharing a trout that Graypool had fished from the river. Blackkit, Skykit, and Reedkit had been giving their faces and paws a thorough wash. Leopardkit had gotten so bored that she'd wondered whether to try hunting the large, lazy dragonfly humming among the reeds behind them. But a game would be more fun. Her pelt tingled excitedly as the others scrambled to their paws.

Sedgekit swished her long tabby tail. "I'll be hunter!" She dropped onto the ground and pressed her paws over her muzzle. "Every cat hide!"

"Keep your eyes closed, Sedgekit!" Leopardkit told her. "You're not allowed to look until we've all hidden."

"If I've got my eyes closed, how will I know when you've all hidden?" Sedgekit's mew was muffled.

Shimmerpelt was weaving willow stems among the reeds to strengthen the den wall. "I'll tell you!" she called.

Leopardkit whisked her tail, happy that her foster mother was watching. "Make sure she doesn't peek," she told Shimmerpelt.

Shimmerpelt nodded gravely. "Of course."

"And give me time to hide properly."

"That's cheating!" Skykit sniffed. "She's not allowed to help you."

Leopardkit puffed out her chest. "It's not helping," she mewed. "It's just making sure Sedgekit sticks to the rules."

Loudkit looked indignant. "Sedgekit *always* sticks to the rules."

"She doesn't even cheat at moss-ball," Reedkit chimed in. "Take that back, Leopardkit!"

Leopardkit looked at them. The three kits always defended each other. It must be because they were littermates and not just nestmates. She wondered if Skykit and Blackkit would stick up for her like that if Shimmerpelt were her *real* mother.

"Hurry *up*!" Frogkit plucked impatiently at the hot, sandy earth.

Sunkit flicked her tail at him. "Leopardkit's just making sure it's fair."

"Leopardkit talks too much," Frogkit complained.

"She can talk as much as she likes," Sunkit snipped back.

Leopardkit blinked at her friend gratefully. *Sunkit* stuck up for her, even though they weren't littermates *or* nestmates. Maybe some cats were just kinder than others.

She turned away from Skykit. "Let's go!"

Charging away, she sped across the clearing. Her paws

burned with the effort. The other kits were older and bigger; if she didn't try her best, they'd outrun her, and she wanted to make sure she found a good hiding place before they stole them all.

Piketooth looked up at her from the mallow leaves he was helping Brambleberry spread in the sunshine to dry. "You're faster than a fish!" he purred as she streaked past.

Leopardkit glanced over her shoulder. Frogkit and Sunkit were pushing their way into the sedge next to the elders' den. Blackkit had scrambled into the willow tree that overlooked the warriors' den. Loudkit and Reedkit were heading for the shadows between its roots. Skykit had stopped in the middle of the sunny clearing and was looking around, clearly scanning the camp for a place to hide.

"Over here." Ottersplash's hushed mew made Leopardkit turn. The white-and-ginger she-cat was Sedgekit, Loudkit, and Reedkit's mother, and she was outside the nursery with Lakeshine. The queens had been sharing tongues while their kits played, but Ottersplash was leaning forward now, beckoning Leopardkit toward her with a nod. Leopardkit hurried over. "Hide behind us," Ottersplash whispered.

Lakeshine shifted to let Leopardkit slide between them. "We'll pretend we haven't seen you."

Leopardkit ducked down behind the two queens as they pressed together, blocking Leopardkit from view.

Shimmerpelt's mew rang out over the clearing. "The prey is hidden!" she called to Sedgekit.

Leopardkit quivered with anticipation. Would Sedgekit find her?

"Be as quiet as you can," Ottersplash warned Leopardkit in a whisper. "Sedgekit is a good hunter."

"I'm good *prey*," Leopardkit mewed back.

Lakeshine's pelt twitched. "Sedgekit's coming this way."

Leopardkit held her breath, fighting the urge to peek out.

Sedgekit's mew sounded in front of the queens. "Have you seen Leopardkit?"

Ottersplash flicked her muzzle toward the medicine den. "Have you looked over there?"

"She's probably hiding behind the apprentices' den," Lakeshine added. The queen's fur tickled Leopardkit's nose, and she held back a sneeze and pressed her belly harder against the earth. The hot greenleaf sun warmed her golden dappled pelt, and her ears were so hot she had to force them not to twitch as Sedgekit's paw steps pattered back and forth in front of the queens.

"Are you sure you haven't seen her?" Sedgekit sounded unconvinced. Leopardkit could picture her denmate tasting the air suspiciously and wished now she'd cleaned the fishy smell of the carp from her whiskers like the others.

"We're sure." Lakeshine's pelt brushed Leopardkit's nose once more.

This time it tickled until Leopardkit could not hold back the sneeze.

Sedgekit darted around Lakeshine, and her pelt fluffed as she spotted Leopardkit. "You lied!" As her denmate glared indignantly at Lakeshine, Leopardkit saw a chance to escape.

She pelted across the clearing, looking back over her shoulder to see if Sedgekit was following. "It doesn't count unless you catch—" She crashed into a wall of thick fur, lost her footing, and tumbled between four hefty paws. A pale brown belly blocked the sky, and she rolled out from beneath it and scrambled to her paws. "Sorry, Crookedjaw!"

The huge warrior blinked at her warmly. "Are you okay?"

But Leopardkit was looking back at the nursery. Sedgekit was charging toward her. "If she catches me, I'll lose!" she gasped.

Crookedjaw seemed to understand. He grabbed her scruff between his teeth and swung her up onto his shoulders. "Hang on," he told her, his deep mew reverberating through his pelt. Leopardkit dug her claws into his thick fur and clung on as Crookedjaw bounded away.

Sedgekit chased after him. "Hey!" she squealed crossly. "That's cheating!"

Leopardkit lifted her muzzle from Crookedjaw's thick ruff and glimpsed Skykit crouching beside the wall of the apprentices' den. Her brown tabby pelt was hardly visible in the shadow, but Leopardkit could see her green eyes flashing.

"Skykit!" She called her name as loudly as she could, so that Sedgekit could hear. "I can see you!" She pointed her muzzle toward the apprentices' den, relief swamping her as Sedgekit pricked her ears and veered away toward Skykit's hiding place.

"That's not fair!" Leopardkit could hear Skykit's outraged mew as Crookedjaw carried her away. She'd escaped! She felt a rush of joy, but then Crookedjaw pulled up suddenly, and she had to dig her claws deeper into his fur as he scrambled to a halt at the camp entrance.

"Don't stop!" she wailed. What if Sedgekit came after her again?

But Crookedjaw was already nodding a greeting to the afternoon hunting patrol as it filed back into camp. Leopardkit's heart leaped as she saw her father heading it. Mudfur held a shiny silver carp in his jaws. Behind him Oakheart, Beetlenose, and Echomist were carrying river prey too.

Mudfur dropped the carp and nodded toward Leopardkit, his eyes shining. "That's a pretty big tick on your shoulder," he told Crookedjaw.

"I'm not a tick!" She slithered from Crookedjaw's back. "It's me! Leopardkit!" She wove around him and ducked through the cool shadow beneath his belly.

He purred as she emerged into the sunshine once more. "What have you been doing?" he asked her.

"Playing hide-and-seek." She nodded toward the apprentices' den, where Sedgekit was nosing Skykit triumphantly from the shadows.

Skykit shot Leopardkit an angry look.

"Come on, Skykit." Sedgekit whisked her tail. "Help me find the others." She steered Skykit toward the warriors' den.

"Did you get caught?" Mudfur asked Leopardkit.

"Crookedjaw helped me get away," Leopardkit puffed out her chest. "Thanks, Crookedjaw."

"You shouldn't indulge her," Mudfur told him. "She needs to stand on her own four paws."

Echomist purred. "You're a fine one to talk, Mudfur." She nudged his catch with her paw. "We'd have been back before sunhigh if you hadn't insisted on bringing a carp home for Leopardkit."

Leopardkit nuzzled Mudfur's shoulder. "That's my favorite," she purred. "Thanks."

As Mudfur nuzzled her back, Sedgekit called across the clearing. "Come on, Leopardkit!" She was beside the warriors' den, her tail high as Blackkit slithered down the willow tree and Loudkit and Reedkit squeezed out from among the roots. "I've found every cat! Blackkit's going to be hunter this time."

Mudfur whisked Leopardkit forward with his tail. "Go and play," he mewed.

"Okay." She blinked at him, happy he was back in camp. "But make sure no one takes *my* carp from the fresh-kill pile while I'm playing!"

As Leopardkit turned away, she heard Echomist's affectionate mew: "You spoil that kit, Mudfur."

"It doesn't seem to do her any harm," Mudfur purred back.

Leopardkit reached her denmates. She looked between them, searching their faces for any signs that they were annoyed at her for winning, or for giving away Skykit's position. "No cat can use the same hiding place again, right?"

"Yeah." Skykit purred, as if excited to play again. Leopardkit was relieved to see that the brown tabby she-kit did not seem angry with her. "You ready, Blackkit?"

Blackkit dropped into a crouch and covered his muzzle with his paws.

Sunkit and Frogkit darted away, heading toward the elders' den. Loudkit followed Sedgekit and Reedkit as they raced for the thick sedge growing at the far end of the clearing. Leopard-kit glanced around, wondering where to hide. Would Hailstar mind if she hid in his den? Maybe Brambleberry would let her hide in the herb store.

"Come with me," Skykit whispered. "I know a great place."

"Okay." Leopardkit's heart quickened. She raced after her nestmate to the reeds edging the camp. The ground was marshy here, and soon she was splashing through shallow water, mud between her claws, as Skykit pushed her way deeper and deeper into the reed bed. She began to slow. Mudfur would be mad at her if he knew she was playing this close to the river, when she'd only just learned to swim. "Wait—"

Skykit turned as she called out and waded back toward her.

Leopardkit saw a flash of annoyance in her nestmate's eyes. "We shouldn't go so close to the riv—"

Before she could finish, Skykit grabbed her scruff with her forepaws and pushed her head under.

Water rushed up her nose and into her mouth. Panic pulsed beneath Leopardkit's pelt. She thrashed her paws in the water, trying to struggle free from Skykit's grip. But Skykit was two moons older and stronger, and she suddenly realized she was helpless. Flailing desperately, she fought the instinctive urge to breathe, as her pounding heart tried to claw its way out of her chest.

Then Skykit let go.

Leopardkit pushed up with her paws and burst dripping from the water. She shook her head and then her body, spraying water among the reeds. She coughed, regaining her breath, and then glared at Skykit. "What was *that*?" She could hardly believe Skykit could be so nasty.

Skykit glared at her. "That's for telling Sedgekit where I was hiding!"

"I only told her because she was chasing me!" Leopardkit bristled. "You didn't have to try to *drown* me!" Water was still running from her nose and whiskers.

"Don't be so dramatic," Skykit snapped. "Stop thinking you're so special, just because every cat makes a fuss over you. You still act like a newborn kit! That's why Blackkit and I don't like playing with you. We only do it because Shimmerpelt makes us."

Hurt pierced Leopardkit's heart. *Don't like playing with me? They only played with her because they* had *to?* She bristled. It wasn't fair. She'd thought they were friends. "I'm going to tell Shimmerpelt what you did," she murmured, keeping her jaws almost closed, to make sure she didn't wail like a newborn. "Then you'll be in real trouble . . . and it'll serve you right!"

Skykit sniffed. "Go on, Leopardkit," she mewed. "Run away and tattle. That's what newborn kits always do."

Leopardkit could hardly believe her ears. Why was Skykit being so spiteful? Her heart pounded in her chest.

Skykit hadn't finished. "You only get special treatment because Brightsky died," she mewed. "If you hadn't killed your own mother, the rest of the Clan wouldn't even bother with you."

"I didn't kill my mother," she hissed back, feeling her claws stretching out.

"That's not what I heard around camp." Skykit's green eyes twinkled with a malicious glee. "I heard your mother was sick when you were born. What could have made her sick? Probably a rotten kit, that's what!"

"Don't say that!" Leopardkit wanted to shut Skykit up and hurt her back. She lashed out, swinging her paw at the brown tabby's muzzle, but Skykit blocked it with her own paw and cuffed Leopardkit around the ear. Leopardkit staggered under the weight of the blow.

"You're going to end up in the Dark Forest," Skykit snarled, "with all the other murderers."

Leopardkit stared at her, the water around her paws suddenly feeling like ice. It seemed to drag her down until she had to struggle to stay standing. Skykit pushed past her and splashed away between the reeds. Leopardkit opened her mouth to call after her, to ask if Skykit had really heard cats say such terrible things. But the words didn't come.

She was afraid of what Skykit would say.

As the sun shone over the camp the next morning, Leopardkit still felt the sting of Skykit's words. They hadn't spoken since, and last night in their nest, Leopardkit had wriggled into the warm space behind Shimmerpelt, as far away from Skykit and Blackkit as she could get. She'd enjoyed sleeping without their annoying paws poking her flank, or their stupid tails flicking her ears. She didn't want to be anywhere near them now that she knew how they really felt about her.

Crouching in the shadow of the sedge that ringed the camp,

Leopardkit watched them playing moss-ball with Loudkit, Sunkit, and Reedkit while Frogkit chased Sedgekit around the warriors' den.

"Come and play!" Sunkit called to her as she sent the moss ball high into the air and Loudkit and Blackkit leaped to see who could catch it first.

Leopardkit tucked her paws tighter beneath her. There was no way she was going to join in and spoil their fun. She glanced at Skykit. Her nestmate was looking at her, but as Leopardkit caught her eye, she quickly looked away. Was that guilt in her gaze? *I hope so,* Leopardkit huffed.

"Come on." Sunkit was bounding toward her. "Join in! You must be bored sitting there by yourself."

"I'm too tired to play," Leopardkit told her. She didn't want to confide in Sunkit her real reason for not playing. She didn't want to repeat Skykit's words. *You're going to end up in the Dark Forest with all the other murderers.* Her pelt felt hot just remembering them.

Sunkit stopped in front of her and frowned. "Are you sure?" she asked.

"I'm sure." Leopardkit faked a yawn to convince Sunkit just how tired she was.

Sunkit looked at her for another moment, then flicked her tail. "Join in after you've rested," she mewed, and headed back toward the others, breaking into a run as the moss ball rolled toward her.

Leopardkit watched her go, her legs twitching like she was going to stand up and run after Sunkit—until a fresh wave of hurt pushed her back down, dragging into her mind all the thoughts that had kept her awake the night before. Was Skykit right? Had she really killed her mother, her littermates? Mudfur never really spoke of it. Was that what the rest of the Clan thought of her? Leopardkit glanced toward Shimmerpelt and Ottersplash, who were dragging the nests from the nursery to air them in the sunshine. *Do they think it's my fault that Brightsky died?* She'd been told that her mother had been sick, but no cat had ever said a queen could be made sick by her kit. That sounded impossible.

But why would Skykit say she had if it was impossible?

Her thoughts chased each other, like fish swimming around and around. *Am I bad?* The idea made her queasy. She didn't want to be bad, but what if she couldn't help it? There had to be some reason that Brightsky had died. Other kits' mothers didn't die. Only hers.

"Leopardkit?" Mudfur's mew took her by surprise. She looked up and saw him stop beside her. Worry clouded his yellow eyes. "Why are sitting by yourself? Why aren't you playing with the other kits?"

She blinked at him and got to her paws. He'd know the truth. Her ears twitched nervously. Should she ask him if she had killed Brightsky? What if he said yes?

He blinked at her anxiously. "You're upset, aren't you?"

She looked at her paws. "It was something some cat said," she mewed.

"Who?"

"It doesn't matter." There was no point blaming Skykit. If

she thought it, the rest of the Clan must believe it too.

"What did they say?" Mudfur pressed gently.

Leopardkit hesitated, her heart pounding. She needed to know. If it was true, she'd just have to accept it and try to make up for what she'd done by being the best warrior she could be, and protecting her Clanmates. She didn't want to end up in the Dark Forest.

Mudfur ran his tail gently along her spine. "Tell me."

She met his gaze. "Did I kill Brightsky?"

His eyes widened.

It made her nervous. He looked like he didn't want to have this discussion.

Because it's true?

"No, Leopardkit," he mewed, pressing his muzzle to her head. "Of course you didn't kill Brightsky." He pulled away and looked at her. "Your mother was sick . . ."

"Because of me?"

"No, little one. It was . . . just a sickness. Brambleberry couldn't help her. Your littermates died with her. None of it was your fault." His eyes began to glisten. "I'm just thankful that StarClan spared you."

"Really?" She realized that she could breathe again. She didn't know she'd stopped. She searched her father's gaze. He was telling the truth. She could see it in his round, anxious eyes.

"Have the other kits been taunting you about it?" Mudfur didn't wait for an answer. He'd clearly guessed why she'd asked him about Brightsky. "You shouldn't listen to them," he mewed. "They're probably jealous because you're special."

"Am I?" Leopardkit looked at him hopefully. "Skykit said I wasn't. She said I was just different."

"You *are* special," Mudfur mewed. "I think StarClan saved you for a reason."

A reason? Leopardkit's thoughts whirled. What could it be?

"Not long after Brightsky died," Mudfur went on, "when you were still a tiny kit, I had a dream. Brightsky told me to take good care of you because you'd be important to River-Clan one day."

"How?" Leopardkit blinked at him eagerly. She liked the idea of being important.

"She didn't say," Mudfur answered. "She just said that one day you'd be important to RiverClan. To all the Clans," he added.

"*All* the Clans?" Leopardkit's ears twitched with surprise. Being important to all the Clans sounded hard.

Mudfur's gaze had wandered, as though he was picturing his lost mate. "That dream, along with my love for you, is what gave me the strength to go on, even though I miss Brightsky so much it still hurts to remember her." He blinked away the sadness glistening in his eyes and focused on Leopardkit once more. "I think one day you'll show us all why StarClan spared you."

Leopardkit fluffed out her fur. StarClan had saved her for a reason. She couldn't wait for Skykit to see her save all the Clans. "Can I start my warrior training early?" she asked Mudfur. She had so much to learn; there wasn't a moment to waste.

"You're too small." His pelt prickled along his spine. "And

being a warrior is harder than you think. You've still got some growing up to do."

But I have to save the Clans. Leopardkit frowned. Didn't Mudfur understand? The Clans were depending on her. She curled her claws into the earth. If StarClan had saved her for a reason, then she needed to learn every battle move and hunting skill that she could. She was going to become the noblest, strongest, bravest warrior RiverClan had ever known.

CHAPTER 2

Leopardkit shook the water from her paws and shuddered. Crossing the stepping-stones had been scarier than she'd imagined— they were so far apart, and the river had swirled hungrily between them as though it were hoping she'd fall in. But this was the only way out of camp, and she didn't want to try swimming. She hurried into the reeds before anyone could see her and hoped none of the other kits would wonder where she'd gone.

She wove between the stems, keeping out of sight. Gray-pool and Willowbreeze had already followed the shore as far as the bulrushes and had taken a path away from the river. She'd overheard them planning to hunt frogs in the water meadow. If Mudfur refused to teach her any hunting skills before she became a 'paw, then she'd have to learn by herself. She wasn't ready to catch fish yet, but frog hunting would be a useful skill, and her mentor would be impressed by how much she knew when she started her training.

Graypool and Willowbreeze were following a narrow path, and Leopardkit shadowed them through the reeds until they opened onto a wide stretch of grass. She watched them cross the water meadow to a puddle that shimmered like a heat haze beneath the hot sun. They began to sniff around the edge.

Graypool dropped suddenly into a crouch, her ears pricking. Willowbreeze froze a tail-length behind. As a frog leaped into the shallow pool, Graypool lunged after it. Leopardkit blinked. She was so fast! The frog hadn't even hit the water before Graypool caught it and hooked it toward her. With a swift bite, she killed it and sat back on her haunches.

"Good catch," Willowbreeze mewed, but her gaze was already scanning the next pool.

Leopardkit leaned farther forward, her pelt tingling. She wanted to try lunging and throwing her paws out just like Graypool had, but she'd make the reeds rattle and the warriors might hear her. She'd practice later, when she was back in camp. She knew that if she tried, she could be as fast as Graypool—perhaps faster if she practiced enough.

Willowbreeze was stalking toward the next pool. Leopardkit noticed how the warrior's ears were half flattened against her head and how she kept her belly low and her tail skimming the grass. The silver tabby moved one paw at a time, placing each gently on the grass as she drew herself forward. Leopardkit tried to mimic her, moving between the reeds as slowly and silently as she could, watching Willowbreeze out of the corner of her eye as she copied every careful step.

Her attention was fixed so intently on Willowbreeze that when the rushes swished behind her, she barely noticed. Only when a familiar scent washed her tongue did her heart lurch. She jerked around as snowy fur flashed between the stems and Whitefang pushed the reeds aside with his broad shoulders.

He stared at her sternly. "What are you doing out of camp?"

She gave him an apologetic mew. "I'm sorry." She nodded toward Graypool and Willowbreeze. "I came to watch them. I thought the meadow would be safe to learn how to hunt."

Whitefang grunted. "Nowhere outside camp is safe for a kit," he murmured. "You don't even know how to stay low and keep out of sight."

"But I'm trying to learn," she mewed earnestly. "Look!" She began to copy Willowbreeze's stalking technique once more.

Whitefang watched her. "Your tail's too high." He stepped toward her. "When you're hunting, your tail should never be higher than your spine. It will give you away."

Leopardkit let her tail droop. "Is that better?"

"Now you're dragging it along the ground." Whitefang nosed the tip a little higher. "There." He stepped back. "Try again."

Leopardkit began to stalk once more, remembering to flatten her ears.

"Keep your ears from twitching," Whitefang told her. "That's right. Now crouch a little lower. Yes, that's good."

Excitement began to fizz in Leopardkit's fur. She was training, like a real 'paw.

"Let the air flow over your tongue," Whitefang added.

Leopardkit opened her mouth. The scent of wet soil and damp stems filled it. She was surprised to find they smelled mustier than the reeds around the camp. Were other smells different too? A thought popped into her mind. "Does live prey smell the same as dead prey?" she asked. She'd only smelled the dead prey that patrols brought back from hunting.

"That's a smart question." Whitefang looked impressed. "Live prey smells sweeter and more delicate, but a frog still smells like a frog and a fish smells like a fish."

"Can we look for a live frog so I can learn what it smells like?" Leopardkit looked at him hopefully.

Whitefang's gaze lit up as though he wanted to show her, and she pricked her ears, excited. Then he frowned. "Mudfur will be mad if he thinks I've been training you," he mewed. He jerked his muzzle toward the camp. "I'd better get you home."

Leopardkit dug her paws into the marshy ground. "Can't we train just a little more?"

"If Mudfur notices you're missing—"

"You could tell him I'm ready to be a 'paw," she pressed hopefully. "He'd listen to you."

"Mudfur doesn't listen to any cat when it comes to his kit," Whitefang mewed. "Come on. We should head back."

Leopardkit sighed. "Are you going to tell him I sneaked out of camp?"

Whitefang pushed the reeds apart and nodded her through the gap he'd made. "I'll have to," he told her. "You smell like meadow water."

Leopardkit padded past him. She was still determined to learn as much as she could while she was out of camp. "Does meadow water smell different from river water?"

He padded after her. "Taste the air," he mewed.

She let it stream over her tongue. It was tinged with sweetness.

As they pushed their way from the reeds and padded along the riverbank, he spoke again. "Taste it now."

She opened her mouth, surprised she hadn't noticed the difference earlier. "Meadow water tastes like grass," she mewed. "River water tastes like stone."

"Exactly," Whitefang mewed. "Of course, it changes with the weather."

"How?"

"When it rains and the river's churned up, it tastes more like mud," Whitefang mewed. "And in leaf-bare it changes again. The cold sharpens the scent of the river, and the meadow tastes of peat."

Leopardkit's pelt prickled with eagerness. There was so much to learn!

She hardly noticed they'd reached the stepping-stones. Her chest tightened as she saw them. Since Skykit's cruel attack, she'd felt less confident about swimming than she had before. She shivered. Even now, as she saw the river swirling around the stones, she could feel the panic that had gripped her when water had flooded into her mouth and nose.

Whitefang paused beside her. "It's probably safer if I carry you across." He grabbed her scruff between his teeth and scooped her up. Her relief at not having to cross the stones turned to hot embarrassment as he carried her all the way into camp.

Sunkit and Frogkit were chasing a butterfly across the clearing. They stopped and stared at her in surprise as Whitefang put her down.

"Where have you been?" Sunkit mewed, her eyes wide.

Leopardkit stuck out her chin. "I went for a walk."

"Come on." Whitefang swished her forward with his tail. "You'd better explain yourself to Hailstar."

Hailstar? She glanced at Whitefang. Did he have to report her to the RiverClan leader? "But—"

"It's best to tell him now," Whitefang mewed. He steered her toward the leader's den, woven among the roots of a willow tree. Leopardkit's legs stiffened.

Whitefang gently stroked her flank with his tail. "Go on. . . . He'll find out anyway. You know how quickly news gets around the Clan."

Leopardkit wondered what the punishment would be for not going to see Hailstar. For turning and running away, and only coming back when this had been forgotten.

But Whitefang was right—Hailstar was going to find out. *And,* she thought, *I'm going to convince my Clanmates I'm ready to begin my apprenticeship, I should act like a 'paw and show some responsibility.* She puffed out her chest and padded ahead of him as though she *wanted* to see the Clan leader.

Mudfur looked up from the fresh-kill pile as they passed. He'd been rummaging for prey. "Leopardkit? Where are you going?"

Leopardkit felt a wave of dismay. "Hi, Mudfur." She tried to sound bright. It wasn't like she'd done anything really wrong. She'd just been trying to learn. But Mudfur's questioning gaze had switched to Whitefang.

"Has something happened?" he asked the snowy warrior anxiously.

"I caught her near the water meadow," Whitefang told him.

"Outside camp?" Mudfur hurried toward them, pelt ruffling.

"I'm taking her to see Hailstar," Whitefang told him. "To explain herself."

Leopardkit's fur was prickling self-consciously. "There's not much to explain," she mewed. "I wanted to learn how to hunt frogs, that's all."

Whitefang nudged her forward and she padded to the entrance of Hailstar's den. Mudfur was following; she could feel his gaze burning her pelt.

"Wait there," Whitefang told her as they reached the root den, and he disappeared through the moss trailing over the entrance.

Leopardkit glanced guiltily at her father.

His eyes were glittering with worry. "What in StarClan were you doing outside camp?"

"Nothing bad happened," she told him. "I was just—"

"Come in, Leopardkit." Hailstar's mew sounded through the moss.

She hesitated, and Mudfur swished her forward with his tail.

"Go on," he mewed.

Paws pricking nervously, she nosed her way inside, relieved when Mudfur followed.

Hailstar was sitting beside his nest, his gray pelt dark in

the shadowy den. Whitefang stood beside him, looking grave.

She braced herself for a scolding, but Hailstar was looking at her thoughtfully. "It's not safe for a young kit to be out of camp," he mewed.

"I'm not a young kit," she objected. "I'll be ready to become a 'paw in a moon or two!"

"Three moons," Mudfur corrected.

Hailstar's ears twitched, but his expression betrayed nothing. Was he angry or amused? "One moon or three, you're still too young to be out of camp," he mewed.

"You've had no training," Mudfur chimed. "And you're still small enough for a hawk to steal you. You should never be more than a tail-length from a warrior."

Leopardkit stuck out her tail indignantly. "That doesn't make sense," she mewed. "When we're playing moss-ball, we're always more than a tail-length—"

"Hush." Hailstar silenced her with a flick of his tail. "It's against Clan rules for a kit to leave camp," he mewed. "If you want to become a warrior, the first thing you need to learn is to follow rules."

Leopardkit opened her jaws to argue some more; then her gaze sank down toward the space between her paws. She couldn't argue against the warrior code.

Hailstar's expression softened. "It won't be long before you begin your training. And then you'll wish you were allowed to stay in camp from time to time. Just wait a moon or two—"

"*Three* moons," Mudfur corrected him.

"I can't wait *three* moons," Leopardkit complained. "The

other kits will be apprentices by then. I don't want to be the last kit left in the nursery."

Hailstar narrowed his eyes thoughtfully. "It must be hard when you've grown up together—"

Mudfur cut in. "It's our duty to keep you safe until you're big enough to start training."

"I'll eat extra prey," Leopardkit mewed. "I'll grow as big as Blackkit and you'll have to make me an apprentice."

Hailstar's whiskers twitched. Did he think this was funny?

"I mean it!" Leopardkit insisted.

"I'm sure you do," Hailstar mewed.

Frustration itched beneath Leopardkit's pelt. She had to start training soon. RiverClan's future might depend on it. "Whitefang would train me now if you let him." She looked imploringly at the white warrior. He'd shown her how to stalk today. He clearly thought she was ready. And he was so kind and strong, she knew she could learn a lot from him. "*He* doesn't think I'm too small."

Whitefang looked at his paws.

"Don't be in such a rush," Mudfur told her. "You'll have plenty of time to be a warrior."

"But you're the one who told me StarClan saved me for a reason," she argued. "That's why I have to start training as soon as possible."

Hailstar got to his paws. "I'm sure whatever StarClan has in store for you can wait," he mewed. "You will start training once I think you're ready."

She dug her claws into the ground. "I'm ready now!"

Mudfur shooed her toward the entrance with his tail. "Don't argue, Leopardkit."

"I'm not arguing. I'm trying to explain." She gazed desperately into Hailstar's eyes. Didn't he realize how much this meant to her? "I have to serve RiverClan . . . to honor my mother, her sacrifice. Please . . . don't make me wait."

He blinked at her, and she saw warmth in his gaze. *Have I persuaded him?*

Hailstar turned to Mudfur. "What do you think?"

Leopardkit felt a stab of dread in her chest. Was her father was going to tell the leader that he still had his doubts? She saw Mudfur glance at her, holding her eye for a long time.

Please agree, she thought desperately. *Please tell him you think I'm ready!*

Mudfur turned back to the leader, dipping his head. "I will agree with your decision," he mewed, "whatever that is."

Hailstar looked back toward Leopardkit. "Very well," he said. "I suppose we can make an exception."

"Thank you!" Leopardkit willed herself not to purr too loudly as she bowed her head, then turned and ducked through the trailing moss, screwing up her eyes as sunshine dazzled her.

Hailstar will be glad he agreed, she thought, *once I become an important RiverClan warrior.* Her belly burned with excitement as she remembered that she was a cat with a destiny. Her father had said so.

And she was going to prove him right.

* * *

Skypaw and Sunpaw followed their mentors into the river. Leopardpaw, watching from the shore, shuddered as she saw the water flowing around their legs and rushing beneath their bellies.

Voleclaw was already midstream, turning to face Sunpaw. "Not so fast," he warned. "The current is strong here."

"I've swum in the river lots of times," Sunpaw mewed.

"Swimming and hunting are not the same thing," Voleclaw said. "Take it slowly."

Sunpaw did as she was told. Beside her, Softwing was treading water, her strong paws holding her steady in the fast-flowing river. "Hold your head up and keep facing upstream," she called to Skypaw.

Whitefang nudged Leopardpaw into the shallows. "Stay close to the others," he advised.

She resisted, her heart pounding. She hadn't gotten more than her belly fur wet in the two moons that had passed since the incident with Skypaw. The thought of water covering her muzzle still made her shudder. "But what if I get swept away?"

For the first time since she'd been given her apprentice name, she felt suddenly aware that she was smaller than her denmates. She'd managed to keep up with them easily when their mentors had taken them on their first tour of River-Clan's territory, and when they'd learned their first battle move, her quickness had made up for her size. But today, faced with her first fishing lesson, she felt sick with fear.

Whitefang blinked at her kindly. "I'll be with you," he mewed. "I won't let you get swept away."

But what if water goes up my nose? She remembered how it had made her splutter and cough, but how could she admit it? She was a RiverClan cat. She wasn't supposed to be afraid of water.

Sunpaw waded in deeper and pushed off into the stream, the water flowing over her shoulders.

Skypaw followed, clearly as comfortable as a water vole in the rushing river. She ducked suddenly beneath the surface, then bobbed up again and shook water from her ears. "Hurry up!" she called to Leopardpaw as she swam easily around Softwing.

Leopardpaw felt a twinge of irritation. *I wouldn't be scared if you hadn't pushed me under.* Did Skypaw even remember what she'd done?

"Come on, Leopardpaw." Sunpaw had swum into an eddy in the middle of the river and was letting it swirl her around. "It's fun!"

Leopardpaw stared at her, wishing she weren't so scared. She tried to force her paws forward, but they felt like they were made of stone.

Whitefang glanced at her for a moment, then swished his tail. "Let's head upstream," he mewed. "There's a pool there. It's shallow enough to wade in, and sometimes fish get caught there. We can check it for prey." He called out to Softwing. "We're going to see if there's anything in the minnow trap," he told her.

"We'll catch up later," Softwing mewed back, nudging Skypaw into a patch of smooth water.

Leopardpaw followed Whitefang, avoiding the gazes of the others. Her pelt prickled self-consciously as they headed upstream. If she didn't get over her fear of the river, her den-mates would start calling her a drypaw. Worse than that, how would she ever fulfil her destiny? She couldn't save RiverClan if she was too scared to swim!

"I'm *not* a drypaw." Leopardpaw glared at Blackpaw.

"Skypaw said you won't even get your belly fur wet," he mewed back.

"That's not true," Leopardpaw snapped. The minnow pool had been so deep, the water had nearly reached her shoulders, and she'd ducked down to let it wash over her back so that her pelt was completely soaked when she returned to camp.

Outside the apprentices' den, Skypaw was dozing after her morning in the river. Leopardpaw could see the brown tabby's ears twitching. Was she listening to her brother tease Leopardpaw? *I'm sure you did tell him I wouldn't swim.*

Frogpaw was lying in the soft grass beside the den. He took another bite of trout and chewed it slowly, his gaze on Leopardpaw. "She's still kind of small," he told Blackpaw. "Perhaps she's scared she'll get eaten by a pike."

Blackpaw's eyes glittered mischievously. "I heard pikes can swallow kits whole."

"I'm not a kit!" Leopardpaw mewed hotly.

"You're only five moons old," Frogpaw pointed out.

"*Nearly* six!" Leopardpaw corrected him. "And I've got my apprentice name."

Blackpaw's whiskers twitched. "That doesn't mean a pike won't swallow you."

Leopardpaw turned her tail on him.

Sunpaw padded out of the dirtplace tunnel and crossed the clearing. She stopped beside Leopardpaw, clearly noticing her ruffled pelt. "What's wrong?" she mewed.

Leopardpaw fluffed out her fur—she wasn't going to tattle—but Frogpaw answered for her. "Blackpaw's teasing her about being a drypaw." He took another mouthful of trout.

Sunpaw jerked her nose toward Skypaw. "I told you not to say anything."

Skypaw opened her eyes and blinked at her denmate innocently. "He asked how training went, that's all." She sat up and stretched. "And I just mentioned how Leopardpaw preferred fishing in the minnow pool rather than the river."

"That was Whitefang's idea," Sunpaw reminded her sharply.

"Only because he saw the look on Leopardpaw's face," Skypaw mewed casually. "When he nosed her toward the river, she looked as if he'd asked her to jump off Sunningrocks."

I did not. Leopardpaw choked back the words. She wasn't going to get into an argument. It would make her seem even more like a kit. But she was going to stop being scared of the water. She was going to show her denmates that StarClan had a plan for her. Crossly, she sat down beside Frogpaw and took a bite of the trout.

"Wouldn't it be better to practice battle moves instead?" She gazed eagerly at Whitefang as they stood on the riverbank. "The others were fishing here earlier. They've probably frightened all the best fish away."

Whitefang frowned thoughtfully. "I guess we'd have a better chance of catching something if we waited until tomorrow," he agreed.

Leopardpaw felt a rush of relief. Battle moves were important. She could get over her fear of the water tomorrow. It would be easier then, with more fish to distract her.

Tomorrow came and went. Then another and another. There was so much to learn —about RiverClan's territory and battle skills and tactics and which fish swam in which part of the river. Leopardpaw became skilled at fishing in shallow pools where fish found themselves trapped. Whitefang didn't seem to argue when she found other ways to hunt that kept her pelt dry. Perhaps he was pleased she was so resourceful. He seemed impressed that she was always the first to find patches of shade near the bank where fish sheltered from the sun. She could spot a brown trout even in murky water, and she was so fast, she could hook it out before it saw her shadow and tried to swim away.

As her warrior assessment grew steadily closer, she felt surer and surer that tomorrow she'd face her fear of the river and simply dive in. But every day, she found another excuse to put it off.

"Do it again!" Timberfur circled Leopardpaw and Frogpaw as they faced each other in a clearing beside the camp. Leopardpaw dropped into a battle crouch, her muscles aching. How many times would they have to practice this move?

"Keep your belly low," Timberfur told her. The dark brown tom touched his tail-tip to Frogpaw's shoulder. He thrust a paw suddenly into Frogpaw's haunch, and the gray tom wobbled and fought to stay on his paws. "You need to be properly balanced."

Whitefang stood back and watched, and Leopardpaw felt her mentor's gaze run along her flank. She tried not to tremble from the effort of keeping still while Frogpaw eased himself back into the battle stance.

"Ready?" Timberfur looked from Leopardpaw to Frogpaw. They nodded at the same time.

"Attack."

Frogpaw leaped at Leopardpaw, but she was a moment faster and was already rearing as he reached her. She hooked her paws into his scruff, unbalanced him with a sharp jerk, and sent him staggering away.

"Good." Timberfur nodded at her, then nudged Frogpaw back to the center of the clearing and whisked his tail. "Again!"

Leopardpaw blinked at him, her heart sinking. "Again?"

"You'll keep doing it until you've both got it perfect," Timberfur told her.

Leopardpaw nodded, and tried not to sigh as she retook her original position, wondering once more how many times she would have to repeat these battle moves.

It wasn't always fun, being a cat with a destiny.

"I really thought I'd do it this time." Leopardpaw felt anxious as she whispered to Sunpaw. They were curled in their nests at the end of a hard day's training. Moonlight was filtering though the woven willow roof of the den, and the other apprentices were already asleep. The sound of their gentle breathing filled the air, while frogs croaked in the distance and a curlew called out across the water meadow. Leopardpaw rested her chin on the side of her nest, feeling weary with disappointment. "But I just froze."

"Again?" Sunpaw blinked at her sympathetically, her amber eyes reflecting the silvery light.

"Whitefang pointed out a chub in the middle of the river and I tried to go in. The water was past my belly, but I just couldn't dive under." Leopardpaw's belly tightened. She was beginning to think she'd never have the courage to swim like other River-Clan warriors. How was she going to save their Clan?

"Was Whitefang angry?" Sunpaw asked.

"No." Leopardpaw was beginning to wonder if her mentor had simply given up hope that she'd ever swim. "He just pointed out a tiny trout near the edge where I could reach it. He sounded really disappointed."

"Would it be easier if he wasn't watching?" Sunpaw asked.

"I don't know." Whitefang was so kind and patient; she couldn't believe he was the problem. It was her own lack of courage that was to blame.

Leopardpaw watched Skypaw and Blackpaw drag a tattered old nest from the elders' den. She was relieved she hadn't been given cleaning duty. She'd woken early that morning and was already hunting for frogs in the reed bed with Loudpaw and Sedgepaw by the time Shellheart began handing out the day's assignments.

Frogpaw padded to her side. "Should we help them?" he asked.

"After we've eaten," Leopardpaw mewed. It wasn't her fault they'd woken late. Besides, her belly was rumbling with hunger. She padded toward the fresh-kill pile, but Reedpaw was already carrying a large bream toward the apprentices' den. He dropped it outside and beckoned her with his tail. "Let's share this," he called.

Leopardpaw hurried toward him, Frogpaw at her tail. The bream smelled fresh and tasty. Her mouth watering, Leopardpaw leaned down to take a bite.

"Leopardpaw!" Sunpaw's mew made her jerk around. Her friend was hurrying toward her. "Come with me." She nosed Leopardpaw away from the bream.

"But I'm hungry," Leopardpaw complained, glancing at the fish.

"If you come with me, you can have the best meal ever."

Leopardpaw widened her eyes. "What do you mean?"

"Follow me," Sunpaw told her.

Curious, Leopardpaw followed her friend out of the camp and along the shore to where the river widened and slowed before it tumbled into the gorge.

Sunpaw stopped and looked across the green water. Leopardpaw followed her gaze. The scent of carp touched her nose, and she saw a fat, shiny fish lying on the far bank.

"Carp's your favorite, right?" Sunpaw asked.

Leopardpaw wiped her tongue around her jaws. "Yes."

"Good." Sunpaw looked at her. "That's my catch over there, but if you swim to it, I'll share it with you."

Leopardpaw stiffened. She guessed what her friend was

trying to do; Sunpaw had clearly gone to a lot of effort to set this up and was willing to share her carp. But it would be far easier to go back to camp and eat bream with Frogpaw and Reedpaw. She blinked at the pale gray she-cat. "Can't I try later?" she mewed hopefully.

"The carp won't taste as good later," Sunpaw told her.

And you'll be disappointed in me. Leopardpaw looked back at the fish. A heron was standing on a stone a few tree-lengths upstream. If it caught sight of the carp lying unguarded, it would swoop in and steal it.

Sunpaw glanced at the heron and then at Leopardpaw. "If you don't hurry up, we'll both lose out," she mewed. Her voice sounded like Whitefang's had, the day she hadn't been brave enough to swim to the middle of the river to catch a chub.

Leopardpaw felt no braver now than she had then. She was sure that if she dived into the river, she'd sink before she reached the other side. Water would fill her nose and mouth, and she might never breathe again. Her heart thumped like a trapped badger in her chest.

Sunpaw nudged her toward the river's edge. "Just do it."

Just do it. Sunpaw was watching her with large, hopeful eyes. The heron was shifting on its stone, its gaze flitting over the bank. "Okay." Leopardpaw took a steadying breath. *If I die, then I die.* Drowning might be better than spending the rest of her life as the warrior who never dared to swim. Ignoring the fear churning in her belly, she waded into the water. Panic began to pulse in her paws. She felt sick. But she kept going, feeling the water touch her belly fur, then rise around her flanks until it was lapping over her spine. Closing her eyes, she pushed away from the shore and plunged into the deep water. The chill of it set her blood roaring in her ears. She churned the water. Where was the bottom? Terror sparked in every hair of her pelt as she realized it was out of reach. She flailed her paws, feeling as clumsy as a ThunderClan warrior.

"You can do it!" She heard Sunpaw's mew and glimpsed her friend swimming a tail-length away. "I won't let you drown!"

Leopardpaw fought to stay above the surface. Water splashed up her nose and stung her eyes. *Remember what Mudfur taught you.* She remembered the swimming lessons her father had given her when she was a kit. *Let the water hold you up.* His mew rang in her mind. *It will if you trust it.* She'd swum then, before she knew enough to be frightened. *You're a RiverClan cat,* Mudfur had told her. *Swimming is in your blood.* She pictured her father swimming ahead of her, as easily as a fish, and always looking over his shoulder to make sure she was okay, his tail just a whisker ahead so she could grab it if she needed. Slowly, her panic ebbed, and she felt her paws begin to work together, one reaching out after another and pulling her through the water.

"You're doing it!" Sunpaw called out beside her.

I am doing it! Triumph swelled in Leopardpaw's chest as her paws fell into a rhythm. Mudfur was right: The water was holding her up. It flowed around her, supporting her and letting her pull herself through it until she felt like part of the current. A moment later, she felt the river bottom beneath her paws and was padding onto the far shore, water streaming from her fur. She glared at the heron's eye and arched her back menacingly. Feathers ruffling, it lifted into the air and wheeled away over the reed bed.

Sunpaw climbed out after her. She purred with delight. "You did it!"

"I did, didn't I?" Leopardpaw circled around her, her tail high. She wondered suddenly why it had taken her so long to face her fear. It might be a while before she felt entirely comfortable in the water, but she knew now she could do it if she wanted. *Next time, I won't let fear stop me.*

Sunpaw padded to the carp and carried it back to Leopardpaw, dropping it at her paws. "You can eat it all if you like," she mewed. "You've earned it."

Leopardpaw blinked at her happily. "It'll taste better if we share it," she mewed.

"I knew you'd do it eventually," Whitefang had told her when they got back to camp. "You just needed to find the right time."

Since then, her mentor had made her swim every day. "You've got a lot of training to catch up on," he'd told her as he taught her to dive into the deepest parts of the river and how to navigate the currents and where to watch out for eddies and hidden rocks. Soon she could tell by the bubbles breaking the surface where a fish was lurking and dive for it, darting so smoothly through the water, it had no chance to escape.

Today, though, had been spent on battle techniques. The countless mornings practicing with Frogpaw and Timberfur had given her patience and skill she hadn't realized until this afternoon, when she had finally beaten Blackpaw in a fight. The tom was bigger and stronger than her, but she'd noticed his weakness—a tendency to put his weight too much on his hind paws—and had first unbalanced him, then, fast as a snake, changed her attack so that he didn't have time to avoid the lunge that knocked him to the ground and let her pin him there.

Now she lay back as the sun, soft and orange as duck feathers against the pale evening sky, sank behind the moor. The long spine of the carp she'd shared with her denmates curved in front of her. Sunpaw was washing beside her while Skypaw was licking the last scraps of flesh from between the bones.

"When I'm a warrior," Skypaw mewed between nibbles, "I'm going to volunteer for every patrol." She scooped out a fish flake with her tongue. "And I'll ask Hailstar if I can lead one."

"I don't want to lead patrols," Sunpaw mewed. "I'm happy just being part of one."

Leopardpaw looked toward the camp entrance, hoping Mudfur would return soon. She'd saved him a small rainbow trout that she'd caught while she'd been training. Trout was his favorite, and she couldn't wait to show him how she'd fished it out of the water without breaking the skin except for the neat bitemark where she'd killed it. "I wonder when the border patrol will be back," she mewed.

"Soon," Sunpaw guessed. "They were only going to check the Sunningrocks border."

"If they see any ThunderClan warriors, I hope they shred them." Leopardpaw ruffled her pelt crossly. ThunderClan had stolen Sunningrocks a few moons ago, and she hadn't forgiven them. "Those squirrel-chasers are so greedy. Isn't the forest enough for them?"

"I guess they think Sunningrocks is part of the forest," Sunpaw mewed.

"Why?" Leopardpaw flicked her tail. "Sunningrocks has always belonged to RiverClan. They have no right to it and they know it."

"Reedpaw said that if he was leader, he'd take Sunning-rocks back," Skypaw mewed.

Leopardpaw sniffed. She wondered why Skypaw seemed to care so much about what *Reedpaw* said. "Why are you always so impressed by Reedpaw's bragging?" She narrowed her eyes. "Do you *like* him?"

Skypaw sat up. "So what if I do?" she mewed. "He's going to be a great warrior. And he's so handsome."

Sunpaw glanced shyly at her paws. "Beetlenose is handsomer."

Skypaw's eyes widened. "Do you like *Beetlenose*?"

"Maybe." Sunpaw glanced at Leopardpaw. "Who do *you* like?"

"Me?" Leopardpaw hadn't thought about it. She didn't care about toms. She was too busy with her training. "No cat."

"Really?" Skypaw blinked at her. "What about Frogpaw? You two seem close."

"We just train together," she mewed. "That's all."

"Are you sure?" Skypaw pushed the fish carcass away. Her eyes sparkled teasingly. "He's quite cute."

"I thought you liked Reedpaw," Leopardpaw mewed back.

Before Skypaw could answer, the camp entrance rustled and Hailstar padded through it. Voleclaw followed, with Crookedjaw at his heels.

Mudfur was leaning heavily against the RiverClan deputy. Leopardpaw sat up, her belly tightening with alarm. Her father was limping. Clumps of fur stuck out from his pelt, she could see gashes along his flank, and his muzzle was scratched and bleeding.

"Mudfur!" She raced across the clearing.

Hailstar waved her away. "He's okay," he told her. "But his wounds need dressing. Go back and wait with your denmates while Brambleberry sees to him."

"But—"

"Go." Hailstar's eyes were dark. "This is warrior business."

Leopardpaw backed away but couldn't bring herself to leave. She stared anxiously at Mudfur.

"I'm okay," her father promised. "Do as Hailstar says."

Leopardpaw held her ground. "What happened?"

"Mudfur fought for Sunningrocks." Crookedjaw guided Mudfur toward the shade of the willow.

Leopardpaw began to follow. "On his own?"

"Against Adderfang, to decide who they belonged to," Crookedjaw told her.

Troutclaw circled the patrol as it crossed the clearing. "Who won?"

"Mudfur," Voleclaw told him. "Sunningrocks belongs to RiverClan again."

As Brambleberry hurried from the medicine den, a wad of herbs in her jaws, warriors began to cluster around the returning patrol. Leopardpaw shifted one way, then the other, trying to keep her father in sight.

"Go back and wait with your denmates," Hailstar told her again, more sternly this time. "We have important matters to discuss."

Reluctantly, Leopardpaw backed away.

Skypaw padded to her side. "Why did Mudfur have to fight alone?"

"I don't know." Leopardpaw didn't care. She just wanted to know how bad her father's injuries were. Her belly churned as she tried to get a glimpse of him, but more and more warriors were getting in the way, clustering eagerly around Hailstar and the others while Brambleberry tended to Mudfur. Ottersplash and Piketooth paced around them, their tails twitching excitedly as Hailstar conferred with Timberfur and Rippleclaw.

Leopardpaw swallowed back frustration. What was happening?

She felt Skypaw's nose brush her ear. "I'm sure he'll be okay," the pale brown tabby mewed. "You'll be able to talk to him soon."

She stiffened as Ottersplash hurried toward them. "Did you hear?" Ottersplash's ears twitched. "Mudfur's going to become a medicine cat!"

Leopardpaw blinked. "What are you talking about?"

"He's just told Hailstar he wants to give up being a warrior and train as a medicine cat," Ottersplash mewed.

Leopardpaw could hardly believe her ears. Mudfur was one of the strongest warriors in RiverClan. He'd just won back Sunningrocks, single-pawed! "Why?"

Ottersplash retuned her gaze blankly. "You'll have to ask him yourself."

"I'm sure he has his reasons," Skypaw told her.

"But he's never mentioned wanting to be a medicine cat." *He'd have told me if this was something he'd been thinking about, right?* she thought. *Of course he would have. So maybe, he's only saying this now because he's not thinking all that clearly, after his fight.*

Time dragged as she waited for a chance to speak to Mudfur. She paced, her heart pounding, as the sun began to sink toward the distant moor, until, at last, the crowd of warriors began to disperse. Hailstar led Ottersplash and Piketooth to the edge of the camp. Willowbreeze padded to the fresh-kill pile and took a trout to the elders' den. Voleclaw called to his Clanmates, organizing a patrol.

Softwing began to tidy a pile of frog bones away from the warriors' den. "Come and help me," she called to Skypaw.

Skypaw hesitated. "Will you be okay?" she asked Leopardpaw.

"Yeah." Leopardpaw didn't look at her. "Thanks." She was staring at Mudfur. As Skypaw headed away, she hurried to her father's side.

"Mudfur?" She inspected his pelt, relieved to see that the bleeding had stopped.

Mudfur had propped himself up on his forepaws as Brambleberry laid more cobwebs over a wound on his leg. His eyes brightened as he saw Leopardpaw. "Don't worry. I'm fine."

Leopardpaw crouched beside him. "Are you sure?"

"Of course." He gave a weak purr.

Brambleberry looked up from her work. "He'll need to take it easy for a while."

"That shouldn't be hard"—Mudfur gave a husky snort—"now that I won't be a warrior."

Leopardpaw felt a sharp tug in her heart, like snagged claws. *He's serious . . . ?* "But why?" She stared at her father. "Was the fight that bad?"

Mudfur nudged her shoulder with his muzzle. "I'd do it again if I had to," he mewed. "I just don't *want* to."

Leopardpaw didn't understand. She couldn't imagine not wanting to be a warrior. "But why not?"

"I'm tired of fighting the same battle over and over again," he told her. "Nothing ever seems to get settled."

Brambleberry was chewing herbs. She spat the pulp onto her paw and began to work it into a bitemark on Mudfur's tail. "There are more ways to help your Clan than fighting."

"But Mudfur trained as a warrior," Leopardpaw argued. "RiverClan needs him."

Brambleberry didn't look up from her work.

Mudfur spoke instead. "RiverClan needs medicine cats too," he mewed.

Leopardpaw looked at him, suddenly noticing the gray hairs flecking his pelt. Was he just feeling old? She felt suddenly protective. "I'm sure you'll be a great medicine cat." But she still didn't understand how he could give up being a warrior. "Maybe one day RiverClan won't have to fight battles," she mewed."

Mudfur looked unconvinced. "Life isn't that simple," he mewed. "But you're too young to understand."

"No, I'm not." Had he forgotten that he'd told her she was special, that one day she'd save RiverClan? "What if I make RiverClan so strong we never have to fight again?"

He purred indulgently. "That would be great."

She could tell he didn't believe her, but she would show him. She'd make him see that RiverClan didn't have to fight the same battles over and over again. She lapped his ears gently. He must be in pain. As she worked at them, cleaning the blood from his fur, her thoughts quickened. Perhaps it had been Mudfur's destiny to become a medicine cat all along. If it was, did it mean that when he'd said she was special—special enough to save all the Clans—his words had been a *prophecy*?

A half-moon later, Leopardpaw crouched on the riverbank. She'd been far too busy training for her warrior assessment to worry about Mudfur's prophecy, or his minnow-brained idea of becoming a medicine cat. Whitefang had worked her hard, and she'd tried her best to impress him. Now assessment day had arrived, and she and her denmates were being tested.

She sniffed the two dead voles that lay at her paws. The apprentices had been told to bring back land prey, and now she was wondering if the water voles she'd caught counted as land prey or river prey. Perhaps she should head into the strip of forest that lay on this side of the river and catch a mouse. She glanced among the trees. Was Whitefang watching from the undergrowth? She knew he'd be keeping an eye on her progress. Had she done enough to earn her warrior name?

A branch, jutting out over the river, shivered above her. Leaves showered down and she looked up, her ears pricking as she saw Skypaw padding unsteadily along the branch. Her denmate's eyes were fixed on a squirrel that she'd cornered by the trunk. Excitement sparkled in Skypaw's eyes. The assignment to catch land prey had been hard for apprentices used to hooking fish from the river, and a squirrel would be an impressive catch.

Leopardpaw felt a twinge of envy. Why hadn't she tried to catch a squirrel?

At the end of the branch, the squirrel had frozen. Its eyes flashed with panic. Skypaw crouched lower against the branch. Her hind paws were trembling, and Leopardpaw could see she was about to lunge for the squirrel. She held her breath as Skypaw launched herself forward, but the squirrel darted suddenly upward and disappeared into the leaves above her head.

Skypaw landed on the empty branch tip. It dipped under her weight. She hissed in frustration as she fought to get a grip, but the branch snapped, and her hind legs swung down. She dangled for a moment before losing her hold, slithering from the branch, and splashing into the river below.

Leopardpaw darted to the edge, her heart lurching as Skypaw disappeared for a moment, but soon her head burst back through the surface.

The tabby's gaze burned with rage as she swam to the shore

and hauled herself out a few tail-lengths downstream.

"Bad luck," Leopardpaw called.

Skypaw scowled at her. "Why did they tell us to catch land prey?" she snapped. "It's not fair. I've been practicing fishing! They should have warned us."

"You can have one of these." Leopardpaw pushed a vole toward Skypaw. Her sympathy for her denmate wrestled with the wry thought that she was only good at catching land prey because of that day Skypaw had given her a fear of water. It had been just a moon or so since Leopardpaw had stopped hating her for it.

The pale brown tabby whisked her tail irritably. "Do you want me to be accused of cheating?" With a huff, she headed into the forest. "I'll catch my own prey, thanks."

Leopardpaw decided not to go after her. Skypaw was right. She had to do this alone.

Back at camp, Loudpaw, Sunpaw, and Blackpaw had already returned with their catch. As Leopardpaw padded into the clearing, Hailstar was looking pleased, and Oakheart and Voleclaw were purring, their pelts fluffed with pride. Leopardpaw guessed that the three apprentices had passed the assessment.

Whitefang was standing beside the RiverClan leader.

Leopardpaw dropped her voles at his paws, blinking at him anxiously. "Do these count as land prey?" she mewed.

"You caught them on land," he told her. "So they count."

She felt a wave of relief. "Then I passed?"

Whitefang touched his muzzle to her head. "Yes."

Happiness surged in her chest. As she began to purr, Frog-paw and Reedpaw trotted into camp, Sedgepaw at their heels. All three of them were carrying prey.

Hailstar nodded approvingly as they laid their catch in front of him. It seemed every cat had passed the assessment.

The RiverClan leader looked toward the camp entrance. "Where's Skypaw?"

"I just saw her," Leopardpaw told him. "She was heading into the forest."

"Without prey?" Hailstar frowned.

Leopardpaw avoided the leader's gaze. She didn't want to tell him that Skypaw had let a squirrel escape. It had been a difficult catch and she'd been brave to try. Hailstar's tail twitched impatiently. He glanced at the sky. It was past sun-high. All the apprentices should have returned by now. "She'll be back soon," Leopardpaw promised him.

Her paws prickled anxiously. *Please, StarClan, help her catch something.* She hurried toward her denmates. "If Skypaw doesn't get back in time," she whispered, "we should ask for our naming ceremonies to be delayed until she has a chance to take the assessment again."

Blackpaw frowned. "But I want my name now."

Frogpaw nudged him. "An extra day or two won't make a difference."

Reedpaw sniffed. "What if she doesn't pass next time, either?"

"She will," Leopardpaw insisted.

Sunpaw glanced hopefully toward the camp entrance. "We

don't know for sure she's failed."

As she spoke, Skypaw stomped into camp. She was carrying nothing, and Leopardpaw's heart sank.

Tail drooping, Skypaw crossed the clearing to Hailstar. "I nearly caught a squirrel," she grunted.

He shook his head sadly. "Nearly is not enough," he mewed.

Softwing hurried into camp, blinking sympathetically at Skypaw. "Her technique was excellent," she told Hailstar. "I watched her; she did well."

"Technique doesn't feed a Clan," he mewed. "Until she brings home prey, I can't give her a warrior name."

Leopardpaw hurried forward. "We don't want our warrior names either, until Skypaw gets hers." She glanced back at her denmates. Blackpaw was looking cross, but he didn't argue.

Sunpaw padded forward. "Skypaw will pass next time," she mewed. "And we don't mind waiting until then for our ceremonies."

Hailstar looked around at the apprentices. His eyes glowed with warmth. "It's good to see such loyalty in our youngest warriors," he mewed. "The naming ceremony can wait until Skypaw is ready to join you."

Skypaw looked gratefully between Sunpaw and Leopardpaw. "I don't want to hold you back," she mewed.

"We can still take care of our Clan even without our warrior names," Leopardpaw told her. "Besides, you'll pass soon. I know you will."

Skypaw lifted her chin. "I'll make sure I do."

A pale sliver of moon hung low in the sky. The moortop was rosy in the setting sun.

Leopardpaw forced her paws to stop trembling as she waited between Mudfur and Whitefang. Her Clanmates had gathered and were ringed around the clearing, watching as Hailstar conducted the naming ceremonies. Loudbelly, Blackclaw, Skyheart, and Reedtail were already sitting proudly among the other warriors. Frogleap, Sunfish, and Sedgecreek had just made their promises to Hailstar to protect their Clan. It would be her turn next. She would finally receive her warrior name.

Mudfur smoothed down the fur between her ears with his tongue. "Brightsky will be watching," he mewed. "She'll be as proud of you as I am."

Leopardpaw's heart seemed to swell. She purred at him. "I'm going to make you even prouder," she promised.

As she spoke, Whitefang nudged her forward. "It's your turn," he whispered.

Hailstar was looking at her expectantly as Frogleap, Sunfish and Sedgecreek padded away to join the others. She hurried across the clearing, her pelt hot as she felt the eyes of the whole Clan on it.

She stopped in front of the RiverClan leader. She hadn't expected to be so nervous. She swallowed back the butterflies swarming in her belly.

"I call upon my warrior ancestors . . . ," Hailstar began slowly. Her heart seemed to burst with excitement. This was it. This was the beginning. He went on. ". . . to look down on this apprentice. With no mother to guide her, she has been raised by the Clan, and it is with special pride that we watch her today pass from apprentice to warrior. She has trained hard to understand the ways of your noble code, and I commend her to you as a warrior of RiverClan."

Leopardpaw held her breath, knowing what he would say next, willing him to hurry.

"Leopardpaw," he mewed at last. "Do you promise to uphold the warrior code and to protect and defend your Clan, even at the cost of your life?"

"I do," Leopardpaw mewed. "I really do."

Hailstar's whiskers quivered. "Then, by the powers of StarClan, I give you your warrior name. Leopardpaw, from this moment on you will be known as Leopardfur. StarClan honors your determination, your independence, and your loyalty, and we welcome you as a full warrior of RiverClan."

Leopardfur looked back at Mudfur, pressing back a purr as his eyes lit up with pride. Whitefang blinked at her happily. Her heart seemed to rise like a bird in her chest. She was a warrior. At last, she could begin to follow her destiny.

CHAPTER 3

❧

Leopardfur shook out her pelt. The rain was freezing and it seemed like it had been longer than six moons since she'd been a 'paw, relishing the sunshine and warmth of greenleaf. She glanced at Sunfish, but her friend hardly seemed to notice the downpour, though it was dripping from her whiskers. She had that starry-eyed look again. *She must be thinking about Beetlenose.* "Aren't you cold?" Leopardfur mewed.

"Yes," Sunfish mewed. "But we'll be home soon, and Beetlenose promised to catch a trout for me. We're going to share it."

Leopardfur huddled deeper against the rain. It seemed to have started at the beginning of leaf-bare and fallen for a moon without stopping. The only time she'd felt warm was when she was curled in her nest in the warriors' den. "I don't suppose he'll share the trout with me too," she grunted.

Sunfish looked at her, surprised. "Of course," she mewed. "If you want some."

"No, thanks." Leopardfur wasn't going to butt in on her friend's budding romance. "I'll eat with Reedtail and Frog-leap." Sunfish had had a crush on Beetlenose since they were 'paws, and the handsome black warrior had finally seemed to notice that the pretty gray she-cat wasn't a clumsy apprentice anymore.

Leopardfur glanced along the shore. She hadn't seen a bird or vole all morning. "I think even river prey is smart enough to stay in its burrow today," she mewed.

Sunfish looked at the river, swollen by the rain. "Beetle-nose says that any fish worth catching has headed upstream to look for warmer water."

Leopardfur sniffed. Did Sunfish believe everything that tom told her? The fish hadn't gone to look for warmer water; it was just harder to catch them when the river was churning and the currents were fierce. She kept the thought to herself. She was only feeling grumpy because she was cold and hungry; there was no need to take it out on her friend. If Sunfish wanted to end up in the nursery, surrounded by kits, that was her choice. Leopardfur was more interested in being a warrior.

She looked at the trees lining the riverbank. The thin strip of woodland was RiverClan's only forest territory, and they hardly bothered hunting there. No cat in RiverClan, besides Graypool and Willowbreeze, liked forest prey; it tasted too musky. But in weather like this, it might be the only place they could find food. "Shall we hunt here?"

Sunfish followed her gaze. "At least we'll be out of the wind," she mewed.

Leopardfur headed for the trees, slowing as she reached a small clearing. She let her eyes adjust to the gloom.

Sunfish stopped beside her, her eyes wide as she scanned

the shadows. "Don't ThunderClan cats miss fresh air?" she mewed.

"I guess they're used to breathing in leaf-mold," Leopard-fur sniffed.

Sunfish wrinkled her nose. "How can they detect prey when everything smells like wet bark?"

Movement caught Leopardfur's eye. "Over there." She nodded toward a birch. Something was rummaging between its roots. Dropping low, she padded toward it, her tail skimming the ground as her gaze fixed on the twitching leaves.

Sunfish drew level with her as she stopped a paw-length from the tree. A tiny tail showed for a moment between the leaves, then disappeared.

"It's a mouse," Leopardfur breathed excitedly. The pile rippled as the mouse burrowed deeper. "I think it's looking for food."

"Beetlenose says mice are the hardest prey to catch," Sunfish whispered. "They move faster than fish."

Leopardfur suddenly had the overwhelming urge to prove Beetlenose wrong. Without waiting to gauge the mouse's movements, she leaped at the leaf pile and slammed her paws down on either side. She had it trapped, and when it ran for the fork in the roots, she'd catch it. She held her breath, waiting for the mouse to burst from the leaves in panic, ready to lunge for it and hook it into a killing bite.

Nothing moved. The leaves between her paws lay still. Confused, Leopardfur slapped her paws down again, hoping to flush the mouse out. There was still no sign of it. Frustration flared in her belly. She began to scrabble through at the leaf pile. Where had the mouse gone? Surely there was nowhere for it to escape?

Sunfish padded toward her and peered over her shoulder. "Did you catch it?"

Leopardfur flashed her a look. "Does it look like I did?" She dug a space in the leaves, dismayed as she saw a gap beneath one of the roots. It was so tiny she wondered how a mouse could have squirmed through, but when she sniffed it she smelled the fear-scent of her quarry. She followed the scent around the tree, but it had disappeared. The mouse was gone.

Her heart sank. Graypool and Softwing were in the nursery, and there were kits. RiverClan was depending on her. She paced around the birch one more time.

Sunfish watched her. "I guess Beetlenose was—"

Leopardfur cut her off. "Don't you dare tell me Beetlenose was right," she snapped.

Sunfish blinked at her. "But he was."

Leopardfur glared at her friend. Her fury melted at once as she saw Sunfish's wide, innocent eyes. Having a crush seemed like a waste of time to Leopardfur, but if it stopped Sunfish from feeling cold and hungry, why spoil it?

Splinters of bark showered around them. Leopardfur looked up. A squirrel was darting along a bare branch high above. She dropped against the earth, flattening herself among the leaves. "Hide," she ordered Sunfish.

Sunfish darted toward the trunk and ducked down beside a root, her gray pelt melting into the shadow. Together they watched the squirrel as it reached the trunk. Leopardfur's heart leaped as it began to scrabble down the bark toward them.

Don't move until it's within reach. She willed Sunfish to understand, but Sunfish was smart. She would know as well as any cat that they only had to stay completely still and wait. Squirrels were fast, but they weren't as cautious as ground prey. Which was probably why ThunderClan cats grew so fat during greenleaf.

Her heart pounded harder as the squirrel scurried down the trunk, its paws spread as it gripped on with nimble claws. Sunfish's gaze was following the squirrel, but not even a hair on her pelt twitched. Leopardfur held her breath as it raced closer. Her muscles tingled with the urge to leap for it, but she forced herself to stay still until, with a sudden burst of speed, the squirrel swarmed down the final tail-length of the trunk and darted along a root.

Leopardfur exploded from the leaves, her ears flattening as she streaked after it. Sunfish shot after her, veering one way as Leopardfur veered the other. Together, they flanked their prey as it pelted for an oak. *It mustn't reach it.* There was no way they'd be able to keep up with it if it reached the trunk. She glanced at Sunfish.

Sunfish caught her eye and seemed to understand. She slowed and fell in behind the squirrel as Leopardfur gave a final push and lunged in front of it. Blocked ahead and behind, the squirrel changed course. Panic flared in its eyes as it looked for escape. Faster than an eel, Leopardfur switched her weight from one paw to another and swerved deftly after their prey. Flinging out her forepaws, she pinned it to the ground, and before it could even squeal, she delivered the killing bite.

Sunfish pulled up beside her and sat back on her haunches, panting. Her whiskers twitched with distaste as the squirrel's blood filled the damp air with a warm, earthy smell. "How do ThunderClan cats eat these all the time?" she mewed.

"I guess a cat can eat anything if they're hungry." Leopardfur lifted the squirrel's limp body with a claw. Her belly rumbled. It was no fish, but it was food, and Graypool and Softwing would be grateful for it. Grabbing its fur between her teeth, she picked it up, and they headed back to camp.

The rain kept pounding the camp through the night, and when Leopardfur slid from the warriors' den the next morning, the clearing was slick with mud. She flattened her ears against the downpour. The sky was laden with heavy gray clouds; it looked as though there'd be no break in the weather today.

"Come and help," Sedgecreek called to her from beside the nursery. "The roof's leaking." She was stuffing leaves between the stems of the woven willow den.

Petaldust was working beside her. "We might be wasting our time fixing the nursery," she mewed. "The water's rising so much, Graypool and Softwing might have to move to the elders' den."

Leopardfur glanced at the water washing through the reed bed and lapping the edges of the clearing. Beyond, the river swirled, muddy and fast. The currents would still be too dangerous for fishing today.

She hurried to help Petaldust and Sedgecreek, grabbing a pawful of wet leaves from the pile and pushing them into a gap. The tips of the leaves flapped loosely in the wind. "Wouldn't moss be better?" she asked Petaldust. "We could pack it tighter."

"Brambleberry wants to save the moss to line nests," Petaldust told her. "She says it's easier to dry out."

Sedgecreek snorted. "I don't think any cat in RiverClan has slept in a dry nest for a moon," she mewed.

Hailstar and Crookedjaw who'd become deputy after Shellheart had retired to the elders' den—were watching the water rise through the reed bed, their eyes dark with worry.

As Leopardfur pressed another pawful of leaves into a gap, Softwing appeared at the entrance to the nursery and peered out. Mallowkit and Dawnkit tried to nose past her, but she drew them close to her belly with her tail as she gazed anxiously at the swollen river.

"Hi, Softwing." Leopardfur greeted her with a nod. "How's Graypool?" The gray queen was expecting Rippleclaw's kits and had been feeling too sick to eat.

"She's still nauseous," Softwing answered with a sigh.

Perhaps if she had more to eat and a drier nest, she'd feel better. Leopardfur felt a twinge of guilt as she remembered the solitary squirrel she and Sunfish had caught yesterday. She glanced at Petaldust. "Has Crookedjaw sent out any hunting patrols yet?"

"He sent out three at dawn, but none are back," Petaldust told her.

Leopardfur shook out her wet fur, wishing she'd woken earlier and joined one. But she'd been on guard duty until late, and Crookedjaw had told her to sleep in.

Mudfur was heading up the slope toward the elders' den with a bundle of leaves in his jaws. He was almost as skilled with herbs as Brambleberry after his moons of training. Leopardfur was used to him being a medicine cat now. She even felt proud that, though he was no longer a warrior, he worked tirelessly to protect his Clan.

Crookedjaw hurried to meet him. "Are those for Birdsong?"

Nodding, Mudfur ducked into the willow den. Only Tanglewhisker and Birdsong slept there now that Shellheart and Troutclaw had died, and Birdsong had been coughing for days.

As Crookedjaw followed Mudfur inside, Leopardfur scooped up more leaves and began to press them around the bottom of the den wall, sealing a gap where rainwater had been trickling through. She worked her way around the den, wondering if she should head out of camp to gather more. This pile wouldn't be enough to plug every gap in the nursery.

Crookedjaw burst out of the elders' den and hurried toward Hailstar. Leopardfur stiffened. Was Birdsong worse? She watched as Hailstar raised his tail. He looked pleased. Perhaps Birdsong had recovered. As Leopardfur stretched her ears, straining to hear what the two warriors were talking about so excitedly, Hailstar called across the clearing.

"Petaldust, Sedgecreek, Leopardfur!"

Her heart quickened as she heard her own name. She dropped the leaves and hurried toward him.

"We're going to fetch dry bedding," Hailstar announced. "There's a barn just past the dog fence." His eyes were shining. "I used to hunt there when I was a 'paw. I haven't been there for many, many moons."

Crookedjaw was pacing around the RiverClan leader. "We can catch some mice while we're there."

Leopardfur felt a surge of hope. For the first time in days, some of her Clanmates might sleep in dry nests with full bellies. As Hailstar headed for the camp entrance, she hurried after him.

The patrol followed the path around the camp wall. The stepping-stones had disappeared beneath the surface, so they crossed the river at its narrowest point. The current was fierce here, but there was not far to swim. Leopardfur had become such a strong swimmer that it was easy to push through the surging water, and she was pleased to note that she could hardly remember the time when she'd been frightened of getting her paws wet. Climbing out on the far bank, she looked back to check that the others were safe. Hailstar and Crookedjaw waded out, Petaldust following, but where was Sedgecreek? Leopardfur couldn't see her denmate in the frothing river. As she began to splash back into the water, Sedgecreek's head appeared above the waves. Water streaming from her ears and whiskers, the tabby she-cat swam to the bank and climbed out.

"Are you okay?" Leopardfur hurried to meet her.

"Of course." Sedgecreek shook out her fur. "I swam underwater. The current's not so strong there."

I might be a stronger swimmer than I used to be, Leopardfur thought, *but I still don't know the river as well as some of my Clanmates do.*

Hailstar and Crookedjaw were already heading for the beech copse, where rain was rattling the brown leaves. Leopardfur hurried after them with Petaldust and Sedgecreek, and they fell into single file as they reached the marsh beyond. Half blinded by the rain, Leopardfur didn't see the dog fence until Hailstar signaled the patrol to halt with a flick of his tail.

"Wait." He sniffed along the gray fence. "No dog-scent," he told them, sounding relieved, and slid underneath.

Heart pounding, Leopardfur followed the others. She'd never been here before. Was it even Clan territory? The rain made it hard to detect border scents. The field inside the dog fence was wide and grassy, and there was a sour scent in the air she didn't recognize. She felt exposed as she followed her Clanmates across the open meadow, and was relieved when they reached a low gray wall. As they sheltered beside it, Leopardfur gazed nervously at the huge nest beyond. It rose squarely against the pigeon-gray sky, its black wooden sides dark and forbidding.

"What is it?" she whispered.

Hailstar glanced at her. "It's a barn," he told her.

Petaldust leaned closer. "It's built by Twolegs," she explained. "But they don't sleep in it. They just store grass there and raise mice."

Hailstar and Crookedjaw had leaped onto the low wall.

"All clear?" Crookedjaw looked anxiously at his leader. As Hailstar nodded, he glanced down at the others. "Come on."

Sedgecreek was the first over, and as Leopardfur followed, her heart pounding, she saw a wide stone clearing in front of the barn. Hailstar hurried across it, glancing warily one way and then the other. Leopardfur followed with her Clanmates. She felt suddenly very far from home. The sour smell was getting stronger, and her pelt lifted along her spine. Had Hailstar really hunted here when he was young? She knew the RiverClan leader was brave, but she hadn't realized he was so daring. Since her nursery days, he'd kept close to his Clan, guarding them like an anxious mother. She'd forgotten that he'd once been a warrior who'd had adventures of his own.

Her unease grew as Hailstar ducked into the barn through a small, ragged hole low down in the side. Would it be safe in there? It would be drier, at least.

She followed him through, the rough wood scraping her wet pelt, relieved to find the barn airy and dry. The roof was so high that she wondered if it was brushing the gray clouds outside. She sneezed. The air here was dusty. Motes drifted in shafts of light that fell through slits in the walls. The wide stone floor was stacked with golden piles of dry grass. Leopardfur wondered how much they could carry home. If they made bundles, they might be able to make dry nests for every elder and queen.

Crookedjaw had crossed to the nearest grass stack and was ripping out a clawful. Sedgecreek joined him and began adding to the pile he had made. Leopardfur hurried to the stack next to them and began tearing out bundles of hay. Dust billowed around her, and she narrowed her eyes against the sting as she pulled out more and more. Petaldust and Hailstar worked steadily beside her, and soon the pile they'd made was almost as tall as Leopardfur. She gathered it together and began wrapping the stems around her paws, creating bundles they could carry home between their jaws.

Her belly growled with hunger, and she realized that through the hay smell of sunshine and dried leaves, she could smell mouse. She paused and licked her lips. Hailstar had said they could hunt here. The air was certainly rich with the smell of prey.

Crookedjaw and Sedgecreek were already sniffing around the shadows at the back of the barn. Sedgecreek darted suddenly forward and a mouse scurried past her outstretched paws, straight into Crookedjaw's. He killed it quickly and scanned the barn for more.

Hailstar was watching them too, his pelt prickling with excitement. He hurried to join them, and Leopardfur padded closer. The mice here were big. Crookedjaw's catch lay on the stone, plump and large, and there was another, moving in the shadows, that looked even bigger.

She unsheathed her claws. How would they carry so many good things home? They might have to make two trips, first to take home the bedding, another to carry home their catch. The Clan would be pleased to see what they'd brought. She imagined Softwing's eyes shining when she realized her kits would sleep in dry nests tonight.

"Watch out!"

Crookedjaw's warning yowl made her jerk her muzzle around. Was a Twoleg coming? She sniffed the air, sneezing as dust filled her nose. Then a rancid scent hit her. It had the warmth and muskiness of mouse-scent, but there was a sourness that made her shudder.

"Rats!" Hailstar's pelt spiked with alarm.

Sedgecreek squawked with surprise. "They're attacking us!"

Leopardfur's eyes widened. The four creatures darting from the shadows were long and muscular, far larger than mice, their sharp yellow teeth glinting in the dim light, their tails like stiff worms. They were squealing, and their eyes glittered with malice. Fear flared beneath her pelt as one of the rats fastened its jaws around Sedgecreek's hind paw.

Crookedjaw pounced on it, killing it with a single bite, but blood was already welling on Sedgecreek's paw. "Are you okay?" he asked, but there was no time to check the wound. More rats were streaming from every side of the barn.

Leopardfur's pelt spiked as fear flooded her.

Hailstar swiped at one after another, flinging them away, but they kept coming.

"Get help!" Crookedjaw yowled at Petaldust.

"But—" Petaldust began to argue.

"Now!"

Hailstar shook a rat from his forepaw, where it had latched on with its jaws.

Petaldust turned and raced for the gap in the wall. Beside

Leopardfur, Sedgecreek was fighting on three legs, blood pouring from her fourth as she shook one rat off, then another, her balance awkward as she leaned her head away from the vile creatures while clawing at them. Hailstar lunged this way and that, rats on every side.

Pain seared Leopardfur's tail. She felt the weight of a rat dragging behind her. Spinning, she sank her teeth into its neck. It thrashed, paws flailing. As it fell limp, she felt claws dig into her back. Another was clinging to her pelt. Its sharp teeth sank into her flesh. Panic sparked beneath her pelt. The rats were attacking faster than she could fight them off. "Help!"

Crookedjaw darted toward her and hooked the rat off of her back. Its teeth ripped out fur, and she yelped as the sour stench of blood and rats flooded around her.

"Hailstar!" Sedgecreek's wail sounded above the rats' shrieking.

Leopardfur jerked around. The RiverClan leader was staggering, one rat clinging to his spine, another dragging at his hind legs with its teeth. Crookedjaw raced toward him and hauled the biggest rat off with his claws. He flung it into the shadows and knocked another away as Hailstar fought to regain his paws before he was lost beneath the sea of rats.

As a fresh surge poured toward her, Leopardfur batted one with a hefty swipe. But another took its place. She swung blow after blow as the rats kept coming. She felt Sedgecreek slump against her and glanced in alarm at her denmate. Sedgecreek's ears were flat, her eyes wide with terror, but she was still fighting. She pressed harder against Leopardfur as she struggled to stay on her paws. Leopardfur pressed back, doing her best to support her Clanmate as they fought off wave after wave of rats. "Can we get to the entrance?" she called, not daring to take her eyes from their attackers to see if there was a way to escape.

Crookedjaw answered. "If we stop fighting for a moment, we'll be overwhelmed," he yowled.

"But we can't keep this up!" Leopardfur wailed.

"We need to work together." Crookedjaw backed toward them, hooking Hailstar's pelt and jerking the RiverClan leader with him. "Warriors! Tail-to-tail!"

Leopardfur understood. She scuttled backward and pressed her spine against Crookedjaw's. Hailstar and Sedgecreek wedged themselves in between. As one, they reared up onto their hind paws, forming a circle of flashing claws. Hailstar was panting. Leopardfur could feel his flanks heaving against hers and his blood soaking her pelt, but still he thrashed mercilessly at the surging rats.

Her panic rose into rage. How dare prey attack warriors! Drawing her lips back, she hissed at them and flung out swipe after swipe, yowling in triumph each time she sent one flying backward into the swarm.

Sedgecreek was trembling, her hind legs unsteady beneath her. Leopardfur propped her up as best she could, and Sedgecreek fought fiercely, slamming her forepaws down repeatedly on the writhing, squealing bodies. Over and over again, they swiped and clawed at their foul enemies, until exhaustion began to drag at Leopardfur's bones. Crookedjaw was fighting relentlessly, but even he was beginning to slow. How could they win against so many?

"Try to get to the entrance!" Crookedjaw began to steer the patrol through the mass of rats. Leopardfur winced as one nipped at her hind paw. She kicked it away. Desperation welled in her chest. They had to reach the gap. But Sedgecreek was stumbling. Hailstar seemed barely able to stay upright. She and Crookedjaw appeared to be carrying their weight as they flailed blindly now against the onslaught.

Leopardfur glanced at the hole. It was only a few tail-lengths away, but it seemed unreachable. As she longed for the daylight that showed beyond, a face peeked through the gap.

Petaldust!

She was back!

"I've brought help." The tortoiseshell charged into the barn, Rippleclaw and Timberfur streaming after her. Sunfish, Blackclaw, and Owlfur were at their heels. The warriors plunged into the swarm and began hooking rats with their claws and flinging them away. Owlfur lunged at one rat after another, clamping his jaws around their spines and cracking them as easily as killing fish trapped in a pool. Sunfish tore at the rats' oily pelts, and the air grew thick with their fear-scent. The rats scattered, like mist vanishing beneath the sun, and ran, shrieking, for the edge of the barn, flowing back into the shadows.

Heavy with relief and completely exhausted, Leopardfur dropped to her belly. Her heart ached with gratitude toward

her Clanmates as Timberfur, Owlfur, and Rippleclaw chased
the last of the rats back to their dens: "We did it!" She blinked
happily at Crookedjaw.

Crookedjaw turned and lapped blood from her ears. "Yes,
we did."

Sedgecreek groaned and collapsed onto her side. As she lay
bleeding on the stone, Leopardfur stared at her, appalled by
the ragged bitemarks that showed on every paw.

White fur flashed at the corner of her vision. Leopardfur
recognized Brambleberry's pelt. She moved aside to let the
medicine cat examine Sedgecreek, and Sunfish hurried to
watch.

"Fetch cobwebs," Brambleberry ordered.

Rippleclaw and Timberfur streaked away and stretched up
on the huge piles of grass to snatch cobwebs from the walls.

"Hailstar!"

At Owlfur's panicked mew, Leopardfur jerked around.
The RiverClan leader was lying on the stone, blood welling
at his throat.

She felt sick. "Help him," she begged Brambleberry. The
medicine cat glanced from Sedgecreek to Hailstar, her eyes
narrowing as if she was trying to figure out how she could
tend to both her wounded Clanmates at once. She seemed
instinctively drawn to her leader, until Sedgecreek gasped,
and blood gushed from her wound where Brambleberry had
moved the paw that had staunched the bleeding. She resumed
her position.

"It's his last life," Crookedjaw gasped. Leopardfur felt her heart sink into her belly. She knew that Hailstar was an old cat, but she had never thought to ask how many lives he might have left. "You must—"

"I can't!" Brambleberry's blue eyes shone with grief. "I can't leave—"

"It's all right," Hailstar croaked. "Sedgecreek needs you."

Crookedjaw crouched beside Hailstar, his gaze glittering with horror. "I'm sorry. . . . I let you down."

Leopardfur blinked at him. How could that be true? He'd fought beside the RiverClan leader as fiercely as any warrior could.

Hailstar struggled to focus. "Lead the patrol home safely." His mew was so weak that she barely heard the words.

Crookedjaw pressed his paw to Hailstar's throat and flung a desperate look at Brambleberry. But the medicine cat was still fighting to staunch Sedgecreek's bleeding.

"No!" Crookedjaw let out an anguished wail. It seemed to send thorns into Leopardfur's heart. She saw the RiverClan leader's head loll to one side and his eyes glaze as though frost had taken him. She felt sick.

Sunfish nudged Brambleberry away from Sedgecreek, snatching the cobwebs from her. "I'll finish this." She began wrapping her denmate's paws as Brambleberry darted to Hailstar's side.

Crookedjaw had slumped beside him, his muzzle buried in the leader's pelt, and the medicine cat's eyes darkened as she inspected the wound on Hailstar's neck.

"There was nothing to be done," Brambleberry told

Crookedjaw softly. "The wound was too deep to heal. This life could not have been saved. . . ."

Crookedjaw lifted his head and looked around, as though he barely knew where he was. "Is Leopardfur okay?" he mewed huskily.

"I'm fine." Leopardfur limped to his side. She touched her nose to Hailstar's pelt. The stillness beneath it made her shiver.

Crookedjaw straightened and looked at Sedgecreek. Sunfish sat back as the injured tabby struggled to her paws. "Will you be able to make it home?" he asked her.

Her eyes were dull with exhaustion, but she nodded.

"Help her," he told Timberfur.

The brown tom tucked his shoulder beneath Sedgecreek's and began to guide her toward the hole in the wall. Sunfish pressed in on the other side.

Leopardfur felt numb with shock as Crookedjaw crouched and let Rippleclaw and Owlfur haul the body of their dead leader onto their deputy's back. The pain of her wounds seemed far away. This must be a dream. They'd only come here for dry bedding, and now Hailstar was dead. It didn't make sense. Something felt wrong. She was supposed to save her Clan. That was why StarClan had let her live when her littermates and mother had died. How could she ever fulfill her destiny if she couldn't even save her leader?

"Here." Mudfur pushed a pawful of poppy seeds toward Leopardfur's muzzle. "These will help the pain."

"It's only a few nicks and scrapes," she croaked, and yet she could hardly lift her head and lay stiff with pain in the medicine-den nest where Mudfur had settled her. Her injuries stung as though the rats' teeth had been coated with nettle juice. And yet she had been lucky. . . .

When Hailstar was not, she thought, miserably.

Sedgecreek was unconscious in the nest beside hers, the smell of blood still fresh on her pelt. Crookedjaw's fur was ragged and bloody, but the poultices Brambleberry had mixed had eased his wounds enough for him to set out with the old medicine cat on the long journey to the Moonstone to receive his nine lives.

He had laid Hailstar in the clearing, and the Clan had gathered around him. It was as though they'd become suddenly numb to the driving rain that washed their dead leader's fur clean and battered their huddled bodies. Darkness was falling and the Clan was silent.

In the medicine den, Leopardfur could only hear Sedgecreek's labored breathing and the swirling of the river outside. She tried to struggle to her paws. "I should join the vigil."

Mudfur nudged her back into the damp moss. "You need to rest," he mewed.

She didn't fight him. She was too weary and miserable. "I should have saved him."

"You fought bravely, from what I hear." He nudged the poppy seeds closer. "No warrior can do more than that."

"But you said StarClan let me live for a reason." She looked at him hopelessly.

"That reason clearly wasn't to save Hailstar," Mudfur told her.

"He was our *leader*," she mewed.

"He was old, and no cat lives forever," Mudfur mewed softly. "Not even a leader. All you need to do is defend your Clan. Let StarClan take care of the rest."

She met his gaze, wondering what he meant. How could she leave it to her ancestors to protect RiverClan? They were dead and she was alive. She'd failed today, but she was more determined than ever to make sure her Clan never suffered again.

CHAPTER 4

Leopardfur dived deep, relishing the cold water after the heat of the greenleaf sun. She'd spotted the carp on the far side of the river, its scales flashing as it surfaced for a moment to snatch at a fly. Now she followed the deep channel in the middle of the riverbed, heading toward it, holding her breath. Her pelt was slicked along her body as she swam. Her tail kept her steady. Staying close to the bottom, she glanced up and saw the carp above her, silhouetted against glittering sunshine.

She pushed up, kicking out with her legs, swishing her tail to give her more speed. The carp seemed to sense her and darted suddenly forward, but she anticipated it and caught it easily, snatching its tail between her teeth and hauling it close enough to grab with her claws. She killed it with a bite in the water, then carried it back to the shore, wading out and dropping it at Sunfish's paws.

Leopardfur licked her lips. With prey abundant and the fresh-kill pile full every day now, she hoped there'd be enough left to taste a mouthful or two of its plump, tasty flesh. She blinked at Sunfish, expecting her friend to be impressed. But Sunfish was gazing back at the camp again.

"I'm sure Whitekit's fine," Leopardfur told her, swallowing back exasperation. "Beetlenose will keep an eye on him."

"But he's used to having me around," Sunfish fretted.

"He's in camp," Leopardfur reasoned. "What harm can come to him there?"

Sunfish was still staring at the thick reed wall that shielded the camp from the river. "I think we should head back."

"We're hardly more than a tree-length away," Leopardfur pointed out. It had taken all morning to persuade Sunfish to leave the nursery and come hunting. She couldn't *really* want to go home so soon. Whitekit was almost ready to begin his apprentice training. "And you haven't caught a fish yet."

Sunfish glanced at the river rippling past. "Okay," she agreed. "Just one and then we must go home."

Leopardfur shook out her dripping fur and lay down on the warm stones beside the water as Sunfish slid in and dived beneath the surface. She gave the carp a loving lick, a purr rising in her throat as she imagined the sweetness of the flesh beneath the rough scales. She longed to take a bite, but a good warrior fed their Clan first, so she closed her eyes instead and imagined one day carrying home a fish huge enough to feed the whole Clan. Of course, Tanglewhisker and Softwing preferred birds. She shuddered. Why would any cat want to eat their way through smelly feathers when fish came from the river clean and easy to bite into? But she should respect her Clan's tastes and wishes. Especially if she was going to be their leader one day.

As her thoughts meandered drowsily, she heard splashing

and opened her eyes. Sunfish was padding toward her, a skinny perch between her jaws.

Leopardfur heaved herself to her paws. The sun had almost dried her pelt already. She hoped that a taste of fishing had persuaded Sunfish to stay out a little longer. The sky was so blue and the river so refreshing that she wanted to stay here and hunt until sunset. "Are you sure you want to go back now?"

Sunfish laid her catch on the pebbles. "Thanks for bringing me out here," she mewed. "But I want to get back and check on Whitekit. Beetlenose is a good father, but you know what he's like. Whitekit could get into all kinds of mischief and Beetlenose would hardly notice."

Leopardfur didn't agree. Beetlenose fussed over the playful kit even more than Sunfish did. "You weren't this anxious with your first litter," she pointed out. "Vixenleap and Grasswhisker both grew into fine warriors. And Silverstream too." Sunfish had raised Crookedstar's daughter after her mother, Willowbreeze, had died of greencough.

"*They* had each other," Sunfish argued. "Whitekit only has me and Beetlenose, and one kit on his own in the nursery is different. He can get into far more trouble."

"Are you sure?" Leopardfur purred. "There were three litters in the nursery when we were kits, and we got into plenty of trouble."

Sunfish conceded a purr. "I guess," she mewed. "But once I start worrying about Whitekit, it's hard to stop."

"Come on, then. Let's go." Leopardfur didn't want her friend to feel uneasy. She picked up the carp and waded into the river, swam easily to the other side, and pushed her way through the reeds.

Sunfish caught up to her as she padded into the camp, her eyes lighting up as Whitekit dashed across the clearing to meet them.

"Guess what!" He bounced around them, his eyes shining.

Leopardfur laid her carp on the ground and purred indulgently. Out of all Sunfish's kits, she had an especially soft spot for Whitekit. He was so energetic and eager to learn. "Did you come to meet us because you smelled the carp?" she teased.

Whitekit stuck out his tail indignantly. "No!"

"Are you sure?" Leopardfur teased. "It's your favorite fish, isn't it?"

"Yes, but I have something to tell you!" The young tom's eyes were as round as an owl's.

Sunfish laid her fish beside Leopardfur's. "Did you stay close to Beetlenose while I was gone?" Her gaze flitted toward the nursery, where the black tom was dozing outside.

"Of course!" Whitekit hopped from one paw to another. He looked like he was about to burst with frustration. "But listen!"

Leopardfur glanced at Sunfish, wondering if they'd made the young tom wait long enough to share his news.

Sunfish caught her eye. "Let me put these on the fresh-kill pile first—"

"No!" Whitekit slapped his paws onto the skinny perch to stop her picking it up. "You *have* to listen!"

Sunfish purred. "Okay," she mewed. "What is it?"

Relief flooded Whitekit's eyes. "Crookedstar says he's going to give me my apprentice name tomorrow!" He fluffed out his fur. "I'm going to start my training." He glanced around the camp. Oakheart, the Clan's new deputy, was taking a rare nap beside the warriors' den. Echomist and Piketooth were sharing tongues beside him, while Whitefang and Cedarpelt were picking at the remains of a trout. "I wonder who my mentor will be."

Leopardfur's heart quickened. She hoped it would be her. In the two greenleafs since she'd become a warrior, she'd never had an apprentice. Whitekit would be fun to train. He was boisterous and confident, yet warm-hearted like his mother. She was sure he'd learn quickly.

Sunfish's pelt had ruffled. "Are you six moons already?" She sounded anxious.

"Of course!" Whitekit puffed out his chest. "Can't you tell? I'll be as big as Beetlenose soon."

Leopardfur nudged him with her nose. "You'll have to eat a lot of fish to grow *that* big," she mewed.

"I will!" Whitekit told her. "Once I've learned how to hunt, the fresh-kill pile will always be full. And I can eat as much fish as I like."

Leopardfur glanced toward Crookedstar's den, where the leader was talking to Mudfur. Perhaps the RiverClan leader was talking about her, wondering whether she was ready to become a mentor. Surely she had enough experience by now? She figured she'd need to have at least two apprentices before she had any real hope of becoming deputy. An experienced deputy would be better at supporting her leader.

Sunfish followed her gaze. "I hope Crookedstar chooses someone sensible to train Whitekit."

Leopardfur shifted her paws.

"Perhaps he'll choose me," Leopardfur mewed lightly, pretending to joke.

Sunfish blinked at her, looking suddenly brighter. "Perhaps he will."

"Whitekit, you're six moons now, and it's time for you to be apprenticed."

Leopardfur could hardly hear Crookedstar through the pounding of her own heartbeat. Whitekit stood in front of the RiverClan leader, looking suddenly too small for his apprentice name. The Clan was ringed around the clearing, their glossy pelts washed smooth for the naming ceremony, their gazes fixed fondly on the warrior-to-be. Sunfish and Beetlenose sat together, their tails curled proudly over their forepaws while Grasswhisker, Vixenleap, and Silverstream watched beside them.

Will he choose me? Hope still itched in Leopardfur's belly. *He'd have told me by now, surely.* But perhaps he wanted it to be a surprise.

She could see that Whitekit was trying hard not to fidget, his tail twitching as he pressed his paws determinedly into the ground.

Crookedstar went on. "From today, until you receive your warrior name, you will be known as Whitepaw."

Leopardfur leaned forward, her ears pricked.

"And your mentor will be Whitefang."

Her heart dropped like a stone in her chest. Sunfish caught her eye, her gaze sympathetic. But Leopardfur lifted her chin, telling herself that Whitefang was a good choice. He was kind and patient, and just what a bundle of energy like White-paw needed. There would be other apprentices for her—and maybe she *wasn't* ready yet.

Whitepaw was staring excitedly at his new mentor as Whitefang padded toward him.

Crookedstar was still speaking. "I am certain White-fang will teach you well. He has a lot to share." He turned to Whitefang as the warrior reached him. "Whitefang, you have trained some of our best warriors." Leopardfur's paws pricked eagerly. *Does he mean me?* "And I know you will teach Whitepaw the same skills you taught them, and the respect and honor only a true RiverClan warrior understands."

Whitefang dipped his head to Crookedstar and touched his nose to Whitepaw's head. Around her, Leopardfur's Clan-mates began to chant the new apprentice's name.

"Whitepaw!"

"Whitepaw!"

She joined in, pushing away the disappointment still lin-gering in her heart. At least Sunfish would be free of the nursery now and they could hunt and patrol together as much as they liked.

As the cheering died and the Clan returned to their duties, Whitefang glanced at Leopardfur. She lifted her tail to show she was pleased and hurried to congratulate him. "You were a great mentor to me," she purred as she reached him. "I know you'll train Whitepaw well."

Whitepaw was pacing back and forth. "Can we go hunting straight away?" He didn't wait for an answer. "Whitefang's taking me hunting!" he called to Sunfish and Beetlenose, who were heading toward their kit, their eyes bright with pride.

"No, he's not," Whitefang mewed sternly. "I'm going to show you around RiverClan territory."

Whitepaw blinked at him. "Will we see the ThunderClan border? Will we see squirrels? *Alive* ones?"

Whitefang's sternness seemed to melt. He broke into a purr. "Yes. And we'll see the WindClan border too," he told Whitepaw. "It'll be a long trek. I hope you're ready."

"I am *so* ready." Whitepaw ducked away as Sunfish tried to nuzzle him and raced for the camp entrance.

Whitefang caught Leopardfur's eye. "He's going to keep me even busier than you did," he mewed as he hurried after the young tom.

The sun had scorched the camp all morning, and Leopardfur was looking forward to the cool of the night.

"Leopardfur."

She jerked around as Crookedstar called her name. The RiverClan leader was standing with Oakheart in the shade of the sedge wall. Hurrying from the warriors' den, where she'd been helping Sunfish to weave fresh willow into the walls, Leopardfur went to stand in front of them. "Yes?"

"I want you to lead a patrol to Sunningrocks," Crookedstar told her.

Her tail twitched with excitement. Sunningrocks had changed paws so many times in recent moons that any border patrol there had become an important mission. Was Crookedstar showing her that he thought she was ready for more responsibility?

She met his gaze steadily. "Who shall I take with me?"

"You decide."

Her heart quickened. *He trusts me.* Around the clearing, she was aware of her Clanmates' gazes. Whitefang had stopped rummaging through the fresh-kill pile and was looking at her with interest. Stonefur and Frogleap watched her from the patch of grass where they'd been sharing an eel. Skyheart paused as she padded sleepily from the warriors' den, while Rippleclaw and Ottersplash got to their paws, their ears pricking.

"Be careful, though," Crookedstar cautioned.

"I understand," Leopardfur told him. There was always a chance of trouble at Sunningrocks, but she was ready to deal with anything.

"I want the border marked clearly," Crookedstar went on. "ThunderClan needs to be sure where it is."

Oakheart narrowed his eyes. "Take a large patrol," he told her. "Just in case."

"Okay." Leopardfur dipped her head and turned toward the warriors' den, where Sunfish was still working on the wall. Her friend hadn't been on a border patrol since she'd left the nursery a few days earlier. "Sunfish!"

"Yes?" The gray she-cat tucked in the end of a willow stem and turned to look at Leopardfur.

"I'm leading a patrol to Sunningrocks," she called. "Do you want to come?"

"Of course." Sunfish hurried toward her.

Whitepaw, who'd been grooming Tanglewhisker's pelt for ticks beside the elders' den, looked up. "Can I come too?"

Whitefang left the fresh-kill pile and crossed the clearing. "You're staying here," he told his apprentice firmly.

Whitepaw bristled. "But I need to know where the border is." He abandoned Tanglewhisker's pelt and hurried toward his mentor. "You didn't show me that part when you showed me our territory."

"Because it's too dangerous," Whitefang mewed.

Leopardfur shifted her paws. She'd been planning to ask Whitefang to join the patrol, but she didn't want to cause a rift between Whitepaw and his mentor. And yet this was the first time she'd led a patrol to Sunningrocks. She'd feel more confident if Whitefang was there. She pretended she couldn't see Whitepaw's wide, longing gaze. "Will you come?" she asked Whitefang.

Whitepaw's tail twitched with indignation. "That's not fair!"

Whitefang looked at him. "You don't know enough battle moves."

"I could learn," Whitepaw mewed.

"A warrior learns *before* a battle, not during," Whitefang mewed.

Whitepaw's pelt prickled excitedly. "Is there going to be a battle?"

"No." Leopardfur lifted her muzzle. "But it's still too dangerous. If there *is* trouble, you're not experienced enough to handle it."

Whitefang cut in before Whitepaw could argue. "There's plenty for you to do in camp." He nodded toward Tanglewhisker, who was struggling to nibble at an itch on his flank. "You haven't finished pulling out Tanglewhisker's ticks yet. And there's the elders' bedding to be changed."

Whitepaw scowled at his mentor. "I thought I was learning to be a warrior, not a nest cleaner."

Leopardfur blinked at him sympathetically. "Every 'paw has to do things they don't like," she told him.

Sunfish nodded. "It's how you learn to be a true warrior."

Whitepaw turned his tail on them. "I don't see how," he muttered crossly, stomping back toward Tanglewhisker.

Leopardfur was relieved to be leaving the young tom here in camp. Leading a patrol of experienced warriors was challenging enough. She called to Stonefur and Frogleap. "Come with us." Ottersplash and Rippleclaw were staring at her eagerly. They were skilled warriors too. With them, the patrol would be strong enough to deal with anything. "And you." She beckoned them with her tail, relieved when they bounded to join her. It felt strange to be giving orders to such senior warriors.

She headed out of camp, reassured as Whitefang fell in beside her. Ottersplash and Rippleclaw followed as she led the patrol through the reed bed and waded into the river. It was shallow here and easy to cross, and the path on the far bank led straight to Sunningrocks. It would save them from having to follow the river and scramble up the cliff from the shore.

She swam across the river and climbed out.

Sunfish caught up to her as she shook out her fur. "I can't believe you used to be scared of the water," she whispered.

"I might *still* be scared of it if you hadn't put that carp on the other side," Leopardfur purred.

She checked that the rest of the patrol was still with her. Ottersplash, Whitefang, and Rippleclaw were already waiting on the path. Stonefur and Frogleap were climbing out a few tail-lengths downstream. Leopardfur was always impressed by what a strong swimmer Stonefur was.

"Let's go." Leopardfur headed up the path to Sunningrocks. At the top, a broad sweep of ThunderClan's forest edged the wide stretch of sun-drenched stone. It was past sunhigh, but the rock still held the midday heat and burned her paws. She crossed it quickly, signaling the patrol to follow with a flick of her tail.

Beneath the shade thrown by the trees, she nodded to Whitefang. "Take Rippleclaw and Ottersplash and mark the border as far as the cliff edge." She looked at Stonefur, Frogleap, and Sunfish. "We'll mark the trees on the other side." As Whitefang led the others away, she headed for an oak and sniffed it. The scent markers left by the last RiverClan patrol had faded almost to nothing, and she marked it freshly and moved on to the next. Frogleap and Sunfish spread out and marked the trees farther along.

Sunfish paused, lifting her muzzle.

Leopardfur glanced at her. Her friend's pelt was prickling along her spine. "What's wrong?"

"Can you smell ThunderClan?"

As Sunfish spoke, a hiss sounded from the cliff top. Leopardfur whirled around and saw Whitefang and Otter-splash backing away from it.

Rippleclaw was still peering over the edge. "There's a ThunderClan patrol down there," he growled.

Leopardfur stiffened. "What are they doing near Sunning-rocks?"

"They haven't crossed the border," Whitefang mewed, but he sounded wary.

"Yet," Rippleclaw mewed ominously.

Leopardfur's hackles lifted.

"They're climbing the slope," Rippleclaw warned. "It looks like they're heading this way."

Did the ThunderClan patrol know they were here? Had they been waiting for a RiverClan patrol to show up? Oak-heart had been right to suggest bringing so many warriors. Anger pulsed beneath her pelt.

"Stand with me." Leopardfur gathered the patrol and faced the forest where the border met the stones. She curled her lip as she glimpsed pelts through the undergrowth. The stench of ThunderClan bathed her tongue. Bushing out her fur, she glared angrily at the ThunderClan cats as they slid between the brambles and padded into view.

Leopardfur recognized Redtail, ThunderClan's deputy. Lionheart and Whitestorm were with him. Flanking them were Tigerclaw and Mousefur, and, at the rear, Runningwind and Longtail shifted in the shadows between the trees.

She flattened her ears. "What are you doing here?" she snarled at Redtail.

"We're marking our border." Redtail narrowed his eyes. "Just like you."

"You're on our land." Leopardfur gazed pointedly at his forepaws. Their tips reached across the border line and touched the stone.

"Am I?" Redtail blinked at her innocently but didn't move.

He wants *a fight.* Leopardfur swallowed back a hiss.

Whitefang murmured in her ear. "They're trying to provoke you," he mewed. "Let's just finish marking the border and move on."

Leopardfur stared at him. "And let them think they scared us away?"

"I'm not scared," Whitefang told her evenly. "But this isn't the time for a fight. We're not prepared."

"We're warriors," she hissed back. "We're always prepared."

Redtail sniffed. "Are you trying to work out where your border is?"

"We *know* where our border is," Rippleclaw snarled.

"Really?" Tigerclaw narrowed his eyes. "Because we can barely smell it. We thought you'd given up marking it."

Ottersplash flattened her ears. "What do you think we're here to do now?"

"Lie in the sun?" Redtail mewed. "Isn't that what River-Clan is best at?"

"It's not like you're going to *hunt* here," Tigerclaw added.

"RiverClan cats can't catch anything but fish."

Rage churned in Leopardfur's belly. "All ThunderClan cats can catch is greencough," she snapped.

Redtail and Tigerclaw exchanged glances, and Redtail slid his paw forward a little more.

"Get off our land!" Leopardfur wasn't going to leave until they did. Whatever Whitefang said, ThunderClan was clearly planning to trespass as soon as RiverClan turned their backs.

Whitefang leaned closer. "Let's go back and report this to Crookedstar," he whispered.

"And let them spread their stink all over our land?" Leopardfur showed her teeth.

Sunfish looked at her nervously. "Should I go and fetch help?"

"We don't need help." Leopardfur didn't take her eyes off Redtail. If he made a move, she was ready. "There are enough of us here to chase them off."

Whitestorm, the white ThunderClan warrior, glanced at Redtail. "Let's mark the border and leave," he mewed.

Rippleclaw lashed his tail. "Yeah," he snarled. "Just leave."

Tigerclaw stuck out his chest. "RiverClan doesn't tell ThunderClan what to do!"

Ottersplash glared at him. "Go home, squirrel-chaser."

Redtail's pelt was twitching. Looking Leopardfur in the eye, he mewed slowly, "We'll leave when you leave." As he spoke, his paw slid forward a little more.

"He's just trying to rile you up," Whitefang urged.

But Leopardfur hardly heard him. Rage roared in her ears.

She remembered Mudfur's words. *All you need to do is defend your Clan.* She wasn't going to let this bunch of mangy mouse-chewers take a single tail-length of RiverClan territory.

Redtail slid his paw forward again. With a hiss, she leaped for the ThunderClan deputy and bundled him to the ground. Wrapping her paws around him, she rolled him onto the stone, churning at his belly with her hind legs. Around her, yowls exploded, echoing around the trees as the two patrols flew at each other.

Redtail slithered like a fish between her paws and ducked free. Turning on her, he knocked her forepaws from beneath her. Leopardfur's shoulder hit the hard stone with a thump, and she felt him clawing at her ears. Beside her, Rippleclaw brought his forepaws slamming down on Whitestorm's shoulders, while Sunfish and Frogleap fought back Lionheart with slashing claws. Rage drowned out the sting of Redtail's claws, and she pushed herself up and reared, raking the Thunder-Clan deputy's nose.

Claws hooked her shoulders and tugged her backward. Staggering, she fought to keep her balance and glanced back to see Mousefur snarling at her ear. Redtail's eyes lit up as he saw her struggle. He lifted a paw and flung a blow at her cheek. It hit her with such force that she reeled to one side. But Mousefur kept hold of her, dragging her down onto the stone. For the first time, panic flared through her. She kicked out, pushing Redtail away with a hefty shove, and tried to shake Mousefur free.

A striped tail flashed at the corner of her vision. Frogleap!

He'd leaped across the rock, skimming her by a whisker and slamming into Mousefur. He knocked the ThunderClan she-cat away and pinned her to the rock with such ease that Leopardfur blinked, impressed by the deftness of his movement. She hadn't realized that he'd become such a skilled warrior. She'd thought of him only as the clumsy kit who'd tripped over his tail every time they'd played moss-ball.

A shriek made her jerk her muzzle around. Sunfish was staggering, her eyes bright with pain. Redtail had turned his attack on the gray tabby, and his claws were wet with her blood. As Sunfish dropped to her belly, a red stain spreading across her flank, Redtail reared for another attack.

Leopardfur leaped for him, thrusting him away with her forepaws so ferociously that he yowled in surprise as he fell back against a tree. Falling clumsily among the roots, he struggled to find his paws.

Leopardfur turned. "Sunfish, are you okay?"

Whitefang and Lionheart whirled in front of her. She froze. The great toms were slashing at each other, their massive paws swishing through the air. Blood sprayed the stone as Whitefang caught Lionheart's ear. With a roar of pain, Lionheart struck back, lashing out at Whitefang with a swipe that caught the white warrior's neck.

Leopardfur froze as she saw Whitefang's eyes widen with disbelief. Around her the battle seemed to stand still as Whitefang's throat turned red, his soft fur crimson in the afternoon sun. Whitefang slowed, staggered, then fell to the ground. He landed with a thump, and the two patrols fell back, seeming to sense that something terrible had happened.

Redtail waved Tigerclaw away with his tail, staring in horror at Whitefang as he collapsed onto the stone.

Leopardfur's heart missed a beat. Her breath caught in her throat as Whitefang's body grew limp and his eyes turned dull. She darted to his side and crouched beside him. "Whitefang." She shook him with her paws. "Whitefang. Wake up."

"He's dead. . . ." Rippleclaw touched her shoulder with his muzzle. "Let's get him back to camp."

Leopardfur glanced at the ThunderClan patrol. They were watching in silence, but they hadn't withdrawn. Sunfish was struggling to her paws, blood welling on her flank. Ottersplash and Stonefur hurried to help her. This wasn't a battle they could win now. Leopardfur met Rippleclaw's gaze and nodded.

The black-and-silver tabby tom grabbed Whitefang by the scruff and nodded to Frogleap. Frogleap ducked beneath Whitefang's body and let Rippleclaw heave him onto his shoulders. Holding Whitefang in place, Rippleclaw guided Frogleap toward the river path. Ottersplash and Stonefur limped slowly behind him, supporting Sunfish.

Leopardfur didn't move. Her paws felt rooted to the stone as she stared at the ThunderClan patrol. How had this happened? It made no sense. They should have chased the ThunderClan patrol off. No cat was supposed to get hurt.

Redtail was watching her, his gaze narrow with interest. Tigerclaw's eyes betrayed nothing. Runningwind, Mousefur, and Whitestorm looked blank. Only Lionheart seemed shocked, his pelt rippling uneasily as Frogleap and Rippleclaw carried Whitefang off.

Leopardfur said nothing and turned away. Words would only emphasize her defeat. She padded stiffly after her Clanmates.

I will not forget this.

It took three of them to carry Whitefang across the river. Frogleap supported him on his back while Leopardfur and Rippleclaw held him on either side. The water ran red behind them as the injured patrol staggered out on the far side. Pushing through the reed bed, they carried Whitefang home.

"Leopardfur?" Mudfur hurried from the medicine den as the patrol reached the clearing. Had the scent of blood alerted him? His gaze flitted over her pelt and across the rest of the patrol before he began to give orders. "Take Sunfish to the medicine den," he told Ottersplash and Stonefur. "Lay Whitefang down here."

Crookedstar was running across the clearing, Oakheart at his heels. Leopardfur stared at the RiverClan leader wordlessly as he stopped beside Whitefang.

"Is he dead?" Crookedstar's eyes were wide with horror.

"Yes." Mudfur touched the white warrior's cheek with his paw. "He's with StarClan now."

Leopardfur was aware of her Clanmates clustering around them. She could hear them murmuring but didn't try to make out the words. Whitefang was dead. The kind, thoughtful mentor who had taught her the first hunting move she'd ever learned was gone. He'd never sleep in the warriors' den again, or cross the clearing to rummage through the fresh-kill pile, or hunt beside her on the riverbank.

"Leopardfur." Mudfur was nudging her shoulder with his nose. "Come and help me with Sunfish." He steered her toward the medicine den. "She'll need you."

Beetlenose was already inside. He was crouching beside Sunfish as she lay in a moss-lined nest, her eyes still wide with shock. Stonefur and Ottersplash blinked nervously in the gloom.

"Every cat out except Leopardfur," Mudfur ordered.

"But—" Beetlenose began.

"Go and reassure your kits that she'll be all right," Mudfur told him.

"Will she?" Beetlenose's eyes were glittering with worry.

"It's just a battle wound," Mudfur told him. "You can come and see her when I've cleaned and dressed it." He shooed Beetlenose from the den with his tail, along with Ottersplash and Stonefur. Leopardfur blinked at him, still numb with shock.

"Talk to her while I make a poultice," he told her.

She nodded and crouched down beside Sunfish's nest.

Sunfish was sniffing at the wound on her flank, her whiskers trembling. "Is it deep?"

Leopardfur forced herself to focus. She looked at the wound, at the long scratches where Redtail had torn Sunfish's flesh. "Not too deep," she lied. The scratches looked red and angry, and she was relieved when Mudfur brought a leaf wrapped around a sharp-smelling poultice. She leaned back to give him room to smear it into the wound.

"You'll feel better in no time," Leopardfur promised. "And I'll tell Whitepaw how bravely you fought."

Sunfish winced as Mudfur worked the poultice in. "I'm just glad Whitefang told him to stay behind."

How would Whitepaw react to his mentor's death? Leopardfur's belly tightened. She shouldn't have let the ThunderClan patrol insult them. She should have attacked straight away. Perhaps they could have caught them off guard.

"Come outside." Mudfur was looking at her.

She glanced toward Sunfish. "Don't we have to . . ."

"The poultice needs time to work before I dress it." He padded toward the entrance, nodding at Sunfish. "Lie still," he told her. "The poppy seeds I gave you will start to work soon, and you'll feel more comfortable."

Leopardfur glanced at her friend. "I'll be back in a moment," she promised. She followed Mudfur outside, relieved he was here. She could still hardly believe Whitefang was dead.

He stopped in the shade of the sedge and faced her. "What happened?"

"A ThunderClan patrol was planning to take Sunning-rocks," she told him. "We fought them off."

"You chased them away?" Mudfur stared at her.

"Not exactly."

"They're still there, then?"

"We had to bring Whitefang and Sunfish home." Should she have kept fighting?

"So Whitefang died for nothing."

Leopardfur felt suddenly cold. She blinked at him. Was he angry?

He went on. "And was Sunfish wounded just so you could say you defended RiverClan?"

"I *did* defend RiverClan." Leopardfur's pelt began to prickle with indignation. Mudfur was being unfair.

"So ThunderClan attacked *you.*"

"They crossed the border."

"And *attacked* you," Mudfur pressed.

"They didn't attack us," Leopardfur told him. "But they were going to."

"And you know that because you can read minds." Mudfur was trembling. Fury blazed in his eyes.

"I could read their faces!" Leopardfur mewed hotly. "I had to defend our territory."

"There's a difference between defending territory and starting an unnecessary battle," Mudfur growled.

"How do *you* know?" Leopardfur flattened her ears. "You weren't there."

"I know warriors," Mudfur growled. "They think that land is more important than life, and pride is more important than anything. They fight the same battles over and over again, pretending that fighting solves problems, when really it just makes them worse."

Leopardfur's heart pounded. "Don't dump your issues on me," she hissed. "Just because you can't stomach fighting anymore doesn't mean I have to be less of a warrior. I'm not going to back down from a fight! If you don't understand what being a warrior means anymore, that's not my problem. Thunder-Clan started this. ThunderClan killed Whitefang and hurt Sunfish. If I stood up to them, that doesn't make me the villain."

Mudfur stared at her, then turned and headed back into the medicine den. Her heart suddenly ached with grief. The battle should never have happened. Whitefang should still be alive. But it wasn't her fault, it was ThunderClan's, and Mudfur wasn't going to persuade her that a true warrior could have made any other choice.

Gray skies hid the sun, but the air felt thick, and Leopardfur longed for the storm to bring cool, fresh wind to the camp. Her heart had sat like a stone in her chest as she'd crouched beside Whitepaw during Whitefang's vigil. Through the long, sticky night, the Clan had sat with the dead warrior's body as it lay in the middle of the clearing, dressed with flowers from the meadow and nestled in a bed made of reeds.

At dawn, Crookedstar had led the patrol that carried the body out of camp and buried it downstream. He returned now with Oakheart, Stonefur, and Piketooth, their paws still muddy from digging, and padded to the middle of the camp.

"Let all cats old enough to swim gather to hear my words," he yowled.

Ottersplash and Timberfur padded from the sedge wall. Tanglewhisker led Birdsong from the elders' den. Skyheart stood close to Blackclaw and Loudbelly as their Clanmates gathered in a circle around their leader. The remains of

Whitefang's bed of reeds still sat in the clearing, and Crooked-star glanced at it for a moment before he began.

"ThunderClan has once more taken the life of a brave RiverClan warrior." He looked at Leopardfur. "Once again, we've had to bravely defend the rocks given to us by StarClan countless moons ago. But Whitefang will be remembered. He gave his life to preserve our land." The RiverClan cats glanced at one another, their gazes heavy with grief. Crookedstar lifted his chin. "Whitefang was training a young warrior who will always carry with him the lessons his mentor taught him. In this way, no warrior ever truly leaves RiverClan. By teaching others, we leave behind our skill and our wisdom." His gaze flitted to Whitepaw, who was standing beside Beetlenose, his eyes glistening. "But just because Whitefang is dead doesn't mean Whitepaw will stop learning. His new mentor will be Leopardfur."

Surprise sparked through Leopardfur's pelt as Crookedstar went on. "Whitefang taught her well, and she will be able to pass on his knowledge to Whitepaw. She has proved herself a loyal and strong warrior and more than ready to train an apprentice." He beckoned her forward with a nod, and she hurried across the clearing.

Whitepaw blinked at her and padded forward, glancing uncertainly at Crookedstar, who gave him an encouraging nod. "Leopardfur will be a fine mentor," he mewed.

Leopardfur's paws pricked nervously. Was Whitefang watching from StarClan? Would he approve? "I'll be the best mentor I can," she promised Whitepaw.

As her Clanmates began to call Whitepaw's name, Leopardfur caught her father's eyes. Mudfur was watching her, his eyes dark. She looked away. It didn't matter what he thought. She'd defended her Clan, and that was the greatest thing a warrior could do.

"How's Whitepaw doing?" Sunfish blinked at Leopardfur, her eyes dull with fever.

"He's really talented." Leopardfur shifted closer to Sunfish's nest. It had been a quarter moon since the fight with ThunderClan. Sunfish should have been out of the medicine den and in her own nest by now, but the wound on her flank was taking time to heal; even from here, Leopardfur could smell the sourness of infection.

"Is he learning quickly?" Sunfish didn't wait for an answer. She sounded fretful. "He always was smart. Does he do as he's told? I hope he's not being a bother."

Beetlenose shifted beside her. He'd been with Sunfish day and night since the battle. "Of course he's not being a bother," he mewed.

"He's easy to train." Leopardfur lapped Sunfish's ear with her tongue, alarmed at how hot it felt. "I love being his mentor." It was true. Whitepaw was a fast learner and eager to improve, and he was quick on his paws. But she was concerned: He was still grieving for Whitefang, and he was worried about his mother. So she'd kept him busy, taking him out for most of the day and giving him chores in camp until late. He never complained, which worried her even more. In the past, he would have objected to fetching fresh moss for the nursery or picking fish bones out of the elders' nests. But now he just dipped his head obediently and followed her orders without question. She forced a purr to reassure Sunfish. "He's going to make a great warrior."

Beetlenose looked up as Mudfur padded into the den. "Have you tried every herb?" he asked the medicine cat anxiously.

"Yes." Mudfur padded to Sunfish's nest and looked gravely at his patient. "If she rests and tries to eat, she'll pull through."

Beetlenose blinked at him gratefully, but Leopardfur recognized doubt in her father's mew. His uncertainty scared her.

"Do you want me to fetch you some prey?" she asked Sunfish.

Sunfish shook her head slowly.

"Maybe just a minnow?" Leopardfur pressed.

"No thanks."

Beetlenose's eyes darkened. "I've been trying to persuade her to eat all day, but she has no appetite."

"I'll give her some more feverfew," Mudfur mewed. "That might help."

As he padded away to his herb store, Leopardfur got to her paws. Whitepaw was waiting outside with Vixenleap and Grasswhisker. They'd visited Sunfish earlier, but Mudfur didn't want his patient worn out. Silverstream was with them, staying close to the medicine den in case of news.

Leopardfur touched her nose to Sunfish's warm head. "Rest," she murmured. "I'll visit you again tomorrow."

Beetlenose moved closer to his mate as she left the den.

Outside, fluffy white clouds dotted the afternoon sky. Whitepaw hurried to meet her. "Is she any better?" His eyes were round with worry.

"She seems a little brighter," Leopardfur told him, knowing it wasn't true but wanting to put his mind at rest. He seemed relieved, his pelt smoothing a little, and guilt prickled in her belly. "Check on Tanglewhisker and Birdsong," she told him. "They might need something."

"Okay." He hurried away, and she hoped his apprentice duties would be enough to distract him.

As she crossed the clearing, Frogleap fell in beside her.

"Is Sunfish any better?" he asked.

She glanced at him, wondering if she could be honest. Sunfish was his littermate.

He looked back at her steadily. "It's okay," he mewed. "I can handle it."

She felt relieved and sad all at once. "I think she's getting weaker."

"But she's strong." Frogleap guided her toward the fresh-kill pile. "If any cat can fight this infection, she can." The prey was already starting to stink. Leopardfur's nose wrinkled. Frogleap hooked a small carp from the bottom, where the shade had kept it cool. He laid it at her paws, then took a limp sparrow from the top for himself. She picked it up and followed him to a shady spot beside the sedge.

As he dropped the sparrow on the grass, she settled beside him and stared at the carp. Guilt was still pricking her belly, and not because she'd lied to Whitepaw. "I should have protected her," she mewed. "I should have stopped Redtail from hurting her."

"I think about that every time I close my eyes," Frogleap told her. "If only I'd been quicker or stronger . . ." His gaze drifted toward the medicine den. "But we can't change what happened." He pushed the carp closer to Leopardfur. "And starving ourselves won't help the Clan."

Leopardfur watched him take a bite of his sparrow, noticing for the first time how broad his head was now and how tightly his muscles bunched beneath his pelt as he moved. He seemed so different from the gangly kit she'd grown up with. She pushed the thought away and bit into the carp, forcing herself to swallow a mouthful. How could she eat this prey when Sunfish needed it more than she did?

Leopardfur padded into camp. It was swathed in the purple shadow as the sun sank behind the distant moor. Skyheart, Ottersplash, and Timberfur followed her quietly after a long border patrol. Her paws ached, and she was looking forward to curling in her nest . . .

Until she saw Mudfur hurrying toward her. "Sunfish has been asking for you," he mewed as he reached her.

Leopardfur's chest tightened. She dashed to the medicine den, slowing as she reached the entrance and willing her pelt to smooth before she padded softly in. "Sunfish?"

In the evening light it was hard to make out the gray tabby in her nest, but her eyes glinted in the gloom.

"Leopardfur." She sounded relieved. "I was worried you wouldn't come in time."

In time? Leopardfur swallowed back alarm. What did she mean? "You're not going anywhere, are you?" she mewed, trying to joke away the foreboding in Sunfish's words.

Sunfish blinked at her. "I wanted to talk to you while Beetlenose was resting." She looked at the nest beside her, and Leopardfur realized that Beetlenose was curled inside, his breathing slow and deep as he slept.

She crouched close to Sunfish, alarmed at the warmth flooding her friend's pelt. Her fever must be worse. She lowered her voice. "What do you want to tell me?"

"Look after Whitepaw." Sunfish's mew was husky.

"Of course I will," Leopardfur whispered. "I'm his mentor. I'll make sure he doesn't get hurt."

"I mean, if anything happens to me." Sunfish was gazing at her with an intensity that frightened her.

"The only thing that's going to happen to you is that you're going to get better," Leopardfur told her. She *had* to get better. Anything else was unthinkable.

"But if it does," Sunfish pressed quietly, "I want you to be there for him, like kin." She glanced at Beetlenose. "I know he'll have his father and Grasswhisker and Vixenleap. And Silverstream will look out for him too, but it's not the same."

"Not the same as what?"

"As having a mother." Sunfish's eyes shone. "He's young. He still needs a mother, even though he doesn't realize it. I want you to watch over him as I would. Make sure he's okay. Care for him." She paused, as though trying to catch her breath.

A chill seemed to reach through Leopardfur's pelt despite the warmth of the evening. *I've never been a mother,* she thought. *I've never even* wanted *to be a mother.* Leopardfur felt out of her depth. "You're going to get better," she insisted again.

Sunfish didn't take her eyes from Leopardfur. "But if I don't," she mewed. "Promise me." Leopardfur's mouth grew dry as Sunfish's gaze grew desperate. "Promise you'll take care of him."

Leopardfur heard her friend's words, but they sounded almost as strange as a dog's bark or a bird's chirp. She couldn't bear to agree, because she didn't want to admit to Sunfish how bad things looked. But how could she say no? "Of course I will."

Beetlenose lifted his head and blinked sleepily for a moment before scrambling to his paws. "Was I asleep long?" He hopped out of his nest and nosed his way past Leopardfur to touch his nose to Sunfish's cheek. "How are you feeling?"

Leopardfur was relieved to let Beetlenose take her place. He could comfort Sunfish better than she could.

She backed out of the den, her pelt prickling with unease. She loved Whitepaw as much as she could love any kit, but did she have the skills she'd need to be a mother to him?

"Is she okay?"

Whitepaw's mew made her jump. She whirled around and saw him blinking at her, like a shadow in the evening light. His eyes were hollow, as though he hadn't slept for days. "Yes," she told him, even though she knew it wasn't true.

"I knew it." Whitepaw's ears pricked eagerly. "I visited her earlier and she seemed better."

Leopardfur stared at him. Did he really believe that? "She'll probably be even better after a good night's sleep."

"Do you think so?" Whitepaw held her gaze as though trying to read it. Leopardfur had to force herself not to look away, not to betray her own terrible thoughts.

Her thoughts that Sunfish did not have long.

She shook out her pelt. "Why don't we go practice night hunting," she mewed.

They both needed to stay busy. With any luck, she'd wear Whitepaw out and he'd be able to sleep.

It felt like she'd only been asleep for a moment when she felt her nest shaking. She opened her eyes. The warriors' den was gray as pale dawn light seeped through the woven walls.

Her nest shook again. Whitepaw was tugging at it, his eyes fixed on her, wide and shimmering with grief. "She's dead," he breathed.

Leopardfur stared at him, still dazed with sleep. Beside her, Ottersplash was breathing peacefully in her nest. Timberfur was snoring. All around the den, her Clanmates were sleeping. Was this a dream?

Whitepaw was trembling. This wasn't a dream. This was real. "Sunfish died."

Pain tore at her heart like a vicious dog. She wanted to close her eyes and bury her muzzle beneath her paws until it eased. But how could it ever ease? Sunfish was dead, and the hope

Leopardfur had tried to give Whitepaw last night had become a lie.

He stared at her, his eyes reflecting her own pain so intensely she couldn't bear to see it. She grabbed his scruff and pulled him into her nest. Wrapping herself around him, she held him close. Her heart seemed to beat in time with his sobs until she thought it would break.

Staring at the den wall, she pictured the reed bed and the river and, beyond that, ThunderClan's forest. ThunderClan would still be sleeping, unaware that they'd killed two of the cats Leopardfur had loved best. Mudfur might have blamed her for starting the fight that had killed them, but she knew who was really to blame. ThunderClan had done this—and as Whitepaw wept in the warmth of her pelt, she vowed never to forgive them.

CHAPTER 5

❧

Leopardfur's tail twitched eagerly as the wren that had been flitting from branch to branch of the alder finally fluttered down to the shore. Her patience had paid off. And she'd been impressed with how quietly Whitepaw had waited beside her this time. She hadn't heard him sigh or even so much as shift his paws as they'd crouched behind the rock at the water's edge, waiting for the wren to land.

In the days since Sunfish's death, the young tom had been distracted; it had been hard to make him concentrate on any part of his training. Yesterday, instead of diving for larger fish, he'd splashed around in the shallows, slapping at minnows with his paws. The day before, when she'd tried to teach him how to move silently through a reed bed, he'd crashed through it carelessly, chasing a dragonfly. But today he'd been as quiet as a mouse.

She glanced around at him, ready to signal that they could finally creep out of hiding.

He'd disappeared. Frustration pulsed in her paws. She sat up so sharply that the wren, startled, fluttered up into the safety of the branches. Where was her apprentice? She scanned the shoreline and then the ferns spilling between the trees at the top of the shore.

Dark brown fur rippled between the fronds. She marched toward it, her tail flicking crossly.

As she neared, Whitepaw stuck his head out and blinked at her excitedly. "Guess what!"

Didn't he realize he was in trouble? "What?" she snapped.

"I found a sparrow's nest." He ducked back among the ferns. "Come and look."

Frowning, she pushed her way between the stems and found him standing beside a heap of tangled twigs.

"It must have fallen." Whitepaw glanced up at the branches above his head. Then he poked the twigs. "There are still feathers in it. We could take them back for Beetlenose's nest. It would keep him warm."

"It's greenleaf," she growled. "He doesn't *need* to keep warm."

"But he's used to having Sunfish beside him." Whitepaw stared at her anxiously.

Leopardfur's anger toward the young tom melted. He was still grieving, as she was; of course every thought would still lead him back to Sunfish. She resolved to be compassionate, calming her breath. "Let's catch a duck." She was still his mentor, and they were supposed to be training. "Duck feathers are softer than sparrow." She nodded him toward the riverbank.

Whitepaw hesitated. "But it's so hard sitting still," he mewed. "Can't we practice battle moves instead?"

She remembered how often she'd persuaded Whitefang

to change his training plans to avoid fishing. Perhaps it was
unfair to make Whitepaw sit still when he was still hurting
from Sunfish's death. Practicing battle skills might keep his
paws busy enough to stop him worrying. "Okay," she mewed.

His lifted his tail happily and followed her as she led the
way to a clear stretch of earth beneath the trees and dropped
into a battle crouch, preparing to demonstrate.

"Watch how I shift my weight to one side—"

Paws thumped onto her back.

"I win!" Whitepaw stood on top of her. He gave her a
playful nip behind her ear that reminded of her of the play
fights she'd had with him while he was still a kit. Sunfish had
watched, purring as they played. She should be upset—he was
her apprentice, and he should be taking his training seriously—but he'd suffered such a loss. They both had. Perhaps
it wouldn't do any harm to play a little today.

She reared up and tried halfheartedly to shake him off, but
he gripped on tighter. "I'll squash you," she teased, dropping
onto her belly as if she was about to roll over.

"Too slow!" He leaped off and grabbed her tail, pummel-
ing it with his hind paws. She pulled it free, grabbed him, and
pushed him onto his back. Purring loudly, she pressed her
nose into his belly, and he squealed with delight. They could
train tomorrow.

"Over here!" Leopardfur itched with impatience as Whitepaw sniffed among the weeds at the edge of the water. "Watch!"

For the third time that morning, she nodded toward the

swirling pool in the middle of the river, where green algae gathered and spun. "Fish might be hiding there because it's shady." She waded in, moving slowly so she barely made a ripple. The cool water swirled around her legs and tugged her belly fur. Her hope that indulging Whitepaw in play-fighting yesterday would help him focus today had faded almost the moment they'd left camp and Whitepaw's attention had flashed to every fly, bird, or trembling reed. It seemed as though he found anything that moved more interesting than learning to be a warrior.

He paused and looked at her, but his unfocused gaze told her that his thoughts were still flitting about. He could barely sit still, his fur twitching along his flanks.

"What did I just tell you?" she mewed.

"Fish like shade." Whitepaw's gaze drifted downstream with the current.

"Let's swim toward the algae patch and see if there's anything hiding underneath." She nodded for him to go first, but swallowed back irritation as Whitepaw splashed into the water. "Move your paws slowly!" she snapped. "If you wade into the river like that, you'll frighten the fish."

Whitepaw scowled at her. "Sorry! I forgot," he snapped back, not sounding sorry at all.

"How could you forget?" she demanded. "It's the first thing I taught you!"

"That was ages ago!" Whitepaw stopped beside her and stared sulkily at the patch of algae spinning slowly in midstream.

Leopardfur took a deep breath before trying again. "We're going to swim underwater," she told him. "*Slowly*, so that if there are fish there, they'll think we're just another fish." She ducked under the water and pushed off from the river bottom, slipping out into the current. She glanced back through the water to make sure Whitepaw was following.

Bubbles churned behind her. The water frothed. What in StarClan was he doing? She burst up out of the water and glared at him. He was holding a minnow between his teeth. The ripples he'd made were still spreading across the stream. They reached the algae patch, broke it open, and let the current tear it apart. Any fish hiding in its shade would be gone now.

She swam back to him. "You were supposed to follow me," she snapped, finding her paws and wading toward him.

He tossed his minnow onto the shore. "I caught a fish."

"That's not big enough to feed a kit, let alone a Clan!" At this rate, Whitepaw would still be an apprentice when Emberkit and Mosskit were getting their warrior names. How would that make her look? And what would Sunfish think if she was watching from StarClan? Leopardfur had promised to help Whitepaw grow into a great warrior. But now White-paw just stared at her blankly. "Don't you care about helping to feed your Clan?" she snapped.

"Yes," he mewed quickly.

"It doesn't seem like you even *want* to become a warrior!"

"Of course I do." But there was no enthusiasm in his mew.

Leopardfur's paws pulsed with frustration. "Go and wait on the shore, and stay out of my way while I catch a fish!"

she snapped. "If you won't let me teach you, then at least let me catch prey for your Clanmates." Angrily, she turned back to the river and dived in. Pushing through the water, she spied bubbles breaking the surface near the reeds on the far side. She headed for them and ducked beneath the surface. A large trout was basking between the stems. She swam a little upstream so that she could come at it with the sun glittering through the water behind her. It didn't see her until it was too late, and she grabbed it between her jaws and dragged it flapping from the river.

Whitepaw hadn't moved. He avoided her gaze, his tail down as she dropped the fish beside him and gave it a killing bite.

"At least the morning wasn't entirely wasted," she grunted.

He stared at his paws.

Perhaps he'll start listening to me now. "Come on," she mewed sharply. "Let's take this back to the camp. Then we can go to the water meadow and I'll teach you how to hunt frogs."

He didn't speak, but followed her miserably as she carried the fish toward the camp.

"I'm sorry." His voice was choked with sadness.

She stopped and glanced back at him.

His eyes were round and dark. "I know you're mad. Are you going to stop being my mentor?" There was a tremble in his mew.

She stared at him. Why would he think that? A mentor never gave up on an apprentice, and he was her best friend's kit. She'd never give up on him. She laid the fish on the ground, guilt churning in her belly. She'd been too harsh with him. "Of course I won't give up on you." Leopardfur knew what it was like to grow up without a mother. She padded toward him and looked him in the eyes. "I'll be your mentor until you don't need me anymore," she told him gently. "I'm not going anywhere."

Whitepaw's amber eyes glistened with emotion. "I keep dreaming I wake up and find my den empty, and then I come looking for you and the warriors' den is empty too." He swallowed. "You're gone, and Beetlenose and Vixenleap and Grasswhisker. You're all gone."

"That's not going to happen." Leopardfur touched her nose to his head. Scolding him had made him pay attention for a moment, but it had also made him feel wretched when he was clearly still grieving deeply for Sunfish. And he'd lost Whitefang too. How could she have been so hard on him? "I promised your mother I'd look out for you," she told him. "And that's what I'm going to do. Even when you get your warrior name, I'll still keep looking out for you." She breathed in his warmth. He seemed more like a kit than an apprentice. "I promise."

He pulled away and looked at her, as though wondering whether he could trust her, then dipped his head. "Okay." Padding past her, he headed into the camp.

She picked up the trout and hurried after him, dropping it at his paws. "Take this and share it with Vixenleap and Silver-stream." The two she-cats were stretching in the sunshine outside the warriors' den. Spending time with his kin might reassure him. "When you've eaten we'll go the water meadow."

He looked at her gratefully and picked the fish up, then headed away. Leopardfur was pleased to see Vixenleap and Silverstream lift their muzzles happily to greet him. The poor thing was still missing his mother so badly . . . he needed all the support from his kin that he could get.

Free for a while, Leopardfur scanned the clearing.

Rippleclaw was sitting in the shade of the sedge, with Stonefur, Ottersplash, and Piketooth gathered around him.

"ThunderClan killed two of our Clanmates," she heard Rippleclaw growl as he shot a look at the shady patch outside Crookedstar's den, where the RiverClan leader was talking with Oakheart. The two warriors looked grim. "We should have retaliated by now."

Stonefur followed Rippleclaw's gaze. "*They* didn't watch them die," he muttered.

Leopardfur shivered. *But I did.* She could still picture Whitefang's blood spreading across the sun-bleached stone of Sunningrocks. Surely that kind of cruelty deserved some punishment?

Ottersplash shifted her paws nervously. "I'm sure Crookedstar won't just let this go," she mewed. "He's being cautious. He'll act when the time is right."

"The time is right *now*," Stonefur growled.

"It was right the moment we carried Whitefang's body back to the camp," Rippleclaw grunted. "ThunderClan killed a RiverClan warrior on RiverClan territory."

"StarClan gave us those rocks." Piketooth spoke bitterly,

his tail whipping the dusty earth behind him. "When will ThunderClan accept that they have no claim to them?"

"We need to make it clear to them," Rippleclaw mewed. "And the sooner the better."

Leopardfur's heart was pounding. The warriors were right, and not only because her heart still ached at the loss of Whitefang. They were right because with every day that passed without ThunderClan paying for what they'd done, RiverClan looked weaker. She tensed as Crookedstar looked up, his gaze flitting to Rippleclaw and the others. He watched them thoughtfully for a moment before turning back to Oakheart. Had he overheard them? Was he finally going to send a battle patrol to confront ThunderClan? She wanted to go and tell him in no uncertain terms what her Clanmates thought he should do—what *she* thought he should do. After all, Mudfur had told her that RiverClan's destiny was entwined with her own. If Crookedstar and Oakheart were discussing ThunderClan's crimes, it was the sort of discussion she should be part of.

Paw steps brushed the ground behind her. As if she'd summoned him with her thoughts, Leopardfur smelled her father's scent. She turned as he reached her, a leaf wrap between his jaws, pungent with herbs.

Mudfur laid it down. "Shouldn't you be training White-paw instead of listening to Clan gossip?"

His sharp gaze made her suck in her breath. Was he reprimanding her? But she forced herself not to bristle. She wasn't a kit anymore. She didn't need him to tell her what she was supposed to be doing. Besides, had he forgotten that he'd told her she was special? Their Clan was seething, and she might be the one who could put it right. She met his gaze. "White-paw's sharing a meal with his kin," she mewed stiffly.

"He can eat later." Mudfur glanced toward the young tom, who was chewing happily on the trout's tail while Grass-whisker washed his ears. "Once he's earned it."

Earned it? Leopardfur twitched an ear uncomfortably. Did Mudfur know that he was behind in his training?

"I'm taking him to the water meadow to hunt frogs once he's finished," she told Mudfur, annoyed at feeling she needed to justify herself. She was trying to train Whitepaw the best she could, but she didn't know how to get him to focus. Indulging him hadn't helped, nor had speaking sharply to him. But she wasn't going to admit that by asking her father's advice. Instead she headed toward Whitepaw, noticing for the first time that Frogleap was resting in the pool of shade at the edge of the clearing. He was watching her, and she prickled self-consciously and avoided his gaze. Had he heard Mudfur's rebuke?

"Come on, Whitepaw." She stopped at the edge of the clearing. "You've had long enough to eat." She was relieved when he got to his paws and padded to meet her. At least he obeyed her in front of their Clanmates. "Let's head for the meadow."

They crossed the river and headed past the bulrushes without speaking. As they reached the meadow, Whitepaw sighed.

She glanced at him. "What's wrong?" Her patience was

wearing thin again, but she tried to remember to be kind.

"Do we *have* to hunt frogs?" he mewed. "They taste weird."

Leopardfur looked away, struggling to hide her irritation. "You're hunting for your Clan, not yourself. Birdsong *enjoys* frogs," she reminded him.

He scuffed the grass with his paws sullenly as he followed her across the meadow to a wide dip where water pooled.

She stopped at the edge. "Okay. What can you smell?"

"Grass," he mewed.

"And?"

"Water?"

"What sort of water?" Couldn't he pick up its stagnant scent, which meant frogs might be nearby?

He looked at her. "I don't know. *Wet* water?"

Irritation pricked in her paws. She opened her mouth, ready to scold him, when gray fur caught her eye.

Frogleap was heading toward them, his tail swishing easily behind him, his fur smooth. Had he followed them? He blinked kindly at Whitepaw. "Excuse me, I couldn't help overhearing. Whitepaw, I think Leopardfur wants you to learn the difference between running water and still water," he mewed.

"Um, okay. Why?" Whitepaw sniffed.

"Because river birds prefer running water, and frogs prefer still water," Frogleap explained. "If you can smell the difference, you can tell what prey to look for."

"But you can *see* if it's still or running." Whitepaw stuck his tail out. "Why do I need to smell it?"

"A *great* RiverClan warrior can tell which is which with their eyes closed," Frogleap mewed back, tilting his head thoughtfully. "But if you're fine being ordinary . . ."

Whitepaw opened his mouth to speak, but Frogleap's gaze had flitted toward the water.

"Look!" There was such excitement in the gray tom's mew that Whitepaw followed it. A frog had surfaced on the far side. It hopped onto the grass. Frogleap dropped into a hunting crouch. "It's my namesake. Should we catch it?" he asked Whitepaw. "Or let it go?"

"Catch it!" Whitepaw mewed eagerly.

"Come on, then." Frogleap began to creep around the edge.

Whitepaw copied him, and even though she was grateful for the help, Leopardfur felt a prickle of annoyance. Why hadn't Whitepaw obeyed *her* like that? She stayed where she was and watched, keeping still so that she didn't startle the frog. Another leaped out beside it, and the two frogs sat, blinking, unaware of the toms creeping slowly toward them. Frogleap stopped and, as Whitepaw slid ahead, touched his nose to the young tom's tail to adjust it. She saw Frogleap whisper something, and Whitepaw crouched lower, his belly fur skimming the grass. Frogleap was watching him intently and spoke again. Whitepaw flattened his ears, and, despite her irritation, Leopardfur found herself rooting for her apprentice as he crept closer to the frogs. Her breath caught as Whitepaw leaped, and a thrill of triumph surged in her chest as he landed squarely on one and pinned it to the ground.

Kill it quickly!

She held her breath as Whitepaw bent to give it the killing bite, but the frog bucked and twisted free of his grip.

As her heart sank, Frogleap leaped to block the frog's escape, giving Whitepaw the chance to grab it again, this time with his teeth, and deliver the killing bite.

Leopardfur was relieved that the frog had been caught—Birdsong really would be pleased—but she didn't know whether to feel proud of or irritated with her apprentice. Whitepaw seemed to have learned more in a few moments with Frogleap than he'd learned in days with her. *Maybe I'm not cut out to be a mentor?* Worry sparked in her chest as Whitepaw carried the frog back and dropped it at her paws.

"Well done." She forced a purr.

Frogleap stopped beside her. "He's a natural," he mewed, then nodded toward another stretch of water a little farther along the meadow. "Try catching another frog by yourself," he told Whitepaw.

As Whitepaw headed away, he called after him. "Don't forget! Keep low. Even when you're not stalking. This is open land. You stand out like a duck on a lake here."

Once Whitepaw was out of earshot, Leopardfur glared at Frogleap. Irritation was twitching through her fur. "Well, that was impressive. But why does he listen to you and not me?"

Frogleap blinked at her sympathetically. "You were his friend before you were his mentor," he mewed. "Relationships are hard to change once they're fixed."

"Are you saying he should have a different mentor?" she snapped.

"Of course not." Frogleap's eyes rounded. "You're the best mentor he could have," he mewed. "But he's been through a lot, and perhaps he's afraid that being a good apprentice would mean losing your friendship."

"Can't I be his mentor *and* his friend?"

"I'm sure you can do anything you set your mind to," Frogleap told her. "But Whitepaw needs careful handling right now. Perhaps he's afraid of losing this time with you once he begins to improve and then becomes a warrior. After all, you're the closest thing he has to a mother now."

Leopardfur looked away. She didn't like being lectured. And yet there was truth in Frogleap's words. With a pang, she remembered Sunfish's last request. *I want you to watch over him as I would.*

"Be gentle with him," Frogleap went on. "Take his lead and guide him with love." He headed after Whitepaw, signaling for Leopardfur to follow. "Be patient with him, like Sunfish would."

Whitepaw was crouching beside a smaller pool. But he clearly wasn't looking for frogs. His gaze had drifted toward the hedgerow at the edge of the meadow, where sparrows were flitting from branch to branch.

Take his lead, Leopardfur thought. She nodded toward the hedge. "Do you think you can catch one of those?" she asked Whitepaw.

He looked thoughtful for a moment. "I think so." He straightened, and Leopardfur followed as he began to head toward them.

"Keep low," Frogleap reminded him, and Whitepaw dropped into a stalking crouch.

"Let your tail skim the grass," Leopardfur added. Whitepaw dropped his tail. "Use the shadows." She kept her mew soft, as though she were encouraging a kit rather than training a 'paw. "That's good," she murmured as he ducked down beside the hedge.

The birds were fluttering in and out, making the leaves quiver. Whitepaw squeezed beneath the branches to get closer.

"Keep your weight in your haunches, not your paws," Leopardfur whispered. "It'll make your steps lighter."

Whitepaw adjusted his stance as he crept forward, hardly making a sound on the grass.

"Don't forget to keep your tail still," Leopardfur mewed.

He obeyed.

"And your ears flat," she mewed. "Like you did with the frogs."

He flattened them.

For the first time in days, Whitepaw's attention was completely fixed on his quarry. And he was *listening* to her. Hope rose in Leopardfur's heart. Maybe Frogleap was right, and all she needed to do was to be as gentle and persistent as Sunfish had been when she'd encouraged Whitekit from the nursery.

She hung back and let Whitepaw make the final approach, watching him eagerly.

Fur brushed her flank as Frogleap stopped beside her. "*You're* a natural too," he whispered.

Leopardfur glanced at him, swallowing back a purr.

Whitepaw's gaze hadn't left the sparrows for a moment, and now, as he reached pouncing distance, it fixed on the closest bird.

"You can do it," she breathed gently, her heart in her throat as he made a sudden leap, opening his mouth and catching the bird's leg in his jaws. As he hit the ground, he shook his head violently and then dropped the bird to his paws, taking advantage of the bird's confusion to deliver a killing bite to its throat.

Leopardfur's paws fizzed with happiness. He was learning. He was *really* learning, and *she* was teaching him, just as Whitefang had taught her.

Finally, she was keeping her promise to Sunfish.

Leopardfur watched Whitepaw as he lunged for the pinecone she'd laid out for him. In the past half-moon, he'd grown so much: He looked more like a warrior than an apprentice. Muscle showed below his dark brown pelt, rippling as he hooked the pinecone into the air with a snowy forepaw, leaped, twisted in midair, and batted it expertly down to the ground with the other. It was a hunting move she'd taken nearly a moon to master, but he had learned in half the time. She was proud of him.

As he stalked silently toward the next one, shifting his weight, adjusting his tail, just as she'd taught him, she glanced eagerly toward the reed bed. Was Frogleap here yet? She'd asked him to test Whitepaw's battle skills with a sneak attack. Would the young tom react fast enough? Frogleap was a strong and skillful warrior; Whitepaw wouldn't be hurt, but she was a little worried the ambush might dent his confidence. Perhaps she should have chosen a different way to test him.

The stalks shivered. She smelled Frogleap's scent. He was close. Had Whitepaw picked up the telltale signals? Of course on RiverClan territory, rustling reeds and Frogleap's scent wouldn't be a sign of danger. Were she and Frogleap being unfair? *No,* she told herself; the ambush would teach him the importance of being alert even on familiar ground.

Whitepaw's attention was fixed on the cone. He was pressing his belly to the ground, his ears flattened against his head as he prepared to lunge for it. From the corner of her eye, Leopardfur saw Frogleap's gray fur, barely more than a shadow among the reeds. But he was moving steadily nearer, and she held her breath, her pelt tingling as the reeds split and Frogleap burst through.

He leaped for Whitepaw and the young tom froze, belly still to the earth. But only for a moment. Rearing, Whitepaw turned in a fierce, fluid movement and faced his attacker. Leopardfur saw his gaze flick toward her, as though confirming she was safe before he committed all his energy to defending himself.

Frogleap's eyes widened, as though he hadn't expected such a fast reaction. He quickly adjusted his stance, bracing himself for Whitepaw's blow as the young tom swung a paw at Frogleap's muzzle. Frogleap dodged just in time and ducked beneath Whitepaw's belly, pushing up until the apprentice's hind paws lifted from the ground, then flicking him over onto his spine.

Whitepaw landed with a thump, but scrabbled up in a heartbeat and rushed again at his attacker. Recognition flared in his eyes. He froze. "Frogleap!" He drew back, letting his paw drop, and frowned. "What are you doing?"

Frogleap's fur smoothed. His eyes sparkled with admiration. "We were testing how quickly you'd react to danger." He dipped his head to the young tom. "You defended yourself very well."

Leopardfur padded forward. "He even checked to see that I was okay," she purred approvingly. "His Clanmates' safety is clearly as important to him as his own." She exchanged approving looks with Frogleap, proud that her apprentice had clearly impressed him. "I think he's almost ready for his warrior assessment, don't you?"

"Definitely." Frogleap blinked at her happily.

Whitepaw's fur was still spiked from the attack, but his eyes were glowing. "Really?" he mewed. "Do you think I'm ready?"

"Yes." Her heart swelled. She'd taught Whitepaw with kindness and encouragement, and in doing so, she'd kept her promise to Sunfish. "I'm sure you'll pass, Whitepaw. You've come so far."

He stared at her, his eyes rounding. "I know I've been difficult. But you stuck with me. Thank you. I couldn't have done it without you, I just wish . . ." He glanced toward the sky, his mew trailing away.

Her throat tightened. She knew what he was wishing for, because she longed for it, too: that Sunfish could be here with them. Was his mother watching them from StarClan?

"I'm so proud of you." She leaned forward and touched her nose to his. "And I know Sunfish is, too."

As they headed back to camp, Leopardfur quickened her step. Frogleap and Whitepaw followed at her heels. She couldn't wait to tell Crookedstar that Whitepaw was ready for his warrior assessment. She wondered if he'd give her a say in what his warrior name would be. It would be tempting to name him Whitefang, after his first mentor. But maybe he deserved a name all his own.

She ducked through the reed tunnel and padded into the clearing, her pelt prickling with alarm as she saw Crookedstar standing in front of Mistyfoot, Beetlenose, and Loudbelly. Oakheart was pacing beside him, his dark red fur rippling along his spine. They looked agitated, their gazes dark. Had something happened?

She hurried to join them and blinked questioningly at Crookedstar, but he didn't seem to notice her and addressed the others instead. "If you see any ThunderClan cat anywhere near the border, warn them off, and if they don't leave, attack."

Beetlenose frowned. "What if they don't cross the scent line?"

"Attack anyway." Oakheart swung his gaze toward the broad-shouldered tom. "If they refuse to retreat when they're told, it's a declaration of war," he growled. "This time we leave no doubt about who owns Sunningrocks."

Leopardfur pushed her way between Mistyfoot and Loudbelly. *An attack on ThunderClan!* A chance to avenge Whitefang and Sunfish's deaths. "Can I join the patrol?"

Oakheart looked at her. "The patrol has already been chosen."

"But I wasn't here when you—" Leopardfur began.

"The patrol has already been chosen," Oakheart repeated firmly.

"That's not fair." Leopardfur ignored the glances of the other warriors. She didn't care if they thought she was too outspoken. She'd been there when ThunderClan had killed her mentor and best friend. She had a right to be part of any patrol that was going to defend Sunningrocks. "I want to fight for my Clan. After last time, I have to—"

Oakheart cut her off again. "You were too quick to fight last time."

"But this time you *want* us to fight!" Surely her eagerness to get even with ThunderClan made her the *best* warrior for this patrol?

Oakheart's tail twitched irritably. "You have an apprentice," he told her. "This patrol is no place for 'paws."

"He can stay in camp." Leopardfur turned her gaze on Crookedstar. Surely *he* would see she had to be part of the battle even if Oakheart didn't!

Crookedstar shifted his paws. "Oakheart is right. We need strong warriors to stay here in case ThunderClan attacks the camp."

No! Leopardfur's heart pounded. She needed to be on this patrol. ThunderClan had killed two of the cats she'd loved most. But Crookedstar was avoiding her gaze, and Oakheart stared past her as Beetlenose, Mistyfoot, and Loudbelly shifted uneasily. Oakheart and Crookedstar clearly weren't going to be persuaded. She swallowed back her objections, her belly churning with frustration.

"Frogleap." Oakheart's gaze flitted toward the gray tom as he hung back beside Whitepaw. "I want you on this patrol," he mewed. "You trained with Loudbelly. You'll fight well together."

He trained with me too! Leopardfur forced her pelt not to bristle. This was so unfair. Was she being punished for the last battle at Sunningrocks? She'd only been defending River-Clan territory. Wasn't that what being a warrior meant? Fury throbbed beneath her pelt as Oakheart led Beetlenose, Mistyfoot, and Loudbelly out of camp. Frogleap shot her an apologetic look as he fell in behind them.

Whitepaw bounded across the clearing to join her. "Do you really think ThunderClan might attack?" he mewed excitedly. "Can I help guard the camp?" He glanced at Emberkit and Mosskit, who were playing outside the nursery with Heavykit and Shadekit. "Should I tell them to stay inside until the danger's passed?"

Leopardfur shook her head. "We're not sure the patrol will even fight," she told him. She hoped it wouldn't. She wanted the chance to fight for her Clan and, this time, to win. She couldn't stand the thought of them fighting ThunderClan without her. "But let's go out and check the camp wall and make sure there are no gaps." She flexed her claws impatiently as she led Whitepaw through the reed tunnel. He might have stopped her this time, but Oakheart couldn't keep her from fighting for her Clan forever.

CHAPTER 6

❧

Checking the camp wall didn't take as long as Leopardfur had hoped. There were no gaps to fix, and although she'd kept her eyes peeled for ThunderClan intruders, she'd seen no sign of a threat to the camp. *Now what?* It was harder to keep from thinking about what was happening with ThunderClan when there was nothing else that demanded her attention. But she had to keep Whitepaw busy, if nothing else.

"Fetch fresh bedding for Birdsong and Tanglewhisker," she told Whitepaw as they padded back into camp. "And help them make new nests."

"But that's an apprentice chore," he objected. "You said I was ready for my warrior name."

"You haven't passed your assessment yet," she reminded him.

He frowned. "But it'll take *ages* to change out the bedding by myself."

"Ask Emberkit and Mosskit to help you."

"But they're *kits*," Whitepaw mewed.

Leopardstar bit back an angry retort, reminding herself that Whitepaw was not responsible for her stretched nerves.

"They'll be 'paws any day now. You can show them what it's like to be an apprentice."

Whitepaw looked less aggrieved. Leopardfur figured that getting to boss kits around might take the sting out of the task.

As he headed toward the nursery, Leopardfur called after him. "They can clean out the old bedding while you gather fresh," she told him. "Don't forget they're still too young to leave camp."

"Sure!" Whitepaw trotted away.

Now that her apprentice had been taken care of, Leopardfur let her thoughts stray back to Oakheart's patrol. Had they found any sign of ThunderClan at Sunningrocks? Perhaps Oakheart planned to wait there until they showed up. Leopardfur listened for distant battle yowls, but all she heard was the river and the reeds swishing around the camp.

Frustration was still worming beneath her pelt. The more she thought about it, the more she wondered why Crookedstar and Oakheart had been so insistent about keeping her off the battle patrol. She was a strong warrior, and trusted enough by Crookedstar to take over as mentor for the Clan's only 'paw. Had Oakheart advised the RiverClan leader against letting her fight? He'd said she'd been too quick to start the battle last time, but this time he *wanted* the patrol to pick a fight with ThunderClan. Perhaps he just didn't like her.

She padded grouchily across the clearing. Mudfur might know. She'd been so busy training Whitepaw and hanging out with Frogleap for the past half-moon that she'd hardly spoken to her father. Besides, he was always in the medicine den these days, and she was a healthy warrior. There was rarely any need for her to go there. But now, angry and not knowing what to do to distract herself, she headed for the moss-draped entrance.

"Mudfur?" She poked her head through. Sunshine was filtering through the woven walls, and the wide, dusty floor rippled with light.

Leopardfur glanced at the empty nests around the edge and felt a pang in her heart. The last time she'd come here to visit a sick cat, it had been Sunfish. But that was moons ago—the nest in which Sunfish had died had been cleared away and replaced with fresh bedding, of course. Wondering if she'd ever stop mourning her friend, she pushed away her sadness and made her way inside.

"Hi, Leopardfur." Mudfur blinked from shadows at the back of the den, a bunch of rosemary stalks between his paws. "How's Whitepaw's training coming along?"

"He's ready for his assessment," she mewed distractedly, glancing around the den. She hadn't come here to discuss Whitepaw.

Mudfur's eyes rounded with concern. "Are you okay?"

Leopardfur turned to meet his eyes. "I'm fine. I'm just wondering what's happening at Sunningrocks."

"Crookedstar's sent a patrol there?" Mudfur laid the rosemary stems on the floor and reached into the gap hollowed in the mud wall.

"Yeah." Leopardfur sat down heavily. "He wants them to challenge ThunderClan."

Mudfur's ears twitched as he pulled out a tightly wrapped leaf and began to unfold it. "Well. I suppose you're worried about missing the battle." There was sharpness in his mew.

Her pelt prickled irritably. He could never resist making her feel like there was something wrong with being a warrior. "I just don't understand. I'm one of our strongest warriors. Oakheart should have let me go."

"Not every warrior can go on every patrol." Mudfur reached in for more herbs. "Not even every *strong* warrior. If they did, there'd be no cat left to guard the camp."

"That's what Crookedstar said."

"And? It's true, isn't it?" Mudfur pulled out a string of tattered stalks and began to unknot them.

Leopardfur stifled a sigh. *He doesn't understand.* "But what if there's a fight?"

"You're not the only RiverClan warrior with battle skills," he mewed evenly.

Leopardfur lashed her tail. "But, after what happened with Whitefang and Sunfish, I should be allowed—"

He cut her off. "It's true, you've lost a lot. But fighting isn't the best way to grieve."

"I've *finished* grieving," she snapped. "Now I want to make ThunderClan sorry."

Mudfur put down the knotted herbs. "Part of grieving is learning to leave things like that up to StarClan," he mewed.

"*You're* not even a warrior."

"No." He gazed at her. "I'm not. But I was, and I know there's more to being a warrior than fighting battles." He went

on before she could speak. "Claws and teeth aren't the only way
to protect your Clan." He looked at her. "You've made the Clan
stronger by training Whitepaw. And there's hunting, fishing,
repairing the camp. Why do you need more than that?"

She dropped her gaze. He'd made her feel ashamed again.
"I know," she conceded. "Feeding my Clan is as important as
fighting for it, but fishing every day and training and mending
dens . . ." She hesitated, guilt jabbing her belly. "It just feels so
ordinary."

"We're lucky to have ordinary. There's nothing *wrong* with
ordinary," Mudfur told her.

Then why did you tell me I was special? But Leopardfur kept the
thought to herself. "I know, and I value peace as much as any
other cat. I just thought I'd be able to do more to help my
Clan."

"You mean fight."

He spoke like there was something wrong with defending her Clan. "The other Clans want to take our land," she
mewed. "Doesn't that worry you?"

"Not while we have strong, *brave* warriors like you to protect it." He began unknotting the herbs once more.

Anger warmed her pelt. She heard the sarcasm in his tone,
the way he'd emphasized *brave*, like he was mocking her. He
was determined not to understand. She turned her tail on him
and nosed her way out of the den. She felt as sulky as a kit,
which made his dismissal feel even worse. She wasn't a kit.
She was a warrior, she was right to be annoyed about being left
behind, and nothing Mudfur could say would change that.

She padded to a shady patch beside the sedge wall and settled onto the cool grass.

"Leopardfur!" Skyheart called to her. The pale brown tabby she-cat was following Blackclaw toward the camp entrance. "We're going fishing. Do you want to come?"

"No." Leopardfur wasn't in the mood for swimming. She wanted to think.

Skyheart looked surprised. "Blackclaw says he saw a really big fish basking near the reed bed this morning. We're going to see if it's still there."

Leopardfur flicked her tail in an attempt to look cheerful. "Have fun."

Skyheart looked at her for a moment, then hurried after Blackclaw and disappeared through the reed tunnel. Leopardfur let her tail fall flat and stared across the camp.

Emberkit and Mosskit were already dragging old bedding from the elders' den, their pelts fluffed out proudly as Heavykit and Shadekit watched jealously from the nursery.

"Why can't we help?" Heavykit complained.

"You're too young." Lilystem wrapped her tail around him. "You won't be an apprentice for moons."

"It's not fair." Shadekit moved out of reach of her mother's tail and glowered at Mosskit.

The tortoiseshell-and-white she-kit was shooing Birdsong away. "You don't have to help," she told her as Emberkit darted back inside and dragged out another bunch of crumpled reeds.

Dawnbright was washing outside the warriors' den. Mallowtail and Voleclaw idly batted a moss ball back and forth between them. Crookedstar was sitting at the edge of the clearing, his ears swiveled as though he too was listening for battle sounds.

Leopardfur's thoughts quickened. What was happening at Sunningrocks? Would ThunderClan kill another of her Clanmates? She pictured Whitefang lying on the stone again, his eyes dull, and remembered the sour tang of Sunfish's infected wound and the long, agonizing days of watching her friend die.

She looked toward Sunningrocks. It was hidden by trees. But she could see it in her mind's eye. She could imagine Frogleap standing beside Oakheart. Her paws prickled anxiously. What if he was hurt? Her breath quickened. What if he died? She'd spent nearly every day with him this past half-moon. It wasn't just that he'd helped with Whitepaw's training. He'd seemed, she realized now, to have made any excuse to hunt and patrol with her until she couldn't imagine leaving camp without him at her side. And now she missed him. She glanced around the camp, suddenly self-conscious, as though her Clanmates could read her thoughts. Was it possible that she had feelings for Frogleap? That he'd become more than just a denmate? She pushed the thought away. She wasn't looking for a mate. Kits would slow her down. The thought of being trapped in the nursery made her paws itch. But perhaps she wouldn't always feel this way. One day, she might be ready to take a mate. If she did, could that mate be Frogleap?

A screech of pain ripped the air. Panic sparked like fire in her chest. It was close by. As Dawnbright and Mallowtail sat up sharply, Leopardfur leaped to her paws. Birdsong hurried protectively toward Emberkit and Mosskit as they stared toward the sound with wide, frightened eyes.

It was coming from the river.

Whitepaw! Leopardfur raced across the clearing. He'd left camp to gather reeds. Had he been attacked? Had Thunder-Clan sent a battle patrol to the camp after all? As she neared the entrance tunnel, Whitepaw hurried through.

He dropped the reeds bunched between his jaws and stared at her. "Did you hear that?"

Relief swamped her. He was safe.

But the shriek sounded again. This time, Leopardfur recognized it. "Skyheart!" Had something happened while she was fishing? Leopardfur raced for the reed bed and, shoving her way through, splashed through the shallows until she broke out the other side, where the river swirled at her paws.

The shrieking was continuous now, panicked and interspersed with the pained cries of another cat. *Blackclaw?* She looked downstream, her heart pounding. Skyheart was standing on the bank, her claws hooked into Blackclaw's smoky pelt as she tried to heave him out of the water. *He's injured!*

Not hesitating for a moment, Leopardfur dived in and swam toward them. Her heart pounded in her chest as she wondered what she was swimming toward. Had something attacked them while they were fishing? *Is it still there?*

Skyheart was tugging at Blackclaw's scruff now, but she couldn't seem to get him free of the river's pull. "Be careful!" she screeched when she spotted Leopardfur in the river. "There's a pike!"

A pike! Leopardfur's heart lurched. Pikes rarely came this far upriver. She wasn't sure she'd ever seen one, but she'd heard horrible stories from the elders. Panic fizzed beneath her pelt as she scrambled onto the bank where Blackclaw was clawing at the stones. He was fighting to stay on the shore, but his hind leg was being dragged into the water. The river churned around it, red with blood, and Leopardfur saw, with a gasp, the spined back of a huge fish thrashing beside it. The pike was holding Blackclaw's paw between its massive jaws and fighting to drag him into the water. Skyheart swiped at its nose, but the pike jerked harder. His eyes wild with panic, Blackclaw dug his paws deeper into the pebbles and tried to get a grip with his claws.

"Hold on to him!" Leopardfur told Skyheart. "I'll get the pike off."

As Skyheart held Blackclaw tight, Leopardfur turned on the pike. It was as big as a warrior. Its tail churned the water, and she could see its eyes, dark and fierce, as it tore at Blackclaw's leg, its teeth hooked into his flesh. Leopardfur slashed at its nose, but it held on, pulling harder, hunger gleaming in its eyes. It was terrifying, but she gathered all her courage, plunged into the water beside it, and gripped its long back with her claws. Its spines jabbed her pads, and she let go with a yelp. Its tail thumped against her, knocking the breath from her lungs, and she gasped for air as she fought again to get close enough to grab hold.

She spluttered as water caught in her throat and filled her nose. For a moment the memory of Skyheart pressing her under filled her with panic, but the pike slapped her again with its tail and knocked the memory away. Her eyes narrowed as she squinted through the water. She had to get this fish off Blackclaw.

The shoreline grew blurred as more water streamed into her eyes. Was that another cat beside Skyheart? She saw a familiar brown pelt. *Whitepaw?* The cat plunged into the river on the other side of the pike. *It is!* She recognized his snowy paws. He lunged for the pike, and it struck out at him with its tail. Leopardfur saw her chance. She hooked her claws into its side and curled them tight. The pike writhed in her grip, its tail thrashing between them. Whitepaw slitted his eyes against the spray and hurled himself at it. With a grunt, he wrapped his legs around it and hung on.

The pike panicked. Eyes flashing, it glanced at Whitepaw. *No!* Leopardfur tore harder at its rubbery flesh, and, with a jerk, it released Blackclaw and turned on the apprentice.

"Let go!" Leopardfur wailed at him, alarm shrilling through her fur. "Get to the shore."

The pike writhed in her grip as it snapped at Whitepaw. She unhooked a claw and slashed at its cheek, drawing its rage back toward her. Clinging on, she held it as best she could as Whitepaw made for the shore. Its jaws couldn't reach her. She was holding it too tightly. But how could she let go without it turning on her and dragging her under? Out of reach of the others, she'd be lost.

She pushed back terror and swung another blow at its cheek. It bucked and twisted in her grip. Holding on, she kicked out with her back legs, fighting for the shore. If she could get close enough, she might be able to scramble out before it grabbed her.

It turned over suddenly, spinning her underwater. As the river swallowed her, she saw in its shadowy depths something moving below. Her eyes widened as her fur billowed around her. An even bigger fish was rising up through the water. Terror engulfed her as a new pair of eyes fixed on her, even larger and more vicious. It was another pike, twice the size of the first—so big it could swallow her in one gulp. Her breath caught. She froze as it swam closer, its jaws opening toward her.

Claws hooked her pelt. She felt them haul her away as the massive pike's mouth opened a muzzle-length away and slammed shut around the smaller pike. Surprise, rather than fear, showed in the smaller pike's glassy eyes as its body was torn in two.

Leopardfur closed her eyes, limp with horror as Whitepaw dragged her from the water.

"Leopardfur!" Skyheart leaned over her as she collapsed on the shore.

Whitepaw thumped his paws into her chest. She twitched and coughed up water, then fell limp again, fighting for breath.

"Are you okay?" He searched her gaze, panic clouding his.

She nodded, her head clearing as she forced herself up and glanced back over her shoulder. The huge pike dropped beneath the surface, dragging both pieces of the dead fish with it. The river closed over it and flowed past as though nothing had happened.

On the shore beside her, Blackclaw groaned. He struggled to his paws but immediately swayed. His hind leg hung like dead prey.

Leopardfur heaved herself up and shook out her pelt, pushing away shock. "We need to get him to Mudfur."

Skyheart nodded and placed her shoulder beneath Blackclaw's. Whitepaw ducked under the other side, and together they helped him limp toward the camp entrance.

Leopardfur pushed past them. "Mudfur!" She called to her father as she reached the clearing. "Blackclaw's been attacked by a pike."

Crookedstar leaped to his paws. Dawnbright and Mallowtail watched, their eyes wide as Mudfur raced toward her.

He darted around Blackclaw, one side, then the other, inspecting the wounded leg as Skyheart and Whitepaw guided the injured tom toward the medicine den.

While they helped Blackclaw inside, Leopardfur waited at the entrance. She didn't want to crowd her father while he worked. Besides, Crookedstar would want a report.

The RiverClan leader was already hurrying toward her. "What happened?"

The smell of Blackclaw's blood was still in the air.

"Blackclaw was attacked by a pike." As she spoke, Whitepaw ducked out of the medicine den. She blinked at him anxiously. "Are you okay?"

He nodded, though his eyes were still bright with shock. "I've never seen a pike before." he mewed. "I didn't know they were so big."

Crookedstar frowned. "It's rare they come this far upstream

in greenleaf," he mewed. "The river is too shallow for them."

"There were two of them." Whitepaw's pelt was prickling along his spine.

"The big one probably followed the other one here," Leopardfur guessed.

Crookedstar nodded. "It must have been tracking it for a while."

Skyheart padded from the den. She was trembling.

Crookedstar's tail twitched. "How is he?"

"Mudfur says a few of the bitemarks are deep, but they're clean and they'll heal fully," Skyheart told him.

"He'll be able to use his leg again?" Crookedstar pressed.

"Yes." Relief showed on Skyheart's face. She turned to Leopardfur. "You saved him," she mewed. "I don't know how you dared dive in! When that second pike appeared, I thought you'd be killed for sure."

Leopardfur felt a small surge of pride. As the shock wore off, she could see the bravery in what she had done. The pike had been almost as big as her, with jaws far bigger than any cat's. She'd been scared, but she hadn't let fear stop her. She'd only wanted to save Blackclaw.

"Whitepaw was brave too." Leopardfur blinked at Crookedstar. He should know about her apprentice's courage. "He dived in to help me and grabbed the pike's tail. It gave me a chance to get close enough to attack properly and make it let go of Blackclaw."

Crookedstar's eyes glowed. "You were both very brave." He turned toward the warriors' den, where Ottersplash and Shimmerpelt had joined Dawnbright and Mallowtail and were staring anxiously across the clearing. "I'll warn the Clan not to fish in that stretch of river for a while," he mewed. "We can fish further upstream, where it's too narrow for pike."

As he headed away, Leopardfur began to shiver. Despite the warmth of the day, she felt suddenly cold. She glanced at Whitepaw. "Are you sure you're okay?"

But Whitepaw didn't seem to hear her. He was staring at the camp entrance. She followed his gaze, her ears pricking when she heard paw steps outside. They were slow and uneven, like the cats that made them were struggling. She tasted the air. Frogleap's scent touched her tongue and, along with it, the smell of blood. Her belly tightened as the reed tunnel quivered and Beetlenose limped into camp. Blood was welling on his cheek.

Leopardfur began to cross the clearing, but Whitepaw raced past her, scrambling to a halt beside his father.

"What happened?" he asked.

Beetlenose glanced behind him, grief sharpening his gaze as Mistyfoot and Loudbelly staggered into camp. Across their shoulders lay Oakheart, limp and unmoving. They padded to the edge of the clearing and let the RiverClan deputy slide onto the ground.

Crookedstar raced toward him. "Oakheart?" The River-Clan leader's mew trembled as he crouched down beside his brother and pressed his ear to his flank. "He's not breathing!" He jerked his muzzle toward the medicine den, but Mudfur was already running.

"There was a battle," Mistyfoot mewed huskily. "Thunder-Clan killed him."

Leopardfur felt sick. Another Clanmate lost to Thunder-Clan? She stared at the dead deputy, her mouth growing dry.

Mudfur was leaning close to Oakheart's muzzle. He drew away, shaking his head. "He's gone," he mewed. He looked at Mistyfoot and Loudbelly. Blood matted their pelts. "Fetch cobwebs from my den," he ordered Leopardfur.

But Leopardfur hardly heard him. She was staring at the camp entrance. *Frogleap?* Where was he? She got to her paws and started toward it, her heart beating so loudly she could hear nothing else.

She froze for a moment as he padded through, relief swamping her, then rushed to meet him. She pressed her muzzle against his cheek. "I thought you were dead."

"I'm fine." Frogleap drew away, his eyes hollow with grief as he looked at Oakheart, lying lifeless in the clearing.

Mallowtail was hurrying from the medicine den, cobwebs between her jaws. She dropped them beside Mudfur. "That's all I could find," she mewed. "I'll gather more from the sedge."

"I'll help." Dawnbright hurried away with her.

"Leopardfur." Mudfur called her name and she spun around. "Help me get Loudbelly to the medicine den."

Whitepaw was already helping Beetlenose across the clearing as Mistyfoot limped after them. Loudbelly was swaying on his paws, and Leopardfur thrust her shoulder beneath his to steady him. Crookedstar didn't move from Oakheart's side, but crouched beside him, his emerald eyes shimmering with grief.

"I'll need your help," Mudfur told Leopardfur as he pressed in on Loudbelly's other side. "There are a lot of injuries to deal with."

"But I'm not a medicine cat." Leopardfur guided Loudbelly forward.

"You don't have to be a medicine cat to rub poultices into wounds," Mudfur mewed. "And the sooner we get these injuries treated, the less chance there is they'll turn sour."

Frogleap padded after them, his steps faltering.

Leopardfur glanced back at him. "Can you make it to the medicine den?"

"Yes," he grunted, his eyes dark with pain.

Mudfur was still looking at Leopardfur. "Surely now you can see now how pointless it is to fight over Sunningrocks?"

"*Pointless?*" She could hardly believe her ears. Was Mudfur saying their Clanmates' suffering meant nothing?

Mudfur's eyes flashed angrily. "There's no glory in this!"

Leopardfur glared back at him. How could he say such a thing? The RiverClan deputy was lying dead in the clearing. Loudbelly couldn't walk without help. This might not be glorious, but that didn't mean Sunningrocks wasn't worth fighting for. If anything, it meant they should fight harder.

RiverClan had sacrificed three lives. If they gave up now, their Clanmates would have died for nothing. Even Mudfur must realize that if they let these deaths go unpunished, no RiverClan cat could call themselves a true warrior!

CHAPTER 7
❧

Through the long warm night, while Leopardfur sat vigil for Oakheart, one thought lingered. As the night wore on, it hardened her grief into anger. Would the RiverClan deputy be lying dead in the RiverClan clearing if she'd been allowed to join the patrol? Perhaps she could have changed the course of the battle. She might have saved him. They could have kept Sunningrocks.

Whitepaw and Frogleap crouched beside her, their gazes dull. No cat spoke as the night dragged on. Frogs croaked from the shadowy reed bed, and a warbler sang its long sad song, as though grieving along with the RiverClan cats who sat in the darkness around their dead Clanmate. As dawn began to show, turning the sky pale beyond the trees, Crookedstar got to his paws and signaled to Rippleclaw, Cedarpelt, and Voleclaw. Together they carried Oakheart's body out of camp, to the stretch of soft earth on the far side of the river where they had buried Hailstar, Whitefang, and Sunfish.

Leopardfur must have dozed for a little while. When she woke, Whitepaw was taking a carp from the fresh-kill pile to the elders' den. Frogleap was still beside her, on his paws and stretching out his stiffness.

She got up and shook out her pelt. Her anger had woken with her, still hard in her belly. "I should have been with them," she mewed softly.

Frogleap looked puzzled. "With the burial patrol?"

"No," she mewed. "At the battle. I might have stopped Oakheart from dying."

"And then who would have saved Blackclaw?" He looked toward the medicine den, where the injured warrior was resting, along with Loudbelly and Mistyfoot.

Mudfur was heading inside. He'd sat vigil with the rest of them but kept close to the medicine den, slipping quietly away to check on his patients from time to time.

Leopardfur watched his tail disappear through the trailing moss. He'd said that there'd been no glory in Oakheart's death or in his Clanmates' injuries. But, if she'd been there to help them, maybe it would have ended differently. "Whitepaw would have been here," she told Frogleap. "It would have been fine."

Frogleap looked unconvinced. "Do you really think such a young cat could have saved Blackclaw by himself?" he mewed. "Would he have leaped into the river with that pike if he hadn't seen you jump in first?"

"Of course he would," Leopardfur mewed, though as she said it, she wondered if it was true. She wanted to believe it was. "I trained him, remember! Besides, it wasn't us who fought off the pike in the end. It was a bigger pike."

"You stopped Blackclaw from being dragged into the river," Frogleap insisted. "If you hadn't, he'd probably be dead by now." She sniffed as he went on. "It's a good thing Crooked-star asked you to guard the camp. You saved a life. There was nothing you could have done to change the battle. I was there, remember? ThunderClan was determined to take the rocks, no matter how hard we fought. And you might have been hurt too if you'd gone."

"It would have been worth it, to protect my Clan." Frustration was still itching in Leopardfur's pelt.

"You did that by staying here," Frogleap mewed.

Around them, their Clanmates seemed unsettled. Beetle-nose was shifting from paw to paw beside the warriors' den. Softwing stood beside Dawnbright, her tail twitching, while Mallowtail glanced apprehensively toward the head of the clearing, as though she expected to see something there. Owl-fur and Ottersplash talked softly, while their apprentices, Emberpaw and Mosspaw, sat nearby, glancing at each other anxiously.

Frogleap glanced at them. "I guess everyone's wondering what to do without Oakheart to sort out the morning patrols."

"They should stay busy." Leopardfur swished her tail. She padded toward Owlfur. "We should secure our other border," she told him. "Will you take Reedtail and Piketooth and mark the scent line beside the moor?"

Owlfur nodded. "We can hunt too," he mewed. "The fresh-kill pile needs restocking."

Leopardfur glanced at it. He was right; there was only a chaffinch left. She called to Softwing. "Can you take a hunting patrol to the water meadow?"

Softwing lifted her tail, as though relieved at the suggestion. "Sure."

Beetlenose padded forward. "I'll take out a fishing patrol," he suggested.

"Good idea," Leopardfur mewed. "The Clan will be hungry after the vigil." Her own belly was beginning to grumble. She'd hadn't eaten since yesterday morning. "But make sure you head far enough upstream to be clear of the pike."

Beetlenose dipped his head. He crossed the clearing, calling Vixenleap, Grasswhisker, and Petaldust to him. Softwing gathered Shimmerpelt and Sedgecreek, along with Dawnbright and Mallowtail. Owlfur and Piketooth were already heading for the entrance, but they halted as the reeds shivered and Crookedstar led Rippleclaw, Cedarpelt, and Voleclaw back into camp.

The leader's shoulders were heavy, and he moved with a slowness that betrayed his grief. But his eyes brightened with curiosity as he saw patrols gathered in the clearing, preparing to leave camp. "What's happening?" he asked.

"Leopardfur suggested we go hunt." Beetlenose looked at the fresh-kill pile. "The Clan is hungry." He looked apologetic, as though it was tactless to talk of food when they'd suffered such a loss, but Crookedstar nodded.

"She's right," he mewed. "But first there are other duties to be performed." He looked around the Clan, and they gathered closer, their eyes sharp with interest. "We must recognize the bravery of one of our Clanmates."

For a moment, Leopardfur wondered who the RiverClan

leader could mean; then her heart lifted as she saw Crooked-star's gaze seek out Whitepaw.

"Whitepaw risked his life to save Blackclaw yesterday." Crookedstar beckoned the young tom into the center of the clearing with a nod.

Whitepaw's pelt fluffed nervously as he padded toward the RiverClan leader.

Crookedstar touched his nose to Whitepaw's head. "You showed courage and strength and loyalty," he mewed. "I see no need for an assessment. Leopardfur and Frogleap have both told me how much progress you've made this past moon. You've done more than enough to earn your warrior name."

Whitepaw lifted his muzzle, glancing gratefully toward Leopardfur before meeting the RiverClan leader's gaze.

"For this moment on, you shall be known as Whiteclaw."

"Whiteclaw!" Leopardfur called out his name as pride flowed like sunlight beneath her pelt. Her Clanmates joined in, and the small island clearing rang with their yowls. *Are you watching, Sunfish?* She glanced at the sky, an ache in her heart as she wished Sunfish could be with her son to celebrate this moment.

Crookedstar looked around his Clanmates once more as their chant died away and Whiteclaw padded to Leopardfur's side. She could hear him purring softly as he took his place beside her and she touched her nose to his head. "Well done."

Crookedstar's gaze had grown solemn once more. "There is one more duty I must perform," he mewed. "RiverClan has lost its deputy, and we will miss him. He was smart and brave and a skillful warrior. And he was my littermate. I will be lost without him." His mew grew husky, and he closed his eyes for a moment as though overwhelmed by his grief. When he opened them, he looked at Leopardfur. The intensity of his gaze took her by surprise. Why was he staring at her? Was he regretting not sending her with the battle patrol after all?

His gaze flitted away, moving from one warrior to another. "The warrior I have chosen as RiverClan's new deputy has shown courage and dedication and strength."

Leopardfur glanced around her Clanmates. Who would he choose? There were so many experienced warriors in River-Clan, it would be hard to pick one. Rippleclaw had always been close to Crookedstar, and Beetlenose had fought for his Clan for moons. Ottersplash was clever and quick, and Leopardfur felt sure that she had earned the deputyship many times over.

"Leopardfur."

She turned to face the RiverClan leader as he spoke her name and padded forward a few steps. Did he want her to run an errand while he made his final decision? "Yes?"

"You will be RiverClan's deputy."

She stared at him. Had she heard him right? She glanced at Frogleap, searching his gaze in case she'd misunderstood, but Frogleap's eyes were shining with pride. He nodded her forward. Whiteclaw's purr was loud enough for any cat to hear.

She turned back to Crookedstar. He was looking at her expectantly. "You showed great courage yesterday when you saved Blackclaw's life. And today it seems you instinctively took charge when the Clan was overwhelmed by its loss."

Leopardfur's ears twitched self-consciously. Was Mudfur watching this? She jerked her muzzle toward the medicine den. He was standing at the entrance. But his gaze was not on Leopardfur. He was staring in surprise at Crookedstar.

"I know Leopardfur wanted to be part of the battle yesterday," the RiverClan leader went on. "And part of me wishes I'd let her go. She is one of our best fighters and never backs down from a challenge. But she obeyed me and stayed in camp, and because she did, Blackclaw is still with us. Thanks to her quick thinking and boldness, we are mourning one cat today instead of two."

"But she's so young."

Leopardfur heard Birdsong whispering to Tanglewhisker, and her pelt twitched uneasily as murmurs rippled around the Clan.

"Why her?"

"Does she have enough experience?"

Crookedstar lifted his voice above the whispers. "I have watched Leopardfur closely since she was a kit. I've seen her overcome every obstacle and prove her loyalty again and again. After losing a leader and a deputy in so few moons, it's important that I appoint a warrior whose youth and strength and ability to survive will ensure stability and continuity in River-Clan for many moons to come." His gaze fixed on her, and she felt as though lightning were sparking through her fur. "Will you accept the job, Leopardfur?" he asked.

She dipped her head, her amazement only now giving way to excitement. She could do this, no matter what her

Clanmates thought. "I'd be honored," she mewed.

"Leopardfur!" Frogleap was the first to chant her name. Whiteclaw joined in, and then Skyheart and Sedgecreek too. Soon the whole Clan was calling her name, and she looked around, searching their gazes, wondering how many of them truly approved of Crookedstar's choice. Sedgecreek's and Skyheart's eyes shone, but Rippleclaw looked anxious, and she saw Cedarpelt and Piketooth glance awkwardly at each other.

She lifted her chin. It didn't matter. She would prove that she was the right choice for RiverClan. If she lacked experience, she would make up for it with loyalty and courage. If she was young, she would show them she had strength and energy an older warrior could no longer muster. There was no cat in RiverClan more prepared to put their whole heart into protecting her Clan than she was, and if they'd give her a chance, she'd make them see it.

From the corner of her eye, she saw the moss-draped entrance of the medicine den shiver. Mudfur had slid back inside. Did one of his patients need him? As the cheering died away and her Clanmates gathered once more into patrols and began to head for the entrance, Leopardfur nodded gratefully and made her way to the medicine den.

"Congratulations!" Whiteclaw bounded to her side.

Frogleap fell in beside her. "Crookedstar made a great choice," he mewed. "You're going to be an awesome deputy."

Leopardfur blinked at him, warmed by his confidence in her, but her thoughts were on her father. Shouldn't he be congratulating her, too? "I need to speak to Mudfur," she told Frogleap.

He seemed to understand. "Sure." He flicked his tail toward Whiteclaw. "You'd better join my patrol," he told the young tom. "Now that you're a warrior, we can do some *serious* hunting."

Whiteclaw's eyes lit up, "No more frogs?"

Frogleap purred. "I wouldn't go that far."

As they padded away, Leopardfur nosed her way into the medicine den. Mistyfoot and Loudbelly were asleep, but Blackclaw lifted his head and blinked at her happily. "Hi, Leopardfur."

Mudfur was lining a spare nest with strips of moss. He looked at her, and she leaned forward, hoping to see pride in his gaze. But he just blinked at her. "You must be pleased," he mewed.

For some reason, the words felt likes claws in her heart. "Of course I am." She frowned. "Aren't you?"

He straightened and padded past her, pushing his way out of the den. She followed, leaving Blackclaw staring after them, puzzled.

A few tail-lengths away from the medicine den, Mudfur paused. She stopped beside him, a chill reaching deep into her pelt. "Aren't you happy for me at all?"

He seemed to think for a moment before he spoke. "Of course I am," he mewed. "And I'm glad Crookedstar thinks so highly of you." Leopardfur tensed. His tone was controlled, as though he was holding something back. He went on. "I knew you were destined for great things. I've always thought it, but . . ." He paused.

His hesitation frightened her.

"I just wonder if you're . . ." His mew trailed away again and she felt sick.

"If I'm what?" She didn't want to hear the answer.

"If you're ready."

Uncertainty curled its claws into her belly. Why couldn't he just congratulate her? This was a great chance. But it was scary too. She needed encouragement, not doubt.

"Crookedstar was right in everything he said," Mudfur mewed. "You're bold and smart, and you never back down from a challenge."

She blinked at him. "So why can't you support me?"

His eyes darkened. "You're too quick to anger," he told her. "A deputy becomes a leader, and a leader must be able to keep their temper. I don't know if you—"

She turned away, not wanting to hear any more. She knew Mudfur loved her. He'd always loved her. But now, just when she was finally beginning to realize her dreams, he doubted her. The betrayal was more than she could bear.

She bounded across the clearing and headed out of camp. She had to get away. She needed time to think.

How could he say she wasn't ready to be deputy? Was it really so hard for him just to be happy for her?

CHAPTER 8

Moonlight silvered the leaves of the four great oaks that cornered the steep-sided glade. The sky was clear and Silverpelt shone brightly. Leopardfur puffed out her chest. This was her first Gathering as deputy, and she was eyeing the bushy slopes sharply, waiting for ThunderClan to arrive. It still pained her to see the cats who had killed Oakheart. They seemed to have no reaction: no gloating over their victory or showing shame at his death. How dare ThunderClan kill a warrior for Sunningrocks when they had no right to it?

ShadowClan was already in the clearing. Brokenstar was already waiting beneath the Great Rock, which jutted from the ground like a jagged tooth. His face was broad and flat and he stared around coldly. As Crookedstar joined him, Emberpaw and Mosspaw hurried away to talk with the ShadowClan apprentices. Leopardfur had warned them not to give anything away. Birdsong and Tanglewhisker were already gossiping with ShadowClan's elders as Mudfur exchanged news with Runningnose at the edge of the clearing. She felt a prickle of unease. The tradition of sharing tongues with other Clans simply because it was full moon made her nervous.

They might live side by side, but once the Gathering was over, the other Clans couldn't be trusted. ThunderClan had proven that. She wished Crookedstar would discourage RiverClan from mixing with the others, but from the way he greeted the ShadowClan cats like old friends as he crossed the clearing, she doubted he would.

Leopardfur stayed beneath the shadow of an oak as White-claw and Vixenleap headed toward the ShadowClan cats. She swallowed back the urge to stop them. Crookedstar wouldn't approve of her interfering. Perhaps they could at least pick up some useful gossip.

Rippleclaw and Frogleap were the only cats to hang back with her. They eyed the slopes, their tails twitching. Were they keeping watch for ThunderClan too?

Frogleap had not left her side since they'd started out for the Gathering, and she was glad to have his steady company. They'd had the chance to catch up. In the days since she'd been made deputy, she'd hardly had time to speak with him. She'd been busy organizing patrols, making sure that the borders were well-marked—especially ThunderClan's—and check-ing on Emberpaw and Mosspaw's training. She'd told Owlfur and Ottersplash to focus on their battle skills since Thunder-Clan seemed determined to steal RiverClan territory. And, since prey was rich and hunting still easy, she'd insisted that every warrior spend time practicing fighting moves and often joined them. Indeed, she'd joined almost every patrol, whether it was hunting or training, and shared tongues and prey with as many warriors as she could. She was determined that even

RiverClan's most senior warriors would see that she had her Clan's best interests at heart and that Crookedstar had made the right choice in choosing her as deputy.

Frogleap nodded toward the far slope. "They're here," he whispered.

Shapes were moving like fish through the shadows. Leopardfur wrinkled her nose as she smelled ThunderClan scent and Bluestar led her warriors into the clearing.

Almost at once, three young ThunderClan toms broke away from the group and headed into the crowd. Bluestar padded toward Crookedstar, while Spottedleaf, her medicine cat, hurried to greet Mudfur and Runningnose.

Leopardfur narrowed her eyes. "Where's Redtail?" She knew the ThunderClan deputy had been part of the patrol that killed Oakheart.

Frogleap was already scanning the clearing. "I can't see him."

"Perhaps he's too ashamed to show his face."

"He should be," Frogleap growled.

Leopardfur glowered at Lionheart and Whitestorm as the two ThunderClan warriors crossed the clearing, but they didn't even look at her. They seemed at ease as they moved among the other Clans, as though the deaths of Whitefang, Sunfish, and Oakheart meant nothing to them. Anger burned in Leopardfur's chest.

"WindClan is late." Frogleap was still watching the slopes.

"It's a long way to travel from the moor," Leopardfur mewed.

"They've never been late before."

Leopardfur frowned. It was true. And hadn't Beetlenose reported that morning that the marks on the WindClan border smelled stale? She tasted the air. There was no scent of a WindClan patrol now, and the thick ferns reaching toward the rise where WindClan usually appeared stood undisturbed in the bright moonlight.

A loud yowl sounded from the Great Rock.

"Let us gather!" Brokenstar called from the top. As Crookedstar leaped up beside him, Leopardfur hurried to join the other deputies at the foot. She ignored Lionheart, who seemed to have taken Redtail's place for the night, and gave Blackfoot a small nod. She was going to make it clear that these cats weren't her friends.

Bluestar took her place beside Crookedstar, but she was watching the fern-covered slope with interest, as though curious whether WindClan would appear.

"We can't start yet!" a black she-cat called from among the ThunderClan warriors. "We must wait till all the Clans are here." Anxious mews sounded around her, but the ShadowClan cats seemed only intent on watching their leader as he sat, gazing impassively at the crowd.

Bluestar padded to the edge of the Great Rock. "Cats of all the Clans, welcome." She held her head high, and her mew rang confidently across the glade. Leopardfur narrowed her eyes. Didn't ThunderClan have any shame? "It's true Wind-Clan isn't here," she mewed. "But Brokenstar wishes to speak anyway."

The gathered cats' attention was drawn back to the Great Rock. Brokenstar began yowling harshly. "Leaf-bare left us with little prey. But we also know that WindClan, RiverClan, and ThunderClan lost many kits in the freezing weather that came so late this season. ShadowClan did not lose kits. We are hardened to the cold north wind. Our kits are stronger than yours from the moment they are born." The ShadowClan leader's stare seemed to carry a challenge as he looked down at the gathered cats. "We find ourselves with many mouths to feed and not enough prey to feed them."

Leopardfur frowned. ShadowClan didn't look hungry.

"Our needs are simple," Brokenstar went on. "In order to survive, we must increase our hunting territory. That's why I insist you allow ShadowClan warriors to hunt in your territories."

Shock pulsed in Leopardfur's paws.

Tigerclaw, the fierce ThunderClan warrior, objected first. "Share our hunting grounds?" He sounded outraged. Leopardfur bristled in agreement. What in StarClan was Brokenstar talking about? Clans never hunted on each other's land.

"Should ShadowClan be punished because our kits thrive?" Brokenstar demanded.

Leopardfur felt stunned. She swallowed back anger. It rose so fiercely in her chest that she couldn't find the words to object.

"Do you want us to watch our young starve? You *must* share what you have with us," Brokenstar went on.

"*Must!*" a ThunderClan elder echoed in disbelief.

"Must," Brokenstar repeated. "WindClan failed to understand this, and we were forced to drive them out of their territory."

A chill slid along Leopardfur's spine. *Drive them out of their territory?* Was that why WindClan wasn't here? Was that what would happen to RiverClan? ThunderClan had already stolen Sunningrocks, and who knew what else they planned to steal. Now ShadowClan was demanding hunting rights. If RiverClan couldn't defend itself from ThunderClan, how could it fight off ShadowClan too?

Brokenstar was leaning over the edge of the Great Rock as he spoke now, every word rich with menace. "There may come a time when you'll need us to protect you."

Only one voice spoke up against him. Tigerclaw's dark amber eyes were fixed on Brokenstar. There was a threat in them. "You doubt our strength?" he hissed.

Leopardfur felt a rush of admiration. This warrior wasn't scared to say what he thought, even to another Clan's leader.

Brokenstar ignored him. "I do not ask for your answer now," he mewed. "You must each go away and consider my words. But bear this in mind. Would you prefer to share your prey, or be driven out and left homeless and starving?"

As the warriors, elders, and apprentices exchanged disbelieving glances, Crookedstar stepped forward. Leopardfur looked at him eagerly. He'd tell Brokenstar exactly what he thought about his idea. Hunting on RiverClan land! What warrior would allow such a thing?

But when Crookedstar looked around at the gathered cats,

what he said pierced her heart. "I have already agreed to allow ShadowClan hunting rights in our river."

What? Leopardfur stared at him in shock. What was he saying? He'd *agreed*? Without telling her! It was absurd. ShadowClan cats couldn't even swim, let alone fish. And with the pike making the river downstream unfishable, they needed every tail-length of water for their own hunting.

She saw Frogleap bristle as well. "ShadowClan cats on our territory?"

Leopardstar finally found her voice. "No Clan hunts on our land but RiverClan!"

Tanglewhisker's tail flicked angrily.

Rippleclaw stepped forward. "We weren't consulted!" he yowled at Crookedstar.

"I feel it's the best for our Clan." Crookedstar glanced quickly at the gray tabby tom, then turned to meet Leopardfur's gaze. A warning glittered in his. He wanted her to be quiet. "For all the Clans."

Leopardfur barely heard Bluestar tell Brokenstar that she would talk to her Clan before giving her answer. Anger pounded in her chest. Why hadn't Crookedstar consulted her? She was his deputy. She should have known about this.

Before she knew it, the leaders were leaping down from the Great Rock, and ThunderClan and RiverClan were melting away into the bushes as the Gathering broke up. Crookedstar was heading for the slope that led to the RiverClan border.

"Come on." Frogleap called to her as he turned to follow his Clanmates. Leopardfur stared after him. Was that it? The

decision had been made, and RiverClan land was now open territory for ShadowClan? Her heart was pounding with fury. She
had to speak with Crookedstar. He couldn't let this happen.

She raced after him as he led the RiverClan patrol up the
slope. She hardly saw the ThunderClan tom crossing her path
and, moving too fast to swerve, thumped into his side. She
stumbled to a halt, recognizing Tigerclaw. "Sorry," she mewed.

As she turned to head away, he spoke. "Leopardfur?" He
sounded uncertain. "The new RiverClan deputy, right?"

She stopped and faced him. Was that admiration in his
mew? "Yes," she answered warily.

"I'm glad to see that one of our leaders has the good sense
to appoint a young warrior as deputy." His gaze flitted curiously over her pelt. "Brokenstar chose *Blackfoot*. StarClan only
knows how many moons *he's* been alive. And Bluestar chose
Lionheart." He shot a sour look at the ThunderClan deputy
as he headed up the slope with his Clanmates.

Leopardfur blinked at him. Was he being openly disloyal?
In front of a cat from another Clan?

Tigerclaw went on. "The Clans need fresh energy to sweep
away old beliefs." He looked at her expectantly. "Don't you
think?"

She narrowed her eyes. He was a ThunderClan warrior. She
wasn't ready yet to forgive the deaths of her Clanmates. But
she couldn't help agreeing with him. "I guess," she grunted,
and turned away.

Crookedstar was nearly at the top of the slope. She bounded
after him, weaving between her Clanmates to catch up, and
reached him as he followed the path through the woodland.

"Crookedstar!" Breathless, she scrambled to a halt beside him. "You can't do this!"

Acknowledging her with a glance, he carried on walking.

"You can't let ShadowClan hunt on our land," she pressed.

"And you can't challenge me in front of the Clan." His ears twitched irritably as he looked over his shoulder. Rippleclaw and Timberfur were exchanging glances. "You're my deputy."

Anger flooded out. "Then why didn't you consult me?"

Crookedstar nudged her off the trail, behind a spreading juniper, and glared at her while the rest of the patrol moved on.

"There was no *need* to consult you," he mewed when they'd disappeared. "I knew what you'd say."

"I'd only say what any true warrior would say!" she mewed hotly. "You can't give hunting rights to another Clan!"

"Do you want to be at war with *two* Clans?" he demanded. "Do you really think we could defend ourselves against ShadowClan when we can't even keep Sunningrocks?"

"We need to try!"

"And lose how many more lives?"

"Are we just going to give our territory to any Clan that asks for it?" She couldn't believe he would give up so easily. "Are you going to let them drive us away like they did Wind-Clan?"

"Of course not," Crookedstar growled. "But the only way to survive is to lose this battle. Then we might be able to win the war."

"How?" she demanded. "When we've lost the respect of every other Clan? When we've shown them that they can push us around?"

"Things will change." His tone grew softer. "I understand why you're frustrated, but we need to give ourselves time to find our paws. That's one of the reasons I made you deputy. And you've done well so far. I can see you trying to strengthen RiverClan—the border patrols, the extra battle training—and I want you to keep on doing it."

"Why? When you're not prepared to fight?"

"Because one day we might have to. But that day's not today."

She stared at him helplessly. "You didn't even tell me you'd made a deal with Brokenstar."

"I know." He sighed heavily. "I knew you'd want to fight Brokenstar before you agreed to his terms."

"Would that be so wrong?"

"No," he mewed. "But you need to learn *when* to fight. If a leader reacts to everything with their claws, we'll always be at war. There are ways to protect your Clan without bloodshed."

"I don't understand." She felt hurt. "If you you're not willing to listen to me, why did you make me your deputy?"

"You have the boldness and courage that RiverClan needs," he mewed. "But until you've learned to master your temper, I will take advice from older cats."

"Like who?" Tanglewhisker? Rippleclaw? They clearly didn't want to give hunting rights to ShadowClan any more than she did.

Crookedstar's gaze flitted past her and she followed it, surprise sparking in her fur as she saw Mudfur. Her father had stopped to listen. Why? Was *he* the older cat Crookedstar had gone to for advice?

Mudfur dipped his head, then turned and headed away. Leopardfur's anger rekindled like scorched leaves in the sun. Mudfur might be wise, in his way, but he wasn't even a *warrior*!

Leaving Crookedstar behind, she hurried after her father, her tail lashing. "Did you tell Crookedstar to let ShadowClan hunt on our land?"

"He asked what I thought and I told him." Mudfur kept calmly walking.

"That's my duty!" she snapped.

"But Crookedstar asked *me*." Mudfur gave her a pointed glance.

And he didn't ask me. Leopardfur felt so frustrated she could barely speak. "I guess you think this proves you right," she growled finally.

"About what?"

"You said I wasn't ready to be deputy, and I guess if Crookedstar is asking your advice instead of mine, you must think you're right." *But he's wrong.* She knew he was wrong, and she would prove it.

"I don't care about being right." He stopped and looked at her. "I care about you, and about our Clan. I want you to be the best warrior you can be."

"I'm *deputy*!" she snapped. Wasn't he even a little bit proud of her? "Isn't that good enough for you?"

"Being deputy doesn't make you the best," he mewed.

"But you always said I was special!" Her anger was turning to despair. From her earliest memories, Mudfur had been her biggest supporter. How had he lost so much faith in her?

"I still think you are," he mewed. "You will save your Clan

one day. I'm sure of it. I remember my dream like it was yesterday. But now you're young, and you're too quick to anger."

"Only because you and Crookedstar don't listen to me!" Frustration surged beneath her pelt. *What am I supposed to do?*

He gazed at her softly. "Are you listening to *us*?"

A shiver ran through her fur. She wanted to listen. She wanted to understand. But *did* she? She had no answer.

"A good deputy must know how to listen more than they speak," Mudfur went on. "They must be prepared to fight for their Clan, but it should never be their first choice."

Shame warmed her pelt.

"Fighting should be your last resort," Mudfur mewed. "And I hope that, when you are the one to make all the decisions for your Clan, you won't let anger sway you. I hope that you won't choose war when peace is still an option."

Peace? After what ThunderClan had done? After what Brokenstar was demanding? What was wrong with these old warriors? Tigerclaw was right. The Clans needed fresh energy. Otherwise they'd all end up like WindClan, driven from their home, too frightened to fight for their land and their Clanmates.

But Mudfur was still talking. "You have a chance to lead RiverClan into a more peaceful time." His eyes were shining. "A time when cats don't fight over a pile of rocks. When we don't lose our Clanmates over a border or a piece of prey." He blinked at her eagerly. "What if you could save RiverClan by bringing us peace?"

She stared at him. Didn't he realize that cats like Brokenstar didn't care about reason, and that ThunderClan would keep taking RiverClan territory whenever they could? How could he be so naive? He'd lived among the Clans long enough to realize that peace was not possible as long as one warrior was willing to steal from another. And there would always be warriors in every Clan who wanted to steal from others. That was just how life was. Wishing wouldn't change it. RiverClan needed her to fight. If it was left to these old toms to make the decisions, they'd lose everything.

Mudfur was still looking at her. "Will you think about what I've said?" he asked gently. "I'm sure that if you make an effort to control your anger, if you listen first and *then* speak, you can become the leader I always imagined you'd be."

She blinked back at him. Was that really how he saw her? Hot-tempered and unwilling to listen? She looked away. There didn't seem any point in arguing. If he really believed that giving in to bullies like Brokenstar was the way to save RiverClan, nothing she could say would change his mind. Perhaps she and Mudfur would never see eye to eye—not about her being deputy, and not about how to run the Clan. This knowledge hurt, but Leopardfur couldn't imagine how she might change it. Swallowing back frustration, she dipped her head. "Okay," she murmured. "I'll try to control my temper and listen more."

As Mudfur stretched his muzzle toward her and rubbed his cheek against hers, she closed her eyes. If only life were as simple as her father seemed to believe.

The moon was still high when they reached camp, and she slowed to let Mudfur duck first through the reed tunnel. It had been a long day. She'd been awake since before dawn, planning the day's patrols, and the arguments with Crookedstar and her father had left her weary. The rest of her Clanmates had already disappeared into their dens, and Mudfur looked back at her, blinking fondly, before he turned away and padded to the medicine den.

As Leopardfur headed to the warriors' den, a shape moved in the shadows outside. She recognized Frogleap's gray pelt and striped tail, her heart lifting a little. "You waited for me." She was touched and pressed her nose to his cheek. His warm scent soothed her, and she realized how much she'd missed him these past days.

"I need to talk to you." His eyes glistened in the moonlight. He looked serious.

She tensed. "About what?" Had something happened?

He guided her away from the den. "This is the first time we've been alone since you became deputy," he mewed, stopping in the shadows beside the sedge.

"I know," she mewed guiltily. "I'm sorry. I've just been so busy." She promised herself that she'd try to make time for him tomorrow. Perhaps she would assign them to a patrol together. They could go hunting upstream, maybe fish in the minnow pool like they used to when they were training Whiteclaw.

"You're going to be just as busy from now on, though, aren't you?" Frogleap's eyes sparked with hurt.

She wished they didn't, although she knew what he'd said was at least part true. She wanted to comfort him. "There's so much I need to do." She moved closer. "But I promise, I'll try harder to make time for you."

"I don't want you to have to *make* time for me," Frogleap murmured. "I shouldn't be one of your duties."

"It's not like that." What did he expect? She had to put the Clan first. But that didn't mean he wasn't important.

"I thought we had something special," he mewed.

"We did!" Where was he going with this? She began to feel nervous. "We *do!*"

"I imagined we'd become mates soon," he mewed. "And have kits together. Like Sunfish and Beetlenose."

"Kits?" Leopardfur couldn't hide her horror. "I can't have kits right now. I'm deputy. And one day I might be leader, although I hope nothing happens to Crookedstar. . . ." Her mew trailed away as her thoughts quickened. What if something *did* happen to him? What if he died? She'd have to travel to the Moonstone. She'd be given nine lives. Everything would change. "But if it did   "

"If it did," Frogleap interrupted her, "there'd be no time for me at all."

"I'd make time," she mewed. "Other leaders have mates. Why shouldn't I?"

He was gazing at her, his eyes round. "I guess other cats are less selfish than me," he mewed. "They can put their Clan before their own needs. But I want kits, and a mate who has time for me. And I've come to realize that means I need a mate who's just a warrior, like me."

"You're not *just* a warrior," Leopardfur mewed. "You're special. Like me. Together we can make RiverClan strong."

"That's *your* destiny," he mewed. "Not mine. I want to belong to RiverClan. You want to *lead* it. You want nine lives.

I only want one, and I don't want to waste it waiting for the cat I love to make time for me."

Pain tightened like brambles around her heart, piercing it until she could hardly breathe. "Would a life with me really be wasted?" she mewed hoarsely.

"Not if it was our life to share," he mewed. "But you want to share your life with all of RiverClan. And I don't want to get in the way."

She wanted to tell him that he wouldn't be getting in the way, but she knew he was right. If they were mates, he'd always come second to the Clan. And perhaps that wasn't fair to him. He deserved a mate who would put him first, who would give him the kits and the love he'd dreamed of. Her eyes pricked with sadness as she met his gaze. "I'm sorry," she whispered. "I love you, but I have to follow the path StarClan has laid out for me."

He touched his nose to her cheek, and the warmth of his breath brought a sob to her throat. She swallowed it back and drew away.

He looked at her for a moment more, then dipped his head and padded away. The moonlight seemed to turn his pelt to water, making it shimmer as he crossed the clearing. Grief welled in her chest, but she knew she'd made the right decision. If she was to follow her destiny, she would have to make sacrifices along the way.

She just hoped that this wasn't one that she'd come to regret.

CHAPTER 9

Leopardfur shivered and fluffed out her pelt. It was a chilly morning. As usual, she'd been awake since dawn, organizing the day's patrols. Two were already out hunting, and another was heading for the ThunderClan border to refresh the markers.

She gazed at the distant moor, rosy beneath the early-morning sun. It still felt strange that WindClan no longer hunted there. Frost glittered on the heather and reached down as far as the river, where the shallow, quiet waters at the edge of the camp had grown a thin skin of ice. She could hear Heavypaw and Shadepaw cracking it with their paws as they hunted for minnows in the reed bed.

"Leopardfur!" Rippleclaw called from the entrance. She turned, surprised. She thought he'd already left with his patrol. "There are fox prints along the riverbank."

Her tail twitched indignantly. How dare a fox show its muzzle so close to the camp? "Follow its trail," she told him. "Make sure it heads back into the forest. If it doesn't, cover its scent trail with your own. Make sure it knows that RiverClan doesn't welcome scavengers." She thought, with a grunt, of the ShadowClan patrols that had been hunting on RiverClan land these past moons, and wished a scent trail were enough to scare off those scavengers too. But they still had Crookedstar's permission, and, although anger prickled beneath her pelt every time she imagined them spreading their stench over RiverClan land, she held her tongue and waited.

RiverClan was getting stronger by the day. She was making sure of that. She kept every paw busy—and none more than her own—patrolling and hunting and training so that her Clanmates were fitter than they'd been in moons, and they'd never worked better together. And they seemed to respect her for it. Even the older warriors had stopped muttering under their breath about her youth and inexperience.

Now, as Rippleclaw turned to leave, she called again. "Take Sedgecreek and Lakeshine with you just in case the fox turns nasty." The two she-cats had been weaving moss into the walls of the elders' den to protect Birdsong and Tanglewhisker from the cold. At her order, they stopped work and hurried after Rippleclaw.

Crookedstar was heading for the entrance tunnel. He had gathered his own patrol—Shimmerpelt, Ottersplash, and Piketooth—which was something he liked to do after the early patrols had left. Leopardfur always made sure that a few of the Clan's best hunters were left behind for him.

She crossed the clearing to speak to him before he left. She was worried the river downstream had been overfished this past moon. "Are you planning to hunt river prey?" she asked.

"Yes." Crookedstar searched her gaze. "Why do you ask?"

"I thought you could fish near Sunningrocks." Crookedstar

had avoided that part of the river since ThunderClan had taken it as their territory. If he wasn't willing to fight to get the rocks back, he should at least make RiverClan's presence felt there. She kept her mew casual. "We haven't fished there for moons. It must be teeming with prey. What do you think?"

His gaze narrowed. "You know how I feel about that stretch of the river."

"Yes, I know. Sunningrocks is ThunderClan territory right now." She sat down and curled her tail over her forepaws. "But it seems a shame to waste such a prey-rich part of the river." She tipped her head to one side. "And the river is still our territory."

Beside the entrance, Shimmerpelt, Ottersplash, and Piketooth were shifting impatiently, their breath billowing in the freezing air.

Piketooth pricked his ears. "Fish do shelter in the calm water there," he told Crookedstar.

Leopardfur didn't take her gaze from the RiverClan leader. It was clear from his expression that he had heard her, and recognized that the others agreed with her. Perhaps that was enough for now. "But perhaps it's better not to provoke ThunderClan," she went on. "The peace over the past few moons has allowed RiverClan to find its paws again, as you hoped. And we have plenty of other places to hunt."

Crookedstar eyed her sharply. "I can see that it's not just RiverClan that's found its paws these past moons," he mewed. "I'm glad to see that you've become as skilled with words as you are with your claws. But we won't be fishing near

Sunningrocks today." He headed for the entrance, flicking his tail. Shimmerpelt and Ottersplash hurried after him, but Piketooth hesitated, catching Leopardfur's eye before he followed.

Leopardfur felt a glimmer of satisfaction. She might not have persuaded Crookedstar, but she'd persuaded Piketooth. He might persuade the other senior warriors. And all without losing her temper. Would Mudfur be impressed by her patience?

Tanglewhisker and Birdsong were making the most of a patch of weak sunshine outside the elders' den, and Shadepaw and Heavypaw were still wading through the reed bed, slapping the water as they hunted for minnows. Whiteclaw had stopped nearby to watch them, his tail flicking excitedly each time they grabbed at a shadow beneath the surface.

Blackclaw was still washing the sleep from his eyes. He'd sat guard last night and had slept late.

"What training do you have planned for Heavypaw today?" Leopardfur called to him.

Blackclaw blinked at her. "I was planning to take him to the gorge to teach him white-water fishing."

Stonefur padded from the dirtplace tunnel, pricking his ears. "I'll join you and bring Shadepaw," he called. "There might still be some late salmon heading upstream."

Whiteclaw straightened. "Can I come?" The young warrior was skilled at fishing the rushing torrent that swirled through the gorge, and some days during leaf-fall, he had brought back enough salmon to feed half the Clan.

As they prepared to leave, Mosspelt and Frogleap padded from the warriors' den, their whiskers twitching with amusement as though sharing a joke.

Leopardfur's gaze snapped toward them, a pang of jealousy piercing her heart. They'd been spending more and more time together, sharing prey and tongues away from their denmates. "You missed the patrols," she mewed sharply.

Frogleap looked at her, surprised. "You said last night that you didn't need me for the early patrols."

"That doesn't mean I didn't need Mosspelt." Her pelt prickled self-consciously as she realized how petty she sounded. She knew she shouldn't care if they were close, but it was hard not to feel possessive. Two moons ago, Frogleap had been sharing jokes with *her*. What was going on between Frogleap and Mosspelt? Was it friendship? Or something more? Perhaps if she could figure out what was happening, she could come to terms with it.

"Come hunting with me." She forced her mew to sound cheery. "Both of you. I could do with stretching my legs." *And I can see just how close you are.*

She needed more warriors for the patrol. She didn't want to feel like the extra egg in the nest. But the camp was nearly deserted. She saw, with relief, Reedtail scraping fresh earth over the empty patch where the prey would be piled later. Emberdawn was with him, brushing away discarded feathers with her paw. "Will you join us?" she mewed hopefully.

"Sure." Reedtail blinked at her happily.

The river was so cold as they swam across it that she was

breathless when she climbed out. She shook out her pelt and bounded into the forest to warm up. There would be birds there, looking for shelter from the frost.

Reedtail and Emberdawn caught up to her as she reached the rise where bracken crowded the forest floor. She glanced back, jealousy pricking her belly, as Frogleap paused to let Mosspelt leap first over a jutting root. Mosspelt blinked at him warmly, and together they bounded up the rise.

That could have been me. The thought made her catch her breath. Was he happier now that she'd chosen her duty to her Clan over him? What if Mosspelt meant more to him than she ever had? Mosspelt was a pretty tortoiseshell, and her white chest looked as soft as duck down. Leopardfur curled her claws into the earth, wishing she didn't feel so jealous. She'd made her decision. She needed to live with it without complaining or letting her heart dwell on regret.

Bracken rustled ahead of them. Emberdawn stiffened. Reedtail's hackles lifted. He drew back his lips as Shadow-Clan scent rolled over them. A few tree-lengths ahead, the undergrowth was shivering. Paws thumped the earth, and a gray pelt burst from the fronds as a ShadowClan cat broke cover and veered across the forest floor. More pelts crashed through the bracken.

Leopardfur stared at them. ShadowClan didn't seem to care how much noise they made. A rabbit shot from the bracken and sent fallen leaves fluttering behind it as it tried to escape. But the ShadowClan warriors were gaining on it, yowling in triumph as they closed the gap—three strong warriors bearing down on a single piece of prey. Birds fluttered in panic in the branches above, and Leopardfur looked up to see them fly away. It would be a while before any prey dared return to this patch of forest. Anger rose in her throat as the ShadowClan warriors drove the rabbit down and one gave it a killing bite.

Emberdawn hissed and Reedtail started forward, but Leopardfur swished her tail in front of him.

"Stop," she ordered. She had no choice. "Crookedstar gave them hunting rights here."

"They were given rights to the river, not the forest," Reedtail snapped, as Frogleap and Mosspelt reached the patrol.

Frogleap blinked at Reedtail. "Wouldn't you rather they caught rabbits instead of fish?" he mewed. "We rarely eat them."

"Do they have to be so noisy about it?" Reedtail growled. "We should teach them how to hunt without scaring off the other prey."

Leopardfur grunted. "Why would they care?" she mewed. "Once they've scared our prey, they can go back to their own land and hunt."

Reedtail's tail was lashing. "How long is Crookedstar going to allow this?"

"Peace is better than war," Frogleap mewed.

Reedtail turned on him. "Not when it means starving."

"Who's starving?" Frogleap mewed.

"*Us,* if there's a hard leaf-bare," Reedtail snapped.

"But what can we do?" Emberdawn argued. "Look what happened to WindClan when they refused Brokenstar."

Leopardfur's paws pricked with indignation. Why had Tallstar let his Clan be chased away so easily? She'd rather fight to the death than accept such humiliation.

One of the ShadowClan warriors picked up the rabbit and led the others deeper into the forest. They hadn't even noticed the RiverClan patrol.

Reedtail growled. "They could at least thank us," he grunted.

"I bet they don't even thank StarClan," Mosspelt sniffed.

Frogleap glanced at her sharply.

Leopardfur felt a rush of hope. Was he disappointed that Mosspelt had taken Reedtail's side? But then she reminded herself: It didn't matter what Frogleap was thinking, because she'd already made her choice. The Clan came before love. And in her heart of hearts, she agreed with Mosspelt— ShadowClan had no place here. She was deputy now, though, which meant that she had to support her leader. She lifted her chin. "We have to respect Crookedstar's decision," she mewed. "ShadowClan is only trying to feed their Clan." She caught Frogleap's eye, pleased when he blinked at her approvingly. "Come on." She turned toward the river. "It's pointless hunting here now. Let's look for fish."

She headed upstream, where the river was wider and fish might be lounging in slack water.

Where she padded from the trees, the shore was wide, stretching from the forest's edge to the water. And a strange sight greeted her eyes: a new, soft-sided, brightly colored boulder sat on the pebbles. Leopardfur stared at it, her pelt twitching with alarm as its thin walls fluttered noisily in the breeze. In the opening, she could see a Twoleg. *So this is a kind of Twoleg den . . . ?* The Twoleg was sitting on its haunches like squirrel, a long stick in its paws. A fine thread of what looked like spider's web hung from the stick and dangled in the water, tugged by the current but unable to break free.

Reedtail stopped beside Leopardfur. He seemed more interested than alarmed by the Twoleg. "What's it doing?"

"StarClan only knows," Leopardfur murmured. She felt annoyed. The forest was full of ShadowClan, and now the shore had been taken up by Twolegs.

"What's that?" Emberdawn backed away as she saw the bright den, giving a low hiss.

"A Twoleg seems to have made camp," Leopardfur told her.

"At least it's alone," Mosspelt commented.

"We need to report this to Crookedstar," Frogleap mewed.

"We can tell Crookedstar later." Leopardfur's claws itched with frustration. "Let's head downstream for now. We can't go back without prey." As she began to turn away, the fine thread twitched. It jerked deeper into the water as though something was tugging it below the surface. Leopardfur halted, alarm shooting along her tail as the Twoleg leaped to its hind paws and began straining at the stick. It bowed like a branch heavy with fruit, and the Twoleg pulled at it, trying to draw the tip clear of the water. Was a fish trying to steal the thread?

Suddenly, the stick flicked up, and the fish that had been pulling on it burst from the river. It writhed desperately at the end of the thread as the Twoleg swung it close and grabbed it with a meaty paw. Then the Twoleg dropped the stick, pulled the fish from the thread, and placed it in a small, orange container.

Leopardfur strained to see what else was inside, rearing up onto her hind paws to get a better look. Her eyes widened with surprise. The container was filled with water like a small pond and was teeming with fish. The Twoleg must have been pulling them out of the river since dawn!

Surprise gave way to anger. "No wonder the river's been so empty!" she growled. "I bet that Twoleg has been stealing fish for days!"

Emberdawn's belly growled with hunger as she followed Leopardfur's gaze. "Perhaps we should head for the water meadow and hunt for frogs."

Leopardfur looked at the dark ginger she-cat. "I'm not eating frogs while a Twoleg steals our fish." A plan was forming in her mind. If it worked, they could return to camp with enough fish to feed the whole Clan.

Emberdawn blinked at her. "How can we stop it?"

Reedtail's pelt was bushed with anger. "We could chase it away."

"We can't chase a *Twoleg* away," Mosspelt mewed. "It's huge."

"We could lead it into the forest and push its stick in the water," Frogleap suggested.

"Or we could steal its fish." Leopardfur lifted her tail.

Emberdawn looked surprised. "How?"

Leopardfur glanced toward the brightly colored den. "We just have to distract it for long enough to take the fish from the container."

The patrol stared at her in disbelief, but Frogleap's eyes brightened. "That's a great idea."

Mosspelt looked puzzled. "How do we distract it?"

"You can attack the den with Frogleap, Emberdawn, and Reedtail," Leopardfur told her. "That will get the Twoleg away from the container, and I'll steal the fish."

"It sounds dangerous." Mosspelt frowned.

"Twolegs are slow." Reedtail kneaded the ground eagerly. "And there are five of us and only one of them."

Emberdawn licked her lips. "It's worth trying," she mewed. "We wouldn't even have to get our paws wet."

Frogleap was looking thoughtful. "You'll need help to steal the fish," he told Leopardfur.

"I'll be okay—"

He interrupted. "I'll help Leopardfur." He looked at Mosspelt. "Okay?"

She blinked at him, anxiety flashing in her eyes. "Okay," she mewed quietly.

Despite herself, Leopardfur felt a flash of satisfaction as Frogleap headed down the bank and crept behind the grass edging the beach.

"Be careful," she warned the others. "Run into the forest as soon as the Twoleg gets close to you." She hurried after Frogleap as he slipped behind the brightly colored den and hid with him behind a rock a tail-length away from the container. The Twoleg's gaze was on the thread as it dangled in the water, absorbed in watching it drift in the current.

Reedtail, Mosspelt, and Emberdawn were slinking toward the brightly colored den. As Leopardfur waited for them to take their positions, she breathed in Frogleap's scent. The familiarity made her heart ache. It had been a long time since she'd felt the warmth of his pelt against hers. Had she made the right decision?

Frogleap nudged her. "Ready?"

"Ready." The patrol had reached the den. They looked at her expectantly, and she unsheathed her claws. She flicked her tail, signaling them to start.

Reedtail reached up and, with a yowl, hooked his claws into the den wall and tugged. Mosspelt and Emberdawn clawed at it, spitting as though attacking a badger.

The Twoleg's flat face stiffened. Its sunken eyes widened, and it snapped its head around. The den quivered behind it, the thin walls flopping in and out like river weed caught in a current. The Twoleg hopped to its hind paws, yelping as it saw the warrior patrol tearing at its shelter.

"Quick!" Leopardfur leaped for the container and, rearing onto her hind legs, reached inside. She hooked her claws into one of the squirming fish and tried to haul it out. But it was too heavy to lift alone. "Help me," she mewed Frogleap.

He'd already reached in and snagged the fish and was trying to drag it over the edge of the container. Panicked, the fish thrashed free of their grip. Leopardfur grabbed at another, trying to keep her balance as she tottered on her hind legs. She hadn't expected fish that had already been caught to fight so hard.

The Twoleg was flapping its arms at Emberdawn. Hopping from one leg to the other, it yelped and howled like a dog, then swiped uselessly at the patrol, not daring to get too close as they ripped at the den wall.

Leopardfur leaned further into the container, straining on her hind paws as she fought to grab another fish. "Grab one!"

But Frogleap had frozen, his paws hanging stiffly over the edge.

"Help me grab one!" She tried to catch his eye, but Frogleap was staring at the rest of their patrol. His pelt spiked with alarm and Leopardfur followed his gaze. The Twoleg had picked up a stick. It was thick and had a curved spike like a claw on the end. He lifted it above his head and swung it toward Reedtail.

"Run!" Leopardfur yowled.

Reedtail leaped backward just in time as the hook swished past him, a whisker away. He raced for the trees. Emberdawn chased after him, her eyes wide with panic as she glanced over her shoulder at the Twoleg's stick. It swished through the air behind them.

"Mosspelt!" Frogleap's terrified wail shrilled in Leopardfur's ear.

Mosspelt was trying to drag her claws free of the den wall, but she was stuck, and she pulled in vain, the brightly colored wall stretching as she pulled, but refusing to tear. The Twoleg lifted the stick once again and began to swing it toward her.

Frogleap wheeled away and charged toward the Twoleg like a hawk. He slammed into the back of the Twoleg's hind paws, unbalancing it, and as it staggered to keep its footing, he leaped to Mosspelt's side and ripped at the den wall with his teeth. Mosspelt pulled free and pelted away as the Twoleg regained its balance. It started after her, but she was almost at the trees.

Leopardfur snapped her attention back to the fish. She had to catch one. This had been her plan. She couldn't let it fail now. She leaped in, all four paws sinking between the wriggling fish, and threw her forepaws around one. It was a salmon and it was huge, but she held on to it as it struggled to escape. Pushing up with her hind legs, she tried to lift it over the side. The container began to tip, and she held her breath, still gripping the salmon as it thumped onto its side and Leopardfur and the fish spilled out onto the pebbles. Water splashed up her nose and into her eyes. But she didn't let go of the salmon. Instead she pressed it to the ground as she found her hind paws, and sank her teeth into its spine to kill it.

"Get out of there!" Frogleap's yowl made her look up. He was pelting toward her, the Twoleg lumbering after with its stick.

Leopardfur froze. She had to get her catch back to camp. As the other fish flapped desperately around her, she caught Frogleap's eye. He slowed, as though reading her thoughts, and grabbed the tail of the salmon and began to help her drag it across the shore.

Leopardfur's heart was pounding so hard she thought it would burst, but she couldn't let go, even as the Twoleg thundered closer. Together they hauled the salmon away from the mess of floundering fish. The Twoleg thundered toward them, its stick slicing the air. If they could get the fish into the river, the Twoleg wouldn't follow, surely! But the water's edge was a tail-length away. Could they reach it before the Twoleg's stick reached them?

She pulled harder, bumping the fish over the pebbles. The Twoleg's eyes flashed with fury. It raised the stick and prepared to bring it crashing down on top of them.

Then its gaze flitted over the rest of its catch. The other fish were flapping desperately over the pebbles, getting nearer and nearer to the water's edge. The Twoleg's tiny eyes widened in alarm. It threw the stick, grabbed the container, and, dropping onto its haunches, began to grab desperately at the escaping prey.

Leopardfur tugged harder on the huge salmon. Frogleap bumped against her as together they tugged it to the water. After wading into the shallows, they plunged into the central current and, holding the salmon firmly between them, carried it to the far side.

She was panting as they hauled it between the reeds onto the grass on the opposite bank. She dropped it and sat back to catch her breath.

Frogleap collapsed beside her. "We did it!" He sounded exhilarated.

"Where's our patrol?" Leopardfur pushed her way back through the reeds and scanned the river. She felt a rush of relief as she saw three heads bobbing through the water toward her. Reedtail was the first to climb out, Emberdawn and Mosspelt behind him, and they pushed through the reeds, onto the grass.

186 WARRIORS SUPER EDITION: LEOPARDSTAR'S HONOR

She followed them. "Are you all okay?"

"We're fine," Emberdawn puffed.

Frogleap hurried to Mosspelt's side and leaned down to inspect the claw that had been caught in the den wall. "Is it torn?" he asked anxiously.

"No," she reassured him. She gave her paw a lick, but Frogleap tugged it toward him and began to wash it gently for her.

Mosspelt glanced at him shyly and looked away.

Leopardfur's heart twisted to see how deeply they cared for each other. Once, he'd looked at her that way. She closed her eyes for a moment as sadness swamped her. Then she shook out her fur. This was what she'd chosen. She wasn't going to regret it. Or resent Frogleap and Mosspelt for finding love where she'd left it. She shook out her pelt. "Let's get this back to camp."

Reedtail's eyes were shining. "Wait till we tell the Clan we outsmarted a Twoleg!"

Leopardfur looked at him, stiffening. "We can't."

He frowned. "Why not?"

Leopardfur's pelt pricked. "If we tell them, other cats might try it," she told him.

"It *was* pretty dangerous," Frogleap agreed. "Mosspelt could have been killed."

"We got away with it." Leopardfur swished her tail. "But what if an apprentice tries to do the same? They might not be so lucky."

Reedtail dipped his head. "I guess you're right."

Emberdawn frowned. "Are we going to lie and tell them we caught it?"

"Isn't that better than encouraging our Clanmates to take risks?" Leopardfur met her gaze.

"I guess," she conceded.

Frogleap glanced at the salmon. "I don't like lying to the Clan, but if it means saving our Clanmates from getting hurt in the future . . ." His mew trailed away as though he wasn't totally sure.

"It's for the best." Leopardfur lifted her chin. "Besides, this fish will feed half the Clan, and feeding the Clan is more important than anything."

Mosspelt glanced at Frogleap, as though looking for reassurance.

He blinked at her warmly. "Let's get it back to camp," he mewed, leaning down to grab the salmon's spine between his jaws.

Leopardfur's neck ached by the time they dropped the salmon beside the fresh-kill pile. It was heavy even with Frogleap, Emberdawn, and Reedtail helping to carry it. The few birds and fish brought back by the other hunting patrols looked small beside it. But the effort of carrying it home was repaid by the mews of admiration from their Clanmates.

"How did you catch such a big fish?" Softwing paced around it, her tail twitching with excitement.

Rippleclaw licked his lips. "StarClan was on your side today, Leopardfur."

She shifted her paws self-consciously. Perhaps StarClan *had* guided them to the Twoleg's den.

Crookedstar padded into camp, a sparrow between his

jaws. Shimmerpelt, Ottersplash, and Piketooth followed him. The RiverClan leader was the only cat carrying prey.

He dropped it on the fresh-kill pile and nodded at the salmon. "Did you catch that in the gorge?"

"Upstream," Leopardfur told him.

"Near the bulrushes," Reedtail added.

"Good teamwork." Crookedstar looked impressed. "It must have taken at least two of you catch it."

Leopardfur glanced at Frogleap and Mosspelt. "It took the whole patrol," she mewed.

Heavypaw and Shadepaw pushed between their Clanmates and began sniffing it.

"We didn't see any salmon that big in the gorge," Heavypaw mewed.

"Can I have a bite?" Shadepaw mewed hungrily.

"Take some to Birdsong and Tanglewhisker," Crookedstar told her.

Eagerly, the dark gray apprentice sank her teeth into the salmon's cheek and began to pull away a lump of flesh. "Ouch!" She flinched and jerked away with a yelp and swiped her tongue around her jaws. "It bit me!" she wailed.

Leopardfur's tail twitched with alarm. Blood was welling on the young she-cat's lip. She looked at the salmon, wondering what had happened. It was definitely dead. What could have hurt the apprentice? Guilt sparked in her pelt.

Crookedstar sniffed gingerly at the salmon's cheek, then picked at it with a claw. Gingerly, he drew out a long, silver thorn. It was curved and barbed at the end. Leopardfur's pelt grew hot. The Twoleg must have used the claw to hook the salmon from the water. She glanced at Crookedstar, wondering if he'd guess. She could tell at once that he had.

His whiskers twitched. Amusement sparkled in his eyes. "So you caught this in the river, did you?"

Leopardfur looked at her paws. "Sort of," she mumbled.

Frogleap lifted his chin stiffly. "We stole it from a Twoleg," he confessed. "It was dangerous and we didn't want to encourage the others to try it." He looked gravely at Shadepaw and Heavypaw. "Mosspelt nearly got killed."

Mosspelt blinked at her Clanmates. "It wasn't *that* bad," she mewed quickly. "And Frogleap saved me."

Leopardfur whisked her tail. "The Twoleg had stolen a pondful of fish from the river," she mewed. "We were just taking back what's ours."

"Twolegs!" Ottersplash fluffed out her fur indignantly. "They're always taking what doesn't belong to them."

Piketooth nodded at Leopardfur. "You did well to get it back."

Murmurs of approval rippled around the cats.

Leopardfur felt relieved. "I didn't like lying," she admitted. "But I wanted to protect my Clanmates. It's a risky way to hunt."

Crookedstar blinked at her. "Next time, let me decide what the Clan should be told."

She dipped her head apologetically.

Crookedstar inspected the fish and tore a lump of flesh from the salmon's flank. He tossed it to Shadepaw. "Take this to Birdsong and Tanglewhisker," he mewed again.

As Shadepaw picked it up and hurried away, the RiverClan leader began to tear up the salmon and pass the pieces among his Clanmates. They carried them to the edges of the clearing and settled down to eat.

Leopardfur stayed beside the fresh-kill pile, pleased by the sight of her Clanmates eating. There'd be no empty bellies tonight. She watched Frogleap and Mosspelt pad to a patch of grass beside the camp wall and settle down with a lump of salmon. She couldn't help but remember the warmth of Frogleap's pelt as he'd crouched beside her. She ignored the faint ache in her heart, embarrassed by the hope she'd felt when he'd joined her plan so enthusiastically. Of course he preferred Mosspelt. She could give him all the time and all the kits he wanted. And she was gentle and pretty.

But I was his first choice. The thought soothed her. He'd loved her once, and that would have to be enough. *It's more important that I concentrate on becoming leader one day, for RiverClan's sake.*

"Leopardfur." Crookedstar's mew cut into her thoughts. He was beckoning her away from the fresh-kill pile with his tail.

He led her to his den and nodded her inside. Leopardfur entered, puzzled. Why did he want to speak to her privately?

"Is something wrong?" she asked as he followed her inside. It was warmer here, the willow walls sheltering them from the cold wind.

He blinked at her, his green eyes glittering in the shadow. "Did you see anything strange while you were out hunting?"

Her pelt twitched nervously. "Only a ShadowClan patrol hunting in the forest, but they're allowed to, so I didn't challenge them."

Crookedstar looked away with a soft grunt. He looked worried.

"What's happened?" she pressed. "Have you decided to stop them hunting on our land?" Her heart quickened with hope. *At last!*

"Not yet." He met her gaze solemnly. "Brokenstar has been chased out of ShadowClan."

She stiffened, surprised. "*Chased* out?"

"ThunderClan joined together with his own Clanmates to drive him away," he told her. "Brokenstar's a rogue now, and Nightpelt will become ShadowClan's new leader."

Nightpelt? But Leopardfur's mind leaped past that news to something more important. "That means our agreement with Brokenstar doesn't hold anymore," she mewed, her heart lifting. "ShadowClan will have to stop hunting on our land!" She looked eagerly at Crookedstar. "When will you tell the Clan?" she asked. "We'll need to organize more border patrols and tell everyone to be on alert. I can—"

Crookedstar's gaze sharpened. "It means nothing yet," he told her. "Only that we should wait and see what happens."

"Wait?" What was he talking about? "It's time to *act*. We have to show ShadowClan and ThunderClan that we're strong."

"Let's see how things pan out before we start making decisions," Crookedstar told her. "We should keep this between ourselves for now. Nothing has changed for us. RiverClan is safe."

"But for how long?"

"Let's not cross that river before we reach it." Crookedstar padded past her. "I'm going to try some of that tasty salmon you brought home."

She watched him duck out of the den, belly churning with worry. *RiverClan, safe?* If ThunderClan and ShadowClan were working together, RiverClan was about as safe as kit in a fox den.

CHAPTER 10

The next morning, the chill had given way to milder weather. The reeds were limp, wilting after the frost, and the camp smelled of mud and mildew once more. Heavypaw and Shadepaw were carrying fresh moss to the elders' den. Mudfur was high in the willow tree, gathering cobwebs from between the branches. Leopardfur had sent out a border patrol and two hunting patrols and set Mosspelt to work with Blackclaw and Sedgecreek, strengthening the nursery walls with thick bunches of reeds.

There was a reason Leopardfur wanted Mosspelt to stay in camp. She was worried that her jealousy yesterday had been obvious. Embarrassment warmed her pelt. She needed to show both Mosspelt and Frogleap that she was fine with whatever relationship they had.

She looked across the clearing and caught Mosspelt's eye, beckoning her with a flick of her tail.

Mosspelt left the willow stems she'd been weaving into the side of the nursery and hurried across the camp. "What is it?" she asked as she neared.

Leopardfur guided her to a quiet spot beside the sedge

wall. "Do you want to help me bring back another fish for the Clan?" she mewed softly.

"Hunting?" Mosspelt looked delighted. "Sure."

"Just the two of us. We could steal another fish from the Twoleg." Leopardfur blinked at her. "It's our fish, after all."

"But you said it was dangerous."

"Maybe for apprentices." Leopardfur glanced at Heavypaw, who was dragging old bedding from the elders' den. "But we're warriors, and we've done it before, so it'll be simpler this time." Leopardfur didn't plan to haul fish out of the container. Now she knew it was easier to tip it over and let the fish tumble out. "Of course, with just two of us in the patrol, we'll have to steal a smaller fish." That didn't matter. All that mattered was that Frogleap would see she liked Mosspelt enough to take her on a special mission. It would show him she wasn't jealous at all.

Mosspelt's eyes glittered nervously. "Do you really think we can do it by ourselves?"

"Of course." Leopardfur headed toward the entrance.

Mosspelt followed. "Do you want me to shake the Twoleg's den like last time?"

"No." That had been too dangerous. "We'll wait for the Twoleg to get distracted by something else. We won't need much time to knock the container over and take a fish."

"Okay." Mosspelt lifted her muzzle and looked more determined. "Frogleap will be pleased that we've taken back another fish."

Leopardfur flicked her tail. *And that I invited you to help me,* she thought.

At the shore, they crouched in the bushes at the edge of the trees. Leopardfur was glad to see that the Twoleg was back, sitting on a stump beside the water, dangling a thread from a stick. Its brightly colored den hadn't moved, though there was a patch covering the tears the patrol had made yesterday. She guessed the Twoleg wouldn't be expecting them. It would think they'd be too scared to return. Besides, they'd be smarter and quicker today. It would be too slow to stop them from taking another fish.

The container was sitting beside it, and she could see dark shapes moving inside; the Twoleg had collected quite a feast for itself. Surely it wouldn't miss a few. . . .

"Is it playing dead?" Mosspelt was watching the Twoleg, which sat unmoving, its small eyes gazing dully ahead.

"It must be trying to fool the fish," Leopardfur guessed. Looking at the full container, she had to concede that the Twoleg might be cleverer than it looked.

Mosspelt stiffened beside her. "It's moving!"

Leopardfur's heart quickened as the Twoleg rested its stick against a stone and got to its hind paws. It turned toward the den and disappeared inside. She held her breath, expecting it to pad out again, but it didn't. Instead, the den trembled as though the Twoleg was busy with something inside.

"Quick!" She darted forward, haring down the bank and over the pebbles, running as lightly as she could so that she made no sound.

Her pelt rippled with surprise as Mosspelt raced past her. Before she'd even reached the den, the lithe tortoiseshell had

196 WARRIORS SUPER EDITION: LEOPARDSTAR'S HONOR

swerved around it and grabbed the edge of the container. She hauled it over with a thump, leaping clear as water and fish sloshed out. Leopardfur was impressed, and had to admit that she could see why Frogleap liked Mosspelt. The she-cat was surprisingly brave. She didn't even glance at the brightly colored den; as Leopardfur raced to catch up, she was already grabbing one of the fish that had spilled onto the pebbles.

"Wait for—" Leopardfur choked back the rest of her cry as the den shivered and the Twoleg lunged out. It was holding a long stick with a heavy web at the end. Horror surged in her belly as the webbing billowed down toward Mosspelt.

Mosspelt looked up, still holding the fish, her eyes widening in terror as the webbing ballooned around her and trapped her inside. She dropped the fish and tore at the web. Her shriek of panic rang across the shore as the Twoleg raised the stick and scooped Mosspelt into the air.

Leopardfur backed away as Mosspelt's panicked gaze flashed toward her. She could hardly breathe. She was as helpless as Mosspelt, who was thrashing like a fish in the web, only managing to tangle herself deeper into its folds. *What have I done?*

"Run!" Mosspelt screeched. "Leave me! Just run!"

Leopardfur hesitated. Should she leave? She was deputy— how could she let one of their strongest warriors get taken by Twolegs? And yet, as Mosspelt struggled, Leopardfur had to admit that she had no idea how to free the she-cat. *I need help,* she realized with dismay. Yowling to Mosspelt that she'd be back, she pelted for the woods. She ran into the shelter of the trees and glanced back at the shore, snarling under her breath. She could see the Twoleg carrying the webbed stick into its brightly colored den. "Fox-heart!" It wasn't enough to steal RiverClan's fish; this Twoleg wanted to steal its warriors, too? She felt sick. Would it hurt Mosspelt now that it had caught her? It must be angry about the stolen fish. Would it take its rage out on her?

She began to run. She had to get home. She had to get help.

Crookedstar looked up as she burst through the entrance tunnel. He scrambled to his paws, leaving the trout he'd been sharing with Voleclaw and Cedarpelt, and hurried to meet her. Outside the elders' den, Tanglewhisker stopped washing and looked up, his eyes sharp with curiosity. Leopardfur forced her fur to smooth, glancing self-consciously around the clearing as her Clanmates shared tongues. She was relieved that most of them seemed too occupied to have noticed her.

As Crookedstar reached her, she dropped her mew to a whisper. "Mosspelt has been caught by a Twoleg." She swallowed back guilt. Why had she suggested such a dangerous mission? Why in StarClan had she thought it was a good idea to return to the Twoleg's camp?

Crookedstar guided her quickly to one side of the warriors' den, out of earshot of their Clanmates. Tanglewhisker's eyes narrowed for a moment, then he returned to his washing. "Tell me what happened," Crookedstar ordered.

"We went to steal another fish."

"But—"

Leopardfur cut him off. "I know," she mewed quickly. "It

was dangerous. I just wanted . . ." She hesitated. She couldn't admit that she'd taken Mosspelt there just to prove she wasn't jealous. What kind of deputy would put a Clanmate at risk just to save her own pride? Her pelt burned with shame. "I thought it would be okay," she mewed. "We'd done it before and I figured it would be easier this time. But the Twoleg had a web and he caught Mosspelt in it and took her into his den."

The warriors' den rustled suddenly, and Frogleap burst out. He must have been listening through the wall. He rounded on her, eyes wide with horror. "How could you do something so dangerous?"

She recoiled. "I'm sorry. I—"

He went on, spitting with fury. "Why would you take her there? Didn't you care if she got hurt?"

She bristled. Of course she cared! Mosspelt was a Clanmate. And a *warrior*. He was acting as though Leopardfur had lured a helpless kit to the Twoleg camp. "We were fetching food for our Clan," she snapped defensively. "Why shouldn't I take her?"

Frogleap was trembling now. His blazing anger seemed to crumble into a heap of ash. "Because she's carrying my kits," he said, his voice raw with emotion.

Leopardfur stared at him, as shocked as if he'd lashed out at her with claws. His *kits*? She'd never imagined they were already mates. Her heart seemed to drop through her chest. *I haven't stopped loving him.* The realization stopped her breath. Had she secretly been hoping they'd have a future together after all? That he'd get over Mosspelt? That his affection for the tortoiseshell was only a passing flirtation? Heat flashed through her fur. *I chose the Clan, not him,* she reminded herself fiercely. She was deputy. She'd be leader one day. That was all she'd ever dreamed of.

And that meant she wasn't going to let one of her Clanmates get hurt, especially not one who was carrying RiverClan kits.

She looked at Crookedstar. "I'm going back to get her," she mewed.

"You're not going alone," Crookedstar told her. "Take Vole-claw and Cedarpelt."

"I'm going too," Frogleap growled.

Crookedstar met his gaze. "You're staying here," he told the gray tom. "You won't be thinking clearly, and this is a danger-ous mission. Leave it to Leopardfur."

Frogleap stiffened. "But—"

"If any cat can rescue her, it's Leopardfur." Crookedstar looked at her. "If you're not back by nightfall, I'll send another patrol."

"You won't need to." Determination hardened Leopard-fur's heart and sent energy sparking through her pelt. She was going to rescue Mosspelt even if it meant risking her life. She glanced at Frogleap. The anger in his gaze was sharper than claws. "I'll bring her back."

She signaled to Voleclaw and Cedarpelt, who leaped up from their meal and crossed the clearing. "We're going to save Mosspelt," she told them, heading for the entrance.

As she led them to the riverbank, she explained what had happened, pushing away the memory of the look Frogleap had given her and the knowledge that he was father to Mosspelt's kits. She would focus on fixing this. She would get Mosspelt home.

"That must be her yowling," Voleclaw whispered as they crouched behind the ferns edging the shore.

They were staring at the Twoleg den. Low cries sounded through its thin walls. Mosspelt sounded frightened, but still angry enough to fight. *Good.* Leopardfur felt a glimmer of hope.

"How do we get her out?" Cedarpelt asked.

Leopardfur scanned the den, realizing with a flash of excitement that there was a gap at the bottom. "The wall is thin enough to bend," she mewed, remembering how easily Mosspelt and the others had torn at it yesterday. "If we can get our noses through the gap at the bottom, we'll be able to squeeze underneath."

Cedarpelt squinted past the den, his pelt prickling nervously. "There's a monster here."

Leopardfur followed his gaze. A Thunderpath monster sat silently on the shore a tree-length from the den.

"It's asleep," Leopardfur told him. *Let's hope it stays that way.*

"Where's the Twoleg?" Voleclaw asked.

As he spoke, it emerged from the front of the den and stalked toward the monster.

"Quick!" Seeing her chance, Leopardfur dived forward and ran to the den wall. She pushed a paw underneath, relieved to feel how light it felt. It was easy to pry open. She made a gap and thrust her muzzle through, then scrabbled underneath and burst into the den.

She blinked to adjust to the weirdly orange gloom as Cedarpelt and Voleclaw wriggled after her.

"Leopardfur!" Mosspelt hissed from a corner of the den. She was still trapped in the webbing. "I can't get out."

Leopardfur darted toward her and examined the webbing, following the threads until she found where they were bunched together, tied by some kind of thick vine. If she could break through that, she could open it. "Watch out for the Twoleg," she told Cedarpelt.

As he darted to the entrance of the den and peered out, Voleclaw hurried to Leopardfur's side.

"Help Mosspelt untangle herself," she told him. She began to gnaw through the cord as Voleclaw hooked the webbing with his claws, lifting it carefully so that Mosspelt could free her paws from its folds. She looked up at Cedarpelt. "Where's the Twoleg?"

"Beside the monster," he mewed.

Leopardfur's heart was pounding in her chest. She began gnawing at the thread again, relieved as it started to fray. She tugged, then gnawed again, feeling it grow thinner and thinner until, at last, it snapped. Excitement surged in her belly. She tugged it open and began pulling at the webbing to open a tunnel to let Mosspelt through.

"The Twoleg's coming!" Cedarpelt's alarmed mew set her pelt bristling. Her claws caught in the webbing, and panic sparked through her as she fought to get them free.

Mosspelt was nosing her way forward, wriggling like a

newborn kit as she pushed her way out of the tangled webbing. Cedarpelt was backing away from the entrance, his hackles high and a low growl rolling in his throat.

Leopardfur gave the webbing another tug, relief flooding her as her claws came free, and she opened a space for Mosspelt to slide through. The tortoiseshell squirmed free, kicking out with her hind legs to throw off the last folds of the webbing.

"Let's get out of here." Leopardfur nodded the others toward the gap beneath the den wall. Voleclaw pushed it open with his muzzle and held it while Mosspelt squeezed her way out.

"You next." Leopardfur could hardly hear her own mew over the roaring of blood in her ears as she nudged Cedarpelt toward the gap. She could hear the Twoleg now, its massive paws crunching over the pebbles. Cedarpelt scooted out, and Leopardfur prodded Voleclaw after him. As he disappeared, she heard a howl behind her and turned.

The Twoleg was standing in the entrance, glowering. It lunged toward her, its paws flying at her. She reared and, hissing defiantly, lashed out at it. She felt its flesh tear beneath her claws and, with a yelp, it shrank back and stared at her in shock. As it hesitated, she turned and shoved her muzzle beneath the gap in the wall. Terror throbbed in her chest while she forced her way through. Exploding from the other side, she glanced around, relieved to see Voleclaw and Mosspelt already racing for the ferns.

Cedarpelt was waiting for her. "Are you okay?"

"Yes." She flicked her tail. "Let's get out of here."

He turned and fled across the shore. Pebbles cracked beneath her paws as she raced after him. The Twoleg was howling behind her, and as she dived through the ferns, she glanced backward. It was thundering after the patrol, its face dark with fury, anger glittering in its sunken eyes.

"Keep running!" she yowled, haring after Mosspelt, Vole-claw, and Cedarpelt as they crashed through the ferns. They leaped up the bank and raced into the forest. She pelted after them, her paws burning as she pushed hard against the forest floor. She didn't dare look back.

"This way." She raced ahead and led the patrol along a trail that dipped through bracken and swerved past brambles until she felt sure they'd lost the Twoleg.

She slowed and turned. Mosspelt scrambled to a halt beside her. Voleclaw and Cedarpelt pulled up, panting.

Voleclaw looked back and tasted the air. "We've outrun it."

Mosspelt staggered.

"Are you hurt?" Leopardfur blinked at her in alarm.

Mosspelt lifted her forepaw. It was swollen. "It got caught in the web," she mewed. "I think it's sprained."

Leopardfur met her gaze. "I'm sorry," she breathed. "I should never have taken you back there."

"The Clan was hungry," Mosspelt told her. There was no reproach in her eyes. "And we needed to show that Twoleg that those fish are ours."

When they reached the camp, Frogleap was pacing outside the entrance tunnel. His eyes lit up as he saw Mosspelt limping toward him. He hurried to meet her, pushing Voleclaw out of the way and taking her weight.

Leopardfur felt a rush of sadness. He hadn't even looked at her.

Lakeshine was rummaging through the fresh-kill pile as they padded into camp. She lifted her head, her ears pricking eagerly as she saw Mosspelt limping toward the medicine den. "You rescued her." She purred and hurried to greet Cedarpelt, touching her nose to his.

Crookedstar was pacing the clearing. He turned, relief flooding his gaze. "Is she okay?"

"Just a sprain, I think," Leopardfur told him. "I'll let you know more when Mudfur's checked her over." Mosspelt and Frogleap had already disappeared into the medicine den, and she hurried after them.

"Well done," Crookedstar called after her.

"Thanks." Guilt jabbed her belly. If she hadn't taken Mosspelt to the Twoleg camp, they wouldn't have needed to mount a rescue mission. She ducked into the medicine den.

Her father was examining Mosspelt's paw. "Some comfrey should ease it, and an oak-leaf poultice," he mewed, heading for his herb store.

Leopardfur padded to her side. "How are you feeling?" Her gaze flitted to Mosspelt's belly.

Mosspelt shifted self-consciously. "I'm okay."

"You're trembling." Frogleap pressed his nose to her cheek anxiously. "You should rest."

Mudfur glanced over his shoulder. "She's probably suffering from shock," he mewed. "Help her settle into a nest."

Frogleap began to nose Mosspelt into the nearest nest. As she circled clumsily down into the reeds, he flashed Leopardfur a reproachful look. "She could have been killed!" He padded toward her, hackles lifting. "She could have lost the kits. And for what? To steal an extra fish off a Twoleg? Was it really worth it?"

Leopardfur's mouth grew dry. She'd made a mistake. Would it help if she admitted it? "I just—"

"Don't be so hard on her." Mosspelt looked at Frogleap. "She saved me."

"She's the one who got you *caught*!" Frogleap mewed sharply.

Mosspelt's gaze hardened. "She didn't *force* me to go," she mewed. "I wanted to. I want to feed my Clan like every other warrior, and I may be expecting our kits, but I'm not in the nursery yet." She turned her face toward Leopardfur. "Thank you," she mewed. "It was brave of you to come back for me."

"I couldn't leave you there," Leopardfur told her.

"But you risked your life to save me." Mosspelt blinked. "Please thank Cedarpelt and Voleclaw too."

"I will." Leopardfur felt a rush of warmth toward the tortoiseshell. She dipped her head, glancing at Mudfur as she backed toward the entrance. "I'll leave you in peace. Let me know how she is when you've finished treating her."

"Sure." Mudfur blinked at her reassuringly. "I'm glad you're safe." His eyes glowed for a moment, then he turned back to his herb store.

Leopardfur ducked out of the medicine den. It warmed her pelt to hear that small reassurance from Mudfur. She'd struggled to accept that he would never see the world the same way she did, and she still carried a wound in her heart knowing that he couldn't support her in her new position. But he was her father, and he cared about her, even if they couldn't agree.

On the other paw, she knew it would be a while before Frogleap forgave her. But she'd tried her best to put things right. Perhaps one day he'd see that.

Outside, sunshine had begun to glimmer between the clouds. Leopardfur paused. A thought had been nagging her all the way back to camp. Why had she made such a risky decision in the first place? She knew well that a smart warrior stayed clear of Twolegs, and yet she'd taken two patrols to steal from them. She frowned. Why hadn't she been able to resist the lure of a successful hunt? It wasn't greed that had driven her. Or laziness. Only the knowledge that leaf-bare would be here before they knew it, and prey would become scarce. In another few moons, her Clanmates could be hungry. They needed all the prey they could get. But how could they catch enough with ShadowClan and Twolegs stealing from them and ThunderClan pressing at their borders?

She had to persuade Crookedstar that RiverClan had no choice but to reclaim the land they'd lost to ThunderClan and start chasing ShadowClan off their territory. It was the only way to make sure the Clan survived.

CHAPTER 11

Leopardfur glanced up at the night sky. Her Clanmates were sleeping. Soft snores rose from the dens. Clouds hid the moon. Rain was on its way, and the river would be swollen by morning.

She felt a prickle of frustration. In the days since she'd rescued Mosspelt, she hadn't found the right opportunity to speak with Crookedstar about reclaiming RiverClan's territory. Perhaps it was better this way. He hadn't taken her advice before.

She crossed the clearing, padding away from the medicine den where she'd peeked in to check on Mosspelt. The queen had been sleeping, Frogleap dozing beside her nest, his chin resting on the side. Mudfur had been hardly visible in the shadows, but she'd seen his eyes glint as he looked up at her from his herbs and blinked softly at her. She'd nodded in return and slipped out, not wanting to disturb Mosspelt's rest.

Now she checked the camp, padding quietly along the walls, her mouth open as she tasted the air for anything unusual. She'd have to remember to organize a patrol to fetch fresh bedding for the nursery and to clear out any cobwebs and dusty reeds there, making it ready for Mosspelt. It would be good to have kits in camp once more, even if they reminded her that Frogleap loved Mosspelt now.

Graypool nodded at her as she neared the entrance. The dark gray she-cat, sitting guard with Silverstream, was looking old, her pelt flecked with lighter gray hairs. Was it time she moved to the elders' den? Leopardfur decided she'd let the warrior decide for herself and nodded in return.

Silverstream got to her paws as Leopardfur reached them. "You should get some rest," she told Leopardfur. "You've been awake since before dawn."

"I just want to check outside." Leopardfur knew she slept better when she felt sure the camp was safe.

"Crookedstar's out there," Graypool told her.

Leopardfur's ears pricked with surprise. She'd thought he was asleep in his den. "Has he been there long?"

Silverstream glanced through the tunnel. "Not long," she mewed. "He said he wanted to stretch his legs."

Leopardfur ducked through the reed tunnel, followed the grass path beyond, and looked around. Crookedstar was sitting at the edge of the river. It flowed past him, the surface smooth and dark. He turned as she approached him, his green eyes gleaming like minnow pools. "Hey, Leopardfur."

"Hi." She sat beside him and gazed across the river, comforted by its soft swirl and whisper. It was a sound she'd heard since she was born, and even now it carried with it the gentle breathing of her nestmates and the steady beating of Shimmerpelt's heart. "I thought you were asleep." She caught his eye. Would this be a good time to discuss ShadowClan? "Is something keeping you awake?"

"No." He watched the river. "Mosspelt is safe. Our Clanmates have full bellies." He paused. "Is something keeping *you* awake?"

She hesitated. She wouldn't find a better time than this to talk to Crookedstar. She glanced at him. "How long will the Clan have full bellies?"

He stiffened, avoiding the question. "Are you worried about leaf-bare?"

"I'd be less worried if we weren't sharing our hunting grounds with ShadowClan."

He didn't look at her. "I'm not going back on the agreement I made," he mewed softly.

"But you made it with Brokenstar," she reminded him. "And now he's gone."

"We have peace. I don't want to threaten it."

"But it's getting harder to fill the fresh-kill pile every day," she told him.

"Is that ShadowClan's fault?" he mewed. "They're hopeless fishers. They barely take more than three or four trout in a moon. And the only land prey they take is fur prey. They leave feather prey alone."

"They might not hunt it," Leopardfur pressed, "but they scare it away. They're clumsy hunters. They frighten every bird in the forest just to catch a single mouse, and when they catch those three or four trout, they splash about so much they drive every other fish away."

"Perhaps it's just the price of peace," Crookedstar murmured.

Leopardfur looked at him. "Our land is slowly being stolen," she mewed. "ThunderClan has claimed Sunningrocks, and ShadowClan uses our territory like they own it. What you call peace, the other Clans will call weakness. Before long they'll be claiming more."

"We'll cross that river if we come to it." Crookedstar was still gazing across the water.

How could he be so calm? Didn't he realize the danger? "If we make a stand now, we might never even reach that river."

He turned his head. His round eyes glittered in the darkness. "And what if we make a stand now and find ourselves at war?"

"Then we fight," she mewed urgently.

"And what if we lose?" he asked. "Do you think the other Clans won't call us weak then? Do you think they'd be happy to stop at stealing Sunningrocks and claiming hunting rights? We might lose even more."

"Then we mustn't lose!" He was declaring defeat even before he'd tried to win.

"You can't guarantee that." He turned away again. "And I'm not willing to take the risk. It's too great."

"Big risks come with big rewards," she pressed.

"And even bigger dangers." His shoulders were stiff, and she knew she was wasting her breath. It wasn't fair to River-Clan. They were living like prey, too frightened to leave their burrow in case they were eaten, and she feared that as long as Crookedstar was leader, nothing would ever change.

* * *

It had rained in the night and the river was high. Leopard-fur signaled to Rippleclaw with her tail. "Check that the Twoleg is gone," she ordered. "Take Blackclaw with you, and Reed—"

She stopped as Whiteclaw raced into camp, his pelt wet from the rain, which was still falling. "Nightpelt's here!" he puffed. "He wants to speak with Crookedstar."

Her pelt prickled with alarm as the brown tom skidded to a halt in front of her.

He was scanning the clearing. "Is Crookedstar here?"

As he spoke, the RiverClan leader pushed through the mossy entrance of his den. "Where is he?"

"I left him beside the bulrushes with Emberdawn and Beetlenose," Whiteclaw told him. "He was waiting for us at the border and asked to be escorted to the camp."

"Did he say why?" Crookedstar's eyes glittered with curiosity.

"No." Whiteclaw shifted his paws excitedly. "He said he could only tell you. Will you speak to him?"

"Yes."

As Crookedstar began to follow the brown tom across the clearing, Leopardfur whisked her tail. Rippleclaw could pick his own patrol. "Take whoever you like," she told him. She hurried after Crookedstar, calling back over her shoulder. "But stay clear of the Twoleg if it's still there. It's dangerous."

She caught up to Crookedstar as he ducked out of camp and fell in beside him. "Can I join you?"

"Yes." He glanced at her. "But when we meet Nightpelt, let me do the talking."

"Okay." She felt a prickle of frustration. Would he ever trust her to behave like a true deputy?

They crossed the stepping-stones and headed for the bulrushes.

"I wonder why he's still called Night*pelt*," she mewed.

"Perhaps he hasn't had a chance to travel to the Moonstone." Crookedstar slitted his eyes against the rain. "ShadowClan must be a mess if their last leader was chased out."

Leopardfur wondered what it would take for a Clan to drive their leader away. Would Nightpelt tell them, or would they have to wait to hear the gossip at the next Gathering?

The rain was falling harder now, seeping through Leopardfur's pelt. She flattened her ears to keep the water out. But, even through the downpour, she could smell ShadowClan's stench before they reached the bend in the path.

As they rounded it, Nightpelt got to his paws. His black fur was slicked against his bony frame. His yellow-green eyes seemed as bright as primroses. Emberdawn and Beetlenose flanked him. They fell back as Crookedstar approached.

Nightpelt dipped his head to the RiverClan leader. "Thanks for meeting me."

Crookedstar waved Emberdawn, Beetlenose, and Whiteclaw away with his tail. Leopardfur hung back, her ears pricked. What had brought ShadowClan's new leader here? Was he going to demand even more hunting rights? She unsheathed her claws. She knew Crookedstar was worried about how she might behave at this meeting, but some things were worth getting in trouble over. Even if her leader agreed to expand their hunting arrangement, she couldn't let that pass.

The RiverClan leader waited until the warriors had disappeared behind the bulrushes before he spoke. "I'm sorry to hear that ShadowClan has been suffering."

Nightpelt's gaze flitted around the small clearing, as though he feared being spied on. "Now that Brokenstar is gone, things will change."

Leopardfur narrowed her eyes. *Does that mean you'll hunt on your own land instead of ours?*

Crookedstar sat down and folded his tail over his front paws. He seemed oblivious to the rain, though it streamed from his fur. "I hope that change will bring peace."

Leopardfur's hackles rose. *Ask him why he came!*

Nightpelt's tail was twitching uneasily. "Prey is more important than peace. A hungry Clan is a dangerous Clan."

Leopardfur curled her claws into the muddy earth. Was he planning to demand *more* rights to RiverClan land?

Crookedstar didn't move. "When leaf-bare comes, every Clan faces hunger," he mewed.

Tell him he needs to get off our land! Anger was pressing in Leopardfur's throat.

"Indeed." Nightpelt glanced to where the moor rose and disappeared into the low clouds. "But leaf-bare is many moons away. And now that WindClan has left, there is more hunting land to spare."

Leopardfur blinked in surprise. Why hadn't she thought of that? The moorland would be prey-rich if no cat had hunted there these past moons. Why let it go to waste?

Crookedstar gazed calmly at the ShadowClan leader but didn't speak.

"I came here to propose an alliance," Nightpelt mewed. "I realize that our hunting on your land has caused tension. I'm grateful you've allowed us to take your prey for as long as you have. But even Brokenstar would have admitted that it wasn't a permanent solution."

Leopardfur leaned closer. This ShadowClan leader had sense.

He went on. "Now that WindClan is gone, we should split the moor between us."

Crookedstar was quiet for a moment more. Then he spoke carefully, as though measuring his words. "What do you think ThunderClan would say?"

Nightpelt shrugged. "If RiverClan and ShadowClan have an alliance, it doesn't matter what ThunderClan says."

"Don't you think they'd want their share of the land?" Crookedstar mewed.

"Why?" Nightpelt looked at him. "They don't share a border with the moor. Besides, ThunderClan is not as pragmatic as us. They'd rather starve than cross a border."

Leopardfur bristled. "They crossed *our* border!" she snapped. "They took Sunningrocks."

Nightpelt glanced at her. "Only because they believe Sunningrocks belongs to them."

"But it doesn't—" she began.

Crookedstar silenced her with a warning look. "Sunningrocks is our concern," he growled.

She flexed her claws but held her tongue.

"What do you think of Nightpelt's plan?" he asked her suddenly.

"Me?" She blinked in surprise.

"You." He stared at her expectantly.

Leopardfur's pelt warmed with pride. He was actually consulting her! "I think it's a great plan." She searched his gaze. Surely he agreed?

"I think so, too."

As he flicked his gaze back to Nightpelt, she felt a rush of jubilation. *At last.* Crookedstar was planning to expand River-Clan's territory!

"Moorland prey isn't to our tastes," Crookedstar went on. "But a hungry warrior can't be picky." He got to his paws. "Will you start sending patrols to the moor straight away?"

"Not until after the Gathering," Nightpelt told him. "ThunderClan might oppose it."

"I thought ThunderClan didn't matter as long as we were working together," Crookedstar reminded him.

"They don't," Nightpelt mewed. "But I want to feel them out first. If they're going to cause trouble, we should be prepared."

"If you think they might cause trouble, we should hide our alliance from them," Crookedstar warned. "We don't want to provoke them more than necessary."

"Agreed." Nightpelt dipped his head. "ThunderClan thinks our loyalty lies with them, since they helped us chase out Brokenstar. It would be wise to let them think we're grateful for their help."

Leopardfur swallowed back a growl. She would never put

her Clan in a position where it had to be grateful.

Crookedstar turned to leave. "I'll send Whiteclaw to escort you to the border," he told Nightpelt as he padded away. As he brushed past Leopardfur, he whispered under his breath. "See?" His caught her eye. "Sometimes a leader only has to be patient."

Her belly tightened with frustration, remembering the lean fresh-kill piles, and her Clanmates' annoyance at seeing ShadowClan warriors clumsily hunting territory that belonged to them. She supposed that being patient had worked out this time—they had their territory back now, and WindClan's to split between the Clans. But who knew what might have happened if they'd fought back when they should have?

How much has that patience cost us? she wondered.

Leopardfur wrapped her tail tighter over her paws. The weather had turned cold in the days since the meeting with Nightpelt, and frosty air pooled in the Fourtrees hollow and reached deep into her fur. The warriors of RiverClan, ThunderClan, and ShadowClan bunched together, and the bright full moon lit their billowing breath, the air swirling around them like cloudy water. Leopardfur was sitting with the other deputies beside the Great Rock while the leaders addressed the Gathering.

Cinderfur sat in Blackfoot's place. The old ShadowClan deputy had fled with his leader. Leopardfur eyed Cinderfur as he gazed up at Nightpelt. Did he approve of his leader's plan to share the moor? Tigerclaw sat on her other side. The dark tabby had replaced Lionheart as ThunderClan's deputy. She shifted as warmth from his pelt reached her, unsettled by his musky ThunderClan scent.

"I, Nightpelt, have taken over leadership of ShadowClan," the skinny tom called from the top of the Great Rock.

Tigerclaw leaned closer to Leopardfur. "I notice he still hasn't gone to the Moonstone for his name," he murmured under his breath.

She eyed him suspiciously. There was amusement in his gaze, as though he thought little of ShadowClan's new leader. She looked away. ShadowClan was RiverClan's ally now, and she didn't like the ThunderClan deputy's insinuation that Nightpelt wasn't a true leader.

Leopardfur glanced at her Clanmates, dotted among the crowd. Mosspelt's sprain had healed enough for her to join the Gathering. She sat with Frogleap while Birdsong stood a few tail-lengths away, among the ShadowClan elders. Mudfur was with Spottedleaf, and Rippleclaw, Timberfur, and Shimmerpelt huddled together at the edge of the crowd, their pelts fluffed out against the cold.

The whole of RiverClan knew about the alliance Nightpelt had proposed. Leopardfur knew her Clanmates were excited and anxious in equal measure at the thought of hunting on WindClan's abandoned territory. She guessed that, like her, they were listening to hear what ThunderClan would think of the plan.

Nightpelt was still speaking. "Our former leader, Brokenstar, broke the warrior code, and we were forced to chase him out."

"No mention of *our* help," Tigerclaw muttered.

Cinderfur glared at the ThunderClan deputy, and Tiger-claw blinked back at him.

Leopardfur ignored the animosity sparking between the two toms. She was more interested in the crowd. The space left by WindClan still felt strange, but now she felt it more as an opportunity than a loss, and pictured the great swaths of moorland that were open to RiverClan's warriors. Per-haps she should organize some special training patrols. After all, RiverClan cats were used to hunting fish and birds. It would do no harm to practice chasing fur prey. Would some of RiverClan's hunting moves work as well on hillsides as on riverbanks and in water meadows?

She went through them, one by one, deciding which could be best adapted to hunting among the heather.

"WindClan must return!"

Bluestar's heated mew caught her attention and she looked up sharply. The ThunderClan leader was staring angrily at Nightpelt. But it was Crookedstar who spoke.

"Why?"

Before the ThunderClan leader could answer, Nightpelt added, "Sharing WindClan's hunting grounds will mean more food for all our kits."

"The forest needs four Clans," Bluestar insisted. "Just as we have Fourtrees and four seasons, StarClan has given us four Clans. We must find WindClan as soon as possible and bring them home."

"They must return!"

"Four Clans, not three!"

Leopardfur's pelt twitched uneasily as ThunderClan warriors raised their voices in support of their leader. She glanced up at the Great Rock as Crookedstar spoke again.

"Your argument is weak, Bluestar. Do we really need four seasons? Wouldn't you rather go without leaf-bare, and the cold and hunger it brings?"

Bluestar met his gaze coolly. "StarClan gave us leaf-bare to let the land recover and prepare for newleaf. This forest, and the uplands, have supported four Clans for generations. It is not up to us to challenge StarClan."

Leopardfur held her breath. Was Crookedstar going to press his point home? The RiverClan leader stared blankly at Bluestar. He couldn't be lost for words. He'd made an agreement with ShadowClan. ThunderClan was outnumbered here. He had to speak.

Bluestar was still staring at him, her blue eyes flashing angrily in the moonlight.

Say something! Leopardfur leaned forward, willing her leader to speak. But Crookedstar was silent. If he was going to let ThunderClan steal this chance of feeding their Clan, she wasn't. "Why should we go hungry for the sake of a Clan that cannot even defend its own territory?" she yowled.

Crookedstar shot her an angry look. She shot one back. Did he really expect her to stay quiet in the face of such provocation?

Tigerclaw bristled beside her. "Bluestar is right!" His growl took Leopardfur by surprise, and she drew away as he glared around at the gathered cats. "WindClan must return."

Bluestar spoke again. "Crookedstar." She was still staring at the RiverClan leader, but her gaze had softened. She was reasoning with him now. "RiverClan's hunting grounds are known for their richness."

Not when ShadowClan has spent a moon scaring away our prey and ThunderClan has claimed part of our territory as their own! Leopardfur trembled with indignation as Bluestar went on.

"You have the river and all the fish it contains. Why do you need extra prey?"

Leopardfur's eyes widened as Crookedstar looked away. Wasn't he going to argue?

Bluestar turned to Nightpelt. "It was Brokenstar who drove WindClan from their home. That's why ThunderClan helped you chase him out."

Leopardfur bristled with indignation. The ThunderClan leader was reminding him of his debt to her. Surely Nightpelt wouldn't be manipulated so easily?

"Very well, Bluestar," Nightpelt mewed after a moment's hesitation. "We will allow WindClan to return."

Leopardfur could hardly believe her ears. Nightpelt had betrayed their alliance at the first sign of pressure. Crookedstar hadn't even bothered to fight; he was still staring at his paws. How could these two leaders be so weak? She glared at Bluestar. Her shoulders were broader than Nightpelt's, her gaze more determined than Crookedstar's. The Thunder-Clan leader seemed far more powerful than either of them.

She turned to look at Nightpelt, the sickly Shadow-Clan warrior. He'd given in so easily. Suddenly the thought occurred to her: Was it was just for show? Perhaps he intended sticking to the deal he'd made with Crookedstar. After all, hadn't he and Crookedstar agreed to keep their alliance from ThunderClan secret? Perhaps agreeing with Bluestar was his way of hiding it.

Tigerclaw's mew sounded softly in her ear, disrupting her thoughts. "Are you learning from her?"

She snapped her head around and glared at him.

"She's impressive, isn't she?" he mewed.

"She's a bully!"

"She only reasoned with them."

Leopardfur felt the ThunderClan deputy's gaze searching hers, as though he was curious. She stared back at him. "What do you want from me?" she snapped. "Are you waiting for me to tell you how much I admire your leader?"

"No." Tigerclaw's mew was silky. "I'm just interested in why you spoke out when Crookedstar wouldn't."

She let out a low hiss. "I'm not prepared to let my Clan go hungry just because ThunderClan says they should."

"I'm glad."

She blinked at him. "Why?"

"Didn't I already tell you that the Clans need fresh energy?" he mewed. "I'm pleased you're living up to your promise."

Her pelt prickled uneasily. A few moments ago, this tom had openly contradicted her. Now he was encouraging her. She didn't understand. "But I don't want WindClan to return."

"So?"

"*You* want them back."

"Do I?"

"You just told the Gathering that Bluestar was right." What

kind of snake-tongued warrior was he?

"She's my leader."

Leopardfur suddenly realized that the Gathering was breaking up. Nightpelt had jumped down from the Great Rock and Bluestar, was already pushing her way through the crowd toward the slope that led toward ThunderClan territory. Cinderfur hurried away without saying good-bye, but Tigerclaw didn't move.

He blinked at Leopardfur. "But that doesn't mean I agree with her."

"You mean you *don't* want WindClan back?" Leopardfur was shocked.

"Right now, it doesn't matter what I want," he mewed. "Bluestar is my leader, and so I support whatever she decides. But if we have thoughts and opinions we keep to ourselves, where's the harm? I want what's best for my Clan, just like you do. Isn't it enough that I be loyal with my tongue and my claws? What happens in my own mind is my concern."

She frowned. She couldn't help thinking that Tigerclaw wasn't keeping his disagreement with Bluestar inside his own mind—he was telling her right now, wasn't he? A cat from outside his Clan. Wasn't that disloyal?

Tigerclaw was watching her carefully. "Clearly, there are times you don't agree with Crookedstar," he pointed out. "Perhaps even more than you said tonight?"

Leopardstar flinched. She couldn't exactly deny it—she'd spoken out just moments before. And yet . . . she couldn't admit this to a ThunderClan cat. Could she?

Tigerclaw drew himself up tall. "It's not always easy being deputy, is it? You must support your leader, but at the same time, you're your own cat. That's why your leader chose you, because you can make your own decisions. We have one paw in the present, supporting our leaders, and one paw in the future, planning for the day when *we* will be leader. I would only say, we understand each other—perhaps better than another cat could," he added, looking her up and down. "I would never betray your confidence. I admire you, Leopardfur. Your intelligence, your ambition. I hope that someday we will work together as leaders."

I hope so too. Being leader was all she'd ever wanted. But it seemed a horrible thing to hope for. It meant that Crookedstar would have to die. And it shamed her, in a way, that Tigerclaw could see her ambition so clearly. She got to her paws. "I should go." Her Clanmates were heading for the slope.

"I won't always be deputy, and neither will you," Tigerclaw purred silkily. "The day will come when our Clans will look to us for leadership. And I believe we can do it, Leopard*star*. We just have to be ready. We can bring change for the first time in moons "

Leopardstar. Since she was a tiny kit, Leopardfur had imagined how her leader name would sound, but this was the first time another cat had spoken it aloud. It sounded beautiful, so beautiful that it shamed her a little. *Crookedstar is my leader.* She began to head away, but Tigerclaw blocked her path.

"Change is frightening." His mew was gentle but insistent. "But you have the courage of your convictions. The Clans waste so much time fighting for the wrong things. I know you see that too." She pushed past him, but he followed. "You love your Clan; that's obvious. But you can see its weaknesses. You know how to make it better; you just haven't been given the chance yet. If we could plan together—"

"My Clanmates are leaving." She raced after them, her pelt twitching uncomfortably. As she reached the slope, she glanced back and saw Tigerclaw standing alone in the empty clearing.

The ThunderClan warrior had unsettled her. *Plan together?* There was something treacherous about his words. Should she tell her true thoughts to this ThunderClan deputy, but not her own leader? Surely he was encouraging her to break the warrior code.

And yet—she realized, as she turned the conversation over in her mind—he hadn't. He'd told her to put her Clan first. *If we have our own thoughts and opinions, where's the harm?* That was true, wasn't it? He was right. She truly believed that the Clans needed change. And she *would* be leader one day. What was wrong with admitting that, and thinking about it now?

Was it a crime to have her own dreams for RiverClan? What made Crookedstar's ideas right and her ideas wrong?

Tigerclaw was right, she realized as she headed back to camp. Believing in change wasn't disloyal. Nothing was disloyal so long as she had her Clan's best interests at heart.

CHAPTER 12

❧

The sky was growing pale. It would be dawn soon. The clouds were clearing, and Leopardfur could tell it would be a fine day. She lifted her face to the wind. It tugged her pelt and swished through the reeds. She should return to camp, but she paused at the river's edge and looked out across the water. She'd crept out before dawn and made a circuit of the island to check that no fox, dog, or Twoleg had come close. She wanted to see how the river was running. In the two days since the Gathering, it had rained hard, and the river was swollen and running fast. Fishing would be dangerous in such strong currents, and Leopardfur hoped that the day's hunting patrols would be able to find enough prey in the forest and along the shore.

Her thoughts flitted back to the Gathering. Bluestar had said that WindClan must be found and brought home, and that no Clan should hunt in their territory. Crookedstar's silence—neither agreeing nor disagreeing with the Thunder-Clan leader's demand—still clawed at her belly. Nightpelt had said that ShadowClan would allow WindClan to return. How could the two leaders give in to ThunderClan's demands so easily? They outnumbered them!

Crookedstar had let Leopardfur send only one patrol to the moor. While he'd agreed that RiverClan should maintain their right to hunt there, he'd ordered the patrol to take only one or two pieces of prey. It was as though he felt ashamed, and his furtiveness rubbed her fur the wrong way. Thunder-Clan could talk about bringing WindClan back, but until they did, the moor was open territory as far as Leopardfur was concerned.

A leaf twirled past Leopardfur's paws, carried on the water, and she grabbed for it, unable to resist. She hooked it out easily and dropped it on the bank.

If it were up to her, she'd have sent three patrols to Wind-Clan's abandoned territory every day. The moor hadn't been hunted for moons. It was foolish not to make the most of such rich land, especially when it sat right on RiverClan's border. She'd have told them to leave scent markers too; she wanted RiverClan to show that the other Clans couldn't tell them what to do. And if their markers happened to discourage WindClan from returning, all the better. The scrawny rabbit-chasers hadn't had the courage to fight for their land when Brokenstar claimed hunting rights; why would they fight for it now?

She turned, her tail flicking behind her, and headed back to camp, deciding on the day's patrols. She'd send out three: one to mark the ThunderClan border, two more to hunt in the woods. Timberfur could lead the border patrol and Cedarpelt could—

She ducked into camp, distracted from her thoughts by Mudfur, who was pacing beside the entrance.

His eyes were bright with worry. "Where have you been?"

"Checking the river." Was something wrong?

"Crookedstar's sick," he mewed. "Graypool found him in his den. He has a fever and is barely making any sense."

Leopardfur's paws pricked anxiously. "Have you moved him to the medicine den?"

"Yes," Mudfur told her. "I've given him feverfew and oak leaf, but we'll have to wait to see if it brings his fever down."

"Is it whitecough?"

"Not as far as I can tell." Mudfur flicked his tail uneasily. "But his throat looks a little red. He needs rest and herbs. You're going to have to take charge of the Clan while he recovers."

Take charge. Excitement sparked in her fur. She'd finally get a chance to put her own ideas into practice.

Mudfur narrowed his eyes. Had she looked too eager? "Until he recovers," he mewed.

"I'll do my best," she mewed quickly. "Take good care of him. It's important he recover quickly."

Mudfur looked reassured. "I'll need fresh herbs," he mewed. "Can you send a patrol to collect some tansy, if they can find it, and mallow?"

"Of course." Leopardfur began to turn toward the warriors' den but Mudfur hadn't finished.

"I saw you talking with Tigerclaw at the Gathering."

Why mention that now? It had been two days since they

were at Fourtrees, and there were more important things to worry about now. She blinked at him. "We're both deputies," she told him. "Of course we'd talk."

"Even after the leaders had argued?"

"Surely that makes it more important for the deputies to talk?"

Mudfur stared at her for a moment. He looked wary. Leopardfur forced her pelt to stay smooth. There was no way he could have overheard their conversation. "I had a dream last night," he mewed. "It disturbed me."

"What about?"

"Tigerclaw was holding a fish in his jaws. It was struggling, but it couldn't escape." Mudfur shifted his paws. "He wants power and he'll do anything to get it. You should be careful of him."

Leopardfur swished her tail. "Why wouldn't I be careful? He belongs to another Clan."

"Yes," Mudfur agreed. "And it's the Clan that stole Sunningrocks."

Leopardfur felt irritated by the reminder. Did he think she didn't know that? Besides, Mudfur had turned his back on being a warrior and made it clear he had no interest in Clan affairs. "I thought you didn't believe in petty quarrels between Clans?"

"But you do." Mudfur's eyes rounded. "And I worry about you."

"I'm fine." She glanced around the clearing. Timberfur was pacing outside the warriors' den while Ottersplash peered through the reed tunnel. Beetlenose was picking through the stiff prey left on the fresh-kill pile. They were restless. "I need to organize the patrols." She left her father, her thoughts darting like fish. Of course she'd be careful of Tigerclaw. His ambition was obvious. But it was driven by the desire to protect his Clan. Was that wrong? She stopped in the clearing and shook out her pelt. Of course it wasn't. It was natural. Mudfur worried too much.

She'd sent Timberfur with a patrol to check the Thunder-Clan border; Cedarpelt had taken Ottersplash, Lakeshine, Stonefur, and Shadepaw to hunt birds along the shore. She would lead the third patrol.

"Blackclaw." She called to the lean, smoky-black tom. "I'm taking a patrol onto the moor," she told him. "I want you to come with me, and bring Heavypaw." She nodded to Frogleap and Beetlenose. "You too, with Whiteclaw and Sedgecreek." She flicked her tail, and they hurried across the clearing to join her as she padded toward the entrance.

Frogleap looked worried. "Will Crookedstar be okay with us hunting on WindClan territory?"

"WindClan has left," she told him. "Why shouldn't we hunt there?"

Frogleap looked wary. "But Bluestar said at the Gathering—"

Leopardfur cut him off. "Is Bluestar your leader?"

"No, but Crookedstar—"

"Crookedstar is sick," Leopardfur told him sharply. "And *I* think we need to show ThunderClan that they don't decide what other Clans can and cannot do."

Heavypaw glanced anxiously at his mentor. "Is Leopardfur our leader now?" he whispered.

"Until Crookedstar recovers," Blackclaw told him.

Whiteclaw padded eagerly around them. "Let's catch as much prey as we can," he mewed. "Before WindClan returns."

"*If* they return," Leopardfur mewed.

Sedgecreek glanced toward the moor, which looked golden in the leaf-bare sunshine. "ThunderClan said they must be found."

"ThunderClan can look for them if they want," Leopardfur mewed. "But it'll be a long leaf-bare, and after losing so much prey to ShadowClan and that Twoleg, we need to fill our bellies however we can." She glanced around the patrol. Frogleap still looked unconvinced, and Beetlenose's tail was twitching. They needed reassuring. "Of course, I'd rather *not* eat moor prey," she mewed. "Moor prey is all fur and bone. But I won't let the Clan starve while perfectly good land goes unhunted."

She headed through the tunnel, ducking out into bright sunlight. Screwing up her eyes, she felt a pelt brush hers. Whiteclaw had fallen in beside her.

"Do you think ShadowClan will be hunting on WindClan land too?" he asked.

"Maybe." Nightpelt had said they would share the moor, before he'd backed down at the Gathering. She sniffed. "But ShadowClan doesn't interest me. I only care about feeding my own Clan."

Whiteclaw puffed out his chest. "The moor's probably stuffed with prey," he mewed. "I bet we'll be able to feed the whole Clan from a single hunt."

The young tom suddenly reminded her of Sunfish. Leopardfur purred at him, grateful for his enthusiasm.

The stepping-stones had disappeared beneath the surging water, so they had to swim across. They headed upstream to cross the river where it was smoother and easier to navigate.

At the WindClan border, Leopardfur paused. There was barely any scent left. WindClan's markers had been washed away, and the scent of heather was stronger than warrior scent now. As she crossed the border, Blackclaw scanned the sky.

"Watch out for hawks," he told Heavypaw. "With Wind-Clan gone, they'll be used to having the moor to themselves." He glanced at his apprentice and added, "They might mistake you for a meal."

Heavypaw's eyes widened. "Really?"

"Really," Blackclaw told him solemnly.

Beetlenose winked at the warrior and added, "Don't worry, Heavypaw. A hawk would spit you out after the first bite," he teased. "You taste like fish."

Heavypaw's ears were twitching nervously. "Don't hawks like fish?"

"Not furry fish," Beetlenose mewed.

Sedgecreek moved closer to the young tom. "Don't take any notice of them," she mewed. "They're just teasing."

Blackclaw purred. "I promise I won't let a hawk take you,"

he mewed, adding mischievously, "Not after I've spent so long training you."

Leopardfur blinked reassuringly at Heavypaw. "You'll be safe as long as you stick with us." She felt a fresh rush of affection for her Clan, and her fierce urge to protect them pressed harder in her chest.

As the rest of the patrol crossed the border, Whiteclaw hurried ahead.

"Stay close." Leopardfur called him back. Blackclaw might only have been teasing Heavypaw about hawks, but they were on territory that hadn't been patrolled for moons. Who knew what was hiding in the heather? Whiteclaw dropped back and fell in beside Sedgecreek, and Leopardfur pulled into the lead. If there were dangers here, she would be the first to meet them.

As the land began to slope upward, the grass beneath her paws grew coarser, the terrain rougher. A swath of heather lay ahead, and she ducked through a passage between the bushes, the patrol falling into single file behind her.

As the rough branches closed over her head, she opened her mouth to taste the air. Peat scent bathed her tongue. It smelled sour after the sharp, fresh scents of the river, but if WindClan never returned and they were to hunt this territory regularly, RiverClan would have to get used to the new flavors.

She stopped and marked a bush. For now, the other Clans should know this land was theirs.

Frogleap watched her, his pelt prickling uneasily. "Perhaps we should wait for ThunderClan to search for WindClan before we start marking," he mewed.

"ThunderClan needs to know they can't push us around," Leopardfur told him.

"But Crookedstar told us to stay low—"

"I'm leader right now," she mewed. "If Crookedstar wants to let the land fall into the paws of the other Clans when he's recovered, that's up to him. But I'm thinking of Mosspelt. And you should too. I'm not going to let a queen go hungry just to appease ThunderClan."

Frogleap dropped his gaze, but his pelt was still rippling along his spine. Leopardfur pushed on through the heather, her nose twitching as fresh scent surprised her. *ShadowClan?* So they *were* hunting here. She didn't know whether to feel irritated that she had to compete with them, or relieved that Nightpelt was sticking to the alliance. She ducked along a heather tunnel and slid out into the sunshine, where a grassy clearing opened on the hillside.

A dark pelt shadowed the bushes a few tail-lengths away. She bristled, giving the rest of the patrol a warning glance as they filed out behind her.

"It's ShadowClan," Frogleap mewed, glancing toward the cat.

As he spoke, the warrior called out. "Leopardfur?"

She recognized the gray pelt of Wetfoot, a ShadowClan warrior, as he hurried to meet her. Two other ShadowClan warriors and an apprentice were watching from the heather behind him.

"We've seen WindClan cats," Wetfoot told her.

Leopardfur's belly tightened. Had WindClan returned already? "Where?"

"Over there." Wetfoot nodded upslope where bracken covered the steep hillside. "We were going to warn you before we went back to camp."

"Is WindClan back?" Leopardfur flexed her claws.

"Their camp is still deserted," Wetfoot told her. "And there are no WindClan scent markers on the ShadowClan border."

"There aren't any on our border either," she told him.

"I think it's just a few stragglers." Wetfoot glanced upslope again and stiffened, his hackles lifting.

She followed his gaze. The bracken was rustling a little way up. She could see pelts moving between the stalks. No more than four, she guessed. "Follow me." She bounded toward them.

Her patrol raced after her, Wetfoot at her heels. The other ShadowClan warriors slid from their hiding place in the heather and followed.

She crashed through the bracken, WindClan scent strong in her nose now. Anger pulsed in her paws. WindClan had abandoned their land. If they'd run away, they should stay away and not sneak back like scavengers and steal food from RiverClan's mouths.

She could see three WindClan warriors through the bracken now, bunched together like fish hiding in weeds. They began to run; she smelled their fear-scent and chased them.

They burst from the heather into sunlight, and she raced out after them, pushing harder against the earth, swerving to overtake them and block their escape.

They slithered to a halt as she faced them. They were skinny, their eyes round with panic. One of them held a plump vole between his jaws. Blackclaw and Beetlenose exploded from the bracken with Whiteclaw and the ShadowClan warriors. They fanned out around the WindClan patrol. Only Frogleap hung back, ears twitching as he watched the WindClan warriors huddle defensively in the middle of the clearing.

"What are you doing here?" Leopardfur stalked toward them. She recognized Stagleap, an old WindClan warrior, and two younger cats.

Stagleap returned her glare. "This is our land," he growled. "What are *you* doing here?" He glanced fiercely at the Shadow-Clan and RiverClan patrols, but Leopardfur could see fear sparking in his gaze. He knew he was outnumbered.

She padded closer and turned her attention to the young she-cat holding the vole. "Your Clan left its territory," she snarled. "It's our hunting ground now." She turned toward Wetfoot. "And ShadowClan's."

The WindClan she-cat glanced nervously at Stagleap.

"Don't worry, Sorrelshine," Stagleap reassured her. "The moors belong to WindClan."

Leopardfur looked casually up the slope. "It doesn't look like it," she mewed. "It looks like you're alone here. Wetfoot says your camp is deserted and there are no markers on the borders. Which means this land belongs to any cat who wants to hunt here."

Stagleap's tail began to lash. "*We* want to hunt here," he hissed.

She blinked at him, then thrust her muzzle close to his. "*We're* not going to let you."

The young gray-and-white WindClan tom bristled. "But it's our territory!"

"It *used* to be." Leopardfur didn't even look at him. She kept her attention fixed on Stagleap. "So I suggest you leave."

Blackclaw growled behind her. "Why are you even here?"

Whiteclaw puffed out his chest. "Did your Clan leave you behind?"

Stagleap eyed them angrily. "We chose to stay behind," he mewed. "This is our home."

"Your home is with your Clan." Leopardfur showed her teeth. "Go and find them." With a snarl, she swiped her claws across Stagleap's nose.

He staggered back, fury burning in his gaze, and started to lift his paw, his claws glinting in the sunlight. But the gray-and-white tom darted in front of him.

"Come on, Stagleap," he mewed. "Let's go. This isn't a fight we can win." He glanced around the warriors encircling them.

Stagleap looked at him. Then, finally, his tail drooped. "Okay." He turned and began to head over the grass. The gray-and-white tom padded after him. As Sorrelshine began to follow, Leopardfur cleared her throat.

"Leave the vole," she growled.

Sorrelshine stared at her, her eyes glittering with surprise.

"Leave it," Leopardfur ordered.

Stagleap blinked at his Clanmate. "Leave it," he told her gently. "We can find other prey."

"Not on the moor," Leopardfur dug her claws into the ground. She was already sharing prey with ShadowClan. She wasn't going to give up more to these rogues. They weren't even loyal to their own Clan. "I want you to leave and never return," she hissed. "This is our land now."

The hunt went well. Prey was plentiful and easy to catch. The cover of heather and bracken made it easy to stalk unsuspecting mice and voles, and it was even easier to chase down rabbits on the open grassland. Leopardfur had given the WindClan warrior's vole to Wetfoot and thanked him for his help, secretly hoping she wouldn't see too many more ShadowClan patrols here. ShadowClan must already be fat on the prey they'd taken from RiverClan territory during the last moon. The more prey RiverClan caught here, the less they'd have to take from the already depleted supplies in the river and along the shoreline at home.

Frogleap was sulking. The dark looks he threw her as they carried their catch home made her pelt burn with irritation. At last, in camp, she dropped her rabbit on the fresh-kill pile and turned on him. "What's your problem?"

He met her gaze steadily, but she could see anger in it. "Was that really the right thing to do?"

"What?" she demanded, even though she knew.

"They were WindClan warriors," he snapped. "The moor is their home."

"*Was* their home," she snapped back. "WindClan gave it up."

"That doesn't mean we can hunt there and they can't." His tail lashed behind him.

She narrowed her eyes. "Why are you so concerned about every Clan but your own?" If he didn't care about his own kits going hungry, then she would care for him.

"Because those WindClan cats are warriors, just like us! They don't deserve to starve any more than we do!"

"That's their problem," she growled. "Not ours."

His tail fell still. "Oh, Leopardfur." The anger suddenly left his eyes, and he stared at her sadly. "You're not the warrior I hoped you'd become."

His words stung like nettles. But she held his gaze, refusing to flinch. "Thank StarClan I'm not." This was for the best. She'd given him up and he'd chosen Mosspelt. And now Mosspelt was having his kits. It didn't matter whether he liked her or not. Her duty was to protect the Clan. And yet the pain in her heart seemed to snatch her breath. She glared at Frogleap as he padded away, trying not to tremble.

"Leopardfur." Whiteclaw's quiet mew made her turn. The young tom was standing beside her. "He's being unfair." He nodded after Frogleap. "He doesn't realize that you only do these things for the good of the Clan."

His words soothed the sting in her heart a little. She blinked at Whiteclaw gratefully. "Thank you," she mewed. "I'm glad some cat understands me."

"When it all works out, every cat will see you were right." He straightened as though he'd suddenly remembered something. "Mudfur told me to fetch you," he mewed. "He wants you in the medicine den."

She tensed. "Is Crookedstar okay?"

Whiteclaw glanced toward the medicine den. "He didn't say," he mewed. "He just wanted you to come. Quickly."

"Thanks." Was Crookedstar worse? Leopardfur hurried across the clearing, trying to keep her fur smooth. She didn't want to alarm her Clanmates. She ducked into the medicine den. "Is something wrong?"

Mudfur was crouching beside Crookedstar's nest. "He wants to speak to you."

Leopardfur crossed the den, her heart sinking as she saw Crookedstar's matted pelt. The RiverClan leader was lying stiffly on the reed bed, and for a moment, Leopardfur wondered if she was too late. How many lives did Crookedstar have left? Panic fizzed beneath her pelt as she realized she didn't know. *What kind of deputy am I?* she wondered, looking from the leader to Mudfur. *How can I be ready to be leader when I have no idea how close I am?*

"I've given him every herb I know," Mudfur mewed softly. "But the fever won't break."

"But he's alive?"

"Yes." Mudfur touched his paw against Crookedstar's shoulder. "She's here," he whispered. "She came like you asked."

Leopardfur leaned closer. As RiverClan's leader lifted his head and blinked slowly at Leopardfur, Mudfur straightened.

"He's very weak." He moved out of the way. "Don't tire him."

"Okay." Leopardfur slid into her father's place.

As Mudfur left the den, Crookedstar stared at her, his eyes bright with fever.

She could feel the heat pulsing from his pelt. She remembered the last time she'd been called to the medicine den like this. Sunfish had asked her to take care of Whiteclaw. And then she'd died. She ignored the twinge of grief that pricked in her chest. "What did you want to speak to me about?"

"Leopardfur." He seemed to brighten as he recognized her. "Thank you for coming."

"Of course I've come," she mewed quickly.

"I was worried you'd be busy." His mew was husky. He shifted in his nest, and the effort of it seemed to pain him. He hesitated, catching his breath. "I'm glad you're such a strong deputy," he mewed at last. "RiverClan will have need of you."

"Don't talk like that." He sounded like he didn't expect to recover. "They have you. And they will for many moons." Leopardfur's heart ached. However many lives he did have left, surely this sickness couldn't take every one of them?

"It's okay." His gaze fixed on her. "I know I'll be leaving the Clan in safe paws," he mewed. "I knew I'd made the right choice when I chose you as deputy. We may not always have agreed, but I know you share the same love for our Clan as I do, and that you will sacrifice anything to protect it." His gaze drifted past her, glittering now as though the fever was tightening its grip. His eyes widened as though he saw something, and she followed his gaze, wondering if she should call

Mudfur. He was staring at nothing. "I knew I'd made the right choice," he mewed again. "Even though Mudfur told me to choose a different cat."

Leopardfur froze. Did Crookedstar know what he was saying? "Mudfur did what?"

"I don't know if he was frightened for you or for the Clan, but I told him you were the best choice and the strongest warrior and the bravest."

Leopardfur was hardly listening. Her thoughts were whirling. Her own father had advised Crookedstar to choose another cat to be deputy? How could he? Why? Did he have so little faith in her? He was the one who had told her she would save RiverClan. Had he never really believed it?

She stumbled to her paws as Crookedstar began to mutter, a look in his eyes so faraway that she knew he couldn't see her anymore. She lurched from the den, staring into the leaf-fall sunshine that was glittering on the water beyond the reeds. She let it dazzle her, feeling numb.

Mudfur hurried to meet her. "How is he?"

"I think he needs you," she mewed blankly.

He slid past her and disappeared into the den.

Around the edge of the clearing, her Clanmates were sharing the prey she'd brought back from the moor.

"So much fur," Tanglewhisker complained to Birdsong as he picked apart a rabbit.

"It tastes quite good," Lakeshine told Shimmerpelt, tearing another strip of flesh from a quail. "Try some. It's a bit like musky sparrow."

Leopardfur padded past them. Her heart felt like a huge

stone in her chest, pressing so hard against her throat that she could hardly breathe. She headed for the entrance. She needed to clear her head.

"Is Crookedstar okay?" Whiteclaw trotted after her as she followed the winding path between the reeds. "You look kind of shocked."

"He's very sick."

"Is he going to die?"

"Mudfur will do everything he can to save him."

Whiteclaw pelt ruffled nervously. "What will happen if he dies?"

"I'll become leader." The words seemed suddenly empty. It was what she'd wanted. And yet Mudfur didn't believe in her. The one cat she wanted to impress most thought Crookedstar had made the wrong choice when he'd made her deputy.

Whiteclaw was watching her as they reached the river's edge. His eyes glistened with worry. "Don't be sad," he mewed encouragingly. "Crookedstar will be happy in StarClan, and you'll be a great leader."

She looked at him, her heart aching at his kindness. He was looking at her with the eyes of a loving kit. Was this how Sunfish had felt when he'd looked at her? "I'm not just sad about Crookedstar," she mewed. "There's something Mudfur said. Something . . ." She hesitated. How much should she share? "Hurtful."

Whiteclaw tipped his head. "I thought you two were close."

"We were, once." Leopardfur swallowed back sadness.

Whiteclaw looked at her thoughtfully. "Sometimes our

parents aren't the ones who understand us best."

She looked at him. There was such honest affection in his gaze, she wanted to lick his ears fondly, just as Sunfish used to do whenever he'd done or said anything particularly cute as a kit.

She sat down, comforted suddenly by his presence and the soothing chatter of the river. She was being selfish, unloading all her worries on such a young cat. "Everything will be okay," she mewed. "Crookedstar will recover and I'll talk to Mudfur. We'll work it out." Even if it wasn't true, it would comfort Whiteclaw. She blinked at him. She should distract him by talking about something else. "What's going on with you at the moment?"

He looked away, as though a thought had made him suddenly self-conscious.

"What?" she mewed. Did he have something on his mind?

He stared at his paws for a few moments, his tail fur twitching nervously. "I have a crush," he mewed without looking at her.

"Really?" She purred, her heart lifting. "Who's the lucky cat?"

Whiteclaw didn't reply.

"I promise I won't tell," she coaxed.

He looked at her. "It's Silverstream."

She purred louder. "A good choice," she mewed. "She's a fine warrior, and pretty too."

"But I feel so awkward around her," Whiteclaw mewed. "It's like she's suddenly from another Clan and I don't know what to say to her."

Leopardfur thought for a moment. "Just tell her how you feel," she mewed. "What's the worst that could happen?"

"She could think I'm a mouse-brain."

"Why would she think that?" Leopardfur felt suddenly defensive of the young tom. "You're not a mouse-brain. Besides, if she's that mean, why would you like her in the first place?"

"But what if she doesn't feel the same way?"

"Isn't it better to find out instead of wasting time hoping?" Leopardfur could see he wasn't convinced. She went on. "She'll have more respect for you if you tell her how you feel than if you hide it," she mewed. "And if you truly want your relationship to grow into something stronger, you have to be bold." She nudged his cheek with her nose. "You want Silverstream to be happy, right?"

"Of course."

"Then tell her. And if she turns you down, you'll survive. You're a true warrior. You can survive anything. And it doesn't really matter what she thinks. What matters is that you have the confidence to speak your mind."

"Really?" She saw hope sparking in his eyes.

"Really." She realized, with a rush of surprise, that she hadn't entirely been speaking to him; her advice had been for herself, too. What did it matter if Mudfur thought she didn't have what it took to lead RiverClan? What mattered was that *she* did. She didn't know how many lives Crookedstar had left, or whether he would survive this illness, but she knew that if Crookedstar died, she would be a great leader. And in the meantime, while he was sick, she could show every cat what type of leader she would be. She'd prove Mudfur wrong—and Frogleap, and any other cat who doubted her. Crookedstar *had* made the right choice when he'd chosen her as his successor, and she'd show them.

I am on the right path. She gazed across the river as it churned and frothed downstream. *Every cat will see it soon. I am following in the paw steps StarClan has laid out for me.*

CHAPTER 13

"Graypool." Leopardfur nodded to the smoky she-cat. "Take Otter-splash and Stonefur to the moor to hunt."

"Can I go too?" Shadepaw looked at her hopefully. "I've never hunted on the moor, but I've been practicing stalking in the forest. I even chased a rabbit the other day."

"Did you catch it?" Leopardfur asked.

"No, but I was close." Shadepaw whisked her dark gray tail.

Leopardfur looked at Stonefur. "Is she ready?"

Shadepaw pushed in front of her mentor. "Of course I'm ready!" she mewed indignantly. "Heavypaw went to the moor yesterday, and I've been training just as long as him."

Stonefur's whiskers twitched with amusement. "She's ready," he mewed.

"Okay." Leopardfur dipped her head. "She can join the patrol."

Leopardfur had been awake since dawn. Dreams of chasing elusive prey across the shores and through the reed beds of RiverClan territory had left her feeling frustrated, and she was eager to get on with the day. She'd paced impatiently as her Clanmates padded sleepily from their dens, assigning patrols as soon as enough cats had gathered in the clearing. She'd spent the night wondering what the future held for Crookedstar and herself. What Mudfur had said yesterday—that he'd already given the leader every herb he could think of, to no avail—didn't sound promising, given how sick Crookedstar had seemed. At the least, Crookedstar would need time to recover. And she remembered what Crookedstar had said about leaving RiverClan in the right paws. If he was sick for a long time, this could be her chance to prove him right. If she succeeded, Mudfur would see that she was good for RiverClan, strong and competent. And when he recovered, Crookedstar would see that she held wisdom, too; perhaps he'd listen to her more often. She'd already sent Softwing with a patrol to mark the ThunderClan border, and Rippleclaw had taken another to fish upstream. Now she was determined that a patrol should hunt on the moor. After yesterday's brush with the WindClan warriors, and knowing that ShadowClan was hunting the same territory, she felt it was important to maintain RiverClan's presence there.

"Keep an eye out for those WindClan deserters," she told Graypool as the she-cat led the patrol toward the entrance tunnel. "Chase them off if you see them, and don't let them take prey."

Frogleap flashed her a look from the edge of the clearing, and she met it. "*You* can spend the day repairing gaps in the camp walls," she told him. "Skyheart and Loudbelly can help you."

He nodded, his gaze betraying nothing, and she turned to

Whiteclaw. She had a special assignment for him. "You and Silverstream will be hunting with me this morning."

His eyes widened. "Me and Silverstream?" He swallowed.

"Remember," she told him, keeping her voice firm but encouraging, "you must be bold and confident."

Whiteclaw glanced uncertainly at the warriors' den. "I don't know if she's awake yet," he mewed. "She was on guard duty last night."

"Only because she was too worried about her father to sleep," Leopardfur told him. "She'll probably be grateful for a chance to go hunting this morning. It'll distract her."

Whiteclaw still looked anxious. "She might want to stay in camp to be near him."

"Staying near him won't help," Leopardfur told him. "And he's got Mudfur." She wasn't going to let Whiteclaw wriggle out of a chance to spend time with Silverstream. Especially now, when Silverstream must be feeling anxious. If nothing else, she would need a friend. "Go and wake her. I'll see how Crookedstar is."

She fluffed out her fur and headed for the medicine den. Dark clouds were rolling in over the moor, and she could taste rain on the wind. But she wasn't going to let the weather stop her from helping Whiteclaw. Besides, a good leader should patrol as much as her warriors.

Her belly tightened as she neared the medicine den. Was Crookedstar worse? He'd seemed close to death yesterday, but he must have made it through the night or Mudfur would have told her. She tasted dread, imagining another feverish conversation like they one they'd had the day before. *What else might he tell me that I don't want to know?* But she pushed those thoughts aside, forcing herself to put the Clan first. A Clan whose leader was gravely ill. Had he lost a life already? Or two? She ducked through the trailing moss, steadying her breath as she prepared for the worst, and padded into the den.

Mudfur greeted her with a cheery purr. "I was about to come and find you."

Surprise sparked through her pelt. Crookedstar was sitting up in his nest, his eyes bright, not with fever, but with welcome. "Hi, Leopardfur." There was still a rasp in his mew, but he sounded much stronger. "How's the Clan?"

"They're fine." As sick as Crookedstar had seemed the day before, she wasn't prepared for this speedy recovery. She felt a little dazed. "I've—" She hesitated. She wasn't going to be leader after all. She wouldn't even be temporarily in charge for much longer. "I've sent out the patrols." She wouldn't mention that she'd sent one to the moor. Crookedstar wouldn't approve. Her paws itched with frustration. She wouldn't have enough time to show him that her way was right, which meant she'd be back to apologizing—for this, and for every decision that didn't match his own.

"His fever broke before dawn," Mudfur told her happily. "He's even eaten a little fresh-kill."

Crookedstar tucked his tail over his paws. "I feel much better."

"That's great!" Leopardfur forced a purr. How could she prove to Mudfur that she was a great leader now? Instead, she'd have to go back to being deputy with the memory of Crookedstar's words gnawing at her. *Mudfur told me to choose a different cat.*

Mudfur headed for the entrance. "I'm going to go and check on Mosspelt," he mewed.

"I'm glad you're feeling better." She padded to the edge of Crookedstar's nest and sat down. "You seemed pretty out of it when I spoke to you yesterday."

He looked puzzled. "I spoke to you?"

"After I'd returned from patrol." She searched his gaze, looking for a spark of recollection. Would he remember?

"I must have been delirious," he mewed. "Did I say anything strange?"

"No," she mewed casually. "You just wanted to make sure the Clan was okay."

"Good." He shook out his matted pelt. "Who's leading the patrols today?"

"Softwing, Graypool, and Rippleclaw." She hoped he wouldn't ask where she'd sent them.

"Good choices," he mewed. "Are they fishing in the river?"

"Rippleclaw's patrol is," she told him. "Graypool's hunting land prey and"—she went on quickly—"I sent Softwing's patrol to mark the ThunderClan border."

"We'd better start marking the WindClan border too if ThunderClan wants to bring them back."

"Okay." She gritted her teeth, fighting back an objection. Clearly, he was completely resigned to giving up their newly gained hunting rights. No doubt he'd hear about the patrols she'd sent to hunt on WindClan land and lecture her for risking the anger of ThunderClan. She could survive that, but what would he say when he heard that she'd chased WindClan warriors off the moor? She'd deal with that when it happened. Right now, Whiteclaw and Silverstream were waiting for her. "I have to go."

"Is something wrong?" Crookedstar frowned.

"No," she told him. "I just promised Whiteclaw and Silverstream I'd go hunting with them."

Crookedstar's eyes lit up. "Can you ask Silverstream to come and see me? She must have been worried."

"She was," Leopardfur told him. "But I've been keeping her busy."

"Thank you," he mewed gratefully. "But I hope you can replace her on your patrol. I want to spend some time with her." His eyes glistened.

Heart sinking, Leopardfur dipped her head. "Of course." She couldn't begrudge him. He'd come close to being separated from his daughter. But she was disappointed at how quickly she'd lost the chance to prove herself and defend her ideas. Patrols to WindClan would have to be suspended, and now she couldn't even help out Whiteclaw. She padded crossly from the den.

Whiteclaw was standing beside Silverstream at the camp entrance, looking like a 'paw at his first Gathering. The rain had arrived and the camp was already drenched.

"Crookedstar wants to see you," she called to Silverstream.

Her eyes glittered with alarm. "Is he worse?"

"He's much better." As Leopardfur's mew rang across the clearing, Frogleap let go of the reed he was weaving into a gap in the camp wall.

"Thank StarClan," he mewed.

"RiverClan is blessed," Skyheart mewed beside him.

Silverstream was already hurrying toward the medicine den, her eyes narrowed against the rain. As she nosed her way inside, Leopardfur joined Whiteclaw.

"I'm sorry," she mewed. She'd made him nervous for nothing.

"Never mind." He shook out his wet pelt, but she could see he was disappointed.

"We'll go hunting anyway," she told him. "Let's take Pike-tooth and Sedgecreek."

The two warriors were sheltering beneath the sedge with Voleclaw and Reedtail.

She called to them all. "Join us for a hunt."

The four warriors hurried across the camp, looking relieved to have something to do. Hunting would keep them warm.

She led them out of camp and followed the path to the stepping-stones. The smooth rocks showed above the surface today, but only just; the river would have swallowed them by the time the patrol returned. She leaped them and headed toward the gorge. There was a beech copse on the way where birds would be sheltering in the trees.

They hunted until sunhigh and caught a starling and a thrush.

"Let's bury these and pick them up on the way back," Leopardfur suggested.

Piketooth blinked at her through the rain. "Aren't we heading home?"

"There'll be good fishing beyond the gorge," she mewed.

Whiteclaw nodded. "When the river's been rough like this, there's usually a few fish trapped below the white water," he agreed.

Leopardfur shook rain drops from her whiskers. "Let's head over the top of the gorge," she mewed. "It'll be quicker than going around."

Sedgecreek glanced at the cliff top. "It's a long drop down to the river."

"Don't worry." Whiteclaw nudged her teasingly. "I'll catch you if you fall."

She nudged him back. "I don't intend to get close enough to the edge to fall."

"I won't let any of you fall." Leopardfur mewed gently. She was relieved that, despite the rain, Whiteclaw seemed to have recovered from his disappointment about leaving Silverstream in camp. She headed along the path, following the track as it wound steeply upward.

As she neared the top of the gorge, a familiar scent touched her nose. She stopped, her paws pricking warily.

"What is it?" Voleclaw lifted his muzzle.

"I smell WindClan." Had the warriors they'd found on the moor yesterday come back? Leopardfur stiffened. There was another scent mingled with WindClan's. Her pelt ruffled. "ThunderClan is with them."

Sedgecreek shifted her paws. "Do you think they found out

we were hunting on WindClan land?"

"Perhaps Stagleap asked them for help," Piketooth mewed.

Leopardfur's belly tightened. "It doesn't matter why they're here," she growled. "None of them should be on RiverClan land."

Whiteclaw began to head along the cliff top. "We were too soft on them yesterday." His tail was bushed angrily.

"Wait." Leopardfur narrowed her eyes against the driving rain and hurried after him. He didn't know what he was walking into. It could be an ambush. "Let me go first." She slid into the lead, glancing back to make sure the others were keeping away from the edge. Despite the wind, the scent of ThunderClan and WindClan was so strong now that there was no doubt it was a joint patrol. Anger pulsed in her blood. Was there no Clan that respected RiverClan's borders? She flattened her ears, preparing to confront them. She would give them a chance to explain themselves but their reason for being here would have to be good. Straining to see through the rain, she made out shadows on the cliff-top path, moving toward them.

"I see them!" Whiteclaw mewed behind her.

"Let me do the talk—"

Whiteclaw pushed past her and pelted ahead.

"Whiteclaw!" Leopardfur stared after him.

His yowl rose above the wind as he charged at the intruders. "Follow me!"

She raced after him. Rain battered her face, and she was half-blind with it as the shapes of the WindClan and

ThunderClan cats sharpened. She recognized their pelts. Fireheart and Graystripe were there with Deadfoot and Onewhisker. Her thoughts whirled in confusion. They weren't the WindClan trespassers she'd chased off yesterday. Had the rest of WindClan already come home? Why was Thunder-Clan with them? There was no time to wonder. Whiteclaw leaped for Fireheart and sent him crashing to the ground.

Sedgecreek streaked past her and lunged at Onewhisker. She dragged him from his paws and raked his ears, then, grabbing him with her forepaws, she tumbled him over and over, dangerously near the edge of the cliff.

Leopardfur leaped for them, grabbing Sedgecreek's pelt and dragging her back.

Sedgecreek let go of Onewhisker and turned on Leopard-fur, her eyes widening with surprise as she realized her deputy had pulled her away from the WindClan warrior. "What are you doing?"

"I promised I wouldn't let any of you fall." Leopardfur nodded toward the edge, where Onewhisker was scrabbling to his paws. Her pelt spiked as the WindClan warrior leaped for Sedgecreek, slamming into the tabby she-cat and knocking her past Leopardfur with a snarl. But Sedgecreek stayed on her paws and, rearing, swiped at the WindClan tom's muzzle, landing a vicious blow that sent him staggering.

Piketooth and Voleclaw were driving Deadfoot back along the path, lashing out at him while he stumbled unsteadily backward, his lame hind paw unbalancing him with every step.

Graystripe looked startled as Reedtail leaped for him, but the ThunderClan warrior reacted faster than a snake, batting Reedtail away with a hefty blow. Leopardfur raced at the gray warrior and, as Reedtail found his paws, she hurled herself at Graystripe and felt him stagger and collapse beneath her.

"This is RiverClan land," she snarled in his ear as she wrestled him the ground and began churning his belly with her hind claws. He screeched with fury and struggled to kick her off, but Reedtail sank his teeth in the gray tom's tail and bit down so that Graystripe screeched again, this time with agony.

Satisfaction surged in her chest. This band of intruders had learned their lesson. She loosened her grip. It was time to let them run away. They wouldn't dare put a paw on RiverClan territory again.

But a yowl erupted through the rain, and Leopardfur's pelt spiked afresh. She jerked her muzzle around, her eyes widening in shock as she saw more ThunderClan warriors pounding along the path toward them.

Tigerclaw! She recognized the dark tabby's broad head at once. He was leading a second battle patrol toward the cliff top. Willowpelt, Whitestorm, and Sandpaw raced at his heels. Suddenly RiverClan was outnumbered.

Leopardfur leaped to her paws to face them, but Tigerclaw had already crashed into Voleclaw, knocking him away from Deadfoot. The dark tabby grabbed the RiverClan tom with his forepaws and flung him to the ground. Voleclaw rolled and tried to find his paws, but Tigerclaw snapped like a fox at his hind leg and sank his teeth deep into the RiverClan tom's fur.

Voleclaw's pelt bushed. He clawed his way across the grass, kicking free of Tigerclaw, and pelted into the bushes in panic.

Leopardfur leaped for Tigerclaw. Before she could reach him, Willowpelt clawed her tail, ripping down to the bone. Pain searing through her pelt, Leopardfur turned, hissing, on the ThunderClan she-cat and slashed her claws across her muzzle. Willowpelt glared at her with rage and reared, lifting a paw to hit back. Leopardfur felt alarm flare in her belly. Whiteclaw was grappling with Graystripe. Fireheart and Whitestorm batted Reedtail back down the path. Deadfoot lunged at Piketooth, surprisingly deft despite his lame paw now that he faced only one warrior. Sedgecreek was crouched against the earth, hitting back with desperate jabs as Onewhisker and Sandpaw loomed over her. If Leopardfur and her Clanmates were going to get out of here with their lives, she would have to fight like a fox.

She leaped for Willowpelt, so fast that the ThunderClan she-cat didn't have time to land the blow she'd aimed at Leopardfur's muzzle. Slamming her head into Willowpelt's chest, she knocked her flying, then turned to help Piketooth. She'd drive Deadfoot off first, then deal with the others.

"Help Sedgecreek," she yowled at Piketooth as she darted past him and hooked her claws into Deadfoot's shoulders. Piketooth whirled away, and she pulled Deadfoot onto his weakest paw, feeling a spark of triumph as he collapsed beneath her. She let him drop. He was as helpless now as a wriggling fish. She lunged for his neck, but before she could give him a bite vicious enough to send him fleeing, claws sank into her scruff. Strong paws jerked her backward, and shock pulsed through her as she turned her head and saw Tiger-claw's eyes glittering beside her cheek. How dare he attack her when he'd acted like her ally? "What in StarClan—"

He thrust her viciously to the ground, the full weight of him burying her muzzle into the wet earth. "You see?" His low hiss sounded in her ear as she choked on mud. "I'm pre-pared to hurt even a cat I admire to protect my Clan."

Did he think this was a lesson? Rage roared in her ears. Her heart bursting, she dug all four paws into the ground and pushed up, every hair on her pelt spiking with the effort. She felt him budge and pushed hard as he tilted to one side, his paws slithering in the mud as he struggled to keep his balance. *I've got him.* She adjusted her weight, pressing her advantage, pushing him further over. She felt him slide from her back and, with a final shove, felt a rush of elation as he thumped onto his side. She was about to twist on her hind legs to slash at his ears when a terrified shriek seemed to make the rain-drops shiver around her.

She froze. Around her, the battle stopped as every face turned toward the sound. She saw eyes widen in horror, and her breath stopped as she followed their gazes toward the cliff top.

Graystripe crouched on the grass, staring over the edge, his pelt bushed.

Leopardfur darted to his side. Dread hollowed her belly

and she stiffened, as though her body knew what her mind refused to imagine. She followed his gaze down the sheer cliff face to the water raging below. A dark head bobbed for a moment in the white water, then disappeared.

A yowl ripped itself from Leopardfur's throat. "Whiteclaw! No!"

CHAPTER 14

Leopardfur wasn't sure how she got back to camp. She could remember grass beneath her paws, the river tugging at her pelt, her Clanmates around her; sometimes a shoulder had propped her up.

At the gorge, Fireheart had tried to make excuses. Graystripe had claimed he'd tried to save the young tom. But she heard them as though she were behind a waterfall, their voices lost in the roar of her grief.

When she found herself back at the camp, she felt so numb that it seemed as though she'd died along with Whiteclaw and was no more than a ghost. And then Beetlenose had asked her where Whiteclaw was, and she could only stare at him. Piketooth had to explain, and as he told the young warrior's father that his kit had died, the shock that had wrapped Leopardfur so tightly suddenly loosened its grip, and she'd crumbled like a rotten branch, her thoughts dissolving into darkness.

She opened her eyes now and saw the medicine den. Starlight was filtering through the walls and she blinked, puzzled. "Why am I here?"

"You needed to rest." Mudfur's soft mew seemed to

welcome her back from a long journey. He was gazing into the nest where she was curled, and she stared at him, thinking she should raise her head, but she couldn't. Her body had become like the river, shaped and guided by the earth around it, with no will of its own.

"Am I hurt?" she asked him.

"Not physically," he murmured. "But not all injuries are physical."

She wondered what he meant but didn't ask. She only wanted to sleep and sleep until what happened at the gorge wasn't the only thing she could think about. She closed her eyes and let herself sink into darkness.

"Leopardfur." Sunfish's mew brought an explosion of light. She could feel warmth on her pelt, healing the pain she'd been fighting to escape. She opened her eyes and, dreaming still, saw her friend. Sunfish's pelt glowed with stars. Her eyes shone as though moonlight blazed behind them. She had never looked so beautiful. Leopardfur lifted her muzzle, reaching for the light and happiness that seemed to enfold Sunfish. Then, suddenly, she was at the gorge and Sunfish was beside her and there, lying on the ground, was Whiteclaw's bedraggled body. It was bloody and battered, pounded by the river so that he was barely recognizable. And his eyes were white and empty.

"How could you let this happen?" Sunfish blinked at her. There was no reproach in her eyes, only grief so raw and desperate that Leopardfur's heart seemed to split in two. "You promised to watch over him." Her eyes reflected the deep, sharp pain Leopardfur felt. "You promised—"

A paw prodded her. Some cat was shaking her shoulder. Some cat who was real. Some cat who was alive. *Is it Whiteclaw? Was he here? Was he going to tell her it had all been a night-mare?* She jerked up her head and blinked into sunshine that was slicing through the den.

Voleclaw pulled back his paw and looked at her anxiously.

It wasn't Whiteclaw. Disappointment snatched her breath.

Voleclaw began talking. "You have to recover," he mewed. "I know you're hurting, but you can't stay in the medicine den. The Clan's hurting too. They need to know you're okay. Patrols need organizing. Heavypaw's ready for his assessment and . . ."

She watched him talk, but his words seemed meaningless. What did it matter? The Clan would manage without her. They might do better if she stayed away. "They have Crooked-star," she mewed emptily.

"But you know where prey's been running," Voleclaw mewed. "And which borders have been marked. We need you."

She stared at him. Why couldn't he leave her alone? White-claw was dead. He'd been killed on her watch, just like his mother and his mentor. It was more than she could bear. "I've made too many mistakes." She thrust her muzzle beneath her paw, closed her eyes, and fled back into sleep.

When she woke next, she felt a brittle sense of clarity as she lifted her head and looked around the medicine den.

"Frogleap?" She blinked in surprise as she saw him sitting beside her nest.

He nosed a dripping wad of moss toward her. "You must be

thirsty," he mewed. "Drink from this."

He was right. Her mouth was parched and she was hungry too, as though she hadn't eaten in moons. "How long have I been in here?"

"Nearly five days," he told her. He pushed the moss closer. "Drink."

She lapped the moss, relishing the cold water, then sucked it like a kit, squeezing out the last drops with her tongue.

Whiteclaw was dead. Her heart seemed to recoil as though clawed by the thought, but the grief didn't engulf her entirely this time. She took a breath and let the pain settle like river mud, leaving her thoughts as clear as spring water. "Why are you here?" She looked past him. "Did Mudfur tell you to come?"

"I've been worried about you." His amber gaze was soft.

"Why?" She was puzzled. "You must hate me."

He blinked at her, surprised. "Why would I hate you?"

"It's my fault Whiteclaw died," she mewed. "And I nearly got Mosspelt killed. And your kits would have . . ." She swallowed. Mosspelt was having his kits. Suddenly, all the choices she'd made seemed to have been wrong. She'd been following the wrong path. She should have become his mate and had his kits, and then Whiteclaw would be alive and the Clan would be happy.

"You didn't kill Whiteclaw," Frogleap mewed. "And you *rescued* Mosspelt."

"But I took them both—"

"You took them both on patrol," Frogleap told her. "They

were warriors and your Clanmates. You did nothing wrong." He was looking into Leopardfur's eyes now so intently that she wanted to look away.

Her heart ached with a new pain. "I should have put love first," she mewed. "I should have kept you by my side. I miss you."

She saw the fur around his neck prickle uncomfortably and felt hot with embarrassment. She shouldn't have said anything.

"I miss you too," he mewed quietly. "And I wonder what it would have been like if we'd stayed together." He held her gaze for a moment, then looked away. "But we chose to separate for a reason, and that reason hasn't gone away. I love Mosspelt now, but you'll always be special to me. You must never feel alone." He lifted his chin. "I'll always be here. As your friend."

She felt a twinge of sadness, as though he'd pulled her closer and pushed her away at the same time. But, after everything that had happened, she should be grateful. She *was* grateful. She hadn't lost him as a friend after all.

He fetched her a trout from the fresh-kill pile and stayed long enough to make sure she ate it. When he'd left, she dozed a little, waking after sunhigh to eat herbs Mudfur had prepared for her.

"Silverstream wants to see you," Mudfur told her as she swallowed the bitter mixture. He nosed a fish tail toward her to take away the taste.

Leopardfur lapped it gratefully. "Is she okay?"

"She seems a little distracted," Mudfur told her. "I told her you'd see her." He looked at her hopefully. "Will you?"

"Yes." Leopardfur felt ready to face her Clanmates, if only one at a time and while cocooned in a nest.

Mudfur touched his nose to her ear. "I'm glad you're feeling better," he mewed softly. "I've been worried about you."

"I'll be okay." She blinked at him reassuringly. "I'm your kit, don't forget. I'm a survivor."

He purred and padded from the den. A moment later, Silverstream nosed her way through the moss at the entrance.

"Hi." Her blue eyes glittered in the shadow of the den. She sat down beside Leopardfur's nest. "Are you feeling better?"

"Yes." She sat up. "Is Crookedstar organizing the patrols?"

She nodded. "Timberfur and Piketooth are helping him, but we've been hunting the same places over and over again and prey has been scarce."

Leopardfur guessed that Crookedstar was still avoiding the river around Sunningrocks and probably fretting about sending patrols near the WindClan border. He needed to be reminded that it was unwise to fish the same stretch of river too much, and she knew a few places in the woods that were good for hunting when shore prey was in short supply. She would have to tell him about them.

She looked at Silverstream. Her tail was twitching anxiously. Was something else worrying the gray tabby she-cat? "You wanted to see me?"

"I wish I'd come to the gorge with you," she mewed guiltily. "Instead of staying with Crookedstar."

Leopardfur felt a rush of sympathy. She knew what it was

like to wonder what would have happened if she'd made different choices. "Crookedstar needed you," she mewed. "And you needed to be with him. He nearly died." She shifted in her nest. Strength seemed to be flowing back to her paws. They itched to be outside. "Not even StarClan can change what happened at the gorge. The patrol was outnumbered. Your being there wouldn't have made any difference. It would have just meant another of my Clanmates was in danger." She held Silverstream's gaze. "I'm glad you were safe in camp."

Silverstream stared at her. There still seemed to be a question in her eyes, something that she hadn't said yet.

"What's wrong?" Leopardfur asked gently. "Is something else troubling you?"

"I heard that it was Graystripe who . . ." Her mew trailed away as though she couldn't bring herself to mention Whiteclaw's death.

"You can say it," Leopardfur growled. "Graystripe killed Whiteclaw. He probably organized the whole ambush. I'm going to make him sorry he ever—"

Silverstream interrupted. "But *I* heard that Graystripe tried to *save* Whiteclaw."

Leopardfur's pelt bristled. How had ThunderClan's lies gotten into RiverClan's camp? "Who told you that?"

"I just heard that's what he said," Silverstream mewed quickly.

"It's a lie!"

"Did you see him push Whiteclaw over the cliff?" Silverstream was staring at her.

"I didn't have to!" Leopardfur forced her paws to stop trembling. "Graystripe was leaning over the edge. It was obvious he pushed him."

Silverstream looked away. "I guess." When she lifted her gaze again, the question seemed to have cleared from it. "It's not fair Whiteclaw died. I'm going to miss him. He was a great warrior."

There was an emptiness in her mew. Like a dutiful kit reciting nursery rules. *It must be grief. It must be more than she can bear.* Why else would the she-cat sound so cold?

Leopardfur wondered suddenly if she should tell Silverstream how Whiteclaw had felt about her. They could have been so happy together. She felt her eyes glisten as a wave of fresh grief swamped her. But she swallowed it back. What good would it do to tell Silverstream that Whiteclaw had had feelings for her? If Silverstream didn't feel the same way, Whiteclaw wouldn't want her to know. And, if she did, it would only cause the young she-cat even more pain to think of the future she might have had with him.

Mudfur slid into the den. "Let Leopardfur rest," he told Silverstream.

Silverstream looked at her. "She's going to be okay, though, isn't she?"

"Of course." Mudfur waved her toward the entrance with his tail. "She just needs to get her strength back."

Leopardfur watched Silverstream disappear through the trailing moss. Her paws pricked. Even if it was grief, there had been something in Silverstream's tone and in her questions that left her with a lingering sense of unease. She couldn't help thinking that there was something the she-cat wasn't telling her.

Mudfur padded to Leopardfur's nest. "Do you want something from the fresh-kill pile?"

"Maybe later," she told him. She wanted her Clanmates to have the first pick of prey before he brought her some. She blinked at him, her heart pricking with affection. "Thanks for taking care of me," she mewed, remembering the last time they'd spoken about her being deputy. He still had doubts that she was right for the job. She'd been so frustrated. But now, for the first time in a long time, Leopardstar felt he might be right. Shame burned beneath her pelt. "I don't deserve so much kindness."

His eyes widened. "Why not?"

"We all know it's my fault Whiteclaw died," she told him, another wave of sadness washing over her. *Sunfish's kit. I loved him as my own, and I couldn't protect him.* Despair overwhelmed her, but she might as well be honest about it. Frogleap had let her off easy because he was kind. Mudfur would be more honest. Leopardfur knew she must face up to what she'd done, and she was ready.

"You are not responsible for everything that happens to every cat," he told her firmly.

"But he rushed into battle because of me." The memory of him racing ahead to confront the ThunderClan patrol had stuck with her like a fish bone in her throat. "If I hadn't always been so determined that no Clan should trespass on our land, he wouldn't have been so quick to fight." Guilt wormed beneath Leopardfur's pelt. "You warned me that I'm always too quick to fight. Oakheart and Crookedstar warned me too." Her chest tightened. "I must have taught Whiteclaw to feel the same way. And that's why he died at the gorge."

Mudfur moved closer, fixing her gaze with his. "You taught him how to be a skilled warrior," he mewed. "You taught him how to be brave. And Whiteclaw isn't the only warrior who would have rushed to fight them. Don't forget, ThunderClan *was* on our land."

"But if he hadn't?"

"If he hadn't, would you have let them pass?" Mudfur asked.

"Is that what I should have done?"

"I can't imagine *any* deputy letting trespassers go unchallenged."

She blinked at him, suddenly longing for forgiveness. "Perhaps one who isn't as hotheaded as me."

He looked puzzled. "Are you doubting yourself?"

"Why not? *You* doubt me." She searched his gaze, longing to see that it wasn't true.

He blinked. "No, I don't."

"But you told Crookedstar not to choose me as deputy."

His pelt ruffled uncomfortably along his spine.

She went on. "I'm sorry. I'm not supposed to know that. But he told me when he was delirious with fever."

Mudfur glanced at his paws, his whiskers drooping. "It's not what you think."

"But you *did* tell him not to choose me." Leopardstar

watched him carefully, waiting for him to respond. It was true, this fact that had hurt so deeply when she'd first learned about it. And now, finally, he would tell her what she'd wondered about since the moment Crookedstar had first said it: *Why?*

"I did," he conceded, looking up at her. "But not because I thought you weren't capable. I've seen how you care for the Clan. I've seen your passion and commitment. I still think you'll be a great leader. I haven't forgotten that my vision told me you'd save the Clan one day, and I still believe it. But I worry you'll choose to save them through war instead of peace, and I'm scared you'll live to regret it."

His words pricked at her. There was truth in them. She'd always been ready to fight for her Clan. Perhaps too ready. And so many cats she loved had died.

Maybe now it was time to take a breath. She could try making different choices. She blinked at Mudfur. "There is truth in what you say. But Whiteclaw's death has shown me what happens when a warrior reacts with instinct and not reason."

He pricked his ears. "Really?"

"Really," she promised. "I may never be as tolerant as Crookedstar, but I never want to feel this way again. I never want to have to ask myself again if I'm the reason one of my Clanmates died."

"I'm glad." A purr rumbled in his throat. "I meant what I said when you were a kit, Leopardfur. If you can find the right balance between keeping the peace and protecting the Clan, I think you'll be one of the greatest leaders RiverClan has ever had."

Leopardfur felt her heart lighten, and a little of her guilt melted away. She'd made a mistake, and the ache of it would always be with her. But her father believed she could change. She'd recover and become stronger. Tomorrow, she'd leave the medicine den. She'd let go of the cat she'd been. She'd put reason ahead of instinct, and she'd push away any lingering dreams of a different life with Frogleap. Instead, she'd give her whole heart to being the best deputy she could be—a deputy RiverClan deserved.

CHAPTER 15

Leopardfur paused outside the medicine den. She didn't want to hear more bad news. Cold weather was biting harder into the camp. In the moon since Whiteclaw had died, the fresh-kill pile had dwindled as leaf-bare tightened its grip. The Clan had gone to their nests hungry more than once as land prey grew scarce and heavy rain, then ice, made the river almost impossible to fish.

And now there was sickness. Sedgecreek, Shadepelt, and Mallowtail were already in the medicine den, and now Mudfur asked to see her. Was he going to report that another Clanmate had been stricken with the illness that seemed to be spreading like fleas through the camp?

Her father ducked out into the camp, his eyes dark.

Had she guessed right? Was another Clanmate sick? "Who is it?"

"Tanglewhisker." Mudfur's tail twitched uneasily. "I've moved him to the medicine den, but Birdsong might have already caught it. I'm keeping an eye on her."

"Do you know yet if it's whitecough?" Leopardfur hoped it wasn't more serious. An outbreak of greencough could devastate the Clan.

"I'm still not sure," Mudfur confessed. "I only know that none of my herbs can cure it."

"Will they die?"

"I don't know," he mewed. "Sedgecreek has stopped taking even water. Shadepelt's fever is getting worse. Nothing I give them seems to help."

Leopardfur felt a fresh wave of anxiety. Mudfur spent every moment with his patients. "What if you catch it?"

"We'd better pray to StarClan that I don't," he mewed. "There's no other medicine cat to look after the Clan."

She met his gaze. She wasn't worried about looking after the Clan. She'd find a way to do that if she had to. What scared her most was that Mudfur might die.

He seemed to read her thoughts. "I'm a survivor, don't forget," he mewed.

"Would it help if there were more food to eat?" Had she let her Clan down by allowing the fresh-kill pile to shrink? Guilt tugged at her belly. Could she have sent out more patrols?

Inside the medicine den, Sedgecreek started coughing. Mudfur turned to head back inside.

"Do you need more herbs?" Leopardfur suddenly felt scared of letting him out of her sight.

"Not yet," he answered grimly and disappeared inside.

"Leopardfur!" Blackclaw's mew made her turn. The smoky warrior was heading across the frosty clearing, Heavystep at his heels. The fur along his spine was rippling anxiously.

What now? Leopardfur hurried to meet him. "Has something happened?"

"We've found ThunderClan scent on our territory," Black-claw told her.

"Near Sunningrocks," Heavystep added urgently. "They must want even more of our hunting grounds."

"They must be planning an attack," Blackclaw mewed.

Leopardfur's tail twitched. Could there be another ambush, like the one that killed Whiteclaw? A moon ago, she'd have been bristling with rage, but now only fear pulsed beneath her pelt. "Go back and find evidence," she told Blackclaw. "A twig or some grass with ThunderClan scent on it."

Blackclaw's eyes widened. "Don't you believe us?"

"We'll need proof to take to the Gathering," she told him.

"We can't wait for the Gathering," Blackclaw argued. "We have to deal with this now. ThunderClan cats have been snooping around on our land."

Her ears twitched irritably. "And what would you have me do?" she asked. "Launch an attack on their camp? Ambush one of their patrols?"

"We need to let them know that if they cross our border, they'll face a fight," Blackclaw growled.

Heavystep's tail was lashing. "We should send a patrol to confront them."

"There's sickness in the Clan," Leopardfur reminded him. "It's nearly leaf-bare, and we're hungry. We're in no shape to confront ThunderClan. The last thing Mudfur needs is more cats to care for."

Blackclaw flexed his claws. "I thought you'd want to stand up to them."

He'd watched her chase WindClan warriors from their territory not long ago. She'd been so sure of herself then. How long ago that seemed—before Whiteclaw died on her watch, before leaf-bare, and before the sickness. "The last time we confronted ThunderClan, Whiteclaw died. This time, I want proof before we act," she told him. "Go back and look for it. But keep your heads down. Act like you're looking for prey. Don't make it obvious."

Blackclaw scowled. "Do you want us to act like trespassers on our own land?"

"Of course not," she snapped. "But I don't want you to pro-voke ThunderClan. If they *are* planning an attack, I'm not giving them an excuse."

Blackclaw swished his tail angrily. "I never imagined you'd be intimidated by ThunderClan."

"I just want RiverClan to be safe." Frustration jabbed Leopardfur's belly. Surely Blackclaw understood!

He turned away, growling to himself. Heavystep glanced back at her, then followed his former mentor out of camp.

She watched them leave, pressing back the feeling that she'd let them down. *It's for the best,* she told herself, hoping it was true.

Bright moonlight bathed Fourtrees. Frost sparkled on the grass, and the earth was frozen beneath Leopardfur's paws as she followed Crookedstar across the clearing. Their Clan-mates headed away to share tongues with the other Clans, and Mudfur joined Yellowfang and Runningnose beneath the trees. She'd had to persuade Mudfur to join the Gathering patrol, and he'd only agreed after Shimmerpelt and Beetlenose had promised not to leave his patients and to send for him immediately if they got worse.

Leopardfur kept close to Crookedstar as he wove between the warriors crowding in the clearing. The scent of WindClan make her hackles itch. It was their first Gathering since ThunderClan had brought them home, and the prey-rich moor was beyond RiverClan's reach now. Her Clan was hungry, and the border was freshly marked every morning, as though WindClan was making sure every RiverClan cat knew they would never again be allowed to cross it.

Crookedstar glanced at her as they reached the Great Rock. "Remember, let me do the talking. This is a delicate matter."

She'd told him about the ThunderClan scent found near Sunningrocks, although Blackclaw's second patrol hadn't produced any more evidence than the first. And Crookedstar had agreed with her that there was already enough tension between the Clans now that WindClan was back, and he didn't want to risk a war. But he'd taken Blackclaw and Heavystep's report seriously and wouldn't let the Gathering pass without saying something about ThunderClan's trespassing.

He blinked at her. "Okay?"

"Okay." She had no intention of speaking up. There'd been a time when his caution would have insulted her, but now she understood it. She wanted Crookedstar to see that she was the best deputy she could be. And a good deputy knew it was better to keep quiet than risk starting a war they couldn't win.

As he leaped into the Great Rock, something moved in the shadows beside her. She stiffened as she smelled Tigerclaw's scent.

The ThunderClan deputy stalked into the moonlight and sat beside her. "You'll let Crookedstar do the talking?" He glanced at her. "What happened to the fierce young deputy who was willing to say what she thought at Gatherings?"

She bristled, remembering their strange conversation after the Gathering where she'd spoken out of turn. At the time, she'd found him convincing; now, she was still angry that he'd attacked her at the gorge. She wasn't sure whether he sincerely wanted her to speak her mind, but she did know that this was a warrior that would say one thing and do another. And still, she couldn't help admiring how sure he seemed of himself. She wished she were so confident. Right now she seemed only able to react to events, while he seemed to anticipate them. Remembering how he'd encouraged her to confide in him before, she wondered whether Tigerclaw had actually had a paw in making those events happen. Perhaps he was playing with every cat, like they were mice in his thrall.

He blinked at her coolly. "What delicate matter was Crookedstar talking about?"

"You'll find out at the same time as every other cat," she snapped.

"Do you agree with him this time?"

"Of course I agree with him. He's my leader." She fluffed out her fur self-consciously. Did he think she'd become a pushover? "I can't disagree with him all the time."

His whiskers twitched. "I suppose it's a tricky balance."

"I'll do whatever I think is best for my Clan."

"I'm sure you will." He tucked his tail over his paws. "I should warn you. I'm going to say some things tonight that might ruffle a few pelts. But if I mention RiverClan, don't take it personally." He gazed across the crowd. "I just want to shake things up a little."

Shake things up? She tensed. What did he mean?

Bluestar's angry yowl sounded above. The ThunderClan leader was glaring at Crookedstar while Tallstar and Nightstar watched uneasily.

"RiverClan has been hunting at Sunningrocks!" Bluestar snarled.

Leopardfur's eyes widened. That wasn't true! Was the ThunderClan leader trying to cover her Clan's tracks by making the first accusation?

Crookedstar returned her gaze. "Have you forgotten how recently one of our warriors was killed defending our territory from ThunderClan?"

One of our warriors. Leopardfur's heart lurched. *Whiteclaw.* Would ThunderClan apologize? But Bluestar seemed determined to argue.

"There was no need to *defend your territory*," she snapped. "Our warriors weren't hunting there."

Tigerclaw hadn't moved. His gaze betrayed nothing as the Clan leaders accused each other of trespassing until Leopardfur wondered if RiverClan was the only Clan that *hadn't* crossed a border in the past moon. She scanned the crowd. If the other Clans had been trespassing, would they give themselves away? Her gaze settled on Graystripe and Fireheart. They were sitting close together, like always, resembling a pair of smug owls. As Crookedstar accused a ThunderClan cat of crossing the RiverClan border, Fireheart seemed to stiffen. He glanced at Graystripe, and Leopardfur narrowed her eyes. Why did he look so alarmed? Were they the trespassers?

Suddenly, Tigerclaw growled beside her. "We have scented ShadowClan in our territory as well as RiverClan this past moon. And not just one cat but a whole patrol, always the same cats."

She stared at him. What in StarClan was he talking about? A RiverClan patrol on ThunderClan territory? She hadn't ordered it. Neither had Crookedstar. Her tail quivered. Was this what Tigerclaw had meant by shaking things up?

Nightstar glared indignantly at Tigerclaw. "ShadowClan has not been on your territory!" When Tigerclaw snorted in disbelief, the ShadowClan leader glared down even more angrily. "Do you doubt the word of ShadowClan, Tigerclaw?"

The crowd murmured uncomfortably as Tigerclaw stared back at Nightstar with unconcealed distrust, and for the first time, Tallstar spoke.

"My warriors have also found strange scents in WindClan territory. They seem to be ShadowClan."

Tigerclaw's eyes lit up, as though this was the reaction he'd been looking for. "I knew it!" he snarled. "RiverClan and ShadowClan have united against us."

As Crookedstar spat with indignation and Tallstar bristled, Leopardfur blinked at Tigerclaw.

"Is this what you wanted?" she demanded.

He blinked back at her without answering, his gaze betraying nothing.

Suddenly, the Fourtrees clearing seemed to be swallowed by shadow. Leopardfur looked up. Clouds had covered the moon.

A ThunderClan elder yowled in alarm. "StarClan has sent the darkness!"

Runningnose yowled from beside Mudfur. "StarClan is angry. These meetings are meant to be held in peace."

Within moments, the leaders had leaped down from the Great Rock, and the Clans began to break apart, heading for the slopes. Leopardfur felt suddenly cold. *Have we really offended StarClan?*

Tigerclaw got to his paws and headed away without speaking.

Leopardfur watched him go, unease spreading beneath her pelt. He'd looked so *pleased*. This must be what he'd intended by *shaking things up*. But what exactly was the ThunderClan deputy playing at? He must be lying. As far as she knew, no RiverClan cat had been near ThunderClan territory. Was Tigerclaw *trying* to cause a war between the Clans?

"Wake up."

Leopardfur jerked up her muzzle as paws poked her shoulder. "What is it?" She struggled from sleep, blinking open her eyes. Dawn light was filtering through the den roof, and Skyheart was staring into her nest.

"Nightstar is here," the pale brown tabby mewed. "He's talking to Crookedstar."

Leopardfur scrambled from her nest. She'd slept in late

after last night's Gathering, but the ShadowClan leader clearly had not. "When did he arrive?" she asked Skyheart.

"Just now," Skyheart told her. "He just appeared at the entrance."

"He crossed our territory without an escort?" Leopardfur's pelt pricked nervously. It must be important to risk giving such an insult. Unless Nightstar was becoming as arrogant as Brokenstar.

"He apologized," Skyheart mewed. "But he said it couldn't wait. He had to speak with Crookedstar."

Leopardfur picked her way between her Clanmates' nests. They were beginning to stir, stretching and yawning, though not quite awake. She ducked out of the den and hurried across the icy clearing, following Nightstar's scent to Crookedstar's den.

"Crookedstar?" She paused outside. "Is Nightstar with you?"

"Come in." Crookedstar blinked a welcome as she slid through the trailing moss. He was sitting beside Nightstar in the gloomy half-light, his tail tucked over his paws.

She dipped her head to the ShadowClan leader. "What brings you here so soon after the Gathering?" Couldn't he have said what he wanted to say to Crookedstar last night?

"I want to make sure our alliance still stands," Nightstar told her.

"Why?" Leopardfur stared at him. "WindClan is back. There's no way we can share their land now."

"This isn't about their land," Nightstar mewed. "It's about survival."

Crookedstar's expression was grave. "I'm beginning to

believe that ThunderClan brought WindClan back to start a war," he mewed.

"They've been planning to move against us all along," Nightstar chimed. "They just needed WindClan's support."

Crookedstar nodded. "You heard them last night," he mewed to Leopardfur. "All those accusations. They're just trying to find an excuse to attack us."

"Wait." Leopardfur took a breath, trying to resist the urgency and fear in the two leaders' eyes. If Tigerclaw had intended to shake things up last night, he had certainly succeeded. But he'd lied to do it. RiverClan hadn't been on ThunderClan land. Should she share her suspicions about the ThunderClan deputy? She hesitated. It might make Crookedstar and Nightstar more determined to form an alliance. They'd assume Tigerclaw and Bluestar spoke with the same voice and that his lies were part of ThunderClan's plot. Besides, part of her was still curious about Tigerclaw's motivations; if he had come up with a scheme, she could learn something by watching it play out. "Won't declaring an alliance provoke ThunderClan more?" she mewed. "It might just prove their suspicions about us are right."

Crookedstar narrowed his eyes. "It's not like you to hold back in the face of aggression."

"They haven't attacked us yet," she told him. "I think we should wait."

He frowned. "I should be pleased you've learned to manage your temper. But I wish you hadn't decided to do it now."

Nightstar was staring earnestly at the RiverClan leader.

"We need to declare our alliance sooner rather than later," he urged. "Runningnose had a dream a few days ago that darkness was coming. He thinks war is coming to the Clans. If it is, I want a strong Clan to fight beside. A Clan like River-Clan."

Crookedstar fluffed out his fur proudly, but Leopardfur cut in before he could speak.

"Won't war come sooner if we declare an alliance against ThunderClan and WindClan?" she argued.

"We don't *have* to declare it," Crookedstar told her. "It'll simply ensure our mutual safety."

Leopardfur shifted her paws. He might be right. Blackclaw *had* found ThunderClan scent on RiverClan land. Bluestar could be scouting in preparation for an attack. Leaf-bare hunger—and the sickness spreading through RiverClan—had made them weak. An alliance could be the best way to protect the Clan.

Crookedstar was looking at her expectantly. She dipped her head. "RiverClan needs an ally," she conceded. "And Shadow-Clan has proved trustworthy in the past."

"Good." Crookedstar pulled his tail tighter over his fore-paws. "Then the alliance stands." He blinked at Nightstar. "But it shouldn't simply be a defensive treaty. I'm certain that ThunderClan and WindClan are looking for an excuse to attack us. And I think we should make the first move."

CHAPTER 16

Dawn light glittered on the snow capping the thick heather wall of the WindClan camp. Leopardfur shifted her paws as she sat between her Clanmates. The battle had gone well. Blackclaw, Skyheart, Stonefur, and Heavystep looked pleased. Their pelts hardly showed a scratch. Crookedstar and Nightstar had made the right decision when they'd decided to target Wind-Clan first and take the fight right into their camp. Most of WindClan's warriors were still scrawny from their exile, and though they'd fought bravely, the patrol of RiverClan and ShadowClan warriors had easily overwhelmed them.

Now WindClan was pinned down between the gorse dens of their own camp. RiverClan and ShadowClan warriors ringed them while Crookedstar and Nightstar addressed Tallstar.

"You should never have returned home," Crookedstar growled.

"ThunderClan is using you," Nightstar's tail swished ominously. "Once they've used your warriors to take our land, they'll turn on you too."

Tallstar glared at them, rage glittering in his eyes. "Don't judge ThunderClan by ShadowClan standards."

His warriors crouched behind him, their tails lashing, their eyes slitted. Queens and elders huddled among them, along with Barkface, their medicine cat. Every WindClan cat had fought to defend their camp, and Leopardfur had been impressed how well the skinny warriors worked together, but it hadn't been enough to chase the RiverClan and Shadow-Clan patrol away.

"Just leave." Crookedstar glared at Tallstar. "Before either we or ThunderClan drive you out again."

Tallstar turned away and began talking to his warriors in low whispers.

Blackclaw shifted beside Leopardfur. "They have no choice but to leave," he muttered.

"ThunderClan will think twice about sending spies onto our land once their allies are gone," Skyheart growled.

Heavystep curled his claws into the earth. "We might even be able to take Sunningrocks back."

"Especially if ShadowClan helps." Stonefur pressed his belly lower against the earth.

Leopardfur's pelt tingled nervously. For once, she wasn't sure that RiverClan should press their advantage. It would be enough to drive WindClan away. ThunderClan would have to back off, and, until leaf-bare was over and the sickness gone from the camp, that was all she wanted. RiverClan wouldn't even need Sunningrocks. With WindClan gone, there'd be more land to hunt. Ending the war here, with a single battle, would be the safest choice.

She stiffened as an unexpected scent touched her nose. It was fresh, drifting through the camp wall. *Onewhisker?* Why had the WindClan tom returned? He'd fled the battle. She'd watched him pelt out of camp, his tail bushed with terror, just as they'd forced WindClan to concede defeat. Had he crept back to see what was left of his Clan?

Pelt prickling along her spine, Leopardfur crept toward the entrance. Her whiskers twitched uneasily. There were other scents, faintly discernible through the freezing air. Something was wrong. As she peered warily through the gorse tunnel, a yowl from the clearing made her jerk around.

She bristled. Tallstar had leaped on top of Crookedstar. The WindClan leader was spitting, tumbling Crookedstar across the grass, clawing at him viciously. His warriors streaked from behind him and, despite their wounds, flung themselves at the ring of ShadowClan and RiverClan warriors.

Shock pulsed through her. Was WindClan really willing to fight to the death? Even the queens threw themselves into battle once more. Morningflower leaped at Littlecloud, raking claws across his muzzle and screeching as he dragged her down and began to tear at her ragged pelt.

Leopardfur hesitated. WindClan was hopelessly outnumbered. Her Clanmates were already clawing and slashing at them so fiercely that the battle would be over in moments.

A shriek sounded beyond the heather camp wall. She glanced over her shoulder, her eyes widening as Onewhisker streaked through. Did the WindClan warrior think he could save his Clan single-pawed? She stiffened as another warrior raced after him, then another and another, and she recognized the strong stench of ThunderClan. Onewhisker had fetched help. Alarm shrilled through her fur as a ThunderClan patrol surged into the WindClan camp and spread out.

She recognized Fireheart's flaming pelt as he streaked across the clearing and ripped Littlecloud away from Morningflower. The WindClan queen staggered, bleeding and exhausted, toward the edge of the camp as Fireheart pinned Littlecloud to the ground.

Pain made Leopardfur spin around. Claws sliced her ear. Slitting her eyes and dropping into a battle crouch, she saw Stagleap rear in front of her. The WindClan straggler had rejoined his Clan. He brought his forepaws down on her shoulders with such force it knocked the wind from her, but she rolled, grabbed his pelt with her claws, and dragged him down, churning her hind paws against his belly.

"This time leave with your Clan," she hissed as she flung him away.

As he landed, his paws splaying beneath him, a Thunder-Clan tom lunged at Leopardfur. She struggled to find her paws and he knocked her easily to the ground and held her there, raking her ears with his claws. She struggled free, ignoring the sting of her wounds, but Stagleap had found her again and snarled at her, aiming a blow at her muzzle. She ducked just in time and shot beneath him, heaving him up and twisting on her back paws to swipe at the ThunderClan tom, who was coming at her from the other direction.

She backed away, the two toms glaring at her. The clearing

was a mass of writhing pelts. Yowls and hisses filled the air. Her breath nearly stopped as she saw Graystripe lead a second ThunderClan patrol, howling, into the camp.

WindClan seemed to have revived. Two WindClan toms rose together on their back paws and began to swat Skyheart toward the camp wall.

Leopardfur dodged as Stagleap tried to claw her muzzle, but the ThunderClan tom hooked her scruff from behind and hauled her backward. She smelled his meaty breath and braced herself for his bite, but he staggered suddenly and let her go.

Stonefur had slammed into his side and knocked him off balance. The RiverClan tom aimed blow after blow at his muzzle as the ThunderClan warrior tried to recover his balance.

Leopardfur turned to deal with Stagleap, but Heavystep had already leaped on top of him and was rolling him away, his pelt spiked with rage.

"Fireheart!"

Leopardfur pricked her ears as she heard Tigerclaw's cry. The ThunderClan deputy was hardly visible behind a wall of ShadowClan warriors. He sounded as though he was fighting for his life.

She saw Fireheart charge toward him. Anger flared through her pelt. Tigerclaw would have to fight alone. Leopardfur had unfinished business with the flame-colored tom. As he streaked past, she lunged for him and grabbed his hind legs between her paws.

"You!" she hissed as he thumped to the ground. He was

going to pay for being part of the patrol that killed Whiteclaw.

He kicked out at her. Surprise sparked in her belly as she tumbled away. He was strong. But stupid. As she jumped up, she saw he'd flipped onto his back, exposing his soft belly. Seeing her chance, Leopardfur reared and came down on top of him with all her might. She heard him grunt as she knocked the wind from him and dug her claws into his belly. He screeched in pain, his gaze rolling toward the end of the clearing where Tigerclaw had been battling.

The ThunderClan deputy had ripped free of his attackers and was standing in an empty space in the battlefield. "Tigerclaw," he yowled, "help me!" Leopardfur hesitated, but didn't loosen her grip on Fireheart as he writhed desperately between her paws. Tigerclaw was watching them, his eyes cold with hatred. He didn't move a paw to help.

What is he doing? Leopardfur's thoughts whirled. *Doesn't he realize his Clanmate is in trouble?* She clawed at Fireheart's belly again and again. This tom was going to pay for what his friend had done to Whiteclaw. The smell of his blood filled her nose, and she aimed another blow, rage pounding in her ears. Suddenly, Fireheart kicked out. The speed and fierceness of the blow took her by surprise. It lifted her high and flung her across the clearing.

She landed with a thump, disbelief sparking through her fur, and scrambled quickly to her paws, hoping no cat had noticed. *You won't get rid of me that easily.* Hissing, she shouldered her way through the crowd. She was going to finish this. But Fireheart was gone, swallowed by the battle.

Lakeshine screeched with pain a tail-length away. A WindClan tom had clamped his jaws around her tail while a ThunderClan she-cat slashed at her muzzle. Leopardfur dived toward them, throwing a hefty blow that sent the ThunderClan she-cat reeling away. She clawed the WindClan tom's ears until he let go, and as Lakeshine reared beside her, she lashed out at his nose. Together they batted him backward through the melee.

Whitestorm pushed in front of her and knocked her down with a fierce swipe. The white warrior leaped at her, but she rolled clear just in time and leaped up, digging her claws into his flank. With a snarl, she pulled him close and pummeled him with her hind paws.

Then she heard Nightstar screech. The ShadowClan leader was being driven backward by Fireheart. The ThunderClan tom dived forward and sank his teeth deep into Nightstar's shoulder.

Leopardfur knocked Whitestorm away. Panic was welling in her chest. The ShadowClan leader looked like he was fighting for his life. With a yowl, he struggled free of Fireheart's grip and fled for the camp entrance.

Eyes flashed toward him, and his warriors broke away from the battle and chased after him, racing like rats from the camp.

Mouse-hearts! Dread gripped Leopardfur as she realized that RiverClan was suddenly alone and heavily outnumbered.

Mousefur charged at her in a blaze of brown fur. The ThunderClan she-cat grabbed her pelt and dragged her down. Whitestorm was pushing his way back toward her. Leopardfur

ripped free of Mousefur's claws and reared as Whitestorm
and Mousefur came at her, side by side. Leopardfur backed
away, flailing with her forepaws as she tried desperately to
fight them off.

Where was Crookedstar? She glanced around the clearing.
Her heart dropped as she saw the RiverClan leader face-to-
face with Tigerclaw. The two warriors crouched low against
the grass, their tails lashing menacingly.

Crookedstar leaped first, but Tigerclaw was quicker.
He jumped out of the way and, as the RiverClan leader hit
bare grass, turned, and lunged at Crookedstar's back. The
ThunderClan deputy grasped the RiverClan leader with
his long claws, and Leopardfur froze as Crookedstar went
limp beneath him. As Tigerclaw bared his teeth and lunged
for Crookedstar's neck, a hefty blow from Whitestorm sent
Leopardfur staggering backward.

"Retreat!" Crookedstar's desperate cry rang over the camp.
The RiverClan leader had escaped Tigerclaw's grip and was
pelting for the entrance.

Around her, RiverClan warriors were ripping free of the
fight and racing after him.

Leopardfur glanced at Whitestorm and Mousefur. They'd
dropped down onto all fours and were glaring at her, clearly
waiting for her to run. She snarled at them, humiliation searing her fur, then raced after Crookedstar.

She glanced over her shoulder. Tigerclaw still stood where
he'd defeated the RiverClan leader, watching her with amusement glittering in his eyes. Every hair on her pelt sparked with

rage as she raced through the gorse tunnel and out onto the moor.

The days following the battle were cold and the snow thick, but Leopardfur still sent out patrol after patrol to check for ThunderClan scent inside their borders. Her Clanmates were recovering from their wounds, and the sickness had stopped spreading. But the river had frozen, and prey was so scarce that she'd sent patrols to wait at the WindClan border for any land prey that crossed the scent line.

She'd also taken the time to praise her Clanmates for their courage in battle. Stonefur in particular had shown a skill she hadn't noticed before, and she looked at the young warrior with new respect. There was fierceness and solemnity in him that she admired. She even wondered if he would make a good mate for Silverstream.

The silver-and-black she-cat seemed lonely. She had been keeping herself apart from her Clanmates. Was it possible she was still mourning Whiteclaw?

Leopardfur kept an eye on her, watching her day after day until at last she decided she should speak. Four days after the battle, the snow at last began to melt, and Leopardfur carried a water vole to where Silverstream was sitting alone beneath the sedge. The sun was just beginning to set behind the trees.

She dropped it at Silverstream's paws. "You must be hungry." The young she-cat had been hunting all day, though she'd brought back little prey.

Silverstream dipped her head. "Thanks," she mewed. "But give it to some other cat."

Leopardfur heard Silverstream's belly growl but she didn't argue. Mosspelt had kitted, and nursing three healthy kits was sapping the queen's strength. She'd welcome the extra prey.

Leopardfur blinked at her and decided to come straight to the point. "You seem lonely."

"Do I?" Silverstream looked surprised.

"You keep to yourself too much," Leopardfur mewed.

"Then I can't be feeling lonely, or I'd look for company," Silverstream mewed.

Leopardfur's pelt twitched. Silverstream didn't seem to appreciate her concern. "Are you missing Whiteclaw?"

"Whiteclaw?" Silverstream looked puzzled for a moment, then dipped her head. "Yes," she mewed, as though remembering. "Of course."

"You've been patrolling with Stonefur a lot lately." Leopardfur had made sure they'd shared the same patrols, hoping that they might make a connection. "He's a good warrior."

"I guess." Silverstream eyed her as though wondering what Leopardfur was getting at.

Leopardfur pressed on. "He'd make a good mate, don't you think?"

Silverstream blinked at her. "Are you thinking of taking him as a mate?"

"Me?" Surprise sparked through Leopardfur's pelt. That was not what she'd imagined at all. "No! I thought he'd make a good mate for *you*."

Silverstream looked away quickly. "I don't want a mate."

Perhaps Whiteclaw had meant more to her than Leopardfur had imagined. "You can't mourn forever."

"I *don't* want a mate." Silverstream sounded irritated this time.

"Why?" Leopardfur knew she was annoying the she-cat, but she couldn't help but ask.

Silverstream flicked her ear, annoyed. "I don't need a reason, do I?" she asked. "You don't have a mate. Do *you* have a reason?"

Leopardfur felt a tiny pang in the tender part of her that still questioned what life might have been like as Frogleap's mate. She didn't have a reason that she wanted to share. Perhaps Silverstream felt the same, and Leopardfur would respect that. But she still wondered why.

The sliver of curiosity nagged her through the night, and in the morning, as the sun reached high into a blue sky, it grew as Leopardfur noticed Silverstream heading out of camp. She hadn't assigned the young she-cat to any patrol; she'd wanted to see who Silverstream *did* choose to be with, even if only as friends. But Silverstream hadn't chosen any of the patrols. Instead she was slipping away without saying good-bye to anyone.

Leopardfur waited for a few moments and followed her out of camp. Hanging well back, she trailed Silverstream along the shore, across the newly thawed river and into the line of trees that grew in the direction of the ThunderClan border. She kept downwind, and stayed out of sight as Silverstream finally came to a halt a few tail-lengths away from the scent line.

Leopardfur's hackles lifted as she saw a gray pelt on the

other side of the border. *Graystripe*. Her paws seemed to freeze to the earth as the ThunderClan tom crossed into RiverClan territory and touched noses with Silverstream. The young tabby she-cat's eyes shimmered with pleasure and affection, and Leopardfur fought the urge to rush forward and swipe her claws across Graystripe's muzzle.

How could Silverstream do this? She was Crookedstar's kit. How could she betray her Clan? And with the warrior who'd killed Whiteclaw! Leopardfur's claws itched with rage, but she kept them sheathed. This was not a problem that could be solved with a single confrontation. If Silverstream was as fond of Graystripe as she appeared, this was something that needed to be dealt with carefully and quietly. Leopardfur was not going to sacrifice the harmony of RiverClan by making a scene.

Before she could decide what RiverClan should do about Silverstream's betrayal, she had to decide how she felt about it herself.

CHAPTER 17

Leopardfur had sent out the patrols for the morning but kept Silverstream back in camp. For two days she'd fretted about what to say, or whether to say anything at all. Perhaps the meetings with Graystripe would come to a natural end. But Leopardfur knew she was grasping at thistledown. Silverstream was young and in love. Leaving her alone to sort out the problem was too risky, and Leopardfur wanted to protect her from making a mistake she and RiverClan might live to regret. She'd *have* to talk to her.

She beckoned Silverstream with her tail, trying to sound casual. "Come hunt with me."

"Me?" Silverstream blinked at her in surprise.

Leopardfur glanced around the clearing. Who else would she mean? Sedgecreek, Shadepelt, and Mallowtail were resting outside the medicine den. They were still weak from the sickness that had taken Tanglewhisker but were clearly willing to endure the drizzle for a little fresh air. Mudfur sorted through herbs bedside them while Reedtail cleared Tanglewhisker's nest from the elders' den.

Birdsong was helping Graypool gather reeds. The old gray

she-cat had finally decided to make a nest in the elders' den. Leopardfur was pleased. Graypool had seemed confused on her last few patrols. She needed rest, and Birdsong would be glad of the company.

As Leopardfur headed for the entrance, Silverstream seemed to drag her paws. Had she guessed that Leopardfur planned to use the patrol as a chance to talk?

"Where do you want to hunt?" Silverstream asked as they reached the stepping-stones.

"In the water meadow." Leopardfur bounded across and waited on the far side. She hadn't worked out what to say to Silverstream yet. "Let's catch a frog for Birdsong," she mewed.

Silverstream followed. "She must miss Tanglewhisker. The camp doesn't seem the same without him."

"I'll never get used to losing Clanmates." Leopardfur thought of Whiteclaw with a pang. Had he been watching Silverstream's secret meetings with Graystripe from StarClan?

She stopped at the edge of the water meadow. The pools shimmering in dips among the long grass reflected the overcast sky. Water rippled on one. Something was moving there. She headed toward it, opening her mouth to taste for frog-scent, and stopped a few tail-lengths from the edge. A frog was scrabbling clumsily over the mud. She dropped, ready to pounce, but it dived into the water and disappeared.

Shaking out her pelt, Leopardfur crouched in a patch of marsh grass.

Silverstream nosed her way in and settled beside her.

"I taught Whiteclaw to hunt here." Leopardfur felt a twinge

of sadness. "Frogleap helped me. This is probably where I fell in love with him."

"You loved *Frogleap*?" Silverstream jerked her muzzle around.

"Is that so strange?" Did she think Frogleap had only ever been interested in Mosspelt?

"I guess not." Silverstream turned back to the pool. "I just can't imagine you being in love with any cat."

Leopardfur hesitated. "Really?"

"You're kind of old."

"I'm not that old."

"You're older than me." Silverstream was watching the pool.

"I was probably your age when I fell in love." Leopardfur shifted her paws. This was as good a way as any to start the conversation. "I thought I'd love him forever, and he'd love me forever. But life isn't like that. We have other responsibilities."

"I guess *you* did," Silverstream mewed. "You wanted to focus on being deputy."

"That doesn't mean I don't regret giving up Frogleap," Leopardfur mewed. "But I knew I had to do what was best for my Clan."

"Maybe it was the best thing for you too." Silverstream didn't look at her.

"What do you mean?"

"I guess you wanted to be deputy more than you wanted to be with Frogleap."

Leopardfur was surprised by a jab of irritation. Was Silverstream judging her? "The Clan *needed* me more than Frogleap did."

Silverstream tucked her tail along her side. "It must be nice to be so sure of yourself."

Leopardfur sat up. She didn't like Silverstream's tone. "I'm sure of *RiverClan*," she mewed sharply. "That's what I care about and I'll do anything to protect them."

Silverstream looked at her. "Is that why you dragged me out here?" She sat up too. "Are you scared I'm a danger to my Clan?"

Leopardfur blinked. Silverstream had clearly guessed why she'd brought her here. *Am I that transparent?* She tried to read Silverstream's gaze. "Aren't *you* scared you might be a danger to them?"

"Why would I be?" Silverstream tipped her head to one side.

"You *know* why," she snapped. After such perceptiveness, Silverstream's obtuseness was irritating. "Graystripe's a ThunderClan tom."

"Graystripe?" Her eyes rounded.

Was she really going to pretend to be innocent? "Don't be cute."

"How did you know I was meeting him?"

"I've seen you together."

"You spied on me?"

"I *watched* you." Leopardfur wasn't going to apologize for keeping an eye on her Clanmates.

Silverstream looked away. "I love him."

"He's our enemy."

"He's not *my* enemy."

Leopardfur's breath caught in her throat. She suddenly realized why Silverstream had come to the medicine den after Whiteclaw had died. *I heard that Graystripe tried to save Whiteclaw.* Silverstream hadn't wanted to find out what had happened to her Clanmate. She'd wanted to defend the cat she loved! "How long has this been going on?" she demanded.

"That's my business." Silverstream pushed her way from the grass. Ripples arced across the pools as a frog fled into the water. Leopardfur didn't care. She could catch a frog for Birdsong later. Right now, she had to try to reason with Silverstream.

"It's the Clan's business." Leopardfur followed her. "Don't you realize you're breaking the warrior code by seeing him?"

"It's not harming anyone," Silverstream snapped.

"It will if it goes on."

"How?" Silverstream glowered at her. "How can loving a cat harm anyone?"

Leopardfur pressed on. "What will Crookedstar say when he finds out?"

Silverstream glanced at her paws. "Who cares?"

"I care," Leopardfur mewed. "I don't want him or you to get hurt."

"No cat's going to get hurt!"

"Do you really believe that?" she snapped.

Silverstream didn't answer. "Can't you just leave me alone?

I'm not going to do anything to threaten your precious Clanmates."

Leopardfur couldn't believe what she was hearing. "They're *your* precious Clanmates too!"

"Yes! They are! And unlike you, *I* trust them. I don't need to sneak around spying on them like a nosy old mother duck!"

Rage burned beneath Leopardfur's pelt, but she forced herself to take a breath. She let her fur smooth. Anger wasn't going to help. "I'm the Clan deputy. I *need* to be a nosy old mother duck. I need to know everything that's going on so that I can help my Clanmates make the right choices and be the best warriors they can be. That's the only way RiverClan can thrive."

"Do you think RiverClan won't thrive because *I* love a cat from another Clan?"

"If every cat broke the warrior code, the Clan wouldn't be a Clan." Leopardfur stared at her. This was basic warrior training. How could she not understand? "It would be a gang of rogues, doing exactly what they pleased with no regard for anyone else."

"But I love him!" For the first time, Silverstream's eyes glittered with pain. "I can't stop loving him just because the warrior code tells me to. You said you loved Frogleap. Did you stop when you decided your Clan needed you more? Did you just decide not to love him one day?" The words were tumbling out now as though she couldn't hold them in anymore. Pity welled in Leopardfur's chest as Silverstream went on. "I wish I could do that. I wish *I* could decide how to feel."

Leopardfur padded closer. "I'll probably always love Frog-leap," she mewed. "Every time I see him with Mosspelt, I feel jealous and I wish I didn't. It hurts. But I know I made the right choice. I know it could never have worked."

Fresh anger flashed in Silverstream's eyes. "And you want me to do the same."

"Don't you see?" Leopardfur mewed desperately. "You have no choice. You can't take Graystripe as a mate. He's a ThunderClan cat." *And he killed Whiteclaw.* She swallowed the words back. They wouldn't help. "The only way to be with him is to leave RiverClan."

Silverstream puffed out her chest. "I might do that."

Shock pulsed in Leopardfur's throat. "And be a *rogue*?"

"I'd join ThunderClan."

"You'd join an *enemy Clan*?" Leopardfur stared at her in disbelief. "Think of what that would do to Crookedstar!"

"He'd get over it."

"He's Clan leader!" Leopardfur snapped. "How would he hold his head up after his own kit betrayed her Clan?"

"It's not a betrayal." Silverstream's fur ruffled. "It's a choice. Like you wanting to be deputy."

Leopardfur snorted. "It's nothing like me wanting to become deputy. I did that for the good of our Clan. You're only thinking of yourself!"

"What's wrong with that!"

"You're a *warrior*." Leopardfur suddenly felt weary. Silverstream couldn't mean these things. She was a good cat. She was loyal and smart. If she weren't caught up in a storm of emotions, she'd never say this.

They stood in silence for a moment, as though both of them realized that they'd gone as far as they could. Then Silverstream spoke.

"Will you tell any cat?" Her mew was trembling now. "About me and Graystripe?"

Leopardfur didn't move. Giving away Silverstream's secret would do nothing but cause upset in the Clan. Cats would take sides. Some would turn on the young she-cat, which could drive her away from RiverClan for good. Wasn't that what Leopardfur was trying to avoid? And Crookedstar would be put in an impossible position. He couldn't defend her, and it would break his heart to confront her. What if he was forced to exile his own daughter? "I won't tell," she mewed.

Relief showed in Silverstream's wide blue eyes. "Thank you."

"But you have to promise to stop seeing him."

Silverstream stiffened. "I can't do that! I love him. And he loves me."

Though she knew this romance was wrong, Leopardfur's heart ached with sympathy for the young warrior. "Whatever you choose will break your heart," she mewed softly. "But you need to decide whether you want to break your father's heart as well." She felt bad using guilt to persuade Silverstream, but it was true. And how else could she convince her that if she continued her relationship with Graystripe, she would only damage herself and her Clan?

"Please don't tell him," Silverstream mewed helplessly.

"Not yet. Give me a chance to sort this out for myself."

Leopardfur shifted her paws uneasily. Dishonesty could harm the Clan, but in this case honesty might do just as much damage. And Silverstream was young. Leopardfur didn't want her remembered as a traitor just because her feelings had gotten the better of her. Leopardfur's responsibility was to protect her. If that meant keeping her secret for a while longer, then she'd do it. But she would still try, in every other way, to stop Silverstream from making a terrible mistake.

In the days that followed, Leopardfur tried not to notice when Silverstream disappeared from camp. With every day that passed, she hoped that the tabby she-cat was closer to ending her relationship with Graystripe. But she feared she was only a day closer to being found out.

The rain battered the camp relentlessly. Crookedstar had been anxiously watching the river rise. Now, as Leopardfur settled into her nest, tired from a day's patrolling, she could hear it thundering past the camp. She was happy the patrols had brought back enough food to ensure no one went to their nest hungry, though fishing hadn't been easy. Most of the catch had been land prey, with only a few fish hooked from the shallows where a bend in the river slowed the current a little. Leopardfur still had tufts of feather between her teeth from the sparrow she'd eaten. She eased them out with her tongue as she huddled deeper into her nest and closed her eyes. Silverstream still worried her, but she was tired and pushed her thoughts away. *I can think about it tomorrow,* she told herself, and let herself to drift into sleep.

An agonized wail cut into her dreams and she jerked up her head. The den was still dark, but some of the nests were empty. In others, her Clanmates were sitting up, their pelts bristling as groans sounded from the clearing.

She blinked at Reedtail, whose eyes were wide with alarm. "What's happening?" she mewed.

"I don't know." He scrambled from his nest and headed for the den entrance.

She ducked out after him.

Mallowtail was crouched beside the medicine den. Birdsong retched nearby. Mudfur was darting from one cat to another as they huddled in the clearing, their fur ruffled, clearly in pain.

Leopardfur raced to Mudfur's side. "What's wrong with them?"

As she spoke, Heavystep vomited violently beneath the sedge wall.

Mudfur's eyes glittered with fear. "It looks like they've been poisoned."

Leopardfur glanced in panic toward the nursery. Mistyfoot had only recently kitted. And Mosspelt's kits were close to trying their first taste of prey. "Are Mosspelt and Mistyfoot okay?"

"There's no sickness in the nursery," he mewed. Leopardfur felt a rush of relief. He nodded to Sedgecreek, who had emerged, blinking, from the warriors' den. "Take any cat who's still well and collect mallow," he told her. "I need as much as you can carry."

Sedgecreek nodded.

"Be as quick as you can," Leopardfur added. Then she paused, a thought sparking in her mind, and added, "What did you eat tonight?"

Sedgecreek glanced at her. "A vole."

Otterplash, Cedarpelt, and Piketooth slid from the warriors' den and looked anxiously at their sick Clanmates.

"What's happened?" Ottersplash mewed.

"They've been poisoned." Leopardfur hurried toward her. "What did you eat tonight?"

"I shared a mouse with Graypool," she answered.

"And you?" Leopardfur asked Cedarpelt.

"A starling."

"I had starling too," Piketooth volunteered.

Leopardfur hurried to Heavystep's side as he huddled beneath the sedge, shivering. "What did you eat tonight?" she asked him gently.

"Trout," he grunted, his eyes bright with pain.

She darted to Mallowtail's side. "Did you eat fish?" she asked.

"I shared a chub with Birdsong," Mallowtail told her, swallowing back sickness.

They ate river food. Prey from the shore hadn't harmed anyone, but the cats who'd eaten fish were sick. Leopardfur felt suddenly cold. The river, on which they had always depended, had somehow poisoned her Clanmates.

CHAPTER 18

They buried Birdsong at dawn. Leopardfur was thankful that the elder was the only cat who'd died from the poisoned fish. Mallowtail, Heavystep, and the others had recovered, but they were weak from the sickness, and the whole Clan was grief-stricken at the loss of their Clanmate. Leopardfur had insisted on being part of the burial patrol, and there was still earth between her claws as she led the search party down to the water's edge and slid into the river.

The tug of the current took her by surprise, and she had to fight to stop herself being swept downstream. Churning her paws to hold herself in place, she glanced back at the rest of the patrol. They were struggling too, but managed to keep close to her as she pushed further out into the stream and made for the far shore.

Her heart was pounding by the time she felt stones beneath her paws and hauled herself out. The water was high even here, where the river was wide and reached as far as the trees. Leopardfur found herself in the middle of a thicket of brambles that used to be several tail-lengths from the shore but now trailed their branches in the water.

Stonefur followed her out. Piketooth and Skyheart scrambled after them. They halted beside Leopardfur, breathless.

Skyheart shook out her pelt. "At least the rain's stopped for now."

Leopardfur looked at the sky. The clouds were still thick; the rain might start again at any moment. They had to find whatever had poisoned the river and get back to camp before it did. If the river rose any higher, it wouldn't be safe to cross, and they might be stranded here until the water receded.

Stonefur's whiskers were dripping. "Do you really think it could be ThunderClan who planted the poison?" he asked Leopardfur.

Her pelt ruffled. "Of course it was. WindClan would never have had the nerve after we defeated them in their own camp."

Piketooth's tail swished irritably. "If Onewhisker hadn't managed to get help, we'd have won the battle and WindClan would be gone by now."

Leopardfur remembered again how pleased Tigerclaw had looked as RiverClan had fled the WindClan camp. His look had stuck with her. It wasn't just a look of victory, but of satisfaction, as though a plan was coming together. But she also remembered how he'd let Fireheart fight for his life without lifting a paw. The ThunderClan deputy was even more ruthless than she'd thought. A cat like him was certainly capable of poisoning the river.

And what about Graystripe? The more she thought about the ThunderClan tom, the more she became convinced that he must have had something to do with the poisoning. Surely he was the warrior who'd been leaving ThunderClan scent on RiverClan land. Was he following Tigerclaw's orders? She wondered if seeing Silverstream was just a pretense. Perhaps he'd been using the RiverClan she-cat to get access to the river. Silverstream might even have inadvertently shown him the secret pools and streams where a piece of rotten prey could be hidden and allowed to fester and infect the whole river.

"We should search the streams that feed the river on this side," she told the patrol.

Stonefur glanced at the roaring water. It was breaking over the banks, washing the shore and lapping between the trees. "It won't be easy," he mewed. "A lot of them will have been swallowed by the flooding."

Leopardfur glared at him. "I don't care how hard it is. We have to find what's caused this. I'm not letting another Clan-mate die."

"Okay." He dipped his head. "Do you think it's definitely rotten prey?"

"I don't know. It might be a bundle of poisonous herbs or berries. Just look for anything unusual."

Stonefur began to pick his way between the brambles, his nose close to the ground. Piketooth headed between the trees.

Skyheart blinked at Leopardfur. "I'll search farther upstream," she mewed.

"Okay." Leopardfur scanned the forest. "Don't get too far away from the patrol. ThunderClan may have crossed the border again." She flexed her claws. She hated to feel her warriors weren't safe on their own territory.

As Skyheart padded away, Leopardfur walked over to where a ditch cut into the earth. Water flowed along it toward the river, and she sniffed it warily and began to follow it back, deeper into the woods. The water smelled fresh, tainted by nothing but earth. She hopped over it and began to look for another ditch.

Frustration hardened into anger as she searched ditch after ditch and found no sign of anything that could have contaminated the river. If Graystripe had poisoned the river, he had timed it well. If he had planted the rotten prey or herbs before the waters rose, they would now be hidden beneath the surface. She hurried further along the shore. She had to find the evidence before he had a chance to retrieve it and hide ThunderClan's crime.

She spotted Skyheart's pelt between the trees. "Have you found anything?"

Skyheart looked at her apologetically. "No," she called.

Piketooth and Stonefur were padding toward her.

She looked at them hopefully. "Any sign of poison?"

"Nothing." Stonefur told her. "You?"

"Nothing."

Stonefur frowned. "I don't think we'll find anything while the river's running so high," he mewed.

"I agree." Leopardfur's pelt twitched with irritation. There was more at stake than finding proof of a ThunderClan plot. If they couldn't find the source of the poison, the river would remain unfishable. With prey already scarce, RiverClan would go hungry, and hunger meant weakness. Another thought was nagging her, too. If she could prove that ThunderClan had caused this, Silverstream would see that Graystripe had just been using her. It would put an end to their relationship without Crookedstar and the rest of the Clan finding out.

But it looked like she wouldn't find the evidence today. Disappointed, she turned back toward the trees. "Let's head back to camp."

"Are you sure it's ThunderClan?" Crookedstar blinked at her through the gloom of his den.

"It has to be," Leopardfur insisted. "First they made an alliance with WindClan; then they made WindClan's battle their own. It's obvious. They want to drive us off our land."

Crookedstar's tail was twitching angrily. "Isn't Sunning-rocks enough for them?"

"They want our woods and the river too."

"What good is the river to them?"

"None." Her tail swished over the den floor. "That's why they're willing to poison it."

A low growl rumbled in Crookedstar's throat.

Leopardfur was relieved to see he was angry. "There's no way to prove it while the river's so high. But we can't let this pass. We have to find the source of the poisoning before they get a chance to cover it up."

Crookedstar nodded. "The other Clans should know that ThunderClan is full of treacherous cats. No true warrior could poison another Clan's prey."

"WindClan wouldn't be able to support them," Leopardfur chimed.

"We'd break up their alliance." Crookedstar flicked his tail.

"When the river starts to recede," he told her, "take another patrol to look for the poison."

"Okay." Satisfied, she headed for the entrance.

Silverstream was waiting outside. She hurried to meet Leopardfur. "Why didn't you take me on your patrol?" Her pelt was rippling angrily along her spine.

"I thought you preferred to go out alone," Leopardfur mewed pointedly.

Silverstream followed her as she headed across the clearing. "You think it was ThunderClan, don't you?" she hissed.

Leopardfur glanced around the clearing. Stonefur was watching with interest from the fresh-kill pile, and, outside the nursery, Mosspelt looked up from her kits as they splashed in a puddle. Leopardfur steered Silverstream the shelter of the sedge wall. "*Every cat* thinks it's ThunderClan," she hissed back. "Including Crookedstar."

"Only because you've convinced them it was." Silverstream glared at her. "Why do you have to blame everything on ThunderClan?"

"You were at the battle, weren't you?" Leopardfur wondered how Silverstream could defend the Clan that had attacked them only a few days earlier. "You watched them hurt your Clanmates!" Didn't she have *any* sense of loyalty?

"Warriors *fight*!" Silverstream growled. "They don't poison rivers."

"ThunderClan does."

Silverstream narrowed her eyes. "But this isn't about *ThunderClan*, is it?" she snapped. "It's about Graystripe. You think he did it. You think that just because he crossed the border, he must be the poisoner. That's why you left me behind. You think I'd cover up for him."

Cover up for him? Leopardfur narrowed her eyes. She never imagined Silverstream would go as far as to hide another Clan's treachery. "Would you?" she asked.

"There's nothing to cover up!"

Leopardfur held her gaze. "I just wanted to leave you out of it," she mewed. "If we do find that Graystripe poisoned the river, I don't want any cat to think you're mixed up with it."

Silverstream stared at her in disbelief. "Do *you* think I'm mixed up with it?"

"Of course not." Leopardfur lowered her mew to whisper. "But you *are* involved with Graystripe, and if *he's* mixed up with the poisoning, you need to stay as far away from the whole thing as possible."

Silverstream was trembling. "How could you think Graystripe would do such a fox-hearted thing?" she demanded.

"He's a *ThunderClan* warrior," Leopardfur snapped back.

"You're just obsessed," Silverstream growled. "Why can't you just keep your muzzle out of my affairs?"

"Because they are endangering the Clan!"

"That's not true!"

"Birdsong is dead," Leopardfur reminded her. "And if ThunderClan is responsible—" She paused. "If *Graystripe* is responsible, then you need to decide whose side you're really on."

Silverstream stared at her without speaking. There was

uncertainty in her eyes. A shiver of fear ran along Leopard-fur's spine. She was really beginning to wonder exactly where Silverstream's loyalty lay. If she had to choose, was it possible that the RiverClan she-cat would take the side of another Clan?

"Silverstream." Leopardfur looked coolly at the she-cat. "I want you to join the patrol." The rain had held off since yes-terday, and the river had receded a little, hopefully enough to find the source of the poison. After a long night of thought, Leopardfur thought she had an idea for how to pull Silver-stream's loyalty back to their own Clan. If Silverstream helped them uncover proof that Graystripe was mixed up in the river poisoning, she'd *have* to realize that her ThunderClan friend wasn't as innocent as she believed. And Leopardfur would no longer have to worry which Clan Silverstream would support if they ever came into conflict.

Silverstream eyed Leopardfur, her gaze sharp with sus-picion as she got to her paws and padded toward the patrol. Stonefur, Skyheart, and Piketooth were already waiting beside the camp entrance.

Leopardfur led them out of camp and across the river where it flowed closest to the ThunderClan border.

"I don't know why we're looking here," Silverstream mut-tered. "The river might have been poisoned farther down."

Stonefur looked at her curiously. "The fish that killed Bird-song was caught here," he mewed.

"Fish *swim*." Silverstream's pelt ruffled. "They don't just stay in one place like bramble bushes. It could have been poisoned anywhere."

Leopardfur whisked her tail. "Let's not waste any time." Her Clanmates might wonder why Silverstream was being difficult. "The shoreline is exposed again today, so we'll concentrate our search along the riverbank. Look out for unusual smells or sights and report to me as soon as you find anything."

As Stonefur, Piketooth, and Skyheart headed away, Silverstream glared at her. "You're determined to prove it was Graystripe, aren't you?"

"This isn't about that," Leopardfur told her.

"Really?" Silverstream sounded unconvinced.

"I'm just looking out for my Clan." *And I wish you were too.*

Silverstream swished her tail. "I'm going to find proof it *wasn't* Graystripe," she snapped, and headed closer to the trees.

Leopardfur padded along the shore, keeping an eye on the she-cat. If Silverstream did find "proof" that vilified Graystripe, she didn't want her to have the opportunity to hide it. The river was less wild today. The channels and ditches flowing into it were easy to see, and she picked her way along them, the chilly water swilling around her legs as she sniffed at the water cautiously.

Her pads grew numb with cold as the morning dragged on. She could see her Clanmates moving along the river, ahead and behind her, checking every inlet and pool along the edge. Worry was beginning to prick at Leopardfur's belly. What if they couldn't find the source of the poison? With every tail-length of shoreline, she cared less about who had caused the poisoning and more about making sure the river was safe for her Clanmates.

As she crossed a pebbly stretch of shore, a sour tang touched her nose. She lifted her muzzle and opened her mouth, letting the air bathe her tongue. It was a scent she'd never smelled here before; it definitely wasn't a river scent. Her nose wrinkled, and she scanned the bank, stiffening as she saw something bobbing beside a clump of rushes at the water's edge. Strange, colored shapes were glinting among the reeds. She hurried toward them, guessing as she got near that they could only be Twoleg trash. There was nothing natural about the smell or look of these shapes. They were bundled together and caught among the stems. She kept her paws dry until she was upstream and then waded in, feeling queasy as the stench of decay grew stronger.

"I've found it!" she called to her Clanmates, signaling with a flick of her tail for them to stay out of the filth that oozed from the trash and clouded the water around it.

Skyheart waded in, her tail bushing as she picked up the scent. "It smells like carrion," she mewed with disgust.

Algae clung to the trash and spread, slimy and putrid, around it. As the water flowed by, the current tore off small patches of algae and swirled them away downstream. There was no doubt that this was the source of the poison that had killed Birdsong. Leopardfur bristled. Had some careless Twoleg left it? Anger churned in her belly. She could challenge a threat from another a Clan, but there was no way to get revenge on a Twoleg.

Silverstream caught her eye. Her look of triumph made Leopardfur even angrier. Graystripe hadn't done this. She felt a flash of frustration. It would have been better for the young she-cat if she'd had been able to prove that Graystripe couldn't be trusted. Instead, she'd have to find another way to end Silverstream's relationship before the rest of RiverClan found out.

CHAPTER 19

Leopardfur woke at dawn. Rain was pounding the roof, and the walls of the den shuddered in the wind. The weather had begun to worsen yesterday as she'd led the patrol back to camp to report the Twoleg trash to Crookedstar. She hadn't been able to hook it free of the reeds even with the help of Piketooth, Stonefur, and Skyheart. If only they'd been able to send it swirling away downriver, past the gorge. She'd planned to take a larger patrol out today in the hope they might dislodge it. But from the sound of the rain, she guessed that the trash would have been submerged again.

She slid from the den, narrowing her eyes against the weather, and, in the gray early-morning light, inspected the fresh-kill pile. A stale thrush, sodden and stiff, was all that was left. But at least there was something.

"Leopardfur." Mudfur's mew made her turn. Her father was padding toward her through the rain. The wind buffeted him, tugging at his thick fur. They were the only cats in the clearing, but Leopardfur could hear her Clanmates stirring in the warriors' den. She'd be able to send out patrols soon. Mudfur glanced at the thrush. "Are you hungry?"

"I was just checking." She poked it with her paw. "Should I take this to the nursery?"

Mudfur shook his head. "Let Mosspelt and Mistyfoot sleep," he mewed. "They must be tired. I heard Dawnkit mewling in the night. She must have kept the whole nursery awake."

Leopardfur tensed. "Is Dawnkit okay?"

"She's fine." Mudfur shook the rain from his fur. "I checked. Just a nightmare."

Leopardfur looked up at the dark gray sky, the rain streaming around her eyes. "We won't be able to reach the Twoleg trash today."

"At least we know where it is," Mudfur mewed. "The fish farther upstream won't be poisoned. You can hunt there today."

"But the river beyond the reed beds is narrow." It had been so long since he'd been a warrior, he must have forgotten. "And it'll be raging after all this rain. It may be too dangerous to fish."

Froglcap ducked out of the warriors' den, hunching against the rain. "Too dangerous to fish?" He sniffed and padded toward them, his fur fluffed out. "Nowhere's too dangerous for a RiverClan warrior."

Leopardfur frowned. "Still," she mewed. "It might be better to hunt in the water meadow today."

"We've had too much land prey," Frogleap snorted. "My kits will grow up thinking they're ThunderClan cats."

"I guess we have spat out a lot of fur lately," Leopardfur conceded.

Frogleap swished his tail. "Besides, I *like* fast-water fishing. It'll be fun." He blinked at Leopardfur and she dipped her head.

"Okay," she mewed. "I'll lead a hunting patrol there once I've organized the others. You can join it." She hooked up the thrush. "But first I'm taking this to Graypool."

Dawn gave way to daylight, which was hardly brighter, but at least the rain was easing by the time Leopardfur led the patrol out of camp. She'd asked Skyheart and Loudbelly to join them, and it almost felt as though they were apprentices again as they trekked upstream. The rain had stopped by the time they'd passed the reed beds. Leopardfur had been right. The river was flowing fast here, churning and frothing as it raced between the steep banks. Farther upstream, she could see trees rocking in the wind. Even from here, she could hear their branches creaking and groaning like grouchy elders.

Leopardfur scanned the water. Twigs and leaves swirled past, the river swallowing them, only to spit them out again a few tail-lengths away as though it didn't like the taste. "Perhaps we should hunt on the shore until the current's less fierce," she suggested.

"Don't be a mouse-heart." Frogleap stood at the edge, his ears pricked eagerly. "I want to give Robinkit, Dawnkit, and Woodkit their first bite of carp." He blinked at Leopardfur affectionately. "They might love it as much as you do."

Leopardfur glanced at him, purring. "Why wouldn't they? Carp is the tastiest fish." She plunged in. The river caught her and pulled her under, but it buoyed her up again and she burst, splashing, through the surface. It was exhilarating. She swam against the current, relishing the challenge and enjoying the rush of water through her pelt.

Skyheart dived after her while Loudbelly slid into the shallows and swam close to the bank. "It's hard to believe you used to be a drypaw," she teased as she surfaced beside Leopardfur.

"I was barely a kit!" Leopardfur splashed her with her paw, and Skyheart darted away through the frothing water, her eyes shining.

"Look!" Skyheart pointed with her nose to a shape racing beneath the surface toward them. She ducked under and surfaced a moment later with a small chub between her jaws. She made for the shore and flung it onto the bank.

Frogleap sniffed it and whisked his tail. "I'm going to catch a carp."

He dived in and Leopardfur watched the water close over him. She waited eagerly for him to surface. It had been a while since they'd fished together. Perhaps they could catch something big, like a salmon. She twisted in the water, looking for him. Where was he? Fighting to hold herself in place, she turned again. Alarm began to spark in her belly. "Frogleap?"

Skyheart was swimming a few tail lengths away, her muzzle in the water as she searched for fish. Loudbelly was nosing beneath the sedge overhanging the bank.

"Frogleap!" Frightened now, Leopardfur ducked underwater, her eyes stinging as she strained to see through the frothing water. The river buffeted her, and she struggled against the current. In a few moments she was out of breath and had to surface for air.

As she bobbed up, she saw Frogleap, swimming toward her.

"There you are!" She splashed toward him, swinging a playful blow at his ear. "You scared me!" she mewed.

He swam away from her, his whiskers twitching. "I was just checking the bottom for lurking fish," he mewed. "But the current's strong down there too. It looks like we'll have to wait for the fish to come to us." He turned and looked expectantly upstream.

His ears pricked as he seemed to spot something moving below the surface. "Get ready!" he mewed. "If I don't catch it, you can." He disappeared under the water again and Leopardfur's heart quickened. She dropped beneath the surface and saw a trout swimming toward her. Frogleap was right behind it, his paws outstretched. As she unsheathed her claws, ready to catch it, it jerked suddenly backward. Frogleap had grabbed it.

Leopardfur bobbed up to the surface, delight surging in her chest as he appeared next to her, the trout between his jaws. He carried it to the shore and flung it out beside Skyheart's chub.

Near the bank, Loudbelly had hooked a perch that must have been hiding among the trailing sedge. He leaped from the water, holding it with his teeth, and placed it beside the others. It was raining again, the water pounding the shore, and before he slid back in again, he moved their catch farther from the edge, as though afraid it might get washed back into the water.

Before long, the pile had doubled.

"We should take these back to camp," Leopardfur called over the roar of the water. Her paws were growing tired from fighting the current, and there were nearly more fish in the pile than they could carry.

"I haven't caught a carp yet," Frogleap called back. He'd swum a little way farther upstream, where the river was even narrower and churned so fiercely it was hard to make out his mew above the noise.

Leopardfur swam toward him, pushing hard against the current. "There won't be carp this far upstream!" she called. He must know that carp preferred to bask in calmer water. "Your kits will have to wait until we've cleared away the trash so we can fish for it."

"There *must* be carp here," Frogleap yowled back. "The only way to get downstream is from upstream." He plunged beneath the water.

Here, the river cut a deep trench in the middle of the channel, and she dived with him, pushing after him through the swirling water.

He was darting back and forth along the trench like an otter, his fur billowing around him. Her heart quickened as she recognized the sleek outline of a carp racing toward him. It was traveling fast, swept along by the current. Would he be quick enough to grab it? She pushed down toward the bottom of the trench, fighting the river as it tried to push her backward. If Frogleap missed the carp, she'd get it.

Frogleap kicked out with his hind legs, shooting through

the water as though it were no more than air. Claws outstretched, he hooked the carp and dragged it toward his jaws
to give the killing bite.

Frogleap's kits would get their first taste of carp after all.
Leopardfur swam happily to the surface and broke from the
water, gulping fresh air.

Then she stiffened. Upstream, something dropped from
one of the trees. It splashed into the river, long, dark, and
heavy enough to send slices of water arcing over the riverbank. A branch! Broken off by the wind. Her heart lurched as
the river grabbed it and sped it downstream. It was heading
straight for them. If Frogleap surfaced now, it would hit him.

She ducked down to warn him and saw him rising through
the water, his eyes bright with triumph as he clasped the carp
between his jaws.

No! Her scream wouldn't carry through the churning water.
She choked as her mouth filled and panic gripped her as the
branch, a dark shadow above them, raced toward Frogleap.

She swam for him, the weight of the water so fierce that
frustration clawed in her belly as she fought to get near. She
reached for him as he surfaced, saw him jerk as the branch hit
him, and watched, frozen, as the current snatched him away.
He spun. His paws flailed for a moment. Then he fell limp
and the river dragged him toward her.

Heart bursting, she grabbed for him again and felt his fur
sweep her claws, just a whisker out of reach, as he tumbled
past. She blinked the water from her eyes and stared, horror-
stricken, as the river carried him away.

"Frogleap!"

Skyheart was watching from the bank, her eyes wide. Loudbelly stared helplessly from the shallows as Frogleap was washed downriver.

Leopardfur launched herself into the current, letting it lift her, swimming with it so fast that the shore blurred beside her. She didn't take her eyes from Frogleap. The river carried him like a leaf on the stream, faster and faster, and then, suddenly, sucked him under and he disappeared.

Skyheart was bounding along the bank. "Leopardfur!" she screeched.

Leopardfur glanced at her.

"Get out of there." Skyheart cry was frenzied with panic.

Leopardfur turned in the water and followed her Clanmate's gaze back upstream. Pieces of broken branch were swirling toward her. The wind must have torn the whole tree apart. The surface of the river was strewn with lumps of wood.

Alarm flashed beneath Leopardfur's pelt. She lunged for the shore, pulling herself out a moment before the branches and bark hurtled past. She stared after them as the river sucked them under, carrying them down to the same dark place it had dragged Frogleap.

She couldn't speak. Skyheart stood stiffly beside her as Loudbelly caught up to them and stared downriver.

"I should have saved him," Leopardfur whispered.

"You tried," Skyheart croaked. "I saw you. He was out of reach."

"I should have swum harder." Grief twisted her heart until

the pain was unbearable. "I should have been quicker."

Skyheart leaned against her. "It was all too fast," she breathed. "There was nothing you could have done."

Leopardfur couldn't speak anymore. She wanted to crumple on the shore. All these moons, a tiny piece of her had wondered what her life might have been if she had done as Frogleap asked and chosen him over being deputy. A not-so-tiny part of her still loved him in a way that defied reason. Now he was gone, and she hadn't been able to save him.

She couldn't pry her eyes from the raging river, wishing it would give back the cat who'd known her best.

CHAPTER 20

❧

Leopardfur padded numbly toward the camp. Loudbelly was trembling beside her, as Skyheart walked ahead, directing them. The weight of Frogleap, slung between her and Loudbelly's shoulders, seemed more than she could bear, but she kept putting one paw in front of the other, staring blindly ahead as her heart ached with more pain than she thought possible. She could feel the last of his warmth ebbing away as they limped through the reed tunnel into the clearing and let him slide from their backs onto the muddy earth.

The rain had started again as they'd searched the riverbank for Frogleap's body. It had beaten down relentlessly as they'd dragged it from the reeds where it had been caught. Leopardfur had hoped for a moment that he might still be alive, but one glimpse of his wide, glazed eyes had told her that he was dead.

Now, back at camp, the rain fell even harder, as though StarClan had no pity for the living. Her Clanmates were sheltering in their dens. Only Sedgecreek and Stonefur were outside, huddled beneath the sedge wall as they shared a bedraggled starling.

Sedgecreek looked up as Frogleap's body thumped to the ground.

Stonefur hurried across the clearing. "What happened?" he asked.

Leopardfur throat tightened. "The river—" The words died on her tongue. She didn't want to relive the accident, or make it more real by speaking of it.

Shimmerpelt slid from the warriors' den. Grasswhisker and Blackclaw followed. One by one, the Clan crept out into the rain and gathered around Frogleap's body. No one spoke, as though they too feared making a nightmare real.

Mistyfoot poked her head from the nursery, her ears twitching nervously as she saw them. "What is it?"

Stonefur turned his head toward her. "Frogleap's dead."

"Does that mean he won't come to the nursery anymore?" Perchkit squeezed past his mother and blinked at her as Pikekit and Reedkit peered from between her paws.

Mistyfoot touched her nose to his head. "Yes," she mewed softly. "Let's go back inside. I want you to play with Robinkit, Woodkit, and Dawnkit for a while. Mosspelt has to—"

"Has something happened?" Mosspelt mewed from inside the nursery.

Mistyfoot disappeared inside. A moment later Mosspelt burst out and ran across the clearing. She stopped beside Frogleap's body and stared at it as though she expected him to move. As though he might not be dead after all. Then she crouched and began to tremble, a low moan rising in her throat as she touched her nose to Frogleap's sodden pelt. The rain battered her, and Leopardfur's chest tightened as she watched.

She felt so helpless. She could not bring Frogleap back, or stop the rain. She could only watch the heartbreaking scene as her Clanmates began to whisper softly around her.

"How did he die?" Heavystep mewed.

"Were you attacked by ThunderClan?" Reedtail asked.

"It was an accident." Leopardfur saw the branch racing toward Frogleap, her breath stopping as she pictured his body jerk and grow limp and the river sweep him away.

Cedarpelt stood beside his body, staring wide-eyed as though he couldn't believe his kit was dead. "RiverClan warriors don't drown," he murmured.

Lakeshine pressed against him, shivering as rain dripped from her whiskers. "He was a strong swimmer."

Leopardfur felt the gazes of her Clanmates settle on her as though they were kits and she were their mother. They wanted her to explain, but the words were too painful. *Frogleap can't be dead. He has kits. He was happy.* She stared at them blankly, her thoughts stuck. *And I loved him.*

"A branch hit him," Skyheart mewed.

Gratitude flickered in Leopardfur's chest as her friend padded forward and began to tell their Clanmates how this had happened.

Mudfur nosed his way through the crowd and stopped beside Leopardfur. He didn't speak but let his fur rest softly against hers.

She glanced at him. "Where's Crookedstar?" The RiverClan leader should be with them.

Mudfur glanced toward his den. "He's in his nest," he mewed. "It's probably best he stay there."

Leopardfur stiffened. "Is he ill?"

"Just tired," Mudfur mewed quietly.

Leopardfur broke away and headed toward the RiverClan leader's den. He had to be told. His Clan needed him. She pushed through the trailing moss and blinked at him.

Crookedstar was sleeping, unaware of the rain dripping through the roof and soaking his nest. He rolled over and began to snore.

"Crookedstar." Leopardfur leaned close. She poked him gently with a paw. "Wake up. Something's happened."

He blinked open his eyes, looking blearily at her for a moment before sitting up.

Leopardfur suddenly realized how old he'd grown. His thick pelt was matted, and there was confusion in his eyes as he struggled awake.

"What is it?" he mewed thickly.

"Frogleap's dead," she told him as gently as she could. "It was an accident. He drowned." The simple words pierced her heart like thorns.

Crookedstar's eyes rounded with grief. "Dead?"

She nodded.

He looked away as though he was having trouble taking it in. Leopardfur felt a flash of panic. She wanted him to talk to the Clan and soften the sharpest edge of their grief. But, looking at him now, she realized he wasn't strong enough. *She* would have to comfort them. She felt suddenly unsteady, remembering how she'd once been ready to snatch leadership from Crookedstar the moment he'd fallen ill. How had she ever thought she could manage such a responsibility? But she must. Crookedstar looked like an elder. He couldn't lead the Clan through something like this.

She closed her eyes, feeling the shelter and warmth of the den, wishing she could stay here and hide in its shadows, alone with the grief that was clawing at her heart. But her Clan needed her. She opened her eyes and looked at Crookedstar.

He was staring at the floor, murmuring to himself. "Frog-leap's dead." His mew was choked with sadness.

"Stay here and rest," she told him. She lifted her muzzle. "I'll speak to the Clan."

It seemed to take every spark of energy she had to force herself back through the trailing moss and across the rain-soaked camp. It was growing dark. Her Clanmates were no more than shadows in the clearing.

She wove among them and stopped beside Frogleap's body. Lakeshine had joined Mosspelt, crouching beside it.

Bright mewls sounded from the nursery.

"Primrosekit! You're the hunter this time!"

"I'm going to catch you!"

"Hey! That's not fair. I was in the nest!"

"Quiet." Mistyfoot's mew was hushed but firm. "Keep your voices down."

"Why?"

As the squeals quietened, Leopardfur looked around her Clanmates. "We lost a beloved Clanmate today," she began slowly. Their gazes were searching hers, looking for comfort. Her belly tightened. "He was a true warrior, loyal and brave.

The Clan won't be the same without him. But he wouldn't want you to grieve for him. We will see him again in StarClan, and when we do, we want him to be proud of us. We want him to see that we never for a moment stopped taking care of our Clanmates. That we never let grief get in the way of keeping them safe."

"True." Timberfur nodded gently.

Piketooth dipped his head. "It's what he would want."

"How could StarClan take him?" Mosspelt turned her agonized gaze toward Leopardfur.

Leopardfur met it. She needed to have an answer, not just for Mosspelt but for the whole Clan. She paused, taking a breath. "I know it feels like StarClan is testing us," she told Mosspelt. Then she lifted her gaze and looked around the others. "We are threatened by ThunderClan and WindClan. Snow and rain have made fishing hard and left us hungry. And the river has been poisoned." She let the words sink in for a moment before she spoke again. "But Frogleap was the first to meet any challenge. He risked fishing in fast water to find prey for his kits. He relished the challenge, and if he were here, he'd tell you to relish it too. He'd tell us a challenge is a chance to prove that a warrior is more than just claws and teeth. A warrior is heart and mind. It is not how we hunt and fight that defines our success, but how we face tragedy, how we rise above it. This is how we prove we are true warriors. That is what Frogleap would have done. That is what he would expect us to do, because he knew, just as I do, that RiverClan warriors are the truest of all, and if we face more challenges than other Clans, it is because we are stronger and braver than any of them."

Her words surprised her. She wondered for a moment where they'd come from. Had StarClan been guiding her thoughts? For a moment her heart lifted as she looked around the Clan and saw their eyes spark with determination. She had reached them, and they were repaying her with loyalty and courage.

And yet Mosspelt was still watching her, eyes shimmering with grief. "How will I tell the kits?" she asked.

Leopardfur had to force her paws not to tremble. She met Mosspelt's gaze steadily. "I'll help."

Mosspelt got to her paws. Her Clanmates parted to let her through as she headed slowly for the nursery. Leopardfur followed, aware of Frogleap's body, lying stiff and cold behind them.

"Begin the vigil," she whispered to Timberfur as she passed him.

He nodded, and she padded after Mosspelt and ducked into the nursery.

The kits were leaping from nest to nest, Mosspelt's kits almost indistinguishable from Mistyfoot's as they chased each other around the willow den.

Mistyfoot looked up as she entered.

Leopardfur nodded to her. "Will you take your kits to the elders' den for a little while?"

Primrosekit stopped and stared at her. "Why?"

"Graypool gets lonely," Leopardfur told her. "It'll do her

good to have some lively, energetic kits around her for a while."

"Can we go too?" Robinkit mewed.

Mosspelt's eyes glinted with pain. "You stay here with me." She blinked at Woodkit and Dawnkit. "You too. There's something I have to tell you."

Perchkit blinked at her eagerly. "Will you tell us too?"

"Mistyfoot will tell you later." Leopardfur shooed him away gently with her tail.

It seemed to take a long time for Mistyfoot to gather her kits and bustle them out of the den. All the while, Leopardfur was aware of Mosspelt trying to stop herself trembling as she watched her kits.

"Is something wrong?" Woodkit seemed to sense his mother's distress. He padded toward her and blinked at her anxiously.

Robinkit and Dawnkit clustered around him.

"What is it?" Dawnkit mewed.

"Why did Primrosekit have to go?" Robinkit asked.

"We were having fun." Dawnkit sounded indignant.

"I have something to tell you." Mosspelt's mew was tight, as though the words were stuck in her throat.

Woodkit moved closer. He was quivering, and Mosspelt sat down and drew him to her with her tail and tucked him close.

"Frogleap has gone to join StarClan," she mewed.

"Why?" Dawnkit blinked at her. "Doesn't he like us anymore?"

"He had no choice," Mosspelt mewed. "There was an accident. In the river. He was hurt, and now he has to live with StarClan."

Woodkit's eyes were round. "But he'll come back when he's better, won't he?"

Mosspelt shook her head. "He can't come back," she mewed. "He died. He can never come back." Her eyes glistened.

Leopardfur padded forward. "He can watch over you, though," she told the kits. "He'll watch you from StarClan."

Woodkit began to wail. "But I want to see him."

"Can we visit him?" Robinkit asked.

"No." Mosspelt leaned forward and grabbed his scruff, pulling him close.

Leopardfur could hardly bear to watch as he huddled against his mother, confused and sad and so small that she wondered how she could ever protect him from all the dangers he would have to face.

Dawnkit sat down and stared at her mother. There was no grief in her gaze. "Can we eat soon?" she asked Mosspelt.

Leopardfur flinched. The kit was too young to understand. She glanced at Mosspelt. What would the queen do?

Dawnkit was still staring at her mother. "Frogleap said we could have our first bite of fish today. He said he'd bring us some." She turned to Leopardfur. "Did he catch anything? He promised."

"Yes." Leopardfur's mew cracked as she pictured him proudly holding the carp. The carp was gone, washed away when the branch had struck him. But the rest of their catch was still on the bank. "We left it behind." How could they have carried home prey along with their Clanmate's body? But she must keep Frogleap's promise. "I'll go and fetch it." She caught Mosspelt's eye. "Will you be okay?"

"Yes," she whispered. "And thank you. They should taste Frogleap's last gift to them." The queen drew Dawnkit close and touched her nose to her head. "It's going to be okay," she promised.

Leopardfur dreamed. The forest was falling. Birds fluttered into the sky as their nests dropped away beneath them. Mice and voles swarmed from beneath crumbling roots. Bark and wood tumbled into the river until it was choked, and the fish were caught in the tangle of branches, and the water, with nowhere left to flow, spread across the land, swallowing the reed beds and water meadows.

Deep in the dream, Leopardfur squirmed in the nest. Panic dragged her deeper into darkness until she could hardly breathe. She struggled to wake, but the long trek to collect the abandoned catch and the vigil for Frogleap afterward—the rain falling harder as the night wore on—had exhausted her. And yet she hadn't even buried Frogleap's body, but had left it in the clearing because the burial patch was flooded. And the entire time, the river was rising around the reed beds and lapping over the edges of the camp.

The wails of her Clanmates filled her dream. They grew shriller and more high-pitched until they became the shrieks of kits. *Kits!* Leopardfur woke at last. The squealing was real! She lifted her head sharply and looked around. Water had pooled at the bottom of her nest. It was swilling through the den. *Flood!*

Pelt spiking, she leaped from her nest. "Wake up!"

Reedtail and Stonefur were already scrambling out of their waterlogged nests.

The kits squealed again as Leopardfur shot from the den and splashed through the water that was swirling across the clearing. The river had burst its banks. It streamed through the camp, so high now that it almost reached the elders' den.

The other dens were awash, and her Clanmates were dashing here and there, grabbing hold of willow stems and bundles of reeds that were floating toward the river. The apprentices' den had been torn apart. The reed wall had been breached, and nests were spinning toward the gap, where the current sucked one out, then another, and swept them into open water.

Stonefur and Silverstream tried to snatch them as they washed past.

"Leave them!" Leopardfur yowled. "Save the nursery!"

The willow den was splitting open because the wind tore at it and water dragged at the base. As Stonefur and Silverstream raced toward it, Mosspelt shot out. Robinkit was swinging from her jaws. Dawnkit and Woodkit clung to her back. The kits shrieked in terror while Mosspelt stared around, her eyes wide with horror.

"Head for the elders' den!" Leopardfur told her. With any luck, the water wouldn't reach it.

As Mosspelt raced away, Mistyfoot burst from the nursery holding Reedkit's scruff. She passed him to Stonefur and turned back inside. A moment later she appeared again, Primrosekit dangling from her jaws.

Silverstream nodded toward the elders' den. "Take her

there! I'll get Perchkit and Pikekit." She pushed her way inside the nursery.

As Leopardfur raced to help, the river swelled and lifted. A wave swept through the camp. It hit the nursery, ripping away the woven walls. Exposed to the storm now, Perchkit and Pikekit squealed in their nest. Silverstream hooked her claws into it, but the water snatched it away.

Leopardfur charged after it, but another wave knocked her sideways. As she floundered and tried to regain her balance, the nest swirled away through the gap in the camp wall and out onto the river. Perchkit and Pikekit stared over the edge, their faces twisted in terror, and she froze, and watched them spin away into the darkness, their squeals drowned by the roaring water.

"No!" The earth seemed to tremble beneath her paws. She was helpless.

Silverstream thrust her muzzle in Leopardfur's face. "Save the others!"

Another swell was howling toward the camp.

Leopardfur snatched her thoughts from the lost kits. She scanned the clearing. "Where's Mudfur?"

Sedgecreek turned from where she was trying to hold the walls of the warriors' den in place as the flood dragged at them. "He's with Graypool."

Leopardfur felt a wash of relief. "What about Crooked-star?" she shrieked.

"I haven't seen him." Sedgecreek grabbed at a bundle of reeds.

Stonefur was helping Loudbelly and Lakeshine gather

pieces of broken den wall from the reeds.

Leopardfur called to him. "Have you seen Crookedstar?"

The gray tom shook his head.

Surely the RiverClan leader wasn't still in his den! Leopard-fur rushed toward it as the water swelled and surged around her. It had reached the elders' den. "Get Graypool out!" she called to Blackclaw. "And the kits!" She turned to Vixenleap and Emberdawn, who were watching the water rise with horror. "Evacuate the camp! Get everyone inland and onto high ground."

As the two she-cats began to round up their Clanmates, Leopardfur slewed to a halt outside Crookedstar's den, sending arcs of water over the root walls. They were already half-submerged with water. A fresh wave swallowed them, and Crookedstar struggled out, coughing. She reached him and put her shoulder beneath his, helping him limp across the flooded clearing.

"Is everyone safe?" he spluttered.

Perchkit and Pikekit were washed away. She didn't dare tell him. What could he do? She was fighting back panic, her thoughts reeling. Could she have saved them? Would they be safe if they managed to cling to their nest? Should she risk sending warriors after them?

Vixenleap and Emberdawn were hurrying their Clanmates through a gap they'd torn in the sedge. The river beyond was no more than a channel. It was raging but narrow. With help, every cat could swim it, even Graypool, who stood at the edge now, her pelt on end.

Crookedstar limped to a halt. "Go and help them." He

nudged her toward them. "I'll follow."

She blinked at him. "I have to get you to safety."

"I want to check the elders' den," he told her. It was the last den left standing.

"Every cat's here," she told him, nodding to where Mudfur was helping Graypool to cross the channel. Mosspelt and Mistyfoot were waiting to follow with their kits.

He looked at her. "I need to make sure no cat is left behind."

Leopardfur let him go and hurried toward her Clanmates. Mistyfoot had crossed the channel with Primrosekit and watched Blackclaw follow with Reedkit. As he scrambled out, she led him into the darkness, where higher ground and safety were waiting.

Mosspelt hesitated on the edge. Dawnkit was dangling from her jaws. Woodkit and Robinkit clung to her back.

"I'll help you." Leopardfur eased herself into the racing water, churning her paws as she struggled not to be swept away. "Come on," she called to Mosspelt.

Tentatively, Mosspelt waded toward her. Dawnkit squealed and struggled. Robinkit and Woodkit buried their muzzles deep into their mother's fur. As Mosspelt pushed out into the channel, a roar sounded from upstream. Leopardfur's pelt sparked with terror when a wall of water thundered toward them. Soon it reached them, curling into a wave that broke over her and pushed her underwater.

She struggled to the surface. Thrashing her paws in panic, she felt Mosspelt's pelt and hooked in her claws. The queen shrieked and floundered in her grip. As the wave receded, Leopardfur stared at her, growing stiff as dread hollowed her belly. Where were the kits?

They'd disappeared. Only Mosspelt remained beside her.

"I couldn't hold on!" Wild with panic, Mosspelt tried to drag herself free of Leopardfur's grip. "I have to save them."

"You can't!" Leopardfur hauled her to the far side. Frog-leap would never forgive her for letting Mosspelt go. As she dragged the queen, wailing, onto the bank, a flash of gray fur dived past them into the channel.

"I'll save them!"

"Crookedstar!" She recognized the RiverClan leader's yowl as he disappeared beneath the water and resurfaced a few tail-lengths downstream. He rolled, flailing for a moment; then, finding his balance, he struck out and swam with the current.

Mosspelt stared as he disappeared into the night, the water frothing around him. Desperation glittered in her eyes.

Leopardfur nosed her inland, following her Clanmates, her thoughts reeling as they trekked to higher ground. Crooked-star would never survive the flood. He wasn't the strong warrior he'd once been, and the water was too fierce even for a young cat.

As the Clan halted, gathering higher up the hill, she gazed down the slope. It was hidden in darkness but she could hear the river roaring as though howling its victory over the fragile camp. Her fur clinging to her body, Leopardfur pressed back a shiver.

Stonefur stood beside her.

"Is everyone here?" she asked him softly.

"All except the kits and Crookedstar," he breathed back.

"They'll never survive," she whispered.

He glanced at her, his eyes dark. "Crookedstar has nine lives."

She nodded. But how many of them were left? Enough to save Mosspelt's kits? Enough to find his way back to shore? Leopardfur's paws felt like stone. The rain was easing, but she barely noticed. How had she allowed so many kits to be lost?

The cold began to reach into her bones, but she didn't move. As the night slowly gave way to dawn, she gazed across the river. The gray light revealed a devastated camp, and her heart seemed to stop as she made out a gray shape on the bank downstream. It lay motionless on a stretch of mud. Reeds, crushed by the flood, were strewn around it.

Behind her, Leopardfur could hear Primrosekit crying. She must be hungry.

She padded to where Stonefur had curled in a bracken patch beside his Clanmates and woke him with the touch of her nose. "Organize a hunting patrol," she whispered softly. "The Clan is hungry and I have to go and check on something."

He looked at her, blinking away sleep. "Where are you going?"

"I can see Crookedstar," she breathed. "I think he'd dead. I'm going to fetch him."

The bracken stirred as Mudfur nosed his way through. "I'm coming with you."

"Me too." Stonefur padded to where Skyheart was curled beside Blackclaw. He poked her gently with a paw. "Can you organize a hunting patrol?" he asked her as she lifted her head.

She scrambled to her paws, nodding.

Leopardfur headed downslope, Mudfur at her heels.

Stonefur hurried to catch up and fell in beside her. They didn't speak as they followed the shore through the gray dawn. She could see Crookedstar's body on the riverbank. It wasn't far now. She slowed as she saw he was curled around three more bodies, as small as ducklings, bedraggled and unmoving.

Mudfur broke into a run. She raced after him. By the time she pulled up beside the bodies, the medicine cat was already kneading Robinkit's chest.

"Rub their chests!" Mudfur nodded toward Dawnkit and Woodkit.

"What about Crookedstar?" Leopardfur asked, dropping down beside Dawnkit and resting her paws on her tiny body.

"He has more lives than these kits," Mudfur mewed. "StarClan will take care of him."

As Stonefur began to work on Woodkit, glancing at Mudfur to learn what to do, Leopardfur's pelt tingled with panic. Dawnkit felt so small beneath her pads, and so cold. Could she really be saved?

"Do it!" Mudfur ordered sharply.

Leopardfur copied him, pumping the she-kit's chest with small rhythmic strokes as though squeezing water from wet moss. Crookedstar hadn't moved. Her thoughts spiraled. Did he have any lives left? After the sickness had nearly killed him, perhaps he'd used his last one to save the kits.

I'll be leader. The idea filled her with fear. *I'm not ready.* The flood had been more powerful that she could ever have imagined. How had she believed she could ever lead the Clan? There were so many dangers. And she was just one cat. *How can I protect them?*

Suddenly, Dawnkit twitched beneath her paws and coughed. The kit rolled over and vomited water onto the shore.

Leopardfur's heart burst with gratitude. "Thank StarClan!" She grabbed Dawnkit and pulled her close, wrapping her tail around her to warm her. "It's okay," she soothed. "You're safe now."

Mudfur sat back on his haunches and stared at Robinkit, his eyes shimmering. Stonefur was still working on Woodkit. He signaled with a nod for the gray tom to stop too. "It's no good," he mewed. "They're gone."

Leopardfur breathed in Dawnkit's scent. Frogleap had died and now two of his kits. As grief threatened to overwhelm her, Crookedstar coughed. A spasm ran along his flank and he twitched suddenly into life.

Mudfur darted to his side and sniffed him anxiously. "Crookedstar?"

Crookedstar sat up slowly, his eyes glittering with shock. He glanced toward the kits and then met Leopardfur's gaze. There was such darkness in his eyes, she shivered. She suddenly understood the responsibility he'd borne all these years—a burden heavier than she'd ever imagined. Holding Dawnkit closer, she dipped her head.

When her time came to lead RiverClan, would she be ready?

CHAPTER 21

✤

"There's no sign of the kits." Timberfur dipped his head to Crooked-star. Though it was nearly sunhigh, his pelt was still damp from the flood. The weak sunshine breaking through the clouds had done little to dry it, or warm the makeshift camp RiverClan had made on the slope above the island. Timberfur lowered his voice. "Or Frogleap's body."

Leopardfur flinched. She should have insisted that Frogleap be laid out somewhere safe while the burial patch drained. Instead he had been washed from the camp along with the nests, the dens, and, worst of all, the kits.

She hadn't moved from where she'd lain down after she'd brought Robinkit's and Woodkit's bodies back from the riverbank, her grief too heavy to bear. Mudfur and Stonefur had placed them gently in a small hollow above the camp and covered them with grass until they could be buried properly.

Mistyfoot had watched them do it, her eyes dark with grief, as though anticipating the moment when Perchkit and Pikekit's drowned bodies would be carried home. She'd begged Crookedstar to let her search for them, but he'd told her to take care of her surviving kits and sent Blackclaw,

Loudbelly, and Timberfur to look for the others. Mistyfoot had led Primrosekit and Reedkit to a stretch of grass beneath the bracken and wrapped herself around them, her eyes on the river, scanning the banks in desperate silence.

How had so many kits been lost? Leopardfur swallowed back guilt. She did not dare go near the bush beyond the bracken where Mosspelt had made a nest for Dawnkit and curled up in it, her back to the rest of the Clan. *Why couldn't I protect them?* She had failed to protect so many of the cats she loved. Suddenly, Mudfur's prophecy that Leopardfur would save RiverClan seemed no more than the foolish dream of a fond father. Why had she ever believed it?

Blackclaw was pacing now in the small clearing of the makeshift camp, his pelt prickling along his spine, while the Clan worked around him, weaving the bushes into dens and bundling reeds together for nests. "I want to go back out," he growled, looking at Crookedstar. Perchkit and Pikekit were his kits, too, and Leopardfur understood his frustration. "I know we didn't find them this morning, but we can't give up," he pressed. "I should have swum after them as soon as they were washed away." He glared at Leopardfur. "Why didn't you tell me they were lost?"

She sat up, hollow with guilt. "What could you have done?" she murmured. "The water was too fierce." She glanced toward the bush where Mosspelt was mourning Frogleap along with her kits. "Did you want Mistyfoot to lose you too?"

Crookedstar swished his tail. "It'll do no good to blame each other for our losses. We must concentrate on rebuilding."

He looked toward the camp. It was screened by the bracken, but every cat had seen the devastation. Water swilled over the clearing where RiverClan's camp had been. The apprentices' and warriors' dens had been washed away along with the nursery, and the elders' den stood, ruptured and bedraggled, its nest floating between the broken walls. "Reedtail, Skyheart, and Heavystep," he mewed. "Hunt for land prey upslope." He nodded to Cedarpelt. "Take a patrol along the shore and look for fish stranded by the flood."

Leopardfur felt a surge of respect for Crookedstar. Since he'd woken on the riverbank, he'd had a new sense of energy and assurance, as though the new life he'd been given had restored the youth and confidence that seemed to have faded over the past moons. While she'd been frozen by grief, he'd been giving orders and reassuring the Clan. Why hadn't she appreciated him earlier? She'd been so hungry to take his place that she hadn't realized how much she could learn just by watching him.

He turned now to Blackclaw. "You must search for your kits until you find them," he mewed. She guessed he was thinking that Blackclaw would be little use to the Clan until he had found out what had happened to them. "Leopardfur." For the first time that morning he addressed her. "Go with him, and take Stonefur," he ordered. "Search the banks and inlets and pools. I want Perchkit and Pikekit brought home."

She got to her paws. Even weighed down by grief, she could follow orders.

Crookedstar padded close to her. "Don't make the Clan's

loss your loss," he murmured. "Let them do the grieving while you keep them safe."

She blinked at him, then dipped her head. She could do that. At least, she could try.

She led Blackclaw and Stonefur through the bracken toward the river. They picked their way around the outside of the flooded camp and took the path that led to the stepping-stones. Although they would still be underwater, it would be the safest place to cross. As they neared the shore, she pricked her ears. She could hear cats mewing beyond the bushes ahead. *ThunderClan!* She could smell their scent. She nodded a warning to Stonefur and Blackclaw and they stiffened.

Stonefur tasted the air, his eyes widening. "What's ThunderClan doing here?"

Blackclaw growled. "An attack?"

Leopardfur unsheathed her claws. ThunderClan must have seen a chance to take advantage of RiverClan's misfortune. Anger pumped energy through her muscles. She plunged through the bushes and burst out, snarling as she saw Fireheart and Graystripe on the shore. They recoiled as she landed in front of them.

"What are you doing here?" she hissed.

Stonefur and Blackclaw skidded to a halt beside her.

Blackclaw drew back his lips. "Why are you trespassing on our territory?"

He stopped, and Leopardfur followed his gaze. It had flicked toward two tiny, bedraggled kits huddled at Fireheart's paws.

She stared at them, her heart pounding. Perchkit? Pikekit? They were barely moving, their eyes closed. She flattened her ears. What had the ThunderClan warrior done to them?

Fireheart spoke. "We're not trespassing," he mewed. "We pulled two of your kits out of the river and wanted to bring them home."

Blackclaw's pelt was twitching. He was staring at the kits in disbelief.

Stonefur padded forward and sniffed them. He glanced back at Blackclaw. "It's true!" His blue eyes widened. "They're your kits!"

Relief and happiness flooded Leopardfur's pelt. This was the first blessing StarClan had sent them in a moon. But she pressed it back and lifted her muzzle. She wasn't going to show weakness to ThunderClan intruders. Blackclaw clearly felt the same. He hadn't moved and his tail was lashing ominously.

"What are you doing with them?" Leopardfur glared at Graystripe. Was this another of ThunderClan's plots? "Were you trying to steal them?"

Fireheart stared at her as though she was talking nonsense. "Don't be such a mouse-brain," he snapped. "Why would we nearly drown ourselves to steal RiverClan kits?"

Blackclaw thrust his muzzle toward Fireheart and snarled. "If I find out you've hurt them, I'll—"

"Blackclaw!" Leopardfur sensed the situation was spiraling out of control. They couldn't fight here; there were kits. "Back off," she told him. "We'll let these cats explain themselves to Crookedstar and see if he believes them." She wasn't going to let them get away without a proper explanation. With a sharp flick of her tail, she beckoned Fireheart and Graystripe to follow her back to RiverClan's makeshift camp.

Fireheart padded stiffly past her. "All right," he mewed. "I just hope your Clan leader can see the truth when it's in front of his nose."

Stonefur and Blackclaw carried the kits past the flooded camp and up the slope beyond, keeping a watchful eye on Graystripe and Fireheart. Even if they had found the kits, why had the two ThunderClan warriors been near the river in the first place? She suspected Graystripe had come to check on Silverstream. But why bring Fireheart? Had Bluestar sent them to spy?

Crookedstar must have spotted them approaching. He met them on the slope, the half-built dens screened by the bracken.

Silverstream slid out behind him with Graypool and Emberdawn. Leopardfur watched her closely as Graystripe stopped in front of the RiverClan leader. The silver tabby's eyes gave nothing away as she watched the ThunderClan tom and his Clanmate with the same coolness as Emberdawn.

Crookedstar narrowed his eyes at Graystripe and Fireheart. "ThunderClan spies?" His pelt rippled along his spine. "As if we didn't have enough trouble!"

Blackclaw and Stonefur placed Perchkit and Pikekit gently on the grass.

"They found Mistyfoot's kits," Leopardfur mewed. Silverstream ducked back into the bracken as she went on. "They claim they pulled them out of the river."

"I don't believe a word of it," Blackclaw spat. "You can't trust a ThunderClan cat."

Crookedstar sniffed Perchkit, then nudged Pikekit with his nose. They looked practically newborn, staring, their eyes open now, and frightened. They must be very cold and hungry.

Graypool hurried toward them and wrapped her tail around them. "Mistyfoot is coming," she whispered. As they began to wail, she pulled them close.

Crookedstar's gaze flitted suspiciously over Fireheart and Graystripe. "How did you come to have them?"

Fireheart glanced at Graystripe. Was that exasperation in his eyes? "We flew across the river and broke into your camp without anyone noticing," he mewed sarcastically.

Leopardfur flexed her claws. She should rake his muzzle for talking to Crookedstar like that, but before she could move, the bracken shivered and Mistyfoot burst through. She rushed to her kits, snatching them from Graypool as though the old queen had stolen them, and pressed them to her belly. As she began to lick them furiously, they pressed against her, mewling, clearly relieved to feel her warmth and familiar scent.

Silverstream slid out behind them, her gaze still cool as it flitted over Graystripe and Fireheart. Mudfur hurried out and began examining the kits, sniffing them anxiously as Mistyfoot washed them. Beetlenose, Lakeshine, and Otter-splash padded out behind him and watched the ThunderClan cats through narrowed eyes, not hiding their distrust.

Crookedstar frowned at Fireheart. "Tell us what happened," he ordered.

Fireheart dipped his head and began to explain. Leopardfur let her hackles fall. At least the ThunderClan tom was showing some respect as he told the RiverClan leader how he and Graystripe had found the kits stranded on a mat of debris floating at the river's edge.

Blackclaw's tail was still twitching, but Leopardfur found herself convinced by Fireheart's story. If they'd wanted to steal the kits, why carry them to the flooded camp? There were quicker ways back to the ThunderClan border. Besides, why would ThunderClan *want* RiverClan kits? Especially in leaf-bare when a Clan had enough trouble feeding its own?

But Silverstream was the first cat to comment. "It makes sense," she mewed. "We saw them being washed away. It's believable that they were swept along the river to where you found them."

Leopardfur shifted her paws. She guessed that Silverstream was more interested in convincing her Clanmates that Graystripe was innocent than in discovering the truth. But Graypool looked convinced too. And Beetlenose, Lakeshine, and Ottersplash were looking gratefully at the ThunderClan toms. Only Blackclaw watched the ThunderClan toms with any kind of hostility. He was probably angry that another Clan had rescued his kits for him. Leopardfur felt a twinge of sympathy for her Clanmate. She knew that even though he must be thankful his kits were alive, his pride must be hurt. The sooner Fireheart and Graystripe left, the better. She was relieved when Crookedstar bowed his head.

"We're grateful to you." His mew was polite but grudging, as though he too was uncomfortable being indebted to another Clan.

Mistyfoot looked up, her gaze soft with gratitude. "Without you, my kits would have died."

Blackclaw's ear twitched irritably.

Fireheart dipped his head. "Is there anything we can do for you? If you can't go back to camp and prey's scarce because of the flood . . ."

How dare he pity us. Leopardfur watched Crookedstar without moving. Would he accept help from this arrogant kittypet?

"We need no help from ThunderClan," Crookedstar growled. She was relieved as he went on. "RiverClan cats can look after themselves."

"Don't be such a fool."

Graypool's mew took Leopardfur by surprise. She jerked her head toward the elder.

"You're too proud for your own good," the old she-cat rasped. "How can we feed ourselves? The river's too fierce to fish and it's practically poisoned; you know it is."

"What?" Graystripe exclaimed.

Graypool explained. "It's all the fault of Twolegs," she mewed. "It's filthy with trash from a Twoleg camp."

"The fish are poisoned," Mudfur added. "Cats who eat them fall ill."

"Then let us help." Fireheart was gushing with good intentions. Leopardfur narrowed her eyes. Were all kittypets this ignorant about warrior pride? "We'll catch prey for you in our territory," he went on, "and bring it to you, until the floods have gone and the river's clean."

Didn't he care about the warrior code at all? Perhaps he didn't even realize he was breaking it. Leopardfur watched Graystripe, wondering if he'd object. Bluestar would never approve of her warriors giving ThunderClan prey to River-Clan. But Graystripe said nothing.

Crookedstar's eyes glittered with suspicion. "Would you really do this for us?"

"Yes." Fireheart puffed out his chest, clearly pleased with himself.

"I'll help too," promised Graystripe. He looked at Silverstream. Leopardfur was relieved that she looked away.

"Then the Clan thanks you," Crookedstar grunted. "None of my cats will challenge you until the floods go down and we can return to our camp. But after that, we will fend for ourselves again."

Leopardfur watched him turn away and hurried after him through the bracken. "Are you really going to let them hunt for us?" Her pelt prickled with unease.

"If they're foolish enough to break the warrior code for anther Clan, let them." He stopped as the bracken opened onto the makeshift camp. Vixenleap and Shadepelt were still working on the dens. Skyheart was carrying a soggy mouse to Mosspelt's den. Crookedstar met her gaze. "You can't deny that we need help."

She held his gaze for a moment. "No," she mewed. He was

right. It would be foolish to let their Clanmates go hungry because of pride. And Fireheart was taking the risk, not them. But anger pricked in her paws. How had RiverClan become too desperate to be proud?

Crookedstar padded away and began to help Vixenleap thread a willow stem through the branches of a bush.

Leopardfur watched him, her thoughts churning. Would ThunderClan hold this over RiverClan in the future? And how would it look to the other Clans if they found out? She shook out her pelt. What would she have done in Fireheart's place? She frowned. She wasn't sure. She wasn't sure *any* other warrior would do what he had.

Suspicion gnawed at her belly and she glanced back at the bracken. Fireheart and Graystripe would be heading home. Were they really just trying to help?

CHAPTER 22

In the quarter moon that followed, Perchkit and Pikekit recovered and Crookedstar seemed stronger than ever. He took the lead in rebuilding the camp, organizing the gathering of willow and reeds to weave into dens and patch the camp wall, and left Leopardfur to make sure the patrols brought back enough prey to feed the Clan. While the work was being done, the Clan slept in the temporary camp upslope. Leopardfur wondered if Crookedstar was delaying the move back to the island, fearing the river a little more than before.

She pushed the thought away. RiverClan cats must never fear the river. It fed them and protected them from attack. It was their ally, not their enemy. But would Mosspelt ever believe that again? It had stolen her mate and two of their kits, and she barely left her nest now, except to fetch food for Dawnkit when she cried.

Catching enough prey had been hard. There'd been a glut of fish at first, left stranded when the water had receded, but most had rotted before they could be eaten, and the flood had left the river empty of prey. The water meadow was still completely underwater and couldn't be hunted yet. Leopardfur had found herself increasingly thankful for the prey Graystripe and Fireheart brought from the ThunderClan forest. But the more thankful she felt, the more resentful she became. It was humiliating to be so dependent on another Clan.

She slid from her nest, hidden among ferns, and glanced around the hillside camp. She was still sleepy after her nap and stretched to wake herself up. The morning patrol had taken her far upriver. She'd wanted to see if the fish were returning. There were one or two darting in the water, but she hadn't let the patrol catch them. Like the Clan, the river needed the chance to recover from the flood; then there would be more fish to hunt as leaf-bare dragged on through another moon.

Vixenleap and Emberdawn were sharing a vole beside their den in a laurel bush. Vixenleap hooked a sliver of bone from between her teeth. "I still can't believe ThunderClan has been sheltering Brokenstar all this time." She was still clearly unsettled by last night's Gathering.

Emberdawn finished chewing. "I thought Nightstar was going to have a fit."

Leopardfur padded toward them. "He's Brokentail now that Nightstar is ShadowClan's leader," she reminded them.

Emberdawn frowned at her, puzzled. "Does that mean he doesn't have nine lives anymore?"

Leopardfur sat down. "I guess not."

"At least the alliance between WindClan and Thunder-Clan has been broken," Vixenleap mewed. "Did you see how mad Tallstar was at Bluestar?"

"*Crookedstar's* the only one who stayed calm," Emberdawn added.

"Brokentail never threatened RiverClan kits—" Vixenleap

paused, catching Leopardfur's eye guiltily. She must be worried that it was too soon to talk of kits while Mosspelt was still mourning.

Leopardfur blinked at her reassuringly. "I guess that's one thing we didn't have to deal with."

"It looked like there was going to be a fight," Emberdawn mewed. "The way the warriors were hissing at each other. And the leaders didn't even try to calm the situation."

"I thought StarClan would cover the moon, but they didn't." Vixenleap pushed the remains of the vole away as though she were suddenly no longer hungry. "Perhaps they *wanted* to see if the Clans would fight."

"There would have been a fight if Crookedstar hadn't made sure ThunderClan had safe passage out of Fourtrees." Leopardfur still felt the anxiety that had prickled through her fur as Crookedstar ordered RiverClan to guard the Thunder-Clan slope so that Bluestar could lead her warriors home. She'd been relieved that WindClan and ShadowClan hadn't challenged them.

"I hope ShadowClan and WindClan don't hold it against us," Vixenleap fretted.

"I guess we *had* to support ThunderClan." Emberdawn's pelt twitched. "After Fireheart and Graystripe have shared so much prey with us."

Vixenleap gave her a warning look. The ThunderClan cats' gift of prey was a touchy subject with the whole Clan. No warrior liked to depend on another Clan.

"It's okay," Leopardfur told her. "We might as well admit it to ourselves, even if we can't let ThunderClan find out."

"Why are Fireheart and Graystripe taking such a risk for us?" Emberdawn's eyes rounded with curiosity. "Bluestar will have their pelts if she finds out they've been feeding another Clan."

"Let's hope they're just being softhearted." Leopardfur guessed that Graystripe was doing it out of concern for Silverstream, but that didn't explain why Fireheart was being so generous. Was he really just being a loyal friend, or was he more like Tigerclaw, with a plan of his own playing out in the background? She pressed back a shudder. Her instinct told her that ThunderClan was not to be trusted. And yet, without the daily deliveries of ThunderClan prey, RiverClan would have gone hungry.

Leopardfur paced along the shore and glanced through the forest toward the ThunderClan border. "Where are they?"

The sun was near the horizon, and Fireheart and Graystripe still hadn't appeared with the day's offering of prey.

Stonefur and Beetlenose followed her gaze, their pelts twitching uneasily.

Silverstream padded toward the trees, her eyes rounding with worry. "I hope they're okay."

"Why wouldn't they be okay?" Leopardfur grunted. "They're only carrying a bit of prey through the forest."

Silverstream blinked at her. "They're carrying it across the border," she mewed. "What if they've been caught?"

Leopardfur didn't care. The ThunderClan toms had made a promise and now they'd broken it. It was typical of Thunder-Clan. Perhaps they'd just wanted to make RiverClan depend on them so they could let them down. "I don't know why I ever trusted them."

Beetlenose flexed his claws. "They're probably watching us right now, purring their whiskers off because they made us wait."

Stonefur was frowning. "Silverstream might be right."

Leopardfur glared at him. Did he expect her to feel sympathy for Fireheart and Graystripe? Guilt pricked her belly. Perhaps she should. They had fed her Clan, after all. *Don't be pathetic,* she told herself. She lashed her tail. "Let's not wait any longer," she mewed. "This might be a trap."

Stonefur looked disappointed. "Shall we hunt along the shore and see if we can catch something to take back to the Clan?"

"Good idea." Leopardfur began to follow the two toms as Stonefur and Beetlenose headed upriver.

Silverstream called her back. "Leopardfur, wait."

She turned, surprised to see how worried Silverstream looked.

The silver tabby's ears were twitching nervously. "Did you tell them not to come?" she asked Leopardfur as Stonefur and Beetlenose disappeared behind reeds.

"Why would I?" Leopardfur tipped her head.

"I know you don't like taking prey from them," Silverstream mewed. "And you hate Graystripe crossing the border."

"If I had stopped them from coming, I'd have been honest about it." Leopardfur was annoyed. "I wouldn't have made Stonefur and Beetlenose wait for nothing."

Silverstream looked again into the forest. Had she been *hoping* Leopardfur was the reason they'd not come? Anything else could mean Graystripe was in trouble. Or that he'd broken his promise to her Clanmates.

Leopardfur felt a glimmer of sympathy for the silver she-cat. "I'm sure he's fine," she mewed. "They probably had other duties today that kept them busy." She padded closer. "It might be for the best." Part of her felt relieved. "We can't keep taking ThunderClan prey forever. We need to fill our own bellies."

Silverstream's eyes still glistened with worry.

"It'll be easier for you if he doesn't come anymore," Leopardfur urged gently. "It's time you started to get over him."

Silverstream stiffened. "I don't *want* to get over him!" Her anger took Leopardfur by surprise. "I'm having his kits!"

Leopardfur felt the cold breeze reach through her pelt. "What?" She stared at Silverstream. This couldn't be true! "You can't be!"

"Yes, I can," Silverstream told her. She stared at Leopardfur. No shame showed in her eyes. "I'm having them and I'm glad."

"How could you!" Leopardfur bristled with alarm. "Don't you know the trouble this will cause! You might drag your Clan into a fight."

"Don't be silly," Silverstream told her. "When I have these kits, the truth will be between me and Graystripe."

"How can you be so dumb?" Leopardfur snapped. "These kits will be half-ThunderClan. Where are you going to raise them? What if Graystripe claims them?"

"He'd never do that!"

"Are you sure?"

"Of course I'm sure."

Was Silverstream really that naive? "How will you explain the kits to your Clanmates?" Leopardfur thoughts were spinning. "You have no mate."

"I have Graystripe."

"You have no *RiverClan* mate!" How did Silverstream think this was going to play out? "Do you think your Clanmates will be happy to raise ThunderClan kits? Do you think Thunder-Clan will *let* you? We could end up at war over them!"

"Who would go to war over kits?" Silverstream snapped. "They're mine and Graystripe's. Our Clans have nothing to do with them."

Leopardfur stared at her. How had Crookedstar raised such a mouse-brain? "Don't tell anyone you're expecting," she growled.

"They're going to notice," Silverstream retorted.

"Then don't say who the father is."

"I'm not denying my relationship with Graystripe!" Silverstream's hackles lifted. "I love him. What don't you understand about that?" Her lip curled. "Oh, I forgot. You think being deputy is more important than love."

"Isn't it?" Leopardfur wanted to claw the silly young warrior's muzzle. Her words brought back a memory of Frogleap's death, and a fresh tear in her heart. But she pushed the feeling down, measuring her next words. "Fine." She steadied her breath. "I want you to end your relationship with Graystripe.

Tell him you will never see him again."

"No!" Silverstream glared at her. "I can't do that."

"Then take yourself to ThunderClan," Leopardfur snapped. "Throw yourself on the mercy of those fox-hearts. See how welcome they make you." She couldn't imagine ThunderClan taking the silver tabby in. Why would they? Silverstream clearly couldn't be trusted, even by the Clan she'd been raised in. "Perhaps ThunderClan likes half-Clan kits."

"Okay." Silverstream narrowed her eyes. "I will." Leopardfur froze as Silverstream went on. "And I'll tell Crookedstar whose kits they are. I'll tell him I love Gray—"

"No!" Leopardfur cut in. Didn't Silverstream realize she'd be exiled forever? RiverClan would have to throw her out. ThunderClan would never take her in. She'd become a rogue. *I can't let that happen!* She stopped her tail from trembling. "Okay," she mewed. "I won't tell anyone. You can sort it out in your own way. Just don't say anything to Crookedstar." She stared pleadingly at Silverstream. "Keep quiet for as long as you can." Perhaps she could find a way around it. Perhaps, if she broke the news gently enough to Crookedstar, and carefully prepared their Clanmates, Silverstream would be allowed to stay. But what about the kits? Would Graystripe let RiverClan raise them? Would Bluestar? Her heart was pounding. She'd been right all along to choose being deputy over love. Look at the trouble cats caused when they let their hearts make decisions.

CHAPTER 23

Leopardfur surveyed the camp. There were no puddles left in the clearing, and the reed wall had been patched. She sat down and swept her tail over her paws, feeling pleased for the first time in days. The dens were freshly woven, and new nests, clean and dry, were ready for the Clan's first night back on the island. It felt strange to see the nursery beside the elders' den, but it made more sense to build it on higher ground.

Perchkit and Pikekit were playing moss-ball outside. Primrosekit and Reedkit were wrestling nearby. It was almost as if the flood had never happened. Only Dawnkit was still in the nursery, watching from the entrance. Her eyes were round, her fur fluffed out. She glanced back inside, as though wondering whether Mosspelt would allow her to join in the other kits' games.

Leopardfur wondered if she should talk to the tortoiseshell queen and remind her that Dawnkit needed to play. *Warrior skills begin in the nursery.* Every Clan cat knew that the games kits played were more than games; they were first steps every cat took on the path to their warrior naming ceremony. When kits played hide-and-seek, or fought in play battles, they were practicing skills they would use every day as a warrior. It was important for kits to hone these skills in a nonthreatening environment, before they began their apprentice training.

Dawnkit put a tentative paw outside and, when her mother didn't call her back, took another step.

"Here!" Primrosekit saw her and batted the moss ball toward her.

Dawnkit's eyes lit up and she pounced on it, her small tail sticking up excitedly.

Leopardfur purred. *I might be leader by the time they get their warrior names*, she thought as she watched the kits chase the ball, pushing each other and tumbling over. Her heart ached suddenly as she thought of the dangers these kits would face in the future. But the fish were returning to the river, the Twoleg trash had been cleared away, and newleaf would come eventually. *I'll protect them*, Leopardfur told herself. *Whatever comes, I'll protect them.*

The reed tunnel shivered and she jerked her head around. Which of the morning patrols had returned first? WindClan scent touched her nose. She stiffened. What was WindClan doing here?

Sedgecreek padded into camp, and Leopardfur flattened her ears as she saw Tallstar and Stagleap behind her, flanked by Beetlenose and Reedtail.

The kits stopped playing and stared at the WindClan cats.

"Who are they?" Perchkit whispered.

Pikekit padded forward a few steps. "Are you Thunder-Clan?" he asked boldly.

Tallstar swung his muzzle toward the dark gray kit and looked at him sternly. "I'm Tallstar," he mewed.

"He's the WindClan leader," Perchkit called out.

"The *leader!*" Primrosekit blinked, clearly impressed. "Why's he here?"

Leopardfur padded forward and narrowed her eyes. "Why *are* you here?" she asked Tallstar.

"You don't know?" He met her gaze, his mew sour, as though he'd come with a grievance.

"Fetch Crookedstar," Leopardfur told Sedgecreek.

The pale tabby dipped her head and hurried toward Crookedstar's den.

"He was waiting for us at the border," Reedtail explained.

"Unlike RiverClan," Tallstar mewed, "I ask *permission* to cross borders."

Leopardfur shifted her paws uneasily. Clearly, the WindClan leader had come with a grievance.

"Dawnkit!" Mosspelt appeared in the nursery entrance, her nose twitching anxiously. Her eyes widened as she saw Tallstar and she darted out. "I told you not to leave the nursery," she chided as she shooed Dawnkit inside.

"But I was bored," Dawnkit complained as she disappeared.

Crookedstar was crossing the clearing, Sedgecreek at his heels. "Tallstar." He stopped in front of the WindClan leader and nodded politely. His eyes glittered warily. "What brings you here?"

Tallstar narrowed his eyes. "There are RiverClan scents inside our border," he told Crookedstar.

Stagleap shot Leopardfur an accusing look. She felt a rush of indignation but forced her fur to stay flat.

Crookedstar turned his head. "Have you sent patrols across the border, Leopardfur?" He spoke lightly, as though he was sure she hadn't.

"Of course not," she told him. Why would she?

Satisfied, he turned back to Tallstar. "Neither have I," he mewed, his gaze unapologetic.

Tallstar bristled. "Are you accusing me of lying?"

"No," Crookedstar mewed. "But if RiverClan warriors have crossed the border, it wasn't on my orders, or Leopardfur's."

"And yet our prey has been taken." Tallstar's mewed deepened. "We've found blood near the scent line and the stench of your warriors near it."

Leopardfur's thoughts were racing. She didn't think Tallstar was lying, which meant one of her Clanmates had been taking prey from WindClan land. She didn't blame them. RiverClan had been hungry. But she didn't like her Clanmates deciding for themselves where to hunt, especially if it brought WindClan warriors to their camp.

Tallstar looked at her directly now. "There was a time when RiverClan considered our land to be their land," he mewed pointedly. "Perhaps they still do."

She met his gaze. Arguing would only make RiverClan seem cowardly. "RiverClan knows that the moor belongs to WindClan," she mewed. "But after the hardships we've been through this past moon, I won't condemn my warriors for crossing the border in search of prey. Letting kits go hungry seems to me to be a worse crime than trespassing."

Stagleap growled. "Or perhaps you're still hoping to give them a taste for moor prey."

She glared at him. Was he determined to turn this into a fight? She'd admitted that RiverClan might be at fault. What more did he want? "It won't happen again," she mewed stiffly. She'd make sure of that. There was no way she was going to be forced into apologizing to *WindClan*. They couldn't even keep hold of their own territory without ThunderClan's help.

Tallstar grunted. "I'm worried that RiverClan thinks that you established some sort of right to hunt on our land while we were gone."

Crookedstar fluffed out his fur. "Of course not," he mewed. "There has clearly been a mistake. But we know the moor belongs to WindClan now, and we will respect your borders in the future."

"It's just a shame you didn't respect them in the past," Stagleap grunted.

Leopardfur swallowed back anger. "Now that the river's back to normal, and the floodwater is gone, we have no need to hunt on your land."

"*Need* has nothing to do with it!" Tallstar's gaze flicked toward her. "No Clan should be hunting on our land, whatever their need."

Crookedstar lifted his muzzle. "I'm sorry my warriors have trespassed. It won't happen again."

"And will the trespassers be punished?" Tallstar growled. "They broke the warrior code."

"If I find out who crossed the border, I will speak to them—"

"*Speak* to them?" Tallstar interrupted the RiverClan leader. "They should be put on den-clearing duty for a moon!"

"I will deal with my warriors as I see fit." Crookedstar's eyes narrowed. "Are you sure you came here because of trespassing?" he asked. "Surely that could have waited until the next Gathering?"

"Why else would I come?" Tallstar snapped.

"Perhaps you're angry with us for protecting ThunderClan at the last Gathering. You and Nightstar seemed ready to claw their pelts off."

"That has nothing to do with it." Tallstar was bristling, and Leopardfur wondered if Crookedstar had touched a nerve. The WindClan leader had every right to resent Thunder-Clan. They had claimed to be his ally while harboring the cat that had driven them from their home. It must have come as a shock to learn that ThunderClan wasn't the friend Wind-Clan had thought it was, and Crookedstar had been the only leader to defend Bluestar's actions at the Gathering. Tall-star's resentment might have spread to include RiverClan. She glanced at the WindClan leader. Surely he could see that RiverClan wasn't anything like ThunderClan. ThunderClan only pretended to be honorable. They'd helped WindClan because it gave them a chance to feel superior and show off their power.

Tallstar's tail was flicking ominously. "If you're not going to punish the warriors that hunted on our land, then you should at least make up for the prey they stole."

"It's leaf-bare," Crookedstar growled. "How are we supposed to find extra—"

"Crookedstar." A mew sounded at the camp entrance. Mistyfoot stumbled in, her eyes glazed with shock.

Crookedstar turned to face her, his eyes wide as though she were a ghost. "Mistyfoot . . . is it . . . ?"

Leopardfur's belly tightened. Why did Crookedstar look fearful? What had happened?

Tallstar and Stagleap turned to look at the RiverClan queen. Sedgecreek hurried to meet her.

"Silverstream." Mistyfoot sounded like she could hardly say the name.

Leopardfur felt cold. Something bad had happened.

"Silverstream's dead," Mistyfoot mewed.

Leopardfur froze. *Dead? How? Why?* Thoughts flashed like lightning in her mind. Silverstream couldn't be dead. She was carrying kits! She looked at Crookedstar.

He was staring at Mistyfoot, barely seeing her. "Silverstream?" He swayed on his paws. "Dead?"

Leopardfur had to take charge. *Let them do the grieving while you keep them safe.* It was too late to save Silverstream. But she could get the Clan through this tragedy. "What happened?" she asked Mistyfoot.

Mistyfoot was staring in confusion at Tallstar, as though not knowing what to say in front of strangers.

Tallstar dipped his head, clearly having decency enough to know that he was not wanted here. "We'll talk about the border crossing another time," he mewed. "I'm sorry for your loss."

Crookedstar stared blankly as the WindClan leader turned and led Stagleap out of camp. "You'll get your prey," he mumbled as though barely aware they'd left.

Leopardfur struggled to hold back panic. How had Silverstream died? *Did I push her too hard into making a decision? Did she do something rash?* Her heart pounded. "Tell us what happened," she demanded, staring at Mistyfoot.

Mistyfoot glanced nervously at Crookedstar. There was an apology in her gaze.

"Tell us," Leopardfur ordered. Whatever the queen was going to reveal, Crookedstar would find out anyway.

Mistyfoot's eyes glistened with grief. "She gave birth to kits."

Crookedstar stared at her, his eyes narrowed.

Mistyfoot went on. "They fetched Cinderpaw, but Silverstream was bleeding too much." She swallowed. "They couldn't—"

"*They?*" Crookedstar was staring at her. "Who are *they?*"

"Fireheart and Graystripe," Mistyfoot told her.

Anger fizzed beneath Leopardfur's pelt. *Fireheart and Graystripe?* How were those two ThunderClan fox-hearts present at every one of RiverClan's tragedies? She knew Graystripe's connection to Silverstream, but why was the former kittypet involved?

"What do they have to do with it?" Leopardfur demanded as the RiverClan leader padded unsteadily toward Mistyfoot, his eyes bright with rage.

"Graystripe is the father," Mistyfoot mewed.

Leopardfur's eyes jumped to her leader. *So now the truth is out for every cat to see.* How would he react?

But Crookedstar didn't seem as angry as she would have expected. Perhaps grief had softened his fury. Instead, he looked lost. "Where are they now?" he mewed thickly.

"Graystripe took them to ThunderClan," Mistyfoot told him. "A ThunderClan queen is nursing them."

"And Silverstream?" Crookedstar sounded like he could hardly say the words.

"Graystripe buried her," Mistyfoot mewed. "At Sunning-rocks."

Leopardfur's shock hardened into anger. "He buried her?" *How dare he?* "By what right? She's not his kin! She's not even his Clan! They didn't even hold a vigil for her!" What kind of rogues were they? Didn't ThunderClan know that a warrior was supposed to have a vigil? Her pelt was bristling now. Rage fired through her. "She was our Clanmate, not his!" What had made ThunderClan so arrogant? They'd protected Wind-Clan while feeding their enemy, and now they were making decisions for RiverClan. And all the time, they acted like they were better than any other Clan. How dare they deny RiverClan the chance to mourn Silverstream? She glared at Mistyfoot. "He should have brought Silverstream and her kits home, where they belong!"

"Home?" Reedtail's pelt ruffled. "ThunderClan kits don't belong here."

Sedgecreek blinked at him. "But they're only half Thunder-Clan."

"Half is too much," Reedtail growled. "If ThunderClan wants them, they should keep them." He met Leopardfur's gaze. "And I won't be the only RiverClan cat to say so."

"If they do"—Crookedstar pushed himself to his paws and glowered at the pale gray tom—"they'll have to deal with me."

Reedtail dropped his gaze, but the fur was still prickling along his spine.

Crookedstar looked at Mistyfoot. "Take me to where Silverstream is buried," he mewed. "We will hold a vigil for her there."

Mistyfoot dipped her head and padded out of camp.

Leopardfur watched him follow her. "I'll wait for the patrols to return, then bring the Clan," she told him. She dreaded setting paw on Sunningrocks. It was full of memories. Cats she'd loved had been killed there in battle. And now Silverstream had died and been buried there. *I should have protected them better.*

Guilt wormed beneath her pelt. *I should have looked after Silverstream.* She'd tried, but she'd failed. She might even have driven the silver tabby to her death by forcing her to choose. Had she chosen Graystripe? Was that why she'd been at Sunningrocks instead of with her Clan? What would have happened if Leopardfur had simply promised to support her no matter what she did?

Leopardfur closed her eyes. The river chattered beyond the reeds. A warbler was singing there. Perhaps Mudfur had been right to doubt her. Perhaps she wasn't cut out to be deputy. Her heart ached. *I won't give up.* She opened her eyes. Perchkit was chasing the moss ball again while Pikekit and Primrose-kit chased after him. Silverstream's kits should grow up here,

beside their kin. They should learn what it was to be a River-
Clan cat.

She unsheathed her claws. *From now on, I'm going to get it right,*
she thought. *I'm going to do whatever it takes to keep my Clanmates safe.
All of them.* And she would begin by getting Silverstream's kits
back from ThunderClan.

The sun was dipping toward the horizon, bringing with it a
chill that reached through Leopardfur's pelt.

Ottersplash and Piketooth were weaving reeds, putting
the finishing touches on the warriors' den. Mosspelt was
sitting outside the nursery, picking apart a trout to give the
softest flesh to the kits while Mistyfoot watched distractedly.
Around the clearing, the rest of the Clan was settling down to
its evening meal, but they were on edge. Every cat had one eye
on the setting sun, and Leopardfur couldn't sit still.

Mistyfoot got to her paws. "I'll be back soon with some
new friends," she told her kits before she crossed the clearing
and stopped beside Leopardfur. "Are you ready?"

Leopardfur nodded. "Yes."

The past days had been difficult. The long vigil at Sunningrocks had made her heart ache, and she hadn't been able to
shake the thought that she could have prevented Silverstream's
death. Mudfur had told her that if a birth went badly, there
was little any cat could do. But perhaps, if Silverstream had
been at home instead of at Sunningrocks with a ThunderClan
apprentice as her medicine cat, she might have lived.

Despite Crookedstar's threat, there had been a long

argument in RiverClan about whether they should demand that ThunderClan return Silverstream's kits. Anger still churned in Leopardfur's belly when she remembered how Reedtail had been only one of many voices calling for the kits to be left with ThunderClan. But it was clear to Leopardfur that Silverstream's kits belonged in RiverClan. No amount of ThunderClan blood would change that. How could her Clanmates even think about letting ThunderClan raise RiverClan warriors?

Thank StarClan Mosspelt had wanted them. She'd begged to be allowed to nurse them. And what cat would deny her after she'd lost Robinkit and Woodkit? After Mosspelt had spoken, even Reedtail had stopped arguing.

But Bluestar had been even harder to persuade. She had sent Leopardfur away the first time she'd led a patrol to ThunderClan to demand the kits back. But Leopardfur had persisted, and the second time she'd gone to the Thunder-Clan camp, Bluestar had conceded that the kits should grow up in their mother's Clan.

Graystripe had promised to bring them at sunset, and now the fiery sun was sinking into the reed bed. Would he keep his promise? He was ThunderClan after all.

Crookedstar was already waiting at the camp entrance as Leopardfur followed Mistyfoot around the clearing.

"Do you think ThunderClan has already named them?" he asked as they padded out of camp. He sounded as anxious as an apprentice waiting for his assessment.

"Who cares?" Leopardfur mewed. "We'll give them

good RiverClan names, whatever they've been called in the ThunderClan camp."

Mistyfoot glanced at her. "We should give them names that suit *them,* not their Clan."

"We need ThunderClan to know that they're ours." Leopardfur headed toward the stepping-stones.

By the time they reached them, the moon was beginning to rise, and the river was a silvery ribbon that reflected the pale sky. In the twilight, Leopardfur could see Graystripe waiting on the other side of the river. Relief washed her pelt. He'd kept his promise. For the first time, she felt a twinge of sympathy for the ThunderClan tom. It wouldn't be easy to watch another Clan take his kits. But he'd made his nest when he'd become mates with a RiverClan warrior. Now he'd have to lie in it.

She stopped and nodded Mistyfoot forward. "You fetch them," she mewed. "We'll wait here." The queen knew Graystripe better than she did, and she didn't want to spook him at the last moment in case he changed his mind.

As Mistyfoot headed away, Crookedstar shifted his weight from one paw to another. She glanced at him. This would be the first time he'd meet Silverstream's kits. Was he scared he'd make the wrong impression? She felt a sudden rush of affection for him. He'd never been this nervous waiting for a battle.

A few moments later, Mistyfoot was hopping back across the stones, a kit dangling from her jaws. Graystripe was following with the other one. She stopped as she reached Crookedstar and placed a small, dark gray tom-kit at his paws. His pelt was thick and long like the RiverClan leader's, but his eyes were amber. As Crookedstar bent down to lick the kit's head, Graystripe hung back, the other kit wriggling as it swung beneath his chin.

Leopardfur beckoned him forward with a flick of her tail, impatience sparking in her pelt. He didn't move, and she glanced nervously at Mistyfoot. Had the ThunderClan tom changed his mind?

"He wants to speak to Crookedstar," Mistyfoot mewed softly.

"He can speak to both of us." Leopardfur didn't trust the ThunderClan tom any more than she'd trust a rat. Both looked harmless, but were dirty and unexpectedly vicious. She glared at Graystripe, remembering all the heartache he'd caused her Clan.

Crookedstar blinked at him. "We'll take good care of them," he promised. "They will be safe and loved, and they'll grow into strong warriors."

Graystripe padded closer. His eyes were glittering anxiously.

Leopardfur tensed. "You can put the kit down and go," she mewed sharply.

He leaned forward and dropped the second kit next to its littermate. It was a she-kit, as pretty as her mother, with blue eyes and a tail that promised to be like a plume of smoke. Crookedstar nuzzled her, purring.

But Leopardfur was still watching Graystripe distrustfully. "Say your good-byes." She tried not to sound too sharp, but she didn't want him to linger. The longer this took, the more chance there was that he'd change his mind.

Graystripe dipped his head, then looked earnestly at Crookedstar.

Leopardfur saw the RiverClan leader tense. Graystripe clearly had something important to say.

"I want to come with them," Graystripe mewed.

Crookedstar looked puzzled. "To the camp?"

Leopardfur cut in. "It's better to leave them here," she mewed. "You're not very popular in RiverClan."

"I know." Graystripe's gaze didn't waver. "And I don't care. I just want to be with my kits. I want to join RiverClan."

Leopardfur stared at him. Did he have bees in his brain? *No way!* She bit back the words. It was up to Crookedstar to tell this ThunderClan tom that RiverClan didn't let enemy warriors join. She blinked at Crookedstar expectantly, but was surprised to see the old tom gazing thoughtfully at Graystripe.

Is he actually wondering whether to agree? "Crookedstar, we should go," she mewed. "The Clan will be waiting to meet Silverstream's kits." *And they won't be waiting for an ugly great ThunderClan tom.*

Crookedstar swished his tail, signaling her to be quiet. His gaze was still on Graystripe.

Mistyfoot watched, her ears twitching anxiously.

"Are you willing to swear complete and unwavering loyalty to RiverClan?" Crookedstar asked Graystripe.

Leopardfur bristled. "What are you saying? Are going to let him join?"

Crookedstar ignored her and went on. "Will you hunt for

RiverClan? Will you protect RiverClan? Will you fight for RiverClan?"

Graystripe held the RiverClan leader's gaze. "Yes."

"Even against ThunderClan?"

Graystripe swallowed. "If it means being with my kits, yes," he mewed. "I swear it. I loved Silverstream with all my heart. I always will. My kits are RiverClan and I will be too."

Leopardfur swallowed back outrage. This was madness. She had to reason with Crookedstar. "He's a ThunderClan warrior," she told him. "He killed Whiteclaw—"

"I didn't kill him!" Graystripe interrupted. "It was an accident."

He was still making excuses! Leopardfur glared at Crookedstar. "How can you trust him so easily? He could swear anything just to worm his way into our camp. You might as well invite a fox to sleep in the warriors' den."

Crookedstar turned his emerald-green gaze on her. The she-kit was sniffing his paws while the tom-kit padded beneath his belly. "I believe him," he mewed. "Some fathers will do anything to protect their kits."

"They won't need protecting! They'll be with us!" Leopardfur snapped.

"He wants what's best for his kits," Crookedstar mewed. "For *Silverstream's* kits. If he's willing to give up his Clan for them, doesn't that show his loyalty and his love, both for the kits and for Silverstream?"

Loyalty? Leopardfur stared at him. How was switching Clans loyal? Crookedstar was letting emotion sway him.

Would he feel the same way if these weren't his daughter's kits? Had he decided to trust Graystripe just because Silverstream had? She curled claws into the ground. "I think you're making a mistake," she growled.

Crookedstar didn't meet her gaze. "This is the best for the kits, and that's good enough for me."

What about the rest of the Clan? Leopardfur swallowed back her objection. She could see that Crookedstar had made up his mind. Pressing back anger, she dipped her head the RiverClan leader. "Okay," she mewed. "Let's take the kits home."

As Crookedstar picked up the she-kit and Mistyfoot grabbed the tom, Leopardfur shot Graystripe a warning look. She hadn't forgotten what had happened at the gorge. And she wouldn't be forgetting any time soon. She'd be keeping a very close eye on the ThunderClan tom, and the first mistake he made that endangered her Clan would be the last.

CHAPTER 24

❧

The full moon shone over the reed beds as though it had been guarding the camp while the patrol had been gone. Leopardfur followed Crookedstar from the river, slowly making their way home. Stonefur shook water from his pelt.

They had taken their time returning from the Gathering, relishing the breeze. It felt deliciously cool after another long hot day. The blazing greenleaf weather had brought prey and peace to RiverClan, and Leopardfur was pleased to see her Clanmates trekking back to camp ahead of her, plump and sleek in the moonlight.

Now that they had crossed the river, Leopardfur felt it was safe to speak her mind without being overheard. "Did anyone hear gossip about Tigerclaw?" She blinked hopefully at Stonefur.

He shook his head. "ThunderClan was tight-lipped," he told her. "They didn't say any more than Bluestar."

"And *she* only said that Tigerclaw had left ThunderClan and Fireheart was her new deputy." Leopardfur frowned.

"Did you ask Fireheart about it?" Crookedstar's eyes gleamed in the moonlight.

"Of course," she replied. "But he was evasive. He just said Tigerclaw was no longer a ThunderClan cat. He mostly wanted to know how Graystripe was." She glanced ahead to where the ThunderClan tom was padding toward camp with her Clanmates. It had been his first Gathering as a River-Clan warrior, and she wasn't sure which had been harder for the ThunderClan tom—leaving his kits or facing his former Clanmates.

She had to admit he'd tried hard to settle into his new Clan, and though his fishing skills were still poor, he brought back more than enough land prey to make up for it. He pretended not to notice when Reedtail and Blackclaw refused to eat it.

"Tigerclaw can't be dead," Crookedstar grunted. "They'd have told us."

"Yes." Stonefur nodded. "It would be the easiest way to explain his absence."

Leopardfur had been unsettled by the news of Tigerclaw's disappearance. She remembered his behavior in the battle over WindClan—how ruthless he'd seemed, how manipulating. And yet she had once felt a true connection with him. He was the only cat she'd ever met who'd been willing to talk about a different future for the Clans, and what their places might be in it. She'd quietly looked forward to seeing him at Gatherings, wondering each time what he would do or say, and while she hadn't fully trusted him in many moons, she'd still imagined herself becoming leader alongside him. It was hard not to admire his forward-thinking determination. *The Clans need fresh energy to sweep away old beliefs.* She still agreed with that. But, now that he was gone, who would help her shake things up?

She glanced at Stonefur. "I don't know why Bluestar didn't tell us everything." She swished her tail. "Tigerclaw's disappearance might affect us all."

Stonefur's eyes were dark with worry. "Could it be linked with the rogues that have been seen in the forest?"

Leopardfur looked at Stonefur, surprised. Not long before Graystripe and his kits had joined RiverClan, she had been part of a group of RiverClan cats sent to help ThunderClan fight off a group of rogues. The cats had been strong fighters, for rogues—but could they best Tigerclaw?

Crookedstar pricked his ears. "How?"

"Perhaps they kidnapped him," Stonefur guessed.

"Why would they?" Leopardfur glanced at him. The gray tom was grasping for butterflies. "Besides, I can't imagine rogues would be able to hold a warrior like Tigerclaw."

"He might have caught the sickness that's been hurting ShadowClan," Stonefur mewed. "Maybe ThunderClan sent him away to stop it spreading."

"That would be harsh, even for ThunderClan," Leopardfur mewed.

"But why keep the reason for his disappearance a secret?" Stonefur looked puzzled.

Crookedstar grunted. "There's no point in guessing," he mewed. "I'm sure Bluestar has her reasons." He hurried ahead and caught up to his Clanmates.

Leopardfur sighed. She'd been hoping he'd say something

about a kittypet becoming ThunderClan's deputy. The thought made her claws itch with annoyance. She hadn't forgotten that Fireheart had been present at the scene of Silverstream's death, or the strange scene when he and Graystripe had turned up during the flood with Pikekit and Perchkit. She had appreciated the prey they'd brought then, but knowing what had come afterward, she couldn't help but question their motives. Besides, how could a kittypet lead *warriors*? And Fireheart was so self-righteous. He acted like he wouldn't take prey from a kit. But he'd clearly been quietly working to become Bluestar's most trusted warrior. At least Tigerclaw had been honest about his ambition. Leopardfur shuddered at the thought of standing next to Fireheart on the Great Rock one day. A *kittypet*, for StarClan's sake! How humiliating. Standing beside Tigerclaw would have been far more dignified.

The juicy carp between Leopardfur's jaws was making her mouth water. Ottersplash and Blackclaw padded beside her, holding their catch. The hunt had gone well, but then, it was hard *not* to catch fish when the days were so warm. The carp had practically swum into her mouth.

Ottersplash stopped as they neared the camp, and Leopardfur stiffened when the sleek ginger she-cat dropped her fish and looked around, her nose twitching.

"What do you smell?" Leopardfur laid her own fish on the ground.

"Blood."

Blood? Before she could taste the air, the reeds rustled behind them.

Graystripe padded out. His pelt was ragged where a clump of fur had been torn out. Stonefur and Skyheart were with him, their muzzles scratched, their ears torn.

"Fetch Mudfur," Leopardfur told Blackclaw. She darted toward the patrol, sniffing their wounds anxiously. "What happened?"

"We were patrolling near Fourtrees," Stonefur told her. His ragged ear was twitching. "We heard yowling and went to check. A ThunderClan patrol was being attacked by . . ." He hesitated, his eyes glittering. "By rogues."

Why did he look so shocked? "We know rogues are roaming the forest," she mewed.

Stonefur shivered. "Tigerclaw was with them."

Tigerclaw? Her gaze flitted to Graystripe. "Did you know about this?"

His pelt ruffled. "Why would *I* know?"

Because you're ThunderClan. The words were on the tip of her tongue, but she bit them back. Even she had to admit that he had been a loyal RiverClan warrior since he'd joined them—at least as far as they knew. She looked back at Stonefur. "Did you drive them off?"

"Of course." Stonefur shook out his pelt. "But they fought hard. Tigerclaw had clearly taught them warrior moves."

Leopardfur's belly tightened. "Why would Tigerclaw attack his own Clan with a bunch of rogues?" She didn't expect an answer. She could barely believe it was true.

Something must have driven him to it.

She looked at Graystripe again. He must know more than he'd told them about what had gone on in the Thunder-Clan camp. "Why did Tigerclaw leave ThunderClan?" she demanded.

"I don't know." Graystripe held her gaze. But she could see he was uneasy. His ear was twitching.

"Did he say anything before he left?" she pressed. "Something that might explain why he's fighting alongside rogues?"

"He didn't say anything," Graystripe dropped his gaze. "He just left."

Was he telling the truth? "You're a RiverClan cat now," she growled. "You can't keep ThunderClan's secrets if it means putting RiverClan in danger."

Graystripe shifted his paws. "I really don't know what Tigerclaw is up to or why he's fighting alongside rogues."

Blackclaw was hurrying back from the camp with Mudfur. The medicine cat held a leaf wrap and cobweb in his jaws. He slid past Leopardfur and began examining the injured patrol.

"Sit down," he told Skyheart, and began smearing a poultice from the leaf warp onto the deepest claw marks beside her muzzle.

Leopardfur frowned. She needed to tell Crookedstar. It was one thing having rogues in the forest; it was another if they were led by Tigerclaw and using warrior battle skills. What could the former ThunderClan deputy be up to? Her pelt ruffled.

She couldn't help feeling there was something Graystripe

wasn't telling her. Tigerclaw had only wanted the best for his Clan. Why would he leave? He'd been planning to become leader and make the Clans stronger and better than they'd ever been. Why would he *attack* them? And with *rogues*?

Her tail quivered. None of this made sense.

Leopardfur lifted her head. An acrid scent had woken her. She blinked and stared into the darkness. What was it?

"Leopardfur!" Loudbelly called through the entrance. His mew was taut. The other nests rustled. Sedgecreek and Vixenleap jerked awake.

Leopardfur scrambled from her nest. "What's happened?"

"Quick!" Loudbelly ducked outside and Leopardfur followed him. The night air was tainted with the smell of smoke.

The dark brown tom blinked at her, fear in his eyes. "There's a fire."

"Where?" Leopardfur flinched as a bolt of lightning streaked across the sky.

"The other side of the river." Loudbelly stared at the trees beyond the reed beds. As Leopardfur followed his gaze, thunder rumbled over the forest. Beyond the river, an orange glow lit the sky.

The Clan began to hurry from their dens, looking around in alarm as smoke drifted across the camp. Graystripe was already awake, pacing in front of the nursery.

"There's fire in the forest," Leopardfur told them. "But it can't leap the river."

Graystripe blinked at her. "What about ThunderClan?"

Crookedstar was crossing the clearing. "Is every cat safe?"

"Yes." Leopardfur hurried to meet him. "There's a fire, but it's on the other side of the river."

"ThunderClan is in danger," Graystripe mewed.

"We must—" Crookedstar broke off, coughing as smoke billowed around him.

Graystripe's pelt was bristling with panic. "We have to help them!"

"You want us to run into a fire?" Loudbelly stared at him as another flash of lightning lit the ThunderClan warrior's frightened face.

"We can't let them die!"

As thunder that rolled around the sky, Crookedstar recovered himself. "Take a patrol to the river," he told Leopardfur. "See what you can do."

Gratitude glowed in Graystripe's eyes.

Leopardfur nodded. She still didn't trust Graystripe, but she could imagine what it felt like to see the Clan you'd been born into in crisis. ThunderClan wasn't their ally, but no warrior should be left to die in a fire. "Graystripe, Blackclaw, Loudbelly," she mewed. "Come with me. Mudfur." She nodded to her father. "You come too. There might be injured cats. And Heavystep, I want you with us."

As the young tom hurried to join the patrol, Leopardfur sprinted out of camp. She led them through the darkness toward the river and burst out on the bank.

ThunderClan's forest was burning. Between the trees, Leopardfur could see the orange glow of fire and hear the roar of it, like a storm howling toward the river. ThunderClan warriors were pacing the shore. Some had already waded in and were struggling to cross.

"Help them," she ordered.

Heavystep dived into the river. He grabbed a floundering ThunderClan she-cat by the scruff and dragged her back to the bank. Blackclaw splashed through the shallows and helped a tom from the water.

Runningwind was struggling toward the shore. Leopardfur waded in and put her shoulder beneath his, guiding him onto dry land.

A yowl made her turn. Further upstream, orange fur flashed in the water. Fireheart was holding an elder, the current sweeping them rapidly downstream. His eyes flashed with panic, and he disappeared beneath the surface as the elder fought to keep his muzzle above the water.

A RiverClan kit could swim better! Leopardfur splashed through the shallows as they sped toward her and dug her paws into the mud. Bracing herself, she reached out and grabbed the elder as he swirled past. She turned and dropped him near the shore, then turned back to grasp Fireheart's scruff between her teeth. With a growl, she hauled the ThunderClan deputy onto the slippery bank, and held on until he'd found his paws.

"Thank you," he spluttered, pulling free.

The bedraggled elder coughed up water beside him, but Leopardfur was scanning the river for more ThunderClan cats.

"Maybe it's time ThunderClan learned to swim," she grunted. She couldn't see any more pelts in the water. "Is that every cat?" she asked Fireheart.

Water was streaming from his whiskers. He took a moment to catch his breath, then looked along the RiverClan shore where his Clanmates were huddled like frightened mice. "I th-think so," he stammered.

"What about that one?" A black-and-white shape lay unmoving on the far shore. The ferns beyond it were on fire.

"That's Patchpelt." Fireheart was trembling. "He's dead."

Leopardfur pushed out into the river. She wasn't going to leave a warrior's body to be burned. It deserved a proper burial. She crossed the river, dodging the sparks that popped and fizzed in the water around her, snatched the dead tom from the shore, and paddled back through the black water. Lightning arced overhead. Thunder cracked and Fireheart flinched, but Leopardfur didn't stop swimming.

She hauled Patchpelt's body onto the shore and laid it at Fireheart's paws. A growl rose in her throat. Graystripe was weaving around the ThunderClan deputy like a kit who'd just found its mother. Separation had clearly done nothing to diminish their friendship. Leopardfur narrowed her eyes but said nothing. It would keep.

She noticed Bluestar lying on the bank a few tail-lengths away. The ThunderClan leader wasn't moving. Had she lost a life? Leopardfur padded toward her and sniffed her wet pelt. The old she-cat was breathing, but she looked like no more than a bundle of fur and bones.

Rain was beginning to fall, great heavy drops that promised a downpour, and wind was blowing the sparks and smoke back toward the forest. They would be safe now.

Leopardfur glanced at Patchpelt's body. "Come on," she mewed to Fireheart. "We'll bury him back at camp."

He blinked at her, confused. "The *RiverClan* camp?"

His words burst forth a new flood of rage in her heart. All she could think of was Silverstream, and how he'd arrogantly helped to bury her body at Sunningrocks rather than give her Clan the chance to mourn and bury her. She was better than that. "Unless you'd prefer to return to your own."

"Thank you." As he dipped his head, Cinderpelt crouched beside Bluestar.

"She's swallowed a lot of water," the ThunderClan medicine cat mewed.

Leopardfur called to Mudfur. "Come and check on Bluestar." He'd had more experience with half-drowned cats than Cinderpelt.

As Mudfur hurried off, Fireheart began to move among his warriors, checking for injuries and making sure they could walk. Leopardfur watched him. He was worried about his Clanmates, which was impressive for a kittypet. But he still irritated her. She waited as the ThunderClan cats gathered themselves. Mudfur helped Bluestar to her paws. Graystripe lifted Patchpelt's body in his jaws.

"Ready?" Leopardfur nodded to Fireheart.

"Yes," Fireheart replied.

She turned and began to lead the smoke-blackened and

drenched ThunderClan warriors back to camp.

The rain was falling heavily as they reached it, pounding the river and drenching the dens. Crookedstar was waiting for them in the clearing. His eyes were rheumy and his pelt was ruffled, and Leopardfur wondered if he'd been coughing again. He scanned the ThunderClan cats, then looked at her anxiously. "Is RiverClan safe?"

"The fire won't cross the river," she told him. He looked relieved as she added, "Especially now that the wind has changed."

Crookedstar blinked expectantly at Bluestar as Cinderpelt and Mudfur guided her into the camp. She looked at him hazily, but before she could speak, Fireheart stepped forward.

"Leopardfur and her patrol showed great kindness and courage in helping us flee the fire," he mewed to Crookedstar. Above him, lightning flickered across the sky and thunder rumbled in the distance, rolling away from the forest.

Crookedstar dipped his head. "Leopardfur was right to help you. All Clans fear fire."

"Our camp was burned and our territory is still on fire," Fireheart went on, blinking away the rain that streamed into his eyes. "We have nowhere to go."

Was he throwing himself on the mercy of RiverClan? Leopardfur narrowed her eyes. At least he was ready to admit his Clan's weakness.

Crookedstar watched him for a moment, then spoke. "You may stay until it's safe for you to return."

Fireheart blinked at him gratefully. "Thank you."

Leopardfur glanced at Graystripe as he laid Patchpelt's

body at the edge of the clearing. She wondered how he felt, surrounded by former Clanmates. Was he pleased to see them? What did *they* think, seeing him in his RiverClan home?

Rain was soaking Patchpelt's body and Leopardfur felt a twinge of pity for the dead warrior. She looked at Fireheart. "Would you like us to bury your elder?"

"You are very generous," Fireheart answered. "But Patchpelt should be buried by his own Clan."

Leopardfur bristled. *By his own Clan.* He'd let Graystripe bury Silverstream at Sunningrocks. Didn't he think she would have liked the same respect? "Very well," she mewed sharply. "I'll have his body moved outside camp so that your elders may sit vigil with him in peace." She glanced at Bluestar. The ThunderClan leader was huddled on the ground and looked pitiful beside Crookedstar. Surely she'd coughed up the water by now. "Is Bluestar injured?" she asked Fireheart.

"The smoke was very bad." There was something careful in his tone. "She was among the last to leave the camp." He dipped his head politely. "Excuse me, I must see to my Clan."

Leopardfur watched him pad away, her ears twitching. Was he trying to hide something? As she wondered what it could be, she noticed Graystripe checking on the ThunderClan cats. The gray warrior leaned close to each one, speaking softly, like a concerned medicine cat. He moved among them with an ease that was disconcerting. The ThunderClan cats were outsiders here, and yet he seemed as relaxed with them as he did with his own kits. She shifted her paws uneasily. Would he ever become a true RiverClan warrior?

* * *

The next day, the weather cleared. The ThunderClan cats still smelled of smoke despite the rain. Leopardfur kept to the edges of the camp, observing them with interest. She noticed how careful Cinderpelt was to keep the other cats away from Bluestar, though she asked for no herbs to treat the Thunder-Clan leader. She also noticed that Graystripe had left camp even before she'd assigned the patrols for the day. He'd returned with prey for his former Clanmates. He'd even taken Fireheart to the nursery to show off Featherkit and Stormkit. Should she have stopped him? She wanted to keep the taint of ThunderClan from Silverstream's kits as much as she could.

After sunhigh, Crookedstar beckoned to her from outside his den. She hurried to meet him.

"I think it's time we spoke to Bluestar," he mewed. The ThunderClan leader was lying in a patch of sunshine beside the camp wall. Cinderpelt hadn't left her side and was watching her own Clanmates as warily as RiverClan.

"If we can get past Cinderpelt," Leopardfur muttered. She followed Crookedstar across the clearing.

The medicine cat looked up as they reached her.

"How is Bluestar?" he asked.

"Recovering," she mewed.

Bluestar opened her eyes and sat up, fluffing out her pelt. She seemed fine, her sky-blue gaze fixing on him. "Thank you for taking us in," she mewed.

"The fire should be out by now," he told her. "After so much rain." Was he hinting that it was time ThunderClan should leave?

"I'll send a patrol to check," she mewed.

Graystripe was heading toward them as Fireheart watched from the camp entrance. He dipped his head his head to Crookedstar as he neared, but before he could speak, Bluestar hurried to meet him. "Graystripe, there you are!" She sounded pleased to see him. "Will you take a patrol to check the camp?" she mewed. "We should make sure it's safe before we return home."

Leopardfur narrowed her eyes. Bluestar was addressing him like a Clanmate. Had she forgotten he wasn't a Thunder-Clan warrior anymore?

Graystripe's pelt ruffled uneasily. "Fireheart has already suggested it." He seemed to be searching Bluestar's gaze. Was he wondering if she'd forgotten too? "But I need Crookedstar's permission to go with him."

Bluestar frowned, then glanced at Cinderpelt, as though for reassurance.

Cinderpelt blinked at her soothingly. "Fireheart will check the camp," she mewed.

"May I go with him?" Graystripe asked Crookedstar.

"Sure." Crookedstar nodded.

Leopardfur blinked at him. "Are you sure it's a good idea?" She wasn't as trusting as Crookedstar. "It might be better if he remembers his old home the way it was before the fire."

But Crookedstar whisked his tail. "If he wants to go, let him."

As the two friends headed out of camp, Leopardfur frowned. They shouldn't be left alone. What was to stop

Graystripe telling Fireheart about RiverClan's patrols and defenses? Even if he didn't mean to, he might let something slip while they were chatting. Especially if Fireheart asked the right questions.

She moved to follow them, but then stopped. She was needed here—and Fireheart would surely turn her away rather than allow the deputy of a rival Clan to see how devastated their territory must be now.

Still she paced, unable to settle, until Graystripe and Fireheart returned and reported that the ThunderClan camp was safe. They'd buried the few cats who hadn't made it out, and since the rest of their Clanmates were all well enough to walk, Bluestar decided it was time to return home.

As the ThunderClan cats circled impatiently in the growing darkness, Bluestar padded toward Crookedstar.

Leopardfur swallowed back a growl as she saw Fireheart lick Graystripe's shoulder and share a few final words before hurrying to take his place beside his leader.

"Thank you for your kindness and for sharing your prey," Bluestar mewed.

Crookedstar dipped his head. "We are all warriors at heart," he mewed. He sounded breathless, and Leopardstar wondered if the smoke he'd inhaled was still bothering him. She should ask Mudfur to take a look.

Bluestar lifted her tail. "ThunderClan is in your debt."

Leopardfur's ears pricked. She narrowed her eyes. It was a debt she would not forget. RiverClan had been generous to the Clan that had stolen Sunningrocks and caused the deaths of Whiteclaw, Sunfish, Whitefang, and Silverstream. And yet she suspected that only she and StarClan truly realized how much ThunderClan owed them. One day, RiverClan would ask for something in return, and when they did, she hoped that ThunderClan would be prepared to honor Bluestar's promise.

CHAPTER 25

"*Deadfoot.*" *Leopardfur dipped her head to* the WindClan deputy. The bright moonlight shining into the Fourtrees clearing gleamed on his black pelt. The air was cold with the first chill of leaf-fall, and, around them, WindClan and RiverClan cats mingled, chatting as they waited for ThunderClan and ShadowClan to arrive for the Gathering.

"Leopardfur." Deadfoot acknowledged her in return with a stiff nod.

"There's no need to be so formal." Leopardfur swished her tail. Was WindClan still holding a grudge just because a few of her warriors had strayed onto their land? She and Crooked-star had never been able to figure out which warriors had done it, distracted as they were by Silverstream's death and Gray-stripe's arrival with the kits. "We've repaid the prey that was taken."

"*Stolen,*" Deadfoot corrected. He lifted his chin. "Have the warriors who stole it been punished?"

"There's no need to punish them," Leopardfur lied, scanning the slopes. Where were ThunderClan and ShadowClan? "They won't do it again."

The WindClan deputy was clearly determined to be

prickly. ShadowClan and ThunderClan hadn't arrived yet, but she wasn't looking forward to chatting with their deputies, either. Suddenly she wished Tigerclaw were here. She missed him. She was still troubled by the news that he'd been fighting with rogues; when and why had he left ThunderClan?

Crookedstar looked frail on the Great Rock beside Tall-star. He hadn't recovered from breathing smoke from the fire and coughed more now than ever. Now he simply looked tired, even though the Gathering hadn't started. As she wondered if Bluestar had recovered, the bracken rustled on the far slope and ThunderClan streamed into the clearing. Leopard-fur narrowed her eyes. Fireheart was leading the patrol. Had Bluestar died? Her ears twitched nervously. What would StarClan think of a kittypet leading ThunderClan? Surely, they wouldn't approve! She sighed. When Tigerclaw had spoken to her about needing "new ideas" to lead the Clans, surely this was not what he'd meant. Had this kittypet's ambitions played a part in his leaving ThunderClan?

"Excuse me." Leopardfur nodded politely to Deadfoot and crossed the clearing, nosing her way through the crowd. She stopped as she reached Cinderpelt. She wanted to speak to the ThunderClan medicine cat before the Gathering began. "Where's Blue—"

Mudfur interrupted. "Don't worry," he mewed. "Bluestar's fine."

"She's still recovering from the fire," Cinderpelt told her.

Leopardfur felt puzzled. "But she wasn't injured." She had just seemed confused.

"She breathed a lot of smoke." Cinderpelt looked at the

Great Rock. Crookedstar was crouching beside Tallstar, his eyes half-closed. "It looks like Crookedstar's still feeling the aftereffects too."

Leopardfur's pet ruffled. Clearly, the ThunderClan medicine was gently warning her not to ask any more about Bluestar. Was she trying to hide something?

Leopardfur noticed Fireheart scanning the clearing. Was he looking for Graystripe? Leopardfur felt a twinge of satisfaction. She had told the former ThunderClan warrior not to come tonight. His concern for his former Clanmates in the RiverClan camp had worried her. He was still a little too close to them for comfort.

Dark pelts moved though the ferns on the slope behind her. *ShadowClan.* They'd brought more warriors than usual. Did that mean they'd finally recovered from the sickness? Where was Nightstar? She frowned. There was no sign of the ShadowClan leader, and some of the faces among the warriors looked unfamiliar.

Then, suddenly, her eyes landed on a face she recognized— but what? *How?* Her eyes widened as she stared at Tigerclaw. What was he doing here, among the ShadowClan cats? Was he planning to disrupt the Gathering? Interest sparked in her pelt as she watched him shoulder his way through the other Clans. He was heading toward the Great Rock.

Something unusual was going on here. Leopardfur nodded quickly to Mudfur and Cinderpelt and ducked away through the crowd. As she reached the Great Rock, she was surprised to see Blackfoot sitting beside Deadfoot. He'd been exiled with Brokenstar—what was he doing here? Where was Cinderfur? Leopardfur's ears twitched. And why hadn't Fireheart joined the other deputies? What was going on with Shadow-Clan and ThunderClan?

Blackfoot nodded to her politely, then turned his gaze toward Tigerclaw. Surprise sparked through Leopardfur's pelt as the dark warrior leaped onto the Great Rock. Murmurs of shock rippled around the gathered cats as Tigerclaw stared down at them.

"I'm pleased to be here with you at the Gathering this night." He spoke with quiet authority. Leopardfur pricked her ears as he went on. "I stand here before you as the new leader of ShadowClan. Nightstar died of the sickness that took so many of his Clan, and StarClan has named me as his successor."

ShadowClan's *leader*? As Leopardfur stared, Fireheart leaped up beside him.

"Our leader breathed smoke in the fire," The Thunder-Clan deputy told the cats below. "She's not well enough yet to travel, but she'll recover."

Leopardfur's thoughts were spinning. Was this how it would be now? Tigerstar leading ShadowClan and Fireheart standing in for Bluestar? And Fireheart was dipping his head to ShadowClan's new leader as though he was fine with it. She felt a glimmer of excitement mingled with trepidation. Was this Tigerstar's new way to shake up the Clans? If so, what was his ultimate goal—and how would it affect River-Clan? Crookedstar looked suddenly old beside the two young warriors, and Tallstar seemed small. Leopardfur shifted her paws, curiosity flickering in her chest. Despite her concerns about what all of this meant, one thought kept echoing in her mind: *What would it feel like to be up there too?*

"Crookedstar." Leopardfur poked her head into the River-Clan leader's den.

She had hoped to talk to him last night about Tigerstar's reappearance and his leadership of ShadowClan, but he'd seemed so worn out by the Gathering that she'd let him walk home in companionable silence. This morning, she hoped a good night's sleep would have restored him, but she found Mudfur with him.

Worry sparked in her belly. "Are you okay?" she asked Crookedstar as she slid into the den.

"Just tired," he answered. He coughed, and Mudfur put his ear to the RiverClan leader's chest.

"You should rest some more," Mudfur told him. "I'll bring you some tansy to chew." He glanced at Leopardfur. "Can you manage the Clan today?"

"Of course." She let him guide her from the den.

"Will he be okay?" she asked, glancing toward the trailing moss entrance.

"If he rests." Mudfur was frowning.

"I'll make sure he's not disturbed." She felt suddenly anxious. She knew that one day Crookedstar would lose his last life, but was that day soon? *Am I ready?* She'd been observing him closely these past moons, trying to learn all she could from him. But there was much more to learn. She just hoped StarClan would give Crookedstar time to teach her. *If not, I must be ready.* She padded across the clearing as Mudfur headed to the medicine den. Whatever happened, she must protect her Clan.

The reed tunnel shivered, and Blackclaw padded into camp. His pelt was rippling along his spine as he glanced uncertainly over his shoulder. Something was worrying the tom.

"Blackclaw?" As Leopardfur headed to meet him, a dark figure padded into camp after him.

"Tigerstar." She was surprised that he'd come alone.

"He was waiting at the border," Blackclaw explained. "He wants to speak with Crookedstar."

"Crookedstar's resting." She met Tigerstar's gaze. "I can give him your message."

Tigerstar tipped his head to one side. "If Crookedstar isn't able to talk, perhaps I can speak to you instead." His gaze flicked to Blackclaw. *"Alone."*

Leopardfur frowned. Could she deal with the powerful tabby warrior by herself? Of course she could. She'd talked to him plenty of times before. She padded out of camp, signaling for him to follow and led him to a quiet spot on the riverbank where reeds screened them from the path. "What is it?" She lifted her chin.

He blinked at her calmly. "I just wanted to tell you that ShadowClan's sickness has eased. Runningnose is treating the last few cases. We've had no new ones for a quarter moon."

"I'm glad to hear it." Leopardfur searched his gaze. It

seemed a long way to come to share news he could have shared at the Gathering last night.

"I also wanted to tell you that ShadowClan will carry on being a friend to RiverClan," Tigerstar went on. "As we have for many moons."

"If you want to renew our alliance, you must talk to Crookedstar," Leopardfur told him. She was uneasy about making a decision like this behind Crookedstar's back. He was still Clan leader.

Was that a glint of amusement in Tigerstar's eyes? "I see you're still loyal," he mewed. "But *you* will be the one making choices for your Clan soon."

"Crookedstar still has lives left," she mewed quickly, though she wasn't sure how many. She didn't want the other Clans to think RiverClan was weak.

Tigerstar dipped his head. "Of course," he mewed. "But every leader dies eventually. Which is sad, but how else can change happen? New ideas come from young minds."

Leopardfur's tail twitched. She remembered how Tigerstar had first talked about bringing fresh energy to the Clans. He was a leader now, just as he'd planned. And, although she didn't feel entirely ready, there was something beguiling about the thought of standing next to him on the Great Rock, leading the Clans, and bringing about real change. She wasn't ready to say good-bye to Crookedstar yet, but it warmed her pelt to know that when she did become leader, Tigerstar would be there with her. If, together, they could challenge the Clans to think differently, it might mean RiverClan would never need to go hungry again.

Tigerstar was watching her. He sat down and swept his tail over his forepaws. He looked relaxed, and there was a calmness and openness in his expression that put her at her ease. He clearly wanted to talk, and she was interested to hear what he would say.

She sat down too. "You've spoken of change before," she mewed. "What changes are you imagining you could make?"

"I'm not thinking of changes I could make," he mewed. "I'm thinking of the changes *we* could make." She stiffened. What did he mean? "We've always been of the same mind," he went on. "Other deputies and leaders are stuck in the past. But not you. You've always had your Clan's future in mind. You have the foresight to realize that RiverClan's future would be far more certain if it didn't rely so much on the river. Why else would you have opposed WindClan's return?"

"Exactly." He understood her.

"Of course," he mewed, "I wouldn't want to make the same mistakes Brokenstar made." His whiskers twitched knowingly.

"Of course not." Brokenstar had pushed his Clan too hard. "If he'd thought further ahead, he'd have been more successful."

"Driving WindClan out was rash," Tigerstar mewed.

"He underestimated ThunderClan's arrogance."

"And the weakness of his own Clan."

"Yes." She'd missed being able to talk frankly. So much of Clan leadership seemed to be about tiptoeing around other

Clans' needs. How refreshing to be honest. "A Clan must be sure of its own strength before it challenges another."

"And the strength of its allies."

Energy was pulsing through her paws. If only all leaders were as open as Tigerstar. "I'm so glad you're not a rogue," she mewed suddenly. "When you disappeared from Thunder-Clan, I was worried. Bluestar and Fireheart wouldn't tell anyone what had happened to you."

Tigerstar bristled. "Fireheart." He curled his lip. "Don't you mean *Rusty*? That was his kittypet name." There was rage in his mew. "He's the reason I left ThunderClan. I'm a *warrior*. How could I stay in a Clan that respects a *kittypet*?"

Leopardfur tilted her head in sympathy. "I've often wondered how that must have felt."

"It was humiliating. And Bluestar treated him as though he had warrior blood. She actually trusted him."

"Why does Bluestar admire him so much?" Leopardfur was genuinely curious.

Tigerstar scowled. "Fireheart's no fool," he mewed. "He knows how to exploit other cats. Kittypets are manipulative. They've learned to use Twolegs. They use other cats too. Blue-star can't see it. She still believes Fireheart has ThunderClan's interests at heart. But he only has his own." He let out a low hiss. "I'd rather be in ShadowClan and risk sickness than stay and see my leader undermined by a *kittypet*."

Leopardfur narrowed her eyes. "Fireheart knows how to act like a warrior," she mewed. "During the fire he took care of his Clanmates when Bluestar couldn't."

"He's always happy to stand in for Bluestar," Tigerstar mewed acidly.

"But you don't think he means it?" Leopardfur suggested. "Do you think he's just playing at being a true warrior?"

Tigerstar snarled. "I'm not sure he knows what a true warrior is. But yes, I think he's clever enough to give the right impression to satisfy his ambitions."

Leopardfur mused on his words. It certainly fit with what she'd observed of the orange tom—always making the right moves, and yet there was something about him she couldn't trust. "He's an impostor," she said finally.

Tigerstar leaned closer, his gaze sharpening. "What do you mean?"

"He *wants* to be honorable but he doesn't truly understand what honor means." She flicked her tail. "When our camp was flooded, he brought us prey." She paused, remembering how desperate RiverClan had been then. How humiliating it had been to allow the former kittypet to help. "*ThunderClan* prey. He didn't seem to realize that, by feeding us, he was betraying his Clan. And Graystripe helped him."

"*Graystripe.*" Tigerstar's nose wrinkled as though he smelled bad fish. "That's another reason I came to talk to you. I wanted to warn you that Graystripe's only true loyalty is to Fireheart."

Leopardfur shifted her paws uneasily.

Tigerstar went on. "He betrayed his Clan by coming to RiverClan, but he'd betray RiverClan in a blink if Fireheart asked him to."

Leopardfur narrowed her eyes. "I can handle Graystripe."

"I'm sure you could," Tigerstar conceded. "*If* he were being honest with you. But have you considered that he might only have joined RiverClan to act as Fireheart's spy? Giving you ThunderClan prey might have been a way to let Graystripe impress Silverstream." Leopardfur's ears twitched uncomfortably as he went on. "And Silverstream could just have been Graystripe's way into RiverClan. Fireheart might have planned it all."

Leopardfur's tail-tip began to flick as she thought his over. She'd also wondered about Graystripe's true intentions toward Silverstream—though she'd assumed Bluestar was behind the gray warrior's ruse, not Fireheart. In a way, this made more sense.

"Think about it," Tigerstar pressed. "Did Graystripe really have any feelings for Silverstream?" Leopardfur became to feel cold, despite the sun. "If he did, would he have buried her at Sunningrocks and stolen her kits without telling her own Clan about it?"

"He told Mistyfoot," Leopardfur mewed.

"Not until the next day."

The next day? What did he mean? Had ThunderClan kept it from them for a whole day? Suddenly, all the grief and fury she felt at Silverstream's death welled in her chest. "Was Silverstream dead for a *day* before ThunderClan told us?" she asked Tigerstar.

He shook his head sadly. "Supposedly, it was Bluestar's decision. But we know who really decided, don't we?"

Leopardfur blinked at him. "It was Fireheart?"

Tigerstar's eyes darkened. "We can't let cats like Fireheart and Graystripe call the shots. We must keep *some* pride, surely? It's humiliating to see the Clans being used by a kittypet. We are supposed to be warriors." Tigerstar's words seemed to reach right to Leopardfur's belly. "We could be great," he went on. "We could make the Clans so strong that no warrior ever goes hungry again. We can rise above petty battles, above borders, above prey. You can see that, can't you? You can see a day when there's prey enough for everyone. When the river and the moor and the forest provide enough for every cat, and no cat has to lift a claw against another. But that can't happen so long as Fireheart and Graystripe are using us. Our weakness is their strength, and they'll take advantage of it until we have enough pride to take back control. To bring true glory to the Clans—to make them what they were always meant to be."

Yes! Before Leopardfur could say it, Tigerstar got to his paws. "I must go," he mewed. "I want to visit Tallstar. But it was important I spoke to you first. I want you to know that if Graystripe and Fireheart give you trouble, you can turn to ShadowClan." He dipped his head respectfully. "RiverClan will always have a friend in ShadowClan."

She bowed her head in return, grateful. "Thanks."

She watched him go, her pelt fizzing. How much should she tell Crookedstar? If Graystripe really was a spy, perhaps she should watch him without worrying Crookedstar. But he needed to hear Tigerstar's warning—Bluestar and Graystripe weren't to be trusted as long as there were being used by a scheming kittypet. She rushed back to camp.

As she crossed the clearing, Graystripe trotted over from beside the fresh-kill pile. His pelt was wet. He must have been fishing.

He stopped in front of her, ears twitching nervously. "I heard Tigerstar was here," he mewed.

She narrowed her eyes. Was he worried the ShadowClan leader had given him away? "That's between me, Tigerstar, and Crookedstar," she mewed icily.

"You shouldn't listen to him," Graystripe urged. "He can't be trusted."

"Really?" Leopardfur flattened her ears. "What about you? Can *you* be trusted?"

Graystripe seemed to freeze. He stared at her without replying. Was that guilt glittering in his eyes?

Tigerstar must be right. "Yeah," she growled. "I thought not." Swishing her tail angrily, she padded toward Crookedstar's den.

CHAPTER 26

❧

She wasn't sure if Crookedstar had taken her warning seriously. There had been something in his eyes when she'd told him how Tigerstar had been driven out of ThunderClan by Fireheart's scheming that made her wonder if he'd entirely believed the ShadowClan leader's story. But he was sick. Perhaps it had been too much to take in. He clearly didn't fully understand what had been going on in the other Clans, how the balance between them had been shifting, and how much Fireheart had been using the situation to advance his own ambitions. How else could a kittypet have become a Clan deputy?

"What about the rogues?" Crookedstar had croaked.

Leopardfur had frowned, puzzled. "The rogues?"

"Tigerclaw attacked a ThunderClan patrol with a gang of rogues," Crookedstar stopped to catch his breath. "And it looks like he took those rogues to ShadowClan with him. You must have seen them at the Gathering."

"Tigerstar recognizes skill and strength." The tabby warrior had always been realistic about warrior life. He saw things how they were, not how he wished they could be. "Shadow-Clan lost warriors to the sickness. Bringing in fresh blood would be the quickest way to make the Clan strong again."

Crookedstar had gazed at her through misty eyes. "When have rogues ever made Clans strong?"

Leopardfur had bristled. "And I suppose *kittypets* can?" she'd mewed sourly.

"I never said that." Crookedstar had held her gaze, though it seemed a struggle. "It's true, Fireheart might be manipulating Bluestar, but that doesn't make Tigerclaw's intentions honorable."

"Tiger*star*," Leopardfur had reminded him gently.

"Tiger*claw*," Crookedstar had rasped again.

He's confused. Leopardfur had dipped her head. "You must be tired," she'd mewed. "I'll let you rest."

Now that she thought about it, she knew he must have been sicker than she'd imagined. A quarter moon had passed with little sign of improvement, and this morning, Mudfur had warned her that the RiverClan leader wasn't going to recover. It was just a matter of time. Worse, while the medicine cat believed Crookedstar had at least one life left, the leader was old enough that Mudfur wondered if the illness could claim more than one. Unlikely though that was, it would rob RiverClan of its beloved leader and place Leopardfur in that position. She didn't feel ready. RiverClan was still mourning Graypool's tragic death—the last thing they needed was to lose their beloved leader, as well.

She'd kept the Clan busy with patrols, and with strengthening the camp wall against leaf-bare floods, and RiverClan had gone about its work quietly, aware that Crookedstar hadn't left his den for days and knowing that he probably never would. One by one, they'd visited him, which had seemed to lift his spirits and theirs. Still, Leopardfur had the sense that they were saying their good-byes to the RiverClan leader. She only hoped he would prove them wrong.

Now, as the wind swirled the rushes, Leopardfur squinted against the sun. It had burst from behind the clouds, turning the leaf-fall afternoon golden. Warriors were resting around the edge of the clearing. Beetlenose and Vixenleap shared a trout in the shade of the sedge wall. Featherkit and Stormkit followed the older kits as they nosed behind the elders' den, hunting ants. Mosspelt was keeping a close eye on them while Graystripe was out of camp, patrolling the WindClan border with Timberfur and Ottersplash.

Mudfur slid through the moss trailing over the entrance to Crookedstar's den. He caught Leopardfur's eye.

She tensed, hurrying to meet him. "Is he . . ." She didn't dare say the word. *Is he dead?*

"He wants to talk to you," Mudfur mewed. "You should be prepared. I'm afraid he's already lost at least one life to this sickness."

Leopardfur's head spun. *This is really happening, then.* Beyond feeling unprepared to be leader, she wasn't ready to lose her friend and mentor. She never would be. She ducked into the leader's den, forcing her pelt to smooth though anxiety was sparking through it.

"Hey," she mewed softly as Crookedstar lifted his head and blinked at her through the gloom. He seemed smaller than ever, worn away by the cough that hadn't left him since the ThunderClan fire. He was wheezing now, and his eyes were cloudy, but they seemed to brighten a little as he saw her.

"Leopardfur." He gave a purr, but it stumbled into a cough, and she sat beside him and waited for it to subside. He recovered himself and went on. "Are you ready?"

"Ready?" She blinked at him, wishing she didn't know what he meant.

"Ready to lead the Clan."

No. She shifted her paws. "I don't know if I'll ever be ready." The closer she came to leadership, the more she felt unequal to the responsibility.

"I know you believe it's your destiny," he mewed. "It might well be, but that doesn't mean it will come naturally. You will have to work hard every day to be the leader RiverClan needs." He hesitated, catching his breath. "The leader River-Clan deserves."

She dipped her head. "I will do my best," she mewed. "I will never stop trying."

His eyes flashed suddenly, affectionate and playful. "I'll be watching you," he mewed. "From StarClan."

"I'm glad." She purred softly. "It means a lot to me to have your support. I'll try to make you proud."

"I've had a good life," he mewed. "And I'm happy to be joining my Clanmates." His eyes clouded with emotion. "I want to see Willowbreeze again. And Silverstream."

She blinked at him, her heart aching at the memory of the rebellious gray she-cat. "Tell her I'm sorry."

"Sorry?"

"I should have done more to help her."

Crookedstar gazed at her for a moment. "I'm sure you did everything you could to protect her," he mewed. "I know you will always protect RiverClan. More than anything else, you have the Clan's well-being at heart. But be fair," he mewed. "Be merciful. And don't let the other Clans push them around."

"Of course." Leopardfur looked fondly at her leader. She wished he could stay and tell her more, but he was looking wearier that she'd ever seen him. It was time to let him go. "Rest now." She touched his head with her nose.

He began to cough, spluttering to begin with, then convulsing as the coughing seemed to grip him and shake him like a fox shaking prey.

Mudfur darted into the den and nosed past her. He began to soothe Crookedstar, running his paws along the old tom's chest, stroking him gently until the coughing gave way to long rattling breaths and Crookedstar relaxed into his nest, his eyes closed.

"Let's give him a moment," Mudfur whispered. He nudged Leopardfur gently from the den.

Outside, Leopardfur drew in a long, deep breath. The fresh air made her realize how stuffy it had been inside the den.

Mudfur was watching her, his gaze solemn. "You know better than anyone how hard it is to lose a cat you care about," he mewed.

She blinked at him, surprised by the softness of his mew. "You're a medicine cat—you've lost cats too," she reminded him.

"Yes." He held her gaze. "And with each loss, I feel a little weaker, as though they've taken something with them. But *your* losses seem to make you stronger."

"Do they?" She didn't feel strong right now.

"They make you more certain about your destiny," he mewed. "Crookedstar's death will bring you closer to that."

The words made her anxious. "Am I ready?" she asked him.

"You're the only one who knows that."

"But you thought I wasn't ready to become deputy," she pressed. "Do you think I'm ready to be leader?"

"I'm not sure any cat is truly ready to be leader," he told her gently. "It might be better that way. If they come to leadership too sure of themselves, they are more likely to make mistakes."

"Really?" His words soothed her. Could it be *good* that she felt so unprepared for this responsibility?

He touched his muzzle to her cheek. "I'm proud of you, Leopardfur," he mewed. "I always have been. I'm privileged in a way most medicine cats aren't: I am a father, and I've lived a full life. I loved being a warrior. But, after your mother died, I lost my appetite for battle. I know Clans must fight sometimes. They will always have something worth protecting." He looked at her, his eyes glistening with hope. "But I still hope that one day they will find a peaceful way to live." He didn't give her a chance to speak, but ducked back into Crookedstar's den.

She gazed after him. He'd been trying to tell her to keep RiverClan from war. Her heart ached for him. Did he really believe that was possible?

"Leopardfur." He called to her through the moss, his

mew tight. Had Crookedstar died?

She hurried into the den. "Is he okay?"

Relief swamped her as she saw Crookedstar breathing in his nest. But he lay awkwardly, as though struggling for every breath.

"It won't be long now," Mudfur whispered. He stepped back, leaving space beside Crookedstar's nest.

Leopardfur slid into it and leaned close to the River-Clan leader. Her heart was beating quickly as grief tightened around it.

Crookedstar seemed to sense her presence. Perhaps he'd felt her breath on his cheek. He opened his eyes. "I have to go," he murmured huskily, struggling to lift his head. "But remember, RiverClan is only part of the Clans, and the Clans are only part of the forest. Fresh dangers face us all, brought by every season, every change in the weather. The Clans must defend themselves, but they must defend each other too. When we're faced with flood or fire, all we have is each other."

He fell back and her heart lurched. "Crookedstar," she mewed. "I'll take care of RiverClan. I promise I—"

He spoke again. "Some cats don't understand that we must share the forest. Some cats think it only exists for them and no other creature matters. Watch out for those cats." He fought for breath. "Watch out for Tigerclaw and . . ."

His mew trailed away. She frowned. He was still calling the ShadowClan leader Tiger*claw*. *He doesn't know what he's saying.* She rested a paw on his flank. *Be at peace now.*

But he went on, barely finding the breath. "Cats like him

will do anything to gain power over others. Don't be that kind of leader. Don't make those kinds of choices."

She felt a prickle of disappointment. Did he really think Tigerstar was like that? That *she* could be like that? If only Crookedstar had spoken to Tigerstar before he'd become ill; if only he'd known him better. Tigerstar only wanted the Clans to be stronger. "I will always protect RiverClan," she mewed, leaning closer. "I will give my life if I have to."

Crookedstar blinked at her, then closed his eyes. "Perhaps Mudfur was right," he breathed. "Perhaps death isn't—"

He stopped fighting for breath, and she felt his flank grow still beneath her paw. Her throat tightened. "He's gone." She moved away, letting Mudfur run his tail over the RiverClan leader's pelt and sniff his muzzle.

"Yes," Mudfur told her softly. "He's with StarClan now."

Leopardfur closed her eyes for a moment. She felt as though she'd reached the edge of a cliff and the river was churning far below. *I can do this.* She bunched energy into her muscles, as though preparing to leap, then pushed her way out of the den.

Mosspelt looked up from the nursery. Beetlenose sat up beside Vixenleap. As though reading her gaze, her Clanmates began getting to their paws, exchanging anxious glances.

Leopardfur announced that it was time for a Clan meeting. Her Clanmates watched her with concern and curiosity as she padded to the center of the clearing and looked at them. "Crookedstar is with StarClan," she mewed. This was the first time she'd addressed them as leader. Though her heart was aching, her mind felt as clear as spring water. "He was a great leader, and we were lucky to know such a warrior. I hope I can live up to his example. He left big paw steps, but I will do my best to fill them." She looked slowly around. Beetlenose's eyes were glistening. Heavystep and Shadepelt were watching with round, anxious eyes. As Loudbelly glanced sadly toward Crookedstar's den, Leopardfur's chest tightened. She wanted to ease her Clanmates' grief. She wanted to reassure them. "Before he died, Crookedstar told me that we are only a part of the forest. That each season brings fresh danger. He said that when there's flood or fire, all we have is each other." He'd been talking about the other Clans, but that wasn't what *their* Clan needed to hear now. Death had made him sentimental. The other Clans weren't their responsibility. Taking care of RiverClan was hard enough without taking care of the other Clans too. A dying leader could make such a generous promise, but how could a living leader ever achieve it?

Her Clanmates were looking at her hopefully. They wanted to know that RiverClan would be safe and that nothing would change even though Crookedstar was gone. She dipped her head respectfully. "Crookedstar was right. We must take care of each other. I will make sure of that. I promise you that, whatever happens, I will protect you." She lifted her muzzle. "I will keep you safe."

CHAPTER 27

"Mudfur?" Leopardfur whispered through the darkness. Her mew echoed around the walls of the cave. "When do I touch the Moonstone?"

"Soon." Mudfur's paws brushed the stone. She could just make him out in the starlight filtering through a hole in the high roof. He was staring up at it expectantly, his pelt fluffed out against the chill of the cavern.

She shifted her paws, the stone like ice beneath them. Which StarClan cats would grant her nine lives? Her belly tightened. There were so many cats she longed to see again, and some she dreaded. Would Whitefang be there? She was glad Mudfur had made the long journey with her across the moor to Highstones. "How long does the ceremony take?"

As she blinked at him, moonlight sliced through the darkness. It touched the Moonstone, and it lit up like sunlight sparkling on water, shimmering on countless ripples.

Leopardfur narrowed her eyes, flinching away. "It's so bright."

"Go on." Mudfur nudged her gently forward.

Nervously, she crossed the stone floor, the cold air reaching deep into her pelt, and stopped beside the brilliant Moon-stone. Closing her eyes, she leaned forward and touched her nose to the rock. The ground seemed to drop away. Her heart lurched as moonlight swirled around her. For a moment she felt she was falling, and then there was soft grass beneath her paws. She opened her eyes to find herself in a dark hollow. She looked up and saw stars spinning in the black sky. Her breath caught as their silvery light swirled around her. She smelled the river and the moor and the forest—the scents of all the Clans were mingled here—and suddenly the slopes glittered with starry pelts. Eyes blazed and pelts sparkled as countless faces stared down at her.

Overwhelmed, Leopardfur fought the urge to crouch against the earth. Was all of StarClan here?

A huge, long-furred gray tom padded forward and dipped his head as he reached her. "Welcome to StarClan." His mew seemed to rumble deep beneath his thick, silver fur. "I am Riverstar."

Leopardfur blinked at him, lost for words. The first leader of RiverClan had come to her ceremony. She bowed her head stiffly, wondering if it was the right way to greet the ancient tom.

"You will bring strength to RiverClan at a time when they need it." He padded closer. "With this life, I give you accep-tance."

"Acceptance?" Leopardfur's pelt rippled with surprise. Surely, acceptance was for the weak, for warriors who had no other choice.

Riverstar's eyes gleamed. Was that amusement in them? "You will need it." He reached out and touched his nose to her head. Agony blazed beneath her pelt as the new life rushed through her. She tried to flinch away, but her paws seemed to be rooted to the earth. Water glittered around her; fish flashed at the edge of her vision; wind roared through trees she couldn't see.

She gasped as he stepped away, feeling as weak as a newborn kit. If this was what it was to receive a life, she didn't know if she could bear eight more. She trembled as Riverstar padded away and disappeared among the starry pelts.

Another cat stepped forward.

"Whiteclaw." Her heart leaped. She wanted to race to greet him. And to apologize. "I'm sorry." Grief long faded became sharp once more. "I trained you to be too much like me."

He blinked at her, his eyes sparkling with starlight. "You trained me to be a loyal RiverClan warrior," he mewed. "It's all I ever wanted to be." He leaned forward. "With this life, I give you empathy, because you always understood me." As he touched his nose to her head, the sadness that had gripped her heart seemed to melt. There was no pain this time. Warmth flowed through her, soft as leaf-fall sunshine. As he stepped away, she opened her eyes and blinked, wishing he could stay. "Whiteclaw." She had so much to tell him, but he turned and slid back among his Clanmates.

Another cat had taken his place. Leopardfur recognized him at once. "Hailstar." She dipped her head quickly. "I'm honored."

"You fought fearlessly against those rats," he mewed. "You have always had the courage and determination to be one of RiverClan's greatest leaders."

She glanced at her paws self-consciously. He'd remembered her courage.

"With this life, I give you bravery." He touched his nose to her head, and, once more, agony pierced her and she had to grit her teeth to stop herself crying out. Hailstar's memories flashed around her like claws—pelts twisting; teeth snapping; enemies shrieking. She pressed back terror as the scent of blood filled her nose. Then it faded and she opened her eyes.

Hailstar was watching her. As she caught her breath, he spoke again. "Protect your Clan with your life."

As he padded away, another cat stopped in front of her. Her heart ached as she recognized Frogleap. She could only stare at him wordlessly and he purred, his starlit eyes filled with affection. "With this life, I give you devotion," he whispered. "Because you are devoted to your Clan." Then he touched her head and she felt water press around her, crushing her until she could barely breathe. She fought, trying to break free. But the water was too heavy. There was no escape. She stopped struggling, and as she did, the water eased its grip and she felt its embrace like a mother's, wrapping her in love.

Leopardfur staggered to keep on her paws as the vision faded. She wondered whether it always hurt this much for a leader to receive their lives—was it *supposed* to hurt this much? She blinked at Frogleap. "Are Woodkit and Robinkit with you?"

His eyes shone brighter. "Yes."

"I'm sorry I couldn't save them."

"They are loved here too." He turned away and another cat took his place.

"Oakheart." She greeted the RiverClan deputy with a polite nod.

"You have grown," he mewed approvingly. "And learned much from Crookedstar."

"Is he here yet?" she asked him. Would she see him?

"He's resting," Oakheart told her. "He's earned it." He touched her head with his nose. "With this life, I give you unity, so that RiverClan may never be divided." She cringed, but as his breath billowed around her ears, she felt only determination hardening in her belly like amber, growing warm and golden inside her as though sunshine drenched it. *That's more like it.*

She managed a nod as he padded away and another cat stepped from the ranks of StarClan warriors. Leopardfur blinked at her. Silverstream was padding toward her.

"I'm sorry," Leopardfur blurted. "I should have given you the help you needed, not the help I thought you should have."

Silverstream's blue eyes were filled with pity. She stopped in front of Leopardfur and gazed at her. "With this life, I give you forgiveness," she mewed, then touched her nose to Leopardfur's head. Guilt seared like flames through Leopardfur until she was breathless with the pain; then it disappeared, quenched by a sense of peace and kindness that felt like the soft brush of a tail on her cheek. Tranquility enfolded her as Silverstream stepped away.

Leopardfur called after her. "Stormkit and Featherkit are safe and happy in RiverClan."

Silverstream glanced back at her. "I know," she mewed. "Thank you for bringing them home."

White fur, brilliant with starlight, dazzled Leopardfur for a moment until she realized that Whitefang was standing before her. Her heart soared as she recognized her mentor's familiar scent.

"I'm proud of you," he mewed. His eyes shone, and she purred, not knowing what to say.

He purred back. "It's not like you to be lost for words." Leaning forward, he went on. "With this life, I give you patience."

She purred again as she felt the touch of his muzzle. What patience had she ever shown? She pictured herself pestering him to teach her battle moves when she was a kit. And then she felt the hurry and rush of Clan life moving around her so fast that the pelts and faces of her Clanmates seemed to blur and become no more than the wind whisking leaves around the clearing while she stood, still and silent, at the center.

When she opened her eyes, Whitefang was gone. A pang of grief pierced her heart. Then she heard a gentle mew.

"Leopardfur." Sunfish's gaze sparkled in front of her.

Leopardfur wanted to press her muzzle against her friend's cheek. But she didn't dare. "Are you happy here?" she asked.

Sunfish blinked at her calmly. "We are all happy here," she mewed.

Leopardfur felt as though a stone had dropped from her heart. She purred as Sunfish leaned close.

"With this life, I give you friendship." At the touch of her nose, Leopardfur felt herself skimming the shoreline, her paws hardly touching the earth, then diving through the water, moving with the current like a fish, while above her, sunshine glittered on the surface. She felt happier than she had since she was a kit, and blinked opened her eyes for one last look at her friend.

But Sunfish was gone, and a white-and-ginger she-cat stood in her place. Leopardfur's nose twitched. Her scent seemed familiar, but she couldn't remember having met this cat.

"I'm Brightsky," the she-cat mewed.

Leopardfur's tail quivered with happiness. It was her mother. She blinked at her. "Mudfur missed you so much." She dropped her gaze, a prick of sadness in her chest. "So did I."

"I know." The she-cat's mew was husky. "I wish I could have raised you. But I've loved you even though I couldn't be with you." She reached toward Leopardfur's head with her muzzle. "With this, your ninth life, I give you love," she mewed. "The love a mother gives her kits."

Leopardfur froze as pain impaled her heart, hardening it until she felt no fear. The strength and ferocity of it took her by surprise. There was no gentleness in it. Was this what a mother's love was like?

Brightsky drew away and blinked at her. "Your Clanmates are your kits now," she mewed. "Their safety depends on your strength. You must fight for them without fear or pity."

"I will." Leopardstar met her gaze. "I promise. I will protect them as though they are my own."

* * *

She and Mudfur arrived back at camp a little before dawn.

"Get some sleep," Mudfur told her, flicking his tail toward Crookedstar's den. It was her den now. But she didn't feel ready to sleep. She wanted to begin the day. She had many plans for RiverClan. There was much to do.

Mudfur nudged her away. "Just a nap," he mewed. "It's the Gathering tonight. You'll need your rest."

She settled into the leader's den, but she wasn't sure if she slept or not. Thoughts filled her mind, whirling so fast that they might have blurred into sleep. She wasn't sure. But her eyes were open when dawn sunshine reached through the trailing moss that covered the entrance of the den. She'd come to a decision. RiverClan had become too dependent on the river since they'd lost Sunningrocks to ThunderClan. The flood had given her stark proof of that. If they were to make it through leaf-bare, they would need more land. Crookedstar was dead; there was no one to object. It was time to take Sunningrocks back.

She climbed out of her nest and stretched. Though the den was freshly woven, Crookedstar's scent still lingered. She'd hoped he would be there to give her one of her lives at the Moonstone ceremony. But perhaps he'd given her all she needed while he was alive.

She nosed her way out of the den and surveyed the camp. Piketooth was stretching stiffly beside the camp wall. Timberfur was nosing through stale prey left on the fresh-kill pile, and Cedarpelt was soaking up the early morning sunshine nearby. Leopardstar narrowed her eyes. The graying toms seemed to sleep less and move slower now, and she realized how old they'd become.

Stonefur padded from the warriors' den. His blue-gray fur glowed in the early-morning light. He nodded to her, picked a stiff perch from the fresh-kill pile, and carried it to the nursery.

Leopardstar watched him as the rest of the Clan stirred and her Clanmates drifted from their dens. Ottersplash nodded a greeting. Blackclaw and Reedtail blinked at her. Graystripe headed for the nursery. The Clan knew she'd gone to receive her nine lives, and they seemed a little wary of her, perhaps because she still carried the scent of StarClan.

Stonefur moved among them, stopping to talk to one warrior, then another, calling into the apprentices' den to make sure Dawnpaw was awake before Heavystep came looking for her, stopping by the nursery a second time to take away the fish bones. Leopardstar had noticed the warrior's concern for his Clanmates before, and she was in no doubt about his skill and courage.

"Let all cats old enough to swim gather to hear my words." She felt a quiver of excitement as she said the words she had heard Crookedstar speak so often. This was her Clan now, and she had much to share with them. She couldn't wait to get started. As they gathered around her, she swished her tail, relishing the respect she saw in their eyes as they waited for her to speak.

"I received my nine lives last night," she mewed. "I am Leopardstar now."

"Leopardstar!" Blackclaw was the first to call her name, and the others joined in, their eyes shining.

"Leopardstar!"

"Leopardstar!"

She swallowed back a purr. "I have decided who my deputy will be." The cheers died away as she looked around the Clan. Reedtail shifted his paws. Loudbelly pricked his ears.

Her gaze rested on Stonefur. He looked at her, a question in his eyes.

"Stonefur has shown his courage and loyalty time and time again. I believe he will make a fine deputy for RiverClan."

"Stonefur!" Mistyfoot hurried to her littermate's side and pressed her muzzle to his cheek as her Clanmates echoed her cheer.

"Stonefur!"

Leopardstar blinked happily. They seemed to be pleased with her choice. She lifted her voice over her Clanmates' and spoke again. "The Gathering is tonight. Voleclaw, Blackclaw, and Beetlenose will join me and Stonefur, along with Misty-foot and Mallowtail." She glanced at Dawnpaw, who was sitting proudly beside her mentor, Heavystep. She'd been the first kit in the nursery to be given her apprentice name, but it wouldn't be long before Primrosekit, Pikekit, and Reedkit joined her in the apprentices' den. "Heavystep." She dipped her head to the thickset brown tabby tom. "I want you to come too, and bring Dawnpaw. She will learn a lot from her first Gathering."

Dawnpaw's pelt bristled with excitement, and she fidgeted

beside Heavystep as Leopardstar turned her gaze toward Piketooth. She dipped her head to the old warrior. "I think it's time you moved to the elders' den." She looked at Timberfur and Cedarpelt. "You too," she mewed. "You have earned your rest. Let others hunt for you. We all feel Graypool's loss, and an elders' den should not stay empty long. It brings warmth and wisdom to a Clan."

Timberfur purred. "And it gives the 'paws something to clean out."

Cedarpelt glanced at Dawnpaw. "You'll be so busy pulling out our ticks, you won't have time for training."

"Don't worry," Leopardstar reassured Dawnpaw as the young apprentice's eyes widened with worry. "You'll have denmates soon enough."

Piketooth arched his back and stretched. "I suppose I could stand a little rest. And if I'm a wizened elder, that means you'll always listen to me, won't you?"

Leopardstar's whiskers twitched with amusement. "I'll certainly take your advice into consideration. That goes for all three of you. Thank you."

The meeting was at an end. She nodded to Stonefur. "I'd like to speak to you before you organize the day's patrols."

"Sure." He crossed the clearing as his Clanmates went back to washing and stretching and gossiping in the clearing. He dipped his head as he reached her. "I'm honored to be your deputy," he mewed. "Thank you for your faith in me."

"I'm lucky to have a warrior like you at my side." She watched the Clan for a moment. "RiverClan needs to be stronger. I want extra border patrols, morning and evening. And I'm going to oversee apprentice training myself, although you should keep a close eye on it too. Dawnpaw and the kits must become some of the finest warriors RiverClan has ever trained. ShadowClan has a new leader, ThunderClan will always want more than they need, and WindClan is starting to flex its claws. We need to be ready to protect our land and our Clanmates."

Stonefur dipped his head. "I agree," he mewed. "I never want to see a Clanmate go hungry again."

Leopardstar blinked at him approvingly. She'd made the right choice. But was he ready for RiverClan to fight? "I've decided that the only way to keep our Clan fed is to expand our territory." She eyed him, trying to read his reaction. His gaze sharp with interest. "I plan to take Sunningrocks back," she told him.

"How soon?"

"As soon as we can be ready."

"Okay."

She felt her shoulders loosen. He was going to support her. "Graystripe must know nothing about it," she mewed.

He frowned. "Don't you trust him?"

"Do you?"

He hesitated. "I want to trust him, but he still seems very friendly with Fireheart. Perhaps we should take him to the Gathering tonight. It could give him a chance to prove his loyalty."

Leopardstar narrowed her eyes. She didn't want Graystripe

anywhere near ThunderClan warriors, but Stonefur had a point. At the Gathering, they could see just how close to his former denmates the tom was. "Okay," she mewed. "Tell him to join the patrol."

Leopardstar led the patrol to the Gathering late on purpose. She didn't want the Clans to have long to speculate about Crookedstar's death before she made the announcement herself. She was RiverClan's leader now; that was all they needed to know.

The clearing was crowded. ShadowClan, ThunderClan, and WindClan had already arrived. Bluestar was sitting on top of the Great Rock, gazing across the Fourtrees hollow, her blue-gray pelt glowing in the bright moonlight.

"Remember," she told Stonefur as they reached the bottom of the slope. "Get as much information as you can from the other deputies and give as little as possible in return."

Stonefur nodded and headed away. The rest of the patrol was already weaving among the crowd. Leopardstar noticed Graystripe nosing his way straight toward Fireheart. He didn't seem interested in staying with his own Clanmates. Leopardstar narrowed her eyes in his direction, thinking that it didn't take very long to show which Clan had his loyalty.

But there wasn't time to worry about that now. She would be addressing the Clans for the first time tonight. She took a deep breath. *You have a voice,* she told herself. *Use it.* Lifting her tail, she shouldered her way through the gathered cats.

Tigerstar and Tallstar stood at the foot of the Great Rock.

They didn't look surprised to see her join them.

"Leopard*star*." Tigerstar dipped his head respectfully. "Congratulations."

Tallstar must have told him she'd received her nine lives. She and Mudfur had run into a WindClan patrol as they'd crossed the moor to Highstones last night, and she'd had to explain to them that Crookedstar was dead and she was on her way to the Moonstone.

"I'm sorry for your loss," Tallstar mewed.

"Crookedstar died a peaceful death, in his nest." She nodded to them politely in turn.

"I'm glad he didn't suffer," Tallstar mewed.

Tigerstar's eyes glittered. "So you're leader now? Who's your deputy?"

"Stonefur." She scanned the crowd. Was the gray tom sharing news with the other deputies yet?

"An interesting choice." There was a sharpness in Tigerstar's mew. It made Leopardstar stiffen. What did he find so interesting? She was irritated by her own curiosity. Why should she care? Tigerstar's opinion on RiverClan business wasn't important.

She leaped onto the rock and nodded a greeting to Bluestar. The ThunderClan leader looked her blankly for a moment, then dipped her head in return as Tigerstar and Tallstar jumped up beside them.

Below, the assembled cats were turning their gaze toward the Great Rock.

Tigerstar nodded Leopardstar forward. "You have the

most pressing news," he mewed.

His tone was respectful, and she pressed back a shiver of excitement. "Thank you."

This was what she'd wanted. To share the Great Rock with a warrior like Tigerstar. She padded to the edge and looked down at the crowd. Seeing so many faces looking back at her made her heart pound. She forced her pelt not to prickle. "Our leader Crookedstar has joined StarClan," she told them. "He was a noble leader, and all his Clan mourns his passing. I am leader of RiverClan now, and Stonefur is my deputy. Last night, I traveled to Highstones to receive my nine lives from StarClan."

Tallstar swished his tail. "Crookedstar will be missed by all the Clans. But may StarClan grant that RiverClan thrives under your leadership."

Leopardstar waited for Bluestar to speak. Surely the ThunderClan leader would offer her congratulations too? But Bluestar was gazing down into the hollow. What was so interesting down there? Leopardstar cleared her throat, but Bluestar still didn't lift her gaze. *Is she ignoring me?* Indignation flared beneath her pelt. She stared at the ThunderClan leader. It seemed as though Bluestar hadn't even realized she was leader now. The old cat's gaze was still fixed on the crowd. What could be distracting her? Older cats could be hard of hearing. Perhaps she hadn't heard Leopardstar address the Gathering. "Bluestar?" she called to her softly.

Bluestar looked at her. She seemed confused for a moment. Then her focus returned. Leopardfur felt a flash of surprise as anger flared in the ThunderClan leader's shimmering blue eyes. Bluestar pushed past Tallstar, knocking him aside as she marched to the front of the Great Rock. Leopardstar hopped quickly out of the way as Bluestar turned her gaze on the gathered cats. "I will speak next," she growled, glancing ferociously at Tallstar.

"Cats of the Clans." Her mew was cold and angry. "I bring news of theft. WindClan warriors have been hunting in ThunderClan territory!"

Angry yowling erupted across the hollow. Leopardstar stepped back, her pelt bristling with alarm as WindClan warriors sprang to their paws, furiously denying Bluestar's accusation.

"Prove it!" Onewhisker yowled at Bluestar. "Prove that WindClan has taken so much as a mouse!"

"I have proof!" Bluestar's eyes blazed.

Tallstar's hackles lifted, but Bluestar seemed fearless, fired with such rage that Leopardstar wondered if a fight would break out on the Great Rock. She glanced at Tigerstar. He was sitting at the back of the rock, his pelt utterly smooth as he watched Bluestar and Tallstar hurl accusations at each other.

"All this is a pile of mouse dung," Tallstar snarled. "Wind-Clan has lost prey as well. We have found rabbit remains on our territory too. I accuse you, Bluestar, of letting your warriors hunt on our land and making false accusations to cover up the theft!"

As Tallstar puffed out his black-and-white pelt, Tiger-star caught Leopardstar's eye. His whiskers twitched with amusement. Did he find the fight funny? Then he padded forward and spoke.

"That seems fair," he told Tallstar calmly. "Every cat knows that prey has been scarce on ThunderClan territory since the fire. Your Clan is hungry, Bluestar, and *some* of your warriors"— he paused, his gaze flitting down toward Graystripe—"know WindClan territory very well."

His words made Bluestar incandescent with fury. She turned on him. "Silence!" she hissed. "Stay away from me and my Clan. This is no business of yours!"

"It's the business of every cat in the forest," Tigerstar replied calmly. "The Gathering is supposed to be a time of peace. If StarClan is angered, we will all suffer."

"StarClan!" Bluestar was spitting now. "StarClan has turned away from us, and I will fight them if I have to. I care only for feeding my Clan—"

Leopardstar stared at the ThunderClan leader. Fight with StarClan? What was wrong with her? How could any Clan leader think StarClan had turned away from them? She narrowed her eyes. Bluestar clearly wasn't herself. And Tigerstar seemed to be enjoying her outburst.

She waited quietly while Bluestar and Tallstar threatened each other, wondering why StarClan hadn't sent clouds to cover the moon. Were their ancestors enjoying the fight too? Tigerstar was looking pleased with himself, as though his intervention had gone exactly as he'd planned. Had he baited Bluestar on purpose?

He seemed to have planted a spark of mischief in

Leopardstar: Suddenly she wondered what would happen if *she* baited the ThunderClan leader too. Would Bluestar explode into rage again? Perhaps now was the moment to announce her plans for RiverClan.

She slid between Tigerstar and Tallstar. The Clans were shifting agitatedly below her like a shoal of nervous fish.

"The fire was a terrible misfortune," she called down to them. "Every cat in the forest knows that, but yours is not the only Clan to have suffered recently." She glanced at Bluestar. "Your forest will grow back as rich in prey as it ever was. But Twolegs have invaded our territory and show no signs of leaving. Last leaf-bare, the river was poisoned and cats who ate the fish fell ill. Who can guarantee that it won't happen again? RiverClan needs better hunting grounds even more than ThunderClan." She knew that every cat in the clearing would have understood the veiled threat in her words. The easiest way for RiverClan was to expand was into ThunderClan territory, and the most obvious place to attack was Sunningrocks. She watched Bluestar, waiting for her reaction. Surely she would be furious?

Bluestar dipped her head graciously. "You're right, Leopardstar," she mewed. "RiverClan has endured hard times. Yet your cats are so strong and noble that I know you will survive."

Leopardstar blinked in surprise. Didn't Bluestar realize she'd been challenged? She tried to read the ThunderClan leader's expression. Was she hiding her anger? There was no sign of it. No ruffled pelt or twitching ear. Bluestar was staring at her calmly.

There was something very wrong with ThunderClan's leader. She didn't seem to be in her right mind. Leopardstar's thoughts quickened. Any Clan was vulnerable without strong leadership. But ThunderClan had been weakened by the fire too. This was a perfect opportunity to take back Sunning-rocks.

She hesitated. Would it be dishonorable to attack Thunder-Clan when they were so weak? She glanced at Tigerstar. What would he do?

He met her gaze, widening his eyes a little, as though he was encouraging her. Was he telling her to go ahead with her plan? He might think she was weak if she didn't. Every cat knew that Sunningrocks belonged to RiverClan. It always had, and it was humiliating to have ThunderClan hunting and patrolling there as though they were the true owners.

This was her chance to put things right. She could finally redress the balance that Crookedstar had refused to. And it would be easier now than ever before. Leopardstar's fur prick-led with excitement. Perhaps StarClan had *arranged* for it to be so easy. They could be hoping that Sunningrocks would finally be returned to the right Clan. Surely, it would be foolish and ungrateful—mouse-brained, even—not to take advantage of the situation?

CHAPTER 28

❧

Leopardstar lashed her tail. She was breathing hard. Battle cries exploded behind her as her Clanmates fought on. They would win this time. This tiny ThunderClan patrol couldn't stop them from taking back Sunningrocks.

She narrowed her eyes against the glare of the sun and stared down into the gully. The early frost was still sparkling there. The claw marks Bluestar had left on her flanks stung. She'd seen the ThunderClan leader try to escape into its shadows, but she wasn't going to let her get away without telling her that Sunningrocks belonged to its rightful owners once more.

She stiffened as she caught sight of Bluestar, cornered at the end of the gully. Her heart quickened with pleasure as she saw that Mistyfoot and Stonefur had already caught up with the ThunderClan leader. They had pinned her to the ground. Would they kill her? She looked closer, frowning. They were frozen.

Leopardstar opened her mouth to ask what they were waiting for when she saw a flame-colored pelt behind the two warriors.

It was Fireheart. He was talking to them. She could hear his mew but couldn't make out the words. As he spoke, Mistyfoot released Bluestar. Stonefur backed away. In an instant, Fireheart leaped past them and, bundling Bluestar against the rock, stood in front of her.

What was he saying to them? Leopardstar pricked her ears, straining to hear as Fireheart went on. Why were they listening to the arrogant kittypet? Rage flared in her belly. *Attack him!*

She'd have to deal with this herself. With a yowl, she hurled herself into the gully.

A cry rang out above her. "Fireheart! Watch out!"

She recognized the mew. *Graystripe!* Her rage hardened. He'd betrayed her. She slammed into Fireheart, blood roaring in her ears. She'd make him pay, and then she'd turn her fury on Graystripe. She pinned Fireheart easily. He was weak from the battle. She raked his belly with her hind claws. She'd put an end to him right now. No kittypet was going to be Clan leader. She'd make sure of that. He writhed beneath her, trying to escape, but her grip was too strong. She saw his throat and lunged at it with her teeth.

Claws hooked her from behind. They hauled her backward, tearing her away from Fireheart. She gasped, shock sparking through her pelt as she was flung to the ground and held there by huge gray paws.

"Graystripe!" She'd been right all along. He'd been nothing more than a ThunderClan spy in her camp. "I had him!" She was so angry she could hardly spit out the words. "I heard you just now. You *warned* him!"

He let her go and backed away. She scrambled to her paws. Where were Mistyfoot and Stonefur? She wanted them to kill this traitor. There was no sign of them. She gave a low warning growl and fixed her gaze on Graystripe.

He was staring at her with round, panicked eyes. "I'm sorry, Leopardstar. But Fireheart's my friend."

She should have done something about this fox-heart as soon as she'd become leader. *I should have listened to Tigerstar.*

Blood was welling in her fur. She shook it out. Fireheart watched her from behind Graystripe. He was injured and barely had the strength to hold himself up. She could smell his fear scent. "You were never loyal to RiverClan," she hissed. "So I'm giving you a choice. Attack your *friend* for me now, or leave the Clan for good." She glared at him. She knew he wouldn't hurt Fireheart. She just wanted to see him own up to his treachery. Of course he'd take the chance to return to ThunderClan. Why wouldn't he? His disloyalty had been so brazen that no warrior would ever again believe that he'd joined RiverClan to be close to his kits. That had been a lie. And his love for Silverstream? Had that been a lie too? She gave a low, long growl as Graystripe stared at her in dismay. "Well," she snarled. "What are you waiting for?"

Graystripe glanced at Fireheart.

Are you waiting for him to answer for you? Leopardfur curled her lip. *Can't you think for yourself?*

"I'm sorry, Leopardstar." Graystripe bowed his head. "I can't do it. Punish me if you want."

"Punish you?" Did he think he'd been caught stealing prey?

Did disloyalty mean nothing to him? Fury stole her breath. "I'll claw your eyes out! I'll set you loose in the forest for foxes to track down. Traitor! I'll—"

Yowls sounded from the rocks above. Blackclaw peered over the top of the gully, his eyes sparking with panic. "Thunder-Clan has sent reinforcements!"

Leopardstar glared at him.

"We're outnumbered," he wailed. "We can't win!"

She'd have to finish this another time. Her Clanmates needed her. She leaped up beside Blackclaw, her pelt spiking as she saw ThunderClan warriors swarming over Sunning-rocks. "Retreat!"

She signaled her warriors toward the river with a flick of her tail and guarded them as they fled past her, frustration pulsing beneath her pelt. She followed them to the river and kept an eye on the slope above, ready to defend them as they leaped in and swam across. Mistyfoot and Stonefur were already climbing out on the far shore. She saw them glance back toward Sunningrocks and exchange words. Their eyes flashed with fear. What had that kittypet said to them to make them run away?

ThunderClan cats were pouring down the slope after them. As the last of her warriors plunged into the river, she leaped after them and swam to the shore. Climbing out, she looked back at Sunningrocks. ThunderClan warriors lined the top and clustered on the shore. They were yowling trium-phantly. Leopardstar glared at them. This wasn't the end. It could never be the end. She would have won this battle, if she hadn't been betrayed.

She lifted her muzzle. "Graystripe is a traitor." She yowled the words clearly so that they rang out across the river. She wanted ThunderClan and RiverClan to hear. "If he's ever seen on RiverClan territory again, I want him killed."

She didn't speak again until she reached camp. She was too angry. Blackclaw and Reedtail limped ahead of her through the reeds. Stonefur had been keeping out of sight. As she padded into camp, she saw him on the far side of the clearing with Mistyfoot. Shadepelt and Loudbelly were already licking their wounds. Timberfur and Cedarpelt watched anxiously from outside the elders' den. They didn't ask any questions. They must have guessed the battle had gone badly.

Mudfur hurried toward Leopardstar. He had a leaf wrap in his jaws. "You're injured," he mewed, laying it on the ground and unfolding it. He inspected the wounds on her flank.

She ducked away, her tail lashing. "See to the others first," she snapped. "I'm fine!"

He glanced at her but said nothing and, picking up his leaf wrap, headed toward Shadepelt.

Leopardstar walked over to Stonefur and Mistyfoot. They watched her coming like rabbits watching a hawk. "What happened?" she snapped as she reached them. "What did that kittypet say to you to stop you from fighting?" Were they traitors too? Had Graystripe managed to turn her these two littermates against her? Her heart was pounding with fury. Blood pulsed in her paws.

They glanced at each other nervously.

Leopardstar narrowed her eyes. "Well?"

Stonefur dipped his head. "Bluestar was so confused," he

mewed softly. "Fireheart said it would be dishonorable to hurt her."

Leopardstar hissed. "You listened to *him*?"

"Only because he was right," Mistyfoot mewed quickly. "She was so confused, she didn't seem to know who was attacking her."

"It was like attacking a kit," Stonefur chimed.

Leopardstar forced her pelt to smooth. He had a point. But it didn't change the fact that they'd lost the battle. "Your *honor* cost us hunting land we can't afford to lose," she snarled. "You'll be doing double patrols for a moon to try and make it up to us!"

Stonefur dropped his gaze. "Okay," he murmured.

At least he seemed to have admitted his mistake. She fixed her gaze on Mistyfoot.

"We're sorry," the gray she-cat breathed, staring at her paws.

Leopardstar's anger ebbed a little. "Killing Bluestar in cold blood would have been wrong," she conceded. "But what about Fireheart? I had to fight him myself. Graystripe attacked me. You'd disappeared and I was outnumbered."

Stonefur looked at her, his gaze glistening with shame. "I'm sorry," he mewed. "I rejoined the battle on the rock."

"We thought you could deal with Fireheart," Mistyfoot added.

"We didn't think Graystripe would actually attack you." Stonefur blinked at her.

Nor did I. She'd never trusted him, but she hadn't thought he'd actually turn on her in battle. She'd been far too tolerant.

She should have banished him the moment Crookedstar had died. She shivered as she imagined what Tigerstar would say. He'd mock her for being so weak. *A real leader would have dealt with this earlier.*

The crisp, dry weather that had set in before the battle lingered, and in the days afterward, the Clan woke to frost. Leopardstar ordered extra hunting patrols and, this morning, led one to the river.

As she reached the shore, her heart sank. It was frozen.

Blackclaw stared at the water. "It's too early to freeze," he mewed in dismay.

Sedgecreek poked the ice with her paw. "It's too thick to break."

Leopardstar pressed back a growl. They sounded defeated. But it wasn't their fault that a cold snap had come so early. And she wasn't going to endanger her warriors by sending them into freezing water to fish beneath ice.

She stared at it, her thoughts quickening. "We'll have to send more hunting parties into the forest," she mewed. "We'll cross borders if necessary. WindClan land will be prey-rich still."

Blackclaw looked at her anxiously. "Won't that cause a battle?"

Leopardstar glared at him. "Are you scared of WindClan?"

"No," he mewed quickly.

Leopardstar looked across the river to where Sunningrocks glowed in the sunshine. Her belly churned with rage. "We'll do whatever we have to," she growled. "I won't let my Clan starve."

Her rage gnawed at her as they hunted along the shore, and even though they caught a warbler and two voles, it hadn't eased by the time they returned to camp.

As Blackclaw and Sedgecreek dropped their catch on the fresh-kill pile, Leopardstar sat down at the edge of the clearing. What if there was no thaw? What if the river stayed frozen through all of leaf-bare? She shifted uneasily. It was only leaf-fall, and her Clan faced hunger already. She gazed distractedly at Primrosekit and Pikekit as they ran past. Featherkit and Stormkit chased after them.

"If we catch you, we'll eat you!" Stormkit squeaked.

Primrosekit and Pikekit squealed in mock terror and ran even faster.

Leopardstar's whiskers twitched. Primrosekit and Pikekit would become apprentices any day now. Stormkit and Featherkit, still with their kit fluff, looked ridiculous chasing after denmates twice their size. But it felt good to watch them play.

She watched as Primrosekit and Pikekit turned on Stormkit and Featherkit and the chase turned into a play battle.

"You'll never beat us!" Primrosekit squeaked triumphantly.

"True warriors will always win over fox-hearts!" Pikekit chimed.

Leopardstar purred. They weren't worried about prey or ThunderClan or Sunningrocks. They were safe and happy, and she'd make sure they stayed that way.

"Now it's our turn," Stormkit mewed, breaking away from

the fight and sitting up. He blinked at Primrosekit. "You chase us this time."

Featherkit leaped to her paws eagerly. "Yes! This time, *you* can be ThunderClan and we can be RiverClan."

Leopardstar pricked her ears.

Primrosekit looked indignant. "But you *have* to be Thunder-Clan," she mewed.

"Why?" Stormkit blinked at her.

"Because you're too weak to win a battle."

Stormkit frowned. "But in real life ThunderClan wins battles all the time."

Leopardstar's breath caught in her throat. *ThunderClan wins battles all the time.* Rage flared fresh beneath her pelt. Stormkit was too young to understand what he was saying, but those were clearly Graystripe's words. That traitor was still undermining the Clan even now that he had left. She got to her paws. She'd have to speak to the kits.

"Leopardstar." Stonefur's mew made her turn.

The RiverClan deputy had stopped beside her. He looked at her anxiously. "Tigerstar's here." He nodded to the entrance, where the ShadowClan leader was flanked by Vixenleap and Mistyfoot.

He was looking around the camp, his eyes gleaming.

Leopardstar fluffed out her fur. "Bring him to my den," she told Stonefur. "I'll speak to him there."

CHAPTER 29

She waited until Stonefur's paw steps had faded before she spoke. The moss trailing at the entrance of her den was still shivering where they'd pushed through, and Tigerstar's eyes gleamed in the half-light.

"Why have you come?" she asked.

He sat down. "To warn you."

She stiffened. "Has something happened?"

"ThunderClan has been hunting in the Fourtrees hollow lately."

Her pelt rippled along her spine. "Fourtrees is neutral territory. No one is supposed to hunt there."

"Perhaps the forest prey hasn't recovered from the fire," Tigerstar mewed. "Or perhaps they just want to leave their mark there."

"Should we challenge them?"

"That's up to you." He tucked his tail over his paws. "I thought you might be thinking of sending patrols there too."

"Why would I send patrols to Fourtrees?"

"The river's frozen, and you didn't manage to reclaim Sunningrocks—"

Had he just come to remind her of her failures? She cut him off. "I don't need advice," she snapped.

He dipped his head apologetically. "I was just trying to be a helpful ally. Forgive me."

She fluffed out her fur. "Are you going to challenge ThunderClan?" she asked.

"I'm not sure ShadowClan is strong enough to challenge them alone." His eyes rounded innocently. Was he hinting that he wanted RiverClan's help? He went on. "Besides, we have enough prey inside our borders. I'm more worried about you. Both you and ThunderClan are struggling to find prey. Since you share a border, it might lead to conflict. All it would take is for one warrior to accidentally chase prey across the scent line . . ." He paused. "Prey doesn't respect boundaries."

"They haven't crossed it so far," she mewed evenly. He was trying to tell her something, but she wasn't sure what it was.

"If they did," he mewed, "you would have ShadowClan's support. Indeed, if perhaps you . . ." He hesitated again.

Leopardstar leaned forward.

"If you *wanted* to cross their border, ShadowClan wouldn't object."

"You want me to steal prey from ThunderClan?"

"I want you to know that ShadowClan supports you whatever you decide." He was staring at her meaningfully.

She narrowed her eyes. He seemed to be encouraging her to provoke ThunderClan. Was this his way of shaking up the Clans—by starting wars?

"Imagine how strong we could be if we worked together," he mewed.

"But we're already allies."

"I'm thinking further ahead," he mewed. "Imagine if there weren't four Clans fighting over borders, but two."

She stiffened. "But there have always been four Clans."

"Why?"

"Because that's what StarClan decided."

"There aren't four Clans in StarClan," Tigerstar pointed out. "Why is there one rule for StarClan and another for us? Do you think StarClan might *enjoy* watching our petty quarrels over borders and prey?"

"Of course not!" Her pelt bristled. What he was suggesting would undermine the warrior code. It would go against everything she'd been raised to believe. And yet, fewer Clans would mean fewer borders. And more prey. RiverClan wouldn't go hungry every time the river froze or flooded. She pushed the thought away. It was mouse-brained. "ThunderClan would never agree," she mewed. "And WindClan can only hunt on the moor. They have no idea how to catch forest prey."

Tigerstar's eyes shone. "Who said ThunderClan or WindClan has to agree?" he mewed. "I'm not interested in rabbit-chasers or kittypets. I'd prefer to work with *you*. We share the same principles. We're forward-thinking, not stuck in the past. We could build a strong Clan of *true* warriors."

Her heart quickened. A Clan of *true* warriors could rule the whole forest. She could take Sunningrocks back from ThunderClan. She could hunt the moor whenever she needed.

Tigerstar leaned closer. His breath was warm, and she could smell the musky scent of mouse on it. "This is the change I've been talking about. This is how we make the Clans stronger than they've ever been."

She stared at him. Two Clans. Was it possible?

She shuddered. *Of course not.* RiverClan was *RiverClan*, and no matter how hard it was to survive, she couldn't imagine giving that up, becoming part of another Clan. "No." She lifted her muzzle. "We can be allies. But nothing more."

He stared at her for a moment, as though waiting for her to change her mind, then got to his paws. "I'm disappointed," he mewed. "But perhaps you're right. Why do the Clans need change? RiverClan is fine the way it is." He turned toward the entrance. "Good luck feeding your Clan." His tail swished past her muzzle as he nosed his way out of the den.

He was irritated. He'd get over it. And yet she couldn't help feeling a twinge of guilt too. She'd said she'd wanted change, and now that Tigerstar had asked her to help him make it happen, she'd let him down. Were his ideas really so unreasonable? After all, he only wanted to make sure their warriors didn't go hungry. Could uniting the Clans be the way to achieve it?

The next day, Featherkit and Stormkit were pacing eagerly at the edge of the clearing while Mosspelt watched them proudly.

Leopardstar called to her Clanmates. "Let all cats old enough to swim gather to hear my words."

Jaggedtooth and Boulder got slowly to their paws as her other Clanmates gathered around the clearing. The two toms pushed their way between Timberfur and Cedarpelt and sat down, watching through narrowed eyes as Mosspelt gathered Featherkit and Stormkit close to her with a swish of her tail.

The kits stared expectantly at Leopardstar, and she felt a twinge of anxiety. It was her duty to help these kits become brave and loyal RiverClan warriors. Could they ever overcome their ThunderClan blood? She glanced at Stonefur and Mistyfoot. Had she made the right decision? Stonefur had been asking questions lately. He clearly doubted her choices. What if he passed on that doubt to his apprentice?

She shook out her pelt crossly. Mudfur and Crookedstar had spent so long doubting her that she'd learned to doubt herself. She wasn't going to let them or Stonefur, or any other cat, make her question her choices. She wanted the best for her Clan, and the decisions she made would always reflect that.

"Featherkit." She called the young she-cat to the middle of the clearing. How she'd grown since the night Graystripe had carried her across the stepping-stones and dropped her at Crookedstar's paws! And how much had changed since then. "You have reached the age of six moons, and it's time for you to be apprenticed," she mewed. Featherkit's eyes were large and shimmered with excitement. "From this day on, you will be known as Featherpaw. Your mentor will be Mistyfoot. I hope she will pass down all she knows to you."

Mistyfoot was standing at the edge of the clearing, looking ready to hurry across to greet her apprentice.

Leopardstar beckoned her forward with a nod. "Misty-foot." She dipped her head to the pale gray she-cat as she reached her. "You have been a loyal and brave warrior. You have already given your Clan kits who will, in their turn, become true warriors."

Primrosepaw, Reedpaw, and Pikepaw were watching from beside Blackclaw, pride glowing in their eyes.

"Now it is time to pass your skills on to a younger cat. I hope Featherpaw will thrive under your mentorship."

She felt suddenly touched by the grave affection with which Mistyfoot pressed her nose to Featherpaw's head. No matter what blood flowed beneath their pelts, these kits were her Clanmates. They would be strong RiverClan apprentices, and soon even stronger warriors.

"Stormkit."

As she called the young tom forward, he hurried from the edge of the clearing. Jaggedtooth muttered something into Boulder's ear, and they exchanged a look that made the fur prickle along Leopardstar's spine.

"Silence!" she growled at them. "This is an important ceremony. Save your gossip until afterward."

Jaggedtooth glowered at her. Boulder tipped his head to one side. But Leopardstar ignored them and looked back at Stormkit. The young tom was staring at her excitedly.

"You have reached six moons, and you are ready to be apprenticed. From this day on you will be known as Storm-paw. Your mentor will be Stonefur." She nodded the deputy forward and dipped her head. "You are one of our Clan's strongest and most skillful warriors," she told him as he stopped beside Stormpaw. "I expect you to pass on your skills to Stormpaw and train him to become as formidable a fighter and hunter as you are."

Stonefur's eyes glowed, and for the first time in days, he looked happy. As he touched his nose to Stormpaw's head, the Clan began to call out the names of the new apprentices.

"Stormpaw!"

"Featherpaw!"

Mosspelt's mew was the loudest, but it was soon drowned out by Blackclaw's and the other warriors' as the island rang to the sound of her Clanmates' cheers.

Leopardstar let her shoulders relax. The apprentices' den would be full again. No wonder Tigerstar had wanted River-Clan to align with him.

As the celebration died down, Leopardstar nodded to her deputy.

"Stonefur, I want to talk about hunting patrols. Ask Black-claw, Sedgecreek, and Ottersplash to join us."

He nodded, leaving the mouse he'd been eating to hurry across the clearing.

Leopardstar paced outside her den. Tigerstar's scent still lingered. She'd turned him down, but she thought he'd still support her if she ran into conflict with ThunderClan. It might be worth testing him.

She dipped her head as Stonefur, Sedgecreek, Blackclaw, and Ottersplash gathered around her. Stonefur blinked at her expectantly.

"Last leaf-bare, RiverClan cats went hungry," Leopardstar mewed. "This leaf-bare, I'm going to make sure that doesn't happen."

"How?" Ottersplash mewed. "The river is already frozen and leaf-bare has hardly begun."

"And ThunderClan still has Sunningrocks," Blackclaw added.

Her fur ruffled. "We have to look elsewhere."

Stonefur shifted his paws uneasily. "What do you mean?"

"If the patrols don't bring back enough prey today, tomorrow I will ask them to cross the ThunderClan border."

Stonefur's pelt rippled along his spine. "That's trespassing!"

Leopardstar tipped her head to one side. "Would you rather your Clanmates went hungry?"

"Of course not." His tail was twitching. "But we can't steal ThunderClan prey to feed ourselves. The warrior code—"

"The warrior code also tells us that we mustn't allow a kit to suffer." She glanced toward the nursery. "Which rule do you think is most important?"

"I know, but—"

"Are you loyal to RiverClan or not?"

He stared at her, his ears twitching.

"Are you loyal or not?" she hissed.

"I'm loyal!" he mewed. "I've always been loyal. How could you even ask?" He fluffed out his pelt, but he looked nervous. "I'd do anything to protect my Clanmates. I always will, even if . . ."

Leopardstar narrowed her eyes. *"Even if?"*

"Even if"—he hesitated again, flustered—"they don't want me to."

"I'm glad to hear it." Leopardstar got to her paws. Why was he acting so suspiciously? "The meeting's over," she mewed. "It's decided. We will hunt across the river if we must."

She dismissed them with the flick of her tail. Stonefur's reaction had unnerved her. She padded out of camp and, pushing among the reeds, sat down beside the river. Ice stretched to the far shore. She could see it was thin at the center. A patrol could probably break through. But she wasn't going to order her warriors to fish beneath ice. It was too easy to get disoriented and lose sight of the breathing hole. She didn't want any cat getting trapped there.

Stonefur's words nagged at her. *I'd do anything to protect them. Even if . . .*

Even if *what*? What had the RiverClan deputy been about to say? Before the incident at Sunningrocks, it had never occurred to her that Stonefur could be disloyal. But Fireheart had said something to him and Mistyfoot that had made them back away. And now Stonefur was objecting to taking ThunderClan prey. Was disloyalty like a sickness that spread through a Clan? Had Graystripe infected him?

Paw steps sounded on the track behind her. She glanced through the reeds and saw a blue-gray pelt moving beyond them. She tasted the air. It was Stonefur. He was treading lightly, as though trying not to be noticed. Where was he going on his own? Didn't he have duties in camp?

She waited for him to pass, then slipped out of the reeds and followed his scent, staying far enough behind that he didn't see her. It led her to the edge of a grassy clearing hidden among the reed beds. She ducked down and wriggled between the reeds until she was close enough to hear. Mistyfoot was pacing on the grass while Stonefur spoke to her.

"We don't have to *do* anything," he mewed. "We just have to stay quiet."

"But Fireheart knows." Mistyfoot looked at him, her eyes sparkling with fear. "Which means Graystripe must know. Perhaps the whole of ThunderClan knows."

"Of course they don't," Stonefur reassured her. "Fireheart only told us so that we wouldn't hurt Bluestar."

Told you what? Leopardstar wriggled closer.

Mistyfoot refused to be comforted. "What if RiverClan finds out?"

"Some of them might already know," Stonefur mewed grimly. "It can't have been easy smuggling two kits into the nursery. And Graypool might have confided in someone. It must have been hard pretending we were her kits all these moons."

Pretending? Leopardstar swallowed. What did he mean? Weren't Stonefur and Mistyfoot Graypool's real kits?

Mistyfoot blinked at her brother. "It must have been hard for Oakheart too," she mewed. "He had to pretend we *weren't* his kits." Her mew cracked. "I wish he'd told us, once we were old enough."

"Bluestar must have made him promise to keep it a secret," Stonefur mewed.

Leopardstar's ears burned with curiosity. What did Bluestar have to do with this?

"Why did she give us up?" Mistyfoot mewed. "When she

gave Featherkit and Stormkit to RiverClan, she said kits belong in their *mother's* Clan. If she believed that, shouldn't she have kept us with her?"

Leopardstar's eyes widened. Had she understood properly? Were Mistyfoot and Stonefur the kits of Bluestar and Oakheart? Was RiverClan's deputy a *half-Clan* cat?

Stonefur frowned. "Whatever Bluestar decided, she must have thought was for the best. All we have to do now is keep it secret."

"Shouldn't we tell Leopardstar?" Mistyfoot mewed. "She should know."

"Have you seen the way she looks at Featherpaw and Stormpaw since Graystripe betrayed her?" Stonefur mewed. "And she nearly bit off my head just now because I didn't want to agree to steal ThunderClan prey." He shivered. "She's far too sensitive after what happened with Silverstream and Graystripe. Let's just keep it quiet."

Leopardstar didn't need to hear any more. She slid backward through the reeds and ducked out onto the track. Hurrying back to camp, her thoughts spun. She'd thought Featherpaw and Stormpaw had been the only half-Clan cats in RiverClan. Now it seemed there were two *more*—and she'd made them Featherpaw's and Stormpaw's mentors. Anxiety wormed beneath her pelt. When water found its way into stone, it could split it. Was that what would happen in River-Clan? Four cats with ThunderClan blood. How could she trust their loyalty? Would they betray her like Graystripe had? She whisked her tail. She should have dealt with him earlier. This time, she wasn't going to make the same mistake.

CHAPTER 30

✿

Leopardstar glanced toward the camp entrance. How long until Tiger-star arrived? She'd sent Blackclaw to fetch him ages ago. She tore off another strip of squirrel and began to chew it. The musky flavor was quite pleasant, and she was getting used to gnawing bones. They were almost tasty, really, once she'd softened them up with her teeth.

The sun was sliding toward the river, turning the reed beds rosy. Her Clanmates had settled around her, sharing the day's catch between them. Satisfaction swept Leopardstar's pelt. Every cat had a piece of prey. They might even come to *enjoy* forest food. They'd have plenty more chances to eat it.

The cross-border patrols over the past few days had gone smoothly. Despite the fire, prey was running well on ThunderClan land, so much so that Leopardstar wondered if ThunderClan would even miss the squirrels and mice her warriors had brought back. As soon as the river thawed, they would return to fishing. But, in the meantime, she wasn't going to let her Clan go hungry.

It felt liberating to ignore borders, and she'd begun to wonder why she'd ever let scent lines decide whether her Clan went hungry or not. If prey was there, why should cats starve? And if ThunderClan objected, she knew ShadowClan would back her up. Slowly, she'd begun to see that borders existed only in the minds of the Clans, and that Clans might be stronger and better fed without them. Tigerstar's plan to unite the four Clans seemed more and more sensible. And hadn't Mudfur and Crookedstar both dreamed of a time without petty battles over prey?

First Tigerstar had suggested that they go from four Clans to two. But recently, he'd asked why they should stop there. She and Tigerstar had similar outlooks; surely they could lead together with little conflict. And if there were only one Clan, there would be no need to fight. Of course, he said, Thunder-Clan and WindClan wouldn't agree at first. WindClan had always kept too much to themselves, and ThunderClan enjoyed bossing the other Clans around too much to accept them as equals. But if RiverClan and ShadowClan worked together, WindClan and ThunderClan would eventually have no choice but to share their land, and, in exchange, she and Tigerstar would guarantee peace.

She pushed the squirrel away and lay back, enjoying the last faint rays of the sun. Happiness flowed beneath her pelt. It looked as though Mudfur's vision was coming true. She would be the cat to save RiverClan. Because of her, there would be prey and peace no matter the season.

She watched her Clan, feeling pleased. Timberfur, Cedarpelt, and Piketooth had settled well into the elders' den. Pikepaw, Reedpaw, and Primrosepaw were apprentices now, and Mosspelt had Skyheart for company.

She could see the queens now, lying in the soft grass beside the clearing. Skyheart was picking at the mouse Reedtail had brought her. Her nose wrinkled as she sniffed the plump piece of prey and pushed it away. Was her pregnancy making her feel queasy?

Leopardstar got to her paws and crossed the clearing. "Are you okay?" she asked as she reached her. "Should I fetch Mudfur? I'm sure he can give you herbs for the sickness."

Skyheart blinked at her. "I'm not sick." She poked the mouse with a claw. "I just don't like *this*."

"You've eaten water vole and warbler before," Leopardstar reminded her. "Mouse isn't so different. You'll get used to it."

"I'm not sure if I want to." Skyheart's tail twitched irritably.

"We can't rely on river prey," Leopardstar told her. "Sometimes forest prey is all we have."

"But this is ThunderClan prey," Skyheart mewed. "Eating it seems"—she hesitated, eyeing Leopardstar—"wrong."

Leopardstar stiffened. *"Wrong?"*

"It's stolen." Skyheart looked at her boldly.

Leopardstar stiffened. "It was caught by your Clanmates so you wouldn't go hungry and so your kits can grow strong."

Skyheart lifted her muzzle. "It was caught on another Clan's land."

Leopardstar's pelt ruffled. "RiverClan hasn't gone hungry even though the river is frozen." Didn't Skyheart appreciate that?

"What about ThunderClan?" Skyheart snapped. "Have they gone hungry because we've stolen their prey?"

"You should be grateful you *have* food." Leopardstar snapped back. Behind her, the entrance tunnel swished. But she didn't turn to see who'd arrived. Anger was sparking in her belly. Were the rest of the Clan ungrateful too? She looked at them, her tail twitching as she noticed them picking at their prey like difficult kits. Didn't they realize they'd be starving if it weren't for her? She turned on Skyheart again. "It's your duty to eat well and make sure your kits grow into healthy warriors!"

Paw steps stopped beside her and Tigerstar's scent swept her muzzle. The ShadowClan leader had arrived. She stiffened. She didn't want him to see how ungrateful her Clan was. But he was already staring at Skyheart's unwanted mouse.

He hooked it with a large claw and dangled it in front of the queen. "You should eat every morsel." He dropped in front of her. "Or Leopardstar might think you don't want your kits to grow up strong."

Skyheart glared at him and pushed the mouse away. "I eat what I like," she snapped.

His tail flicked ominously. "Eat it," he growled.

Skyheart looked at Leopardstar. "Are you going to let him tell me what to do?"

Leopardstar hesitated. It felt strange to let another Clan leader give orders to her Clanmates. And yet, soon they'd be his Clanmates too. That was why she'd asked him here. That was why he'd come. She was going to agree to unite RiverClan and ShadowClan into a single Clan. She nodded at the mouse. "He's right," she mewed. "You should eat it for the good of your kits."

Skyheart blinked at her. Then she looked around the

clearing, as though appealing to her Clanmates.

Tigerstar didn't take his gaze from the queen. RiverClan was watching uneasily. Leopardstar shifted self-consciously. *I must back him up.* He needed to know she would support him, and the Clan needed to know that things were going to change. It was the only way to make sure they would have prey every night.

"Eat it," she told Skyheart.

The gray queen flattened her ears.

"Eat it," she snapped.

Skyheart stared defiantly back for a moment; then she leaned down to take a bite.

"All of it," Tigerstar growled.

Leopardstar's paws pricked as Skyheart slowly ate the mouse. She felt uncomfortable, but the queen would go to her nest with a full belly, and when her kits were born, healthy and strong, they would never know hunger.

As Skyheart spat out the bones, Tigerstar yanked them away. "You should keep her from prey for a few sunrises," he told Leopardstar. "See how she likes going hungry."

Leopardstar glanced at him. Was he this strict with his own Clanmates? "That would certainly teach her to be a little more grateful for her food," she told him. "But she's a queen. We must take care of her kits."

But Tigerstar didn't seem to hear. He was looking at the bones. "Save all your bones from now on." He looked at the small piles collected around the clearing. "I have a plan for them."

What did a warrior want with bones? Leopardstar glanced at him curiously, but she didn't ask. There were more important things to discuss. She jerked her nose toward the reed tunnel. "Let's talk."

As she led him out of camp, she felt a glimmer of satisfaction. The powerful tabby had crossed Fourtrees and walked all the way to her camp to hear what she had to say. He needed RiverClan. She liked it.

Outside, she stopped beside the river. "I've been thinking about what you said," she told him. "And I've come to a decision."

Tigerstar sat down, his sleek pelt glossy in the twilight. "I was pleased to see Blackclaw," he mewed. "Especially when he told me you wanted to speak to me." He pricked his ears. "Good news, I hope?"

"I took your advice and expanded my hunting patrols," she told him.

"You mean you've been hunting on ThunderClan land." His whiskers twitched. "I thought I recognized the scent of ThunderClan prey."

"I can see now how borders cause unnecessary hardship," she mewed. "Why shouldn't warriors hunt where they like? Why do they need to go hungry because of a scent line?"

"Borders create hunger," Tigerstar mewed.

"Fewer Clans means more prey for all."

"Exactly." He licked a paw and ran it over his ear. "Does this mean you're finally ready to shake things up a bit?"

"Yes." Excitement sparked in her belly.

"RiverClan and ShadowClan will become one?"

She hadn't discussed this with Stonefur yet. She knew her deputy would never agree. How could he agree to an alliance against ThunderClan when ThunderClan blood ran beneath his pelt? But this was right. And he would come to see it in the end, as would ThunderClan and WindClan. This was the best for everyone, but most importantly, it was the best for River-Clan. "We'll be equals?" she asked. "We'll lead together?"

"Of course," he mewed smoothly. "Everything will be shared fairly."

"And you'll discuss everything with me before you act?"

"I've always valued your opinion." That was true. He'd treated her with respect even when Crookedstar and Mudfur doubted her. "This will begin a new age for the Clans," he went on. "Once every Clan has accepted that unity is the best way forward, there will be peace and prey for every cat."

Leopardstar's heart was racing. She'd never see her Clan-mates go hungry again. And ThunderClan and WindClan would treat her with a new respect. She lifted her muzzle, energy fizzing through her pelt. "All right," she mewed. "Let's do this. Let's become a single Clan."

Tigerstar's tail swished. "Good." He looked across the river, the light of the rising moon reflecting in his amber eyes. "With RiverClan on our side, ShadowClan will never be defeated. Together, we'll form TigerClan. We'll be the fierc-est hunters and fighters in the forest, just like the ancestors we were named for."

Leopardstar blinked at him. "Or we could be LeopardClan."

He looked at her. "Let's decide the details later," he purred. "We're going to make a great team. We'll remake the forest." He got to his paws. "I can't wait to tell my Clanmates. Let's meet tomorrow at Fourtrees. Bring your Clan. We can get to know each other."

"Sure, but—" she began, but Tigerstar was already bounding away. He was more excited than she'd imagined. His plan was finally becoming a reality.

She fluffed out her fur. This would a fresh start: She'd be remembered for generations for what she'd decided here today.

She stiffened. A shape was moving in the shadows beside the camp wall. She padded toward it, her pelt ruffling. "Who's there?"

As she tasted the air, Mudfur padded into the moonlight.

"Were you listening?" Why did she feel guilty? She'd made a decision for her Clan. She was leader.

"I heard everything." His eyes were dark. "Are you sure you know what you're doing?"

"Of course," she snapped. "Life is going to improve for RiverClan."

"I don't trust Tigerstar," Mudfur padded closer. "There's something dangerous about him."

"He just wants peace."

"By joining ShadowClan and RiverClan?" Mudfur sounded skeptical. "Won't the other Clans see it as a challenge?"

"If they do, they won't dare fight us. We'll be too strong."

"There are more important things than being strong," Mudfur mewed.

Leopardstar bit back anger. "Nothing's more important than feeding the Clan."

Mudfur narrowed his eyes. "Will you be happy following Tigerstar's orders?"

"We will lead equally!" Leopardstar lasted her tail. "Tigerstar said we would."

Mudfur grunted. "Well, if Tigerstar says it, then that's the way it will be, I suppose."

"Stop twisting my words!" Leopardstar tried to keep her pelt smooth. "Have you forgotten your vision? It was you who said I'd save the Clan, and I've found a way to do it. You're just finding problems."

"Joining with ShadowClan won't save the Clan," he mewed darkly. "It will destroy it."

"What makes you so sure?" she snapped.

"He left ThunderClan and became leader of ShadowClan," Mudfur mewed. "Don't you think that's odd?"

"Fireheart got in the way." Leopardstar puffed out her chest. "Agreeing to lead ShadowClan was the only way left for him to bring change to the Clans."

"Do they need changing?"

She couldn't believe he was asking. "Your Clanmates go hungry every time the river freezes or floods! That doesn't have to happen now. *I* can see that. Tigerstar can see it. Why can't you?"

"I think all Tigerstar can see is power."

"You never trust any cat!" Leopardstar's pelt bristled. "You've never trusted *me*!"

"I wanted to," he mewed. "I *still* want to."

"Then why are you questioning me? You told me I'd save the Clans. Let me save them!"

The moon was high now and the sky indigo behind him. Mudfur's eyes shone like water. "When I told you that you'd save the Clans, I believed it with my whole heart. But now . . ." His mew trailed away.

But now? Leopardstar's mouth grew dry. What was he saying? That he'd been wrong? That he'd stopped believing in her? She'd thought the plan to unite with ShadowClan would prove that she was the right leader for RiverClan once and for all, dispelling any doubts he'd had when she became deputy. But was he saying it was the opposite?

All she'd ever wanted was for her father to believe in her. She'd tried so hard to impress him, and yet here they stood. Her heart seemed to crack, but she lifted her chin. "*I'm* leader," she growled. "Not you. Perhaps you should hold your tongue before you say something we'll both regret." But it was too late for that. She wanted him to take back his words. She wanted him to say he'd been wrong, that he'd just spoken out of anger.

Mudfur's eyes darkened. "I'm not the one who will have regrets," he mewed sadly. "You are not the only one here who cares about RiverClan. As your medicine cat, I'm obliged to speak the truth of what StarClan tells me."

Leopardstar widened her eyes. Was he threatening her? Was he planning to undermine her in front of their Clanmates? "What does that mean?" she demanded.

But he didn't answer. Instead he dipped his head and padded back into camp.

* * *

"Let all cats old enough to swim gather to hear my words." Leopardstar stood in the middle of the clearing, the bright morning sun almost warm on her pelt. She'd barely slept. Mudfur's words had echoed in her mind all night. Even when she had drifted off, she'd been woken by dreams where Mudfur had turned his back on her as the river had swept her away.

She fluffed out her fur, trying to push back the weariness dragging at her bones. As her Clanmates gathered around her, she barely noticed them. She could only see Mudfur padding from the medicine den, herb flecks in his pelt, as he joined his Clanmates to listen.

"Mudfur must leave us for a while." Leopardstar ignored the surprised murmuring of the Clan. She kept her gaze fixed on her father.

He stared back at her, his gaze giving nothing away.

"We have lost too many cats to greencough over the moons," she mewed. "Including Crookedstar. But I have heard rumors about loners who claim there is an herb that can cure greencough. It has rosy, round leaves, and it grows in cracks in the rocks in the mountains."

"What's it called?" Sedgecreek was blinking at her eagerly.

"I don't know," Leopardstar told her. "But I'm sure Mudfur will recognize it when he sees it. I know he'll find it. Imagine if we are able to find a cure for this terrible sickness."

Mosspelt flicked her tail happily. "No kit need die of it again!"

"We will be spared at least one hardship," Timberfur mewed.

Cedarpelt looked anxiously at Mudfur. "Will you travel alone?"

But Mudfur's gaze was still on Leopardstar. "Will I?" he asked her.

She dug her claws into the earth. She'd given him no warning that she was going to ask him to leave for a while, and she knew that their conversation yesterday must be fresh in his mind. Was he going to challenge her order in front of the Clan? "You will travel faster alone," she mewed evenly. "And we can't spare warriors now with prey scarce. Feeding our Clanmates is a priority."

Ottersplash frowned. "Why go now? Why not wait until newleaf?" she asked. "When the weather is better?"

"Greencough strikes hardest in leaf-bare," Leopardstar told her. "And I hear this herb is at its most potent now." It was a lie, but it was necessary. There was no herb. She knew it and so did Mudfur. He was still watching her, his tail twitching. But he wasn't going to argue. He would have already spoken.

She had to get him out of the way while she and Tigerstar formed a Clan that would change the whole forest. She didn't want Mudfur second-guessing every decision, planting doubt in her mind. Those days were gone. She was leader now, and she was going to lead without any cat's interference.

CHAPTER 31

❧

"Thank you." Leopardstar nodded to Stonefur as he dropped a rabbit at her paws.

He eyed her warily and padded away, little more than a shadow in the twilight. Perhaps he sensed her distrust of him, or perhaps he was still uneasy about having Jaggedtooth and Boulder stay in the RiverClan camp.

The two ShadowClan cats had been sent by Tigerstar to support her while her Clanmates grew accustomed to the new arrangement. But the two former rogues had done little to win the confidence of RiverClan, refusing to hunt or patrol with the other warriors, claiming instead that Tigerstar had ordered them to stay in camp to make sure it was safe from ThunderClan or WindClan aggression.

The two burly toms sat apart from the Clan now, sharing a mouse and watching the RiverClan cats. Leopardstar had told her warriors that they were all Clanmates and that they should be grateful to have extra fighters in camp. Now that they were TigerClan, they could expect retaliation from ThunderClan and WindClan at any moment.

Blackclaw and Reedtail seemed to appreciate their presence, and Skyheart too. The rest of the Clan seemed less certain, but since Jaggedtooth and Boulder had arrived, they had stopped questioning whether aligning with Shadow-Clan was wise. Leopardstar was relieved that she didn't have to defend her decision anymore. It was for their own good; they would come to see that soon enough. Until they did, they had to admit there was plenty of prey now that they could hunt across Fourtrees and into ShadowClan land, not to mention make forays into ThunderClan and WindClan territory whenever they liked.

Leopardstar glanced toward the entrance tunnel. Tigerstar would come soon. He usually came this time of day to check that the river warriors of TigerClan had enough prey, and Leopardstar always felt a little relieved to see him. She was reassured by his presence, more certain that she'd made the right choice in making RiverClan part of TigerClan.

She heard paw steps beyond the reed wall and began to get to her paws, her nose twitching eagerly as she smelled Tiger-star's scent. He padded through the tunnel but didn't cross the camp to greet her as he usually did. Instead he flicked his tail toward her. "I have something to show you." His eyes gleamed. "Come with me."

Stonefur lifted his muzzle. "Should I come, too?" Leopard-star knew that he didn't trust the dark warrior, though he'd never said so out loud.

Tigerstar glowered at the deputy. "This isn't for half-Clan cats."

Stonefur looked away. The Clan knew now that his—and Mistyfoot's—mother had been Bluestar. Stonefur had told them himself. Perhaps he'd guessed that Leopardstar had discovered their secret and decided it was safer to tell the truth than to have it told for him.

"Are you coming, Leopardstar?" Tigerstar's ears twitched impatiently.

She got to her paws and stepped over the rabbit Stonefur had brought. It would keep. Her paws were itching with curiosity. What did Tigerstar want to show her?

She had to hurry to catch up to him as he headed along the riverbank. "What is it?" she asked, falling in beside him.

"Wait and see." His tail was swishing. There was something on the tabby warrior's mind.

"Is everything okay?" she asked.

He glanced at her. "Are you still planning to make Stonefur and Mistyfoot mentors to Featherkit and Stormkit?"

He didn't approve. But she was still a leader; she could make the final decision. She fluffed out her fur. "Yes."

"I think you're taking a risk," he grunted. "Letting half-Clan cats train other half-Clan cats is dangerous. If you put traitors together, they'll encourage each other."

"They're not traitors." Leopardstar was wary of their ThunderClan blood, but she hadn't seen any evidence of disloyalty. Indeed, they seemed to be trying hard to fit in among the river warriors. "If I show them trust, they're more likely to support me."

"Do you need their support?"

"I need the support of all my Clanmates," Leopardstar told him.

"You don't win support by winning trust," Tigerstar mewed. "You just show them what happens if they don't support you."

She glanced at him, uneasy at the darkness in his expression.

Carrion scent touched her muzzle as she padded beside Tigerstar through the fading light. It grew stronger as he led her past the water meadow to a wide, flat clearing among the reeds. The carrion scent was so strong here that her nose wrinkled. She narrowed her eyes. What was that heap at the far end?

Tigerstar hurried toward it and stopped as he reached it. "I got the idea when Skyheart refused to eat her mouse."

Leopardstar followed, realizing with a start that it was a heap of bones. She frowned. Was this where ShadowClan had decided to throw their waste? "Isn't there anywhere to dump trash on *your* territory?"

Tigerstar's hackles twitched. "It's *all* my territory now," he growled.

"It's all *our* territory," Leopardstar corrected him.

"Of course." He glanced at her. "But this isn't trash." His swept his gaze over the pile of bones. It was a mound big enough to climb. "It's a monument."

"What's it for?" Leopardstar wasn't sure it was wise to create a stinking heap so close to the island camp.

"It's to remind our Clanmates to be grateful for their food," he mewed. "One look at this pile will show them how much they've eaten and how lucky they are to be part of TigerClan."

Leopardstar had to admit that it was an impressive pile

and that any cat who saw it would have to admit TigerClan ate well. But she couldn't stop the shiver of surprise that ran down her spine as Tigerstar leaped on top of it and turned to stare at her.

The bones shifted beneath his paws. A few tumbled down the sides, dislodged by his weight.

"It's a good place to address the Clan." He looked around the dark clearing. "From now on we should hold TigerClan meetings here."

Leopardstar narrowed her eyes. She had been wondering how they'd solve the problem of which camp to choose for Clan gatherings.

He went on. "You said you were worried that whichever camp was chosen would show favor to that Clan," he mewed. "This way, we favor neither."

Leopardstar felt a ripple of satisfaction. The bone pile was on former RiverClan land.

Tigerstar looked around from the top of the pile, imposing against the darkening sky. "I can see over the reed beds too," he mewed. "It will make a good place to look out for enemy attack."

Leopardstar shifted her paws. "Do you think WindClan and ThunderClan will attack?"

"They must," he mewed. "We're stronger than they are now. They'll need to weaken TigerClan if they're to keep their borders and prey safe." He bounded lightly from the bone pile and landed beside her. "Which means we must attack them first."

Leopardstar frowned. "Shouldn't we talk to them first?" she mewed. "We might be able to persuade them to join us. There'd be no need to fight."

"Firestar is a leader now." Tigerstar's lip curled. "Do you think he will want to share power after fighting so hard to gain it?"

Leopardstar knew he was right. "We might be able to persuade WindClan," she mewed.

Tigerstar grunted. "WindClan will do whatever Thunder-Clan tells them to do."

"Even now that Bluestar's dead?"

"Especially now that Bluestar's dead." Tigerstar's eyes flashed. "Firestar will have made peace with Tallstar. They're probably planning retaliation right now."

Leopardstar ignored the flutter of anxiety in her chest. "In that case, we must attack soon," she mewed. "And we must attack both Clans at the same time."

"Is that wise?" Tigerstar leaned closer, his ears pricking.

"We must defeat them both with a single swipe," Leopardstar told him. "If we attack WindClan alone, the survivors will go to ThunderClan. If we attack ThunderClan alone, the survivors will go to WindClan. But if we attack both Clans together, the survivors will have nowhere to go but TigerClan."

"I knew you were skilled at fighting, and brave"—Tigerstar dipped his head—"but I didn't realize you were a strategist too."

Leopardstar puffed out her chest. "It just takes a little reasoning, that's all."

His gaze drifted toward the reeds. "If we're going to attack them both, we'll need more cats."

"Perhaps we can persuade a few WindClan and Thunder-Clan warriors to turn on their leaders. Some of them might see that a single Clan will save them from a future of fighting and hunger." She blinked at him expectantly. Would he be impressed by this idea too?

There was a gleam in his eyes she hadn't seen before. Her pelt ruffled self-consciously.

He padded a little closer. "Why have you never taken a mate?"

She felt warm. Was he flirting with her? "It was a choice," she mewed.

"It seems a shame."

"I wanted to dedicate my life to my Clan," she told him. "Not to a single warrior. And I didn't want to be tied down with kits." She hesitated. "My Clanmates feel like my kin. I wanted to take care of them all, not just my own kits."

His breath touched her whiskers. "That sounds lonely."

"It wasn't." She paused. That hadn't been true in recent moons. "Not to begin with, anyway. But I suppose, now that I'm leader, I'll always feel a little separate from my Clanmates. I'm different from them, I guess."

He held her gaze. "But not so different from me."

She looked away, her heart quickening. He understood her. "I don't mind the loneliness. Although I miss Mudfur. . . ." She paused. Had she been right to send her father away? Even if she disagreed with him, she'd always felt a closeness to him that came with truly being kin.

Tigerstar leaned closer. "Mudfur?"

"It doesn't matter." She drew away. "I don't mind loneliness, that's all. It's not important. What's important is making my Clan as strong as it can possibly be."

Tigerstar was gazing at her wistfully. Then he sighed. "If only our timing had been different."

The fur around her neck prickled.

He whisked his tail. "I should head back to the Shadow-Clan camp," he mewed briskly. "I think I might know how we can get more cats to help us defeat both Clans at once."

"You do?" Leopardstar looked at him eagerly. "How?"

"Let me look into it," he mewed. "I'll tell you later." He padded past her.

She watched him go, the fur twitching at the base of her tail. *If only our timing had been different.* She was intrigued. Could there have been a future for her and Tigerstar? Perhaps there still could be. She pushed the thought away. *Don't be mouse-brained. This is about your Clan,* she told herself firmly. *Not about you.*

The light snow that had fallen all morning had given way to afternoon sunshine, but the wind was still cold. The Clan was waiting for the apprentice ceremony to begin. Stonefur dipped his head to Leopardstar. "It's the half-moon meeting for the medicine cats tonight. Should I meet them on their way to the Moonstone to tell them not to expect Mudfur? They might wonder why he hasn't come."

Leopardstar eyed him sharply. "What would you say to them?"

"That he's looking for herbs."

"No." Leopardstar's tail twitched. The other medicine cats might realize she'd invented the story to get him away from the Clan. "Let's wait to see what Mudfur brings back. I don't want to get their hopes up."

"I hope he returns soon." Stonefur seemed anxious today. "A Clan needs a medicine cat."

"We have Runningnose," Leopardstar reminded him.

"But he sleeps in the ShadowClan camp. If anything happened here, it would take too long to—"

"There *is* no ShadowClan!" Leopardstar mewed curtly. "Only TigerClan."

"He's still a long way away if there's sickness here," Stonefur pointed out.

"Don't meet trouble halfway." Leopardstar turned away. Why was he always finding problems? Was it his way of criticizing her? She flexed her claws. Perhaps Tigerstar was right. Perhaps she shouldn't trust him so much. She swallowed back irritation.

TigerClan was stronger than ThunderClan and WindClan could ever be—and the strongest part of TigerClan was its river warriors.

As pride swelled in her chest, the reed tunnel shivered. Leopardstar's eyes widened in surprise as Tigerstar padded into camp. Blackfoot followed with a tom Leopardstar didn't recognize. His pelt was black and he had one white paw, and although he was small, his icy blue eyes gleamed with a menace that made Leopardstar's belly tighten. He was wearing a collar. Was this a kittypet? Leopardstar looked closer. The collar was purple and studded with something that looked like teeth. Leopardstar shivered. Why had Tigerstar brought such a vicious-looking cat here?

"Hey, Leopardstar." Tigerstar's pelt was fluffed out and his tail was high.

Leopardstar met his gaze. "What are you doing here?"

"I have to keep an eye on you. We all know that some of your warriors have . . . *divided* loyalties." His gaze flicked over Stormpaw and Featherpaw. They glanced nervously at each other as he curled his lip with distaste.

"I trust all of my Clanmates," Leopardstar mewed curtly. He'd told her often enough how much he disapproved of her choice to allow half-Clan cats to remain part of TigerClan.

Tigerstar padded into the clearing. Blackfoot and the other tom followed. As they neared, Leopardstar wrinkled her nose. They smelled of blood. Didn't they have the decency to wash before coming here?

She narrowed her eyes. "It's a shame the river is frozen," she mewed pointedly. "If you'd swum across the river, you wouldn't have arrived reeking like a fresh-kill pile."

The unfamiliar tom's eyes glittered with amusement. "I think your friend is objecting to the smell of rabbit blood," he mewed. "Are all river cats so squeamish about warm-blooded prey?"

Leopardstar met his gaze. "It's not the warmth that's offensive," she snapped. His muzzle and whiskers were stained red. "It's that you're covered in it. Don't you know how to wash?"

Tigerstar's tail flicked ominously. "Show some courtesy to our friend."

He's no friend of mine. Leopardstar kept the thought to herself. Tigerstar seemed belligerent. She didn't want to provoke him. "Who is he?" she asked instead.

"This is Scourge," he mewed. "He's offered to help out with our warrior shortage."

Scourge padded around Featherpaw and Stormpaw, eyeing them with interest. "I hear we have half-Clan warriors here," he mewed.

"They're apprentices, not warriors." Leopardstar felt a twinge of fear. Featherpaw and Stormpaw seemed suddenly vulnerable. "They're too young to fight. They've not yet been given their warrior names."

Tigerstar snorted. "They're no use to us anyway," he sneered. "A patrol of foxes would be more trustworthy."

Featherpaw lifted her tail. "That's not true!" she mewed. "We're as trustworthy as any RiverClan cat."

Tigerstar padded toward her. "Don't you mean *TigerClan?*"

Featherpaw backed away, her pelt rippling. "Of course," she mewed quickly. "TigerClan."

Stonefur stepped in front of her and faced Tigerstar. "Featherpaw and Stormpaw are loyal Clanmates," he mewed evenly. "As are Mistyfoot and I."

Tigerstar leaned toward him. "Loyal to whom?" he hissed. "TigerClan or ThunderClan?"

Mistyfoot pushed in front of her brother. "TigerClan, of course."

Tigerstar looked amused. "Which makes you disloyal to ThunderClan." He didn't give her chance to respond but swept his gaze around the watching Clan. "That's the trouble with half-Clan cats, they can only be *half*-loyal." He stopped as his gaze reached Leopardstar. "Or perhaps they are completely loyal to ThunderClan." He lashed his tail. "For all we know, Stonefur and Mistyfoot could be ThunderClan spies, and yet you let them train other half-Clans." He flattened his ears. "I'm beginning to think I made a mistake aligning with a Clan that has almost as many spies as warriors among its ranks."

Timberfur padded forward, his pelt bristling. "There are no spies in RiverClan!"

"*TigerClan!*" Tigerstar turned on Leopardstar. "Why can't your warriors even remember their new Clan name?" he spat. "Didn't you explain to them who they follow now?"

Cedarpelt padded to Timberfur's side and glared at the tabby warrior. "Who are we *supposed* to be following?" he asked Tigerstar. "*You?*" His gaze flitted to Leopardstar. "Have you given up the leadership as well as everything else?" he asked her.

Leopardstar's heart began to race. Suddenly she felt as though she were grabbing at fish in a shoal and that her claws couldn't hook any of them. Her hackles lifted. "I've given up nothing," she snarled at Cedarpelt. She turned to Tigerstar. He was embarrassing her in front of her Clanmates. "Come with me!" She padded toward the reed tunnel and ducked out of camp, relieved when Tigerstar followed with Blackfoot and Scourge.

The small black tom's eyes gleamed as she stopped and glared at Tigerstar.

Leopardstar forced her pelt to smooth. "Why are you acting like this?" Did he want to alienate half his Clan? "We're supposed to be working together against WindClan and ThunderClan. Right now it feels more like you're working against *me*!"

Tigerstar narrowed his eyes. "I'm worried that you've become too much like Bluestar."

"I'm nothing like her!"

"Really?" His muzzle wrinkled. "She let a kittypet deceive her into giving up her power. Now you're letting half-Clan cats run the place."

"They don't run the place!"

"One of them is your deputy!" Tigerstar snapped.

Stonefur ducked from the camp. He looked anxiously at Leopardstar. "Is everything okay?"

"Everything's fine," she reassured him.

Tigerstar thrust his muzzle toward the gray deputy. *"You're lucky to be alive, half-Clan traitor!"*

The viciousness of his mew sent alarm sparking through Leopardstar's pelt. Stonefur bristled, his eyes widening. The dark tabby had gone too far.

"Stonefur." She nodded to her deputy. "Go and see to Featherpaw. You should be training your apprentice."

But Stonefur was staring at Tigerstar. "I'm staying with you until he leaves," he told her. "I'm Clan deputy. My first duty is my Clanmates' protection."

"*I'm* your Clanmate now," Tigerstar snarled. "And who says you're deputy?" He glanced at Blackfoot. "TigerClan already has a deputy. I'd never appoint a mange-pelt like you."

Leopardstar's tail bushed with outrage. "I didn't agree to that!"

Tigerstar looked at her. "Are you going to *disagree?*"

She stiffened. She didn't want to have this discussion in front of Stonefur. Or Scourge and Blackfoot. She nodded to Stonefur. "I can manage this," she told him. "Go back to the camp."

"Yeah, go on, half-Clan snake," Blackfoot growled. "Go take care of your half-Clan apprentice."

Scourge sat down. He was clearly relishing Stonefur's humiliation.

Stonefur glanced at her. There was a question in his eyes.

Leopardstar shifted her paws uncomfortably. She looked away. "Featherpaw will be waiting for you."

Stonefur turned, his tail lashing, and padded back into camp as Scourge and Blackfoot began to purr loudly.

Leopardstar swung her muzzle toward Tigerstar. "You didn't have to do that," she growled.

He frowned. "Why are you letting half-Clan cats tell you what to do?" he mewed. "Why are you even letting them *stay?* They'll only make TigerClan weak."

Because they're my Clanmates. She swallowed the words. If she broke her agreement with Tigerstar, RiverClan would stand alone against three hostile Clans. She had to appease him. He was just having a bad day. He admired her. He always had. He was just showing off in front of Scourge. He'd realize later how badly he'd behaved. "Let's talk about something else," she mewed.

"I want to talk about this," Tigerstar hissed. "I don't want half-Clan cats weakening TigerClan. As long as there are half-Clan cats among our warriors, we are vulnerable. Stonefur clearly disapproves of our alliance. Can you be sure he hasn't already turned to ThunderClan for help? Firestar might have given him orders to betray us."

Leopardstar's belly tightened. She'd been betrayed before. Graystripe had turned on her in battle. His kits were still part of the Clan. Could they really be trusted? And what if Stonefur *had* turned to ThunderClan? He'd been complaining a lot lately. Her thoughts quickened. She had to make sure her Clan was safe. "Perhaps we could exile them." Sending Mudfur away for a while had been useful. He hadn't been able to make her doubt herself. If she sent Mistyfoot and Stonefur away with their apprentices, she'd be *sure* there were no traitors in the camp. Besides, Mistyfoot and Stonefur would be safer away from TigerClan. Tigerstar clearly wasn't going to make their life easy. And Featherpaw and Stormpaw were still too young to stand up for themselves. If they all left, they'd be safe, and so would TigerClan.

"*Exile* them?" Tigerstar snorted. "You want to send them straight into the paws of ThunderClan?" he went on. "With all of TigerClan's secrets?"

"What else can we do?" she mewed.

"What else can we do?" Tigerstar glanced at Blackfoot and Scourge. They looked at each other knowingly as he looked back at her. "Can't you guess?"

Leopardstar felt a chill reached through her pelt. She fought to stop her tail from bushing. Was Tigerstar threatening Stonefur's life? She'd thought, when he'd told the RiverClan deputy that he was lucky to be alive, that it had just been an empty threat meant to impress the others. But perhaps he'd meant it. Was he planning on killing Mistyfoot too, and Featherpaw and Stormpaw?

She glanced at Scourge. This tom must be having a bad influence on Tigerstar. The tabby warrior had never spoken like this before. *Unless I misjudged him.* The thought made her breath catch. Had the icy determination she'd admired in Tigerstar simply been malice all along?

"You can't kill our Clanmates without my permission." She kept her mew even, meeting Tigerstar's gaze. It glittered back at her, but she went on. "We agreed to share all decisions, remember?"

Tigerstar didn't move, but his eyes gleamed like a snake's. "You still think I need you, don't you?"

Her paws seemed to turn to stone. "You do," she growled.

"Really?" His mew dripped with disdain. "It seems to me that your cats don't listen to you anymore. Why should I?"

"They do listen!"

"How many of them support your decision to join Tiger-Clan?"

"All of them." She held her ground, even though she knew her Clanmates had been grumbling ever since she'd announced that RiverClan was going to become part of a bigger, stronger Clan.

Tigerstar narrowed his eyes. "And yet even the elders defy you." He sneered. *"Have you given up the leadership as well as everything else?"* he mewed, mimicking Cedarpelt. Leopardstar felt a rush of panic as he went on. "I think it's clear who leads TigerClan," he growled. "You might not be able to inspire your Clanmates' loyalty, but I will."

"How?" She lifted her muzzle. If they didn't agree with her, they certainly weren't going to agree with Tigerstar.

He leaned closer. *"Fear."* The scent of blood on his muzzle was overwhelming. Leopardstar felt sick. "Your Clanmates will do anything I tell them because, if they don't, they know what will happen to them. And I will start by imprisoning their half-Clan friends. And when they see you sit back and watch without lifting a paw, there won't be a whisker of doubt about who's really in charge here."

"Who says I won't lift a paw?" Leopardstar only just managed to stop herself from trembling.

"I do," Tigerstar mewed. "And so do Blackfoot and Scourge and all the other warriors who would die for me if I ordered them to."

Leopardstar didn't move. She felt as though she'd turned to ice. He'd *liked* her. He'd respected her. She was sure he had. *If only our timing had been different.* What had changed since she'd spoken to him at the Bonehill? Why was he being like this?

Before she could ask, he turned away. "We'll be back to sort out your half-Clan problem soon," he snarled. "It would be wise for you to back me up."

* * *

"I've brought you a trout."

Leopardstar was dreaming. Warm sun bathed the River-Clan camp as her father carried a fish across the clearing. She raced to meet him, her kit fluff quivering with happiness as he laid it at her paws.

"You're going to grow up into the greatest warrior River-Clan has ever seen," he purred, lapping her ears with his strong, rough tongue.

She blinked at him excitedly. "I want to grow up soon," she mewed. "I want to make you proud."

Her heart ached, even as she dreamed. She knew she would let him down, and she was filled with a longing to see him even though he was standing in front of her. "Don't go away." She brushed around him, rubbing her head against his shoulder. "I need you here."

"I'm still here," he mewed. But as he spoke, a dark shadow flitted across the camp.

Leopardstar looked up and saw a hawk circling above them.

"Run!" Mudfur yowled.

But the hawk had dropped into a dive. It was swooping toward her and Mudfur, its shadow growing until darkness covered them both.

"It's too late," she shrieked. *"It's too late!"*

She woke with a start, swallowing back a yowl of panic. The fear sparked by the dream lingered as she leaped to her paws and shook out her pelt. Night had fallen. She'd only meant to sleep for a few moments. She pushed her way from her den. The clearing lay empty in the moonlight. The dens were

silent. Where had every cat gone? For a moment she wondered if her Clan had deserted her. Then she saw Skyheart
gazing from the nursery.

"They've gone to the Bonehill," the queen told her, her eyes
wide and dark. "Darkstripe and Blackfoot rounded them up
like kits and marched them out of camp. They said Tigerstar
had called a meeting."

"Why didn't they fetch me?" Dread tugged in Leopardstar's belly.

Skyheart stared at her. "I don't know."

Leopardstar raced toward the entrance, her heart quickening. She had a sudden kitlike notion that he could fix this. He
could bring sense to it all. But how?

She ran through the entrance tunnel and hurried into the
moonlight beyond. As she neared the Bonehill, she could hear
snarling, and ahead she saw the willow tree where Stonefur, Mistyfoot, Featherpaw, and Stormpaw were being held
prisoner, barricaded by branches threaded among its tangled
roots. Darkstripe—the ThunderClan deserter—and Jaggedtooth dragged Featherpaw and Stormpaw out. Stonefur
watched from the path, as stiff as prey, while Mistyfoot still
crouched, half-hidden by shadow, in the prison.

"Are they all right?" she yowled. "You're hurting them!"

"They're alive, aren't they?" Jaggedtooth snarled.

"For now," Darkstripe growled as he pushed Stormpaw
along the path toward the Bonehill clearing.

Jaggedtooth grabbed Featherpaw's scruff and dragged her
after them.

Mistyfoot blinked at Stonefur. "Why don't you fight them?"

Stonefur shook his head. He looked helpless, and Leopardstar realized how thin her deputy had grown. His pelt was tattered, his nose scratched. "They'd take it out on the 'paws," he murmured. Slowly, he headed after the TigerClan toms.

Leopardstar was beginning to feel that she'd lost control. That Tigerstar had become more of a fox-heart than she'd ever imagined was possible. But she wanted desperately to believe there had a been a reason—that there was still hope for TigerClan to fix more than it was breaking.

"They're half-Clan cats," Leopardstar mewed to herself. "ThunderClan will use them against us. It's better for them and for us if they're gone."

She lifted her chin as she padded past Darkstripe and Jaggedtooth. They'd stopped outside the clearing with Featherpaw and Stormpaw. Leopardstar avoided looking at them.

"Is this really what you want?" Stonefur growled as she passed.

"Be quiet!" Jaggedtooth raked him with a vicious swipe, but Stonefur didn't even yelp.

Crossing the clearing, Leopardstar saw Tigerstar on the Bonehill. His eyes gleamed as he saw her. "Leopardstar." He sounded surprised. "You're awake. How lucky. Come and join us."

Blackfoot was standing on one side of the great pile of bones and she walked toward the other side, ignoring the gazes of her Clanmates even though they felt like fire on her pelt. They were ringed around the clearing, among Tigerstar's rogue warriors, like prey caught in a trap.

The dark warrior waited for Leopardstar to take her place among the scattered bones, then lifted his muzzle. "It's time for the trial to begin!" he yowled. "Fetch the prisoners."

Trial? Leopardstar glanced at Tigerstar. This seemed like a cruel way to exile the half-Clan cats. Did he have to humiliate them like this? Perhaps he only wanted to deter other cats from betraying the Clan. . . .

At his call, Jaggedtooth dragged Stonefur into the clearing. A moment later, Darkstripe herded Featherpaw and Stormpaw in.

"Cats of TigerClan," Tigerstar mewed. "You all know the hardships that we have to face. The cold of leaf-bare threatens us. Twolegs threaten us. The other Clans in the forest, who have not realized yet the wisdom of joining with TigerClan, are a threat to us."

Leopardstar's heart was pounding so loudly in her ears that she could barely hear Tigerstar's words.

"Bluestar and Graystripe of ThunderClan both flouted the warrior code when they took mates from RiverClan. The kits from such a union, like the ones you see in front of you now, can never be trusted."

Leopardstar swallowed. It was better, she reminded herself, to drive the half-Clan cats out now, before they had a chance to betray them. But she would have chosen a quieter way to banish them. She wished Tigerstar would hurry up.

She wanted this to be over.

Stonefur was glaring at Tigerstar even though he looked like he could hardly stand up. Why was he so weak? She'd ordered the prisoners to be fed while they were in captivity. Had Tigerstar countermanded her orders? Anger twitched through her fur. *This isn't my fault.*

"No cat has ever questioned my loyalty," Stonefur snarled. "Come down here and tell me to my face that I'm a traitor!"

Tigerstar ignored him, glaring at Leopardstar instead. "You showed poor judgment when you chose this cat as your deputy," he growled. "RiverClan is choked by the weeds of treachery, and we must root them out." His eyes burned with fury. Leopardstar dropped her gaze. Why didn't he just hurry up and banish them instead of humiliating her in front of her Clan?

Tigerstar turned his attention back to Stonefur. "I will give you a chance to show your loyalty to TigerClan," he told him. "Kill these two half-Clan apprentices."

Leopardstar's blood ran cold. He'd threatened to kill the half-Clan cats, but that had been in front of Scourge. When he hadn't mentioned it again, she'd convinced herself he'd only been showing off. She fought back dread. How could he make Stonefur kill his own apprentice? Stormpaw and Feather-paw might be Graystripe's kits and the reason Silverstream was dead, but they didn't deserve this. Nor did Stonefur. Did Tigerstar really believe this was how the Clan would become strong?

"Kill them," Tigerstar told Stonefur.

Stonefur turned to Leoparstar. "I take orders from *you*," he growled. "You must know this is wrong. What do you want me to do?"

Leopardstar's mouth went dry. *What do you want me to do?* What could she say?

"These are difficult times," she replied finally, struggling to keep her voice steady. "As we fight for survival we must be able to count on every one of our Clanmates. There is no room for divided loyalties. Do as Tigerstar tells you."

She forced herself to keep her composure, but she could hardly breathe, watching him.

Something had changed inside Stonefur. She'd disappointed him. He took in a deep breath and turned to face the apprentices, who cowered in fear.

After what seemed like an eternity, Stormfur spoke. "You'll have to kill me first, Tigerstar."

Tigerstar's tail twitched with menace. He signaled to Darkstripe. "Kill him."

Horror shrilled through Leopardstar as Darkstripe leaped at Stonefur. She could hardly breathe as she watched Stonefur fight fiercely against the cruel tabby. Though half-starved and beaten, he managed to haul Darkstripe to the ground and dig his claws into the warrior's throat.

Kill him! Leopardstar found herself willing Stonefur on.

"Finish it." Tigerstar flicked his ears at Blackfoot, and his deputy shot forward and dragged Stonefur off Darkstripe. Together, the vicious warriors turned on the RiverClan deputy, and as Darkstripe held him down, Blackfoot scored his claws across Stonefur's throat.

Stonefur struggled, then fell still, his blood staining the ground.

Leopardstar struggled not to sway on her paws. Tigerstar couldn't see that she was disgusted. If she showed weakness, who knew what he might do.

This is wrong. Every hair on Leopardstar's pelt suddenly quivered with horror. *What have I done?* She stood like stone as Jaggedtooth dragged Featherpaw and Stormpaw back to their prison and the others headed silently back to their camps. *What have I let RiverClan become?* And yet it was too late. She'd taken a path with no way back. With a groan, she dropped to her belly. How could she have made such a mistake?

Chapter 32

Leopardstar watched dawn light filtering through the trailing moss at her den entrance. She'd slept for a while, but she'd heard that Mudfur had returned at sunset, and she'd dreamed only of the horrified reaction he would have when she told him what had happened at Bonehill. In her dreams, there had been such sorrow in his eyes that she'd wished she'd died instead of Stonefur. Perhaps she had, as far as Mudfur was concerned. Perhaps the Leopardstar he'd known and loved had ceased to exist. She hadn't the courage to get up and tell him the truth. She hadn't wanted to hear what he might say. Instead she'd stayed in her own den and curled up in her nest, numb to everything but grief. *Let him hear it from some other cat.*

She heard her Clanmates stirring outside. They'd be wondering where to patrol, and who should go. Without Stonefur, they'd be unsure. Leopardstar knew she should go and speak to them, but her pelt felt as heavy as stone.

"Take a patrol to the shore." Timberfur's mew sounded from the clearing. "Blackclaw." The elder sounded brisk. "It's a little warmer today. See if you can break the ice near the gorge. You might be able to fish there."

"Who shall I take?" Blackclaw asked.

"Any cat who wants to join you."

Ottersplash called out to Timberfur. "Shall I take a border patrol out?"

"Not today," Timberfur mewed. "We're not ready to fight."

Tigerstar's mew rang across the camp. "Not ready to fight?"

Leopardstar sat up sharply. She scrambled from her nest but couldn't force herself outside.

"You'll fight if I tell you to, you bunch of fish-brains!" Tigerstar sounded angry. "Haven't you noticed the prisoners have escaped?"

No cat answered. Leopardstar's heart pounded. Did Tigerstar hold her responsible for her Clanmates' escape? She recoiled as Tigerstar burst into her den.

"Didn't you post a guard at the prison?" He thrust his muzzle in her face.

"Jaggedtooth said that only ShadowClan warriors should guard it."

Tigerstar closed his eyes and seemed to take a moment to control himself. Leopardstar's forced her paws to stop trembling.

When he opened them again, he glared at her. "We're attacking WindClan today," he snarled. "We're going to send a message that there's no future outside TigerClan. They join me or we drive them from their land."

"Just WindClan?" She blinked at him. "I thought we were going to attack WindClan and ThunderClan at the same time," she mewed. "That's what we decided."

"The plan has changed," he snapped. "We have to move fast."

Leopardstar forced herself to meet his gaze. She had to stand up to him. "You can't change plans without consulting me."

"Can't I?" Tigerstar leaned close. "What are you going to do about it? Set your Clanmates on me? What do you think my warriors will think of that? You've met them, right? You know what they're capable of."

Leopardstar swallowed.

Tigerstar sat back on his haunches, his tone softening. "Are you going to help me or not?"

Leopardstar felt sick. Who knew what he would do if she refused? "I'll help," she mewed quietly.

"Good."

"But my warriors are grieving," she mewed. "You can't expect them to fight at their best."

Tigerstar's tail twitched. "Grieving?"

Did he really not understand? "They watched Stonefur die yesterday."

"They watched me save them from a traitor." Tigerstar's eyes glittered in the half-light. "They wouldn't have seen anything if you hadn't made a half-Clan cat your deputy. How can any warrior have faith in a leader who makes such dangerous decisions? Stonefur might have betrayed you all. Thunder-Clan was probably waiting for his signal. Your Clanmates are lucky I stepped in. From now on, I'll be making the decisions for TigerClan. You can't be trusted."

"That's not what we agreed!" Leopardstar's hackles lifted. She couldn't let him take over. She slitted her eyes. "I am joint leader of TigerClan," she hissed.

The moss shivered as Blackfoot slid through. Darkstripe followed him. Silently, the two warriors stood beside Tigerstar and glared at her, the fur bristling around their necks.

Her heart seemed to stop beating. Their eyes gleamed with violence. She understood that Tigerstar had brought them in to show her they'd kill her if she opposed them. Who would protect her Clanmates then? She backed away. "Okay," she mewed. "Whatever you say."

Tigerstar's tail whipped the air behind him. "Good," he growled. "I'm glad to hear it. We attack WindClan at sunhigh. Bring a battle patrol and meet me at the WindClan border."

He turned and pushed his way from the den. Darkstripe eyed her menacingly, then followed, Blackfoot at his tail.

Panic pressed at the edge of her thoughts. She wanted to talk to Mudfur. He must have heard the truth by now, but what would he say except I told you so? And Stonefur was gone. Which of her warriors could she depend on? She'd let them down. She'd led them into dangerous water and she had no idea how to get them out. They must hate her.

She closed her eyes. What had she done?

At least Scourge seemed to have disappeared. Leopardstar lifted her chin as she led her warriors to the WindClan border. She hadn't seen the vicious tom since Tigerstar had brought him to her camp. Perhaps Tigerstar had decided not to use him as an ally after all. Did that mean there was still a chance to oppose Tigerstar's warriors? But did her warriors still trust her enough to follow her in an uprising against their new leader?

She glanced at them. When she'd announced the attack on WindClan, no cat had spoken. Loudbelly had eyed her uncertainly, but dropped his gaze when she met it. Ottersplash and Vixenleap had glanced anxiously at each other. Reedtail had only stared blankly ahead. After Stonefur's death, her Clanmates clearly had no stomach for battle.

She pushed the memory away. All she had to do was get them through the fight with WindClan with as few injuries as possible.

She paused as she neared the WindClan border, glancing around at her patrol. "Remember," she hissed, her mew hushed in case Tigerstar and his allies were nearby, "stay out of danger. Let Tigerstar's warriors do most of the fighting. I want you all home in one piece." She looked at each of her Clanmates in turn, her heart sinking as they stared at the ground, their pelts twitching as though they wanted to shrink beneath them. Shame washed her pelt. She'd wanted to believe that when TigerClan attacked WindClan and ThunderClan, they would create one strong Clan that never went hungry and worked together in harmony. But it was all going wrong. She'd trusted the wrong cat. She was forcing her warriors into a dishonorable fight and they knew it.

Loudbelly's gaze flashed nervously toward the bracken lining the border. As she followed it, Tigerstar padded out and glared at her. "Are you coming?" he snarled. Sunlight made his pelt gleam as he lashed his tail.

Leopardstar flicked a signal to her warriors with her tail and headed toward him, her belly churning with dread. She had ordered the apprentices to stay behind. She wasn't risking them in this battle, no matter what Tigerstar said.

Tigerstar's patrol was waiting beyond the bracken. They were pacing on the grass, their ears twitching excitedly. Tigerstar watched as Leopardstar's warriors lined up beside them. She was relieved when he didn't seem to notice that there were no apprentices in their ranks.

"The battle must be fast," the dark warrior growled. "And it must hurt. WindClan is bound to send for help, the mouse-hearts. We have to be out before ThunderClan arrives, but we must leave WindClan in no doubt as to what they will suffer if they continue to defy me."

Leopardstar glanced at her Clanmates, relieved to see them lift their chins and square their shoulders. Tigerstar had to believe they wanted this. If he didn't, she was sure there would be reprisals.

They crossed the moor swiftly and chased away the two WindClan guards so easily that, when they entered the camp, the Clan was unprepared for their attack.

Leopardstar glanced at Blackclaw as they hurried after Tigerstar. Had he remembered her orders? Relief swamped her as he hung back and let Tigerstar's warriors charge ahead. Vixenleap and Sedgecreek fanned out with Loudbelly, Beetle-nose, and Voleclaw, keeping to the edges of the battle as

Tigerstar's warriors hurled themselves, hissing, at WindClan.

WindClan met them, claws flashing, at the center of the wide, grassy clearing. Screeches filled the air as Leopardstar pushed her way into the melee. Tigerstar had to see her in the thick of the fight. Then he might not notice her warriors staying on the fringes.

She ducked beneath a WindClan warrior's belly, heaving him away with a sharp thrust, relieved to see that she was the only RiverClan warrior deep in the battle.

A WindClan she-cat glared at her. Hatred gleamed in her amber gaze as she flung herself at Leopardstar. The lithe tabby she-cat slammed into her, the ferocity of the attack taking Leopardstar by surprise. The tabby gripped her pelt and knocked her hind paws from under her with a nimble kick that sent Leopardstar thumping onto her side. Pain arched like lightning through Leopardstar's belly as the WindClan warrior churned it with her hind claws. She struggled free, lashing out with her forepaws and landing a powerful blow on the tabby's cheek. More claws hooked her from behind and dragged her backward into a knot of writhing pelts. She flattened her ears and slitted her eyes as claws sliced the air around her. Fur flashed at the edges of her vision, and she felt her pelt tear as paws grabbed at her and dragged her deeper into the fight. She hit out, not sure who she was fighting, relieved when she ripped free and found her paws. Pushing herself up, she lunged, using her power against the WindClan warriors' agility, slashing and swiping as warriors shrieked around her. *Survive.* The word echoed in her mind. *Survive.* That was all she needed to do.

Claws raked her muzzle, and she ducked away and lashed out, jerking around to aim a blow at the warrior pulling at her tail. She ripped it free and sent the warrior reeling with a blow that sliced his ear and left blood beneath her claws.

"Finish it!" Tigerstar yowled to his warriors. The snarls and shrieks around Leopardstar hardened. Then the battle began to ease. The WindClan cats were scattering to the edges of their camp. They crouched, trembling and bloody, beneath the heather wall. Leopardstar straightened, scanning the battlefield for her Clanmates, relieved when she saw them hanging back as Tigerstar's warriors clawed and hissed at the last of WindClan's fighters. A moment later, the camp was silent.

Tigerstar stood at the center of the clearing and looked around, triumph glittering in his eyes as he surveyed the bleeding and ragged WindClan cats. He was holding a young WindClan apprentice, pinning him to the ground with a single massive paw.

"Gorsepaw!" A WindClan she-cat whimpered from the edge of the clearing as she stared in horror at the young tom in Tigerstar's grip.

Tallstar's black-and-white pelt was torn and covered in dust. He faced Tigerstar from the head of the clearing. "Let him go!"

Tigerstar stared back at Tallstar as Blackfoot padded around the WindClan leader, scorn twisting his lip. Darkstripe walked slowly around the camp, snarling at any WindClan warrior who dared to meet his eye.

"He's an apprentice, for StarClan's sake!" Tallstar growled.

Tigerstar eyed the WindClan leader. He leaned down and hissed something softly into the WindClan apprentice's ear. Then his eyes lit with cold fury and he slashed his claws across the young tom's trembling neck. Blood spurted from the wound, and with a screech, the apprentice jerked and twisted and then fell still.

As Tallstar's eyes widened with shock, the WindClan she-cat who'd whimpered before wailed in horror, her cry echoing over the camp.

Leopardstar felt dizzy. Her mind whirled. Stonefur's final growl as he tried to fight Blackfoot and Darkstripe still rang in her ears. *And now an innocent apprentice is dead.* Would Tigerstar ever stop killing? She glanced at Blackclaw, then at Vixenleap, and then around at the rest of her Clanmates. They all watched the dark warrior with same expression of fear.

"I have a message for Firestar when he gets here," Tigerstar snarled. His gaze fixed on Tallstar. "Tell him to meet me, with WindClan, at Fourtrees tomorrow at sunhigh. I'm tired of waiting. I want his decision about joining TigerClan." He lifted Gorsepaw's lifeless body with a claw. "If he refuses, he knows what to expect."

Tigerstar's jubilation as they trekked back across the moor made Leopardstar feel sick. He crowed with Blackfoot and Darkstripe about how easy WindClan had been to beat.

"We should have killed more of them," he mewed as he pushed through the heather. "It would've saved us the trouble of killing them tomorrow."

"Do you think Firestar will turn you down?" Darkstripe asked eagerly.

"At first," he mewed.

At the border, Leopardstar told him that her warriors must return to the river camp so that Mudfur could deal with their wounds. She was relieved when he didn't object and led his own warriors toward the pine forest.

Cedarpelt got to his paws as she led the battle patrol into camp. Dawnpaw hurried across the clearing to meet Moss-pelt, falling in beside her and sniffing at her wounds as she lay down, exhausted, beside the sedge wall. Primrosepaw, Pikepaw, and Reedpaw stayed close to the apprentices' den. Their eyes glittered with worry. They knew Mistyfoot had escaped with Featherpaw and Stormpaw, but they would not relax until they knew their mother was safe.

"What happened?" Cedarpelt blinked at her.

"Tigerstar left WindClan with an ultimatum for Firestar," she told him. "He wants to meet ThunderClan and Wind-Clan at Fourtrees tomorrow at sunhigh."

Timberfur padded froward. "Are we going too?"

Leopardstar couldn't meet his gaze. "Yes." What choice did she have? If she didn't support Tigerstar, Primrosepaw or Pikepaw could be the ones lying dead in their own camp.

Mudfur hurried from the medicine den, cobwebs and herbs dangling between his jaws. His eyes met hers, and he stared at her for a moment, more disappointment in his gaze than Leopardstar could bear. As Leopardstar sat down, her heart so heavy that she wondered how it could still beat, he padded past her and began checking on his Clanmates.

Leopardstar closed her eyes. She felt as though she'd been pushed deep underwater and she couldn't find the surface. Time seemed to slow as she listened to the soft murmuring of her Clanmates. They must wish Crookedstar had never made her deputy. She shuddered. Mudfur had been right from the beginning. She was not cut out to be a leader. Her Clan was in tatters, and soon her Clanmates would be no more than Tigerstar's minions.

It was no good. She had to talk to Mudfur. No matter what he might say. At the very least, she had to confess she'd been wrong.

She opened her eyes. The afternoon had drifted into evening and she'd barely noticed. Her Clanmates were still licking their wounds at the edges of the camp. She got to her paws and headed for the medicine den. Bracing herself, she pushed through the moss at the entrance.

The air was pungent with herb scents. Sedgecreek and Vixenleap were sitting beside the nests. They glanced at her as she padded in.

"Hi, Leopardstar," Sedgecreek mewed.

Leopardstar felt a flicker of surprise. The brown tabby sounded friendly. "How are you?" she asked.

"I'll be fine in a day or two," Sedgecreek mewed.

"Just a few scratches," Vixenleap told her.

Mudfur padded from the shadows at the back of the den. "I've treated them," he mewed. "They can go back to their den."

Sedgecreek dipped her head to the medicine cat. "Thanks, Mudfur."

"Thanks." Vixenleap blinked at him gratefully and the two warriors left the den.

Leopardstar held her breath as Mudfur looked at her. What could he possibly say to her that she hadn't already said to herself? She'd been wrong. She'd been stupid and gullible. She'd destroyed the very Clan she'd wanted to save. She met his gaze, trying not to tremble.

"You did well to tell the patrol to hold back," he mewed. "No one was badly wounded. There were only a few bites and scratches."

He was being kind. Her throat tightened. She wanted to bury her nose in his soft neck fur as she'd done when she was a kit. "I'm sorry," she mewed huskily. "I should have listened to you."

"Yes," he mewed. "You should have. But you've always thought you knew best and rushed in without thinking."

She hung her head, almost relieved by his reproach. She deserved it. She'd put her Clan in terrible danger. She'd gotten Stonefur killed.

"What are you going to do about it?"

She lifted her head, surprised by Mudfur's question. "What *can* I do?"

"You were born to save RiverClan."

She shook her head. "Don't you see? Your vision was wrong," she mewed. She'd given up so much to follow it. She could have become Frogleap's mate. He might have lived. They could have had kits by now. "It was just a dream you had. It was never going to come true. I was dumb to believe it."

He looked at her steadily. "Are you blaming me for setting you on this path?"

"No," she mewed quickly, alarmed that he thought she would. "It's all my fault. I've done everything wrong."

"I still believe my vision."

Leopardstar stared at him. "How can you? I've failed. I've destroyed everything. There's no RiverClan left. Only Tiger-Clan, and it's . . ." She swallowed. "It's evil."

"What are you going to do about that?"

That question again. She looked at him. Were there bees in his brain?

"There's nothing I *can* do," she mewed miserably. "It's hope-less."

"Who's going to stop Tigerstar if you don't?" Mudfur mewed.

"No cat can stop him."

"Some cat must." He hadn't moved. "Do you remember exactly what my vision was?"

How could she forget? "Brightsky told you to take care of me because I'd be important one day," she mewed.

"Yes," he mewed. "She said that one day you'd be impor-tant, not just to RiverClan, but to all the Clans."

Leopardstar stared at him helplessly. Not only had she let down her own Clan, she'd let down *all* the Clans. "I've failed every cat." Her mew caught in her throat.

"Not yet, you haven't." Mudfur padded closer and looked at her intently. "Tigerstar was always going to threaten the Clans. If he hadn't used you, he'd have used some other cat. He was always the reckoning the Clans were going to have to face." He blinked at her. "Don't make them face it alone," he mewed. "Help them."

"Help them?"

"Yes," he mewed. "You have to."

She looked at him, surprised to see affection still in his eyes. After everything she'd done, he still had faith in her.

She could do this. She had to. She tried to concentrate. What if ThunderClan and WindClan *weren't* her enemies? What if they were her allies? "We could all beat Tigerstar together," she mewed.

His eyes brightened. "Tigerstar has done nothing to earn your loyalty."

She nodded. "I'm only following him now so that he doesn't hurt my Clanmates."

"But if he were gone, he couldn't hurt them."

Her heart lifted. "If I help ThunderClan and WindClan defeat him, he could never hurt RiverClan again."

Mudfur's purr seemed to warm the air around her.

She sat down and tucked her tail over her paws, thinking hard. "Tigerstar wants a battle tomorrow, and he thinks RiverClan will be on his side." She looked excitedly at Mudfur. "But what if we're not? What if he has to face three Clans and not one?"

"Then he'll lose." Mudfur swished his tail. "You'll be the one who decides the fate of the Clans. They are depending on you."

CHAPTER 33

✤

"*Remember,*" *Leopardstar hissed softly to Blackclaw.* "Once the battle starts, fight ShadowClan, not ThunderClan."

He nodded, his gaze flashing toward Tigerstar.

"What are you whispering about?" Tigerstar glared at Leopardstar, his eyes glittering with distrust.

She lifted her head. "Do you want to win this battle or not?" She didn't wait for an answer. "If you do, you need to let me speak to my warriors."

He grunted and turned away, giving his own warriors instructions. "Start fighting when I tell you."

TigerClan was ranged across the top of the Fourtrees hollow. Above them, heavy gray clouds threatened rain. Leopardstar kept close to her RiverClan warriors, leaving distance between them and Tigerstar, Blackfoot, and Darkstripe. Tigerstar's warriors stood like stones around him, their dark pelts ruffling in the stiff breeze and their ragged ears twitching as they waited for the order to advance down the slope. They still bore the wounds of the previous day's battle with WindClan, and Leopardstar wondered how WindClan's warriors were doing after TigerClan's vicious assault. Would

they be strong enough to fight again? They might not even
dare turn up.

Jaggedtooth and Boulder stood among the other forest
warriors. Their days on the island had made them no more
loyal to their river Clanmates; even now they were eyeing
Loudbelly and Heavystep as though they were as much the
enemy as ThunderClan and WindClan. Turning on *them*
when the battle started would be easy, Leopardstar thought
with relish.

"Tell the apprentices to stay close to the slope and away
from the thick of battle," she whispered to Blackclaw.

"I already have," he murmured under his breath.

Dawnpaw, Primrosepaw, Pikepaw, and Reedpaw were
shifting nervously beside their mentors. This would be their
first battle. Leopardstar felt a pang of regret. She hoped their
next would be more honorable. She wanted to see them fight
for RiverClan, not for Tigerstar. Longing tugged in Leopardstar's belly. All she wanted was RiverClan back and for her
Clan to be healthy and safe.

Tigerstar looked down the slope. "Any sign of Firestar and
his mouse-hearted friends?"

Darkstripe tasted the air. "I can't smell them."

Tigerstar glanced at the sky. The sun was piercing the thick
cloud, high overhead. "He should be here by now."

"Perhaps he's not coming," Blackfoot mewed.

Leopardstar stiffened. What if ThunderClan and Wind-
Clan decided not to respond to Tigerstar's ultimatum? Would
RiverClan have to endure Tigerstar until they did?

"Firestar's probably trembling in his den like prey," Darkstripe sneered.

Blackclaw narrowed his eyes and stared at Tigerstar. "ThunderClan and WindClan are good fighters. Are you sure we can beat them?"

"Yes." The dark warrior's eyes were already gleaming with triumph. "Because we won't be fighting alone." He signaled with a flick of his tail, and the bracken on the rim of the hollow nearby shivered.

Leopardstar stiffened as Scourge padded into the open. The teeth on his kittypet collar glinted as, around him, more cats emerged from the bushes. Her heart sank.

"Don't you remember I said we'd need help if we took on ThunderClan and WindClan at the same time?" He looked at Leopardstar. "RiverClan isn't as strong as I'd hoped, so Scourge has provided enough warriors to destroy Thunder-Clan and WindClan forever." Cats were still padding from between the bushes. They crowded the top of the slope, too many to count. They looked skinny, their fur ragged, but Leopardstar could sense strength in their wiry limbs. Their eyes glittered with a hunger she'd never seen in any warrior's gaze. Her throat tightened. RiverClan would pay heavily for any betrayal.

"Meet BloodClan." Tigerstar's gaze swept over them proudly, as though he'd trained them himself. "They've agreed to help us win the forest."

Scourge narrowed his eyes. "We've agreed to fight, that's all," he growled.

"Of course," Tigerstar mewed smoothly. "That's all I need you to do. I'll take care of the rest."

Scourge watched the dark warrior as he turned to Blackfoot.

"Now that we're all here, let's head down to the clearing." Tigerstar pushed through the bushes covering the slope and headed into the hollow. Blackfoot followed, his warriors pouring after him.

Leopardstar couldn't move. Fear had hollowed her belly. She hadn't realized Scourge was coming. She'd thought Tigerstar had abandoned the idea of bringing help from outside the Clans.

"We can't fight them too," Blackclaw hissed in her ear.

"I know." Her heart was pounding. She'd pictured carrying news home to Mudfur of her victory over Tigerstar. But that was impossible now. The only way for her warriors to survive this battle was to fight with Tigerstar's side. If they didn't, this army of rogues would tear them apart. Hopelessness swamped her. Once ThunderClan and WindClan had been defeated, there would be no hope for RiverClan, or any Clan. Every warrior in the forest would be at the mercy of Tigerstar's hunger for power. There would be no code, no honor, no loyalty left. Only fear.

She closed her eyes. *StarClan, help me.* How had she ever hoped she could save the Clans?

Blackclaw nudged her. "What do we do?"

She pushed back despair. She'd chosen her path; she must follow it. StarClan would decide her punishment. She flattened her ears and straightened her tail. "We have no choice," she told him softly. "We fight for TigerClan."

His shoulders slumped.

"We have no choice," she murmured.

"I know." He looked at her, his eyes hollow with defeat.

"Tell the others."

As he weaved among their Clanmates, whispering the change of plan, Leopardstar noticed that Scourge and his cats hadn't moved. They were staring down the slope as Tigerstar and his warriors reached the bottom.

"Aren't you coming with us?" she asked him.

"I'll wait for the Clans to gather before I join you," he mewed. "You probably have warrior business to discuss." His whiskers twitched and he caught the eye of the large black-and-white tom beside him. Together they purred with amusement, as though warriors were no more than a joke to them.

Leopardstar fought back fury. She flicked her tail, signaling to her Clanmates, and headed downslope after Tigerstar.

She smelled ThunderClan and WindClan scent as she reached the bottom.

"Wait," Tigerstar flicked his tail across her path before she could push her way through the bushes to the Fourtrees clearing.

She peered between the branches. Firestar and Tallstar stood side by side beneath the great oaks. Behind them, ThunderClan and WindClan shifted nervously. The Wind-Clan warriors were still bloody from their last battle. The ThunderClan warriors looked stronger, but she could see fear sparking in their eyes. Guilt wormed beneath her pelt. If she'd never agreed to align RiverClan with ShadowClan, this battle might never have happened. She shook out her pelt. She could do nothing about it now. She only had to fight and make sure her Clanmates escaped Fourtrees with their lives.

She glanced at Tigerstar, waiting for his signal, and when he nodded, she followed him from the bushes with Blackfoot and Darkstripe.

Firestar's pelt was bristling, but not from fear. His emerald eyes seemed to flash with energy as he saw Tigerstar. "Greetings, Tigerstar," he mewed coolly. "You came, then. Not still looking for those prisoners you lost from RiverClan territory?"

Leopardstar pricked her ears. Had he helped Mistyfoot, Featherpaw, and Stormpaw escape? Her heart lifted for a moment. Were they safe in ThunderClan's camp?

Tigerstar snarled. "You'll regret that day's work, Firestar."

"Try and make me," Firestar retorted.

Behind Leopardstar, TigerClan began to stream from the bushes and fan out around the clearing. Firestar still looked undaunted. Her paws pricked nervously. Did the young ThunderClan leader really think he could win this fight? She felt a wave of pity. He had no idea that Scourge and his army were waiting at the top of the slope.

Tigerstar took a pace forward. "Have you thought about my offer? I'm giving you a choice: Join me now and accept my leadership, or be destroyed."

Firestar glanced at Tallstar. Tallstar dipped his head. They must have already decided.

"We reject your offer," Firestar mewed. "The forest was

never meant to be ruled by one Clan, especially not one led by a dishonorable murderer."

Leopardstar felt a flicker of admiration for the Thunder-Clan leader. If only she'd been so ready to reject Tigerstar's offer. But Firestar clearly knew far more about the dark warrior than she ever had. He'd shared a Clan with him.

Tigerstar swished his tail. "With or without you, Firestar, one Clan will rule the forest. By sunset today, the time of four Clans will be over."

The bushes rustled farther up the slope. BloodClan was coming like a wave ready to crash over the Clans and sweep them away.

She moved quietly away from Tigerstar and whispered in Blackclaw's ear. "Defend the 'paws, whatever happens."

"Okay."

"And make sure every RiverClan cat is seen fighting," she breathed. "There will be repercussions if Tigerstar thinks we didn't pull our weight."

As she spoke, Blackfoot raised his tail in a signal. Behind him, BloodClan padded out. Firestar's ears were twitching. He was clearly struggling to maintain his composure as more and more cats emerged into the clearing, row after row of them, lining up behind the TigerClan warriors.

"Well?" Tigerstar demanded silkily. "Are you still sure you want to stand and fight?"

Firestar didn't reply. His Clanmates shifted nervously, exchanging hushed mews.

"You see, Firestar?" Tigerstar sounded triumphant. "I am even more powerful than StarClan, for I have changed the

Clans in the forest from four to two. TigerClan and Blood-Clan will rule forever."

Alarm showed now on Firestar's face. Leopardstar wanted to catch his eye, and try to show him she was sorry this was ever happened. She was as much a hostage as he was to Tigerstar now. And yet the ThunderClan leader lifted his muzzle.

"No, Tigerstar," he mewed quietly. "If you want to fight, let us fight. StarClan will show you who is more powerful."

Leopardstar's breath quickened. He was so fearless. She'd underestimated this kittypet.

"You mouse-brained fool!" Tigerstar spat. "I was prepared to come and talk with you today. Just remember that it is you who drove us to this. And when your Clanmates are dying around you, they will blame you with their last breath." He swung around to face the mass of cats ranged behind him. "BloodClan, attack!"

Leopardstar's heart lurched. Energy bunched in her muscles as she prepared to spring into battle.

But no cat moved.

She watched Tigerstar's eyes widen.

"Attack! I order you!" Fury edged his shriek.

Still no cat moved, except for Scourge. He took a pace forward and glanced at Firestar. "I am Scourge, leader of BloodClan," he mewed icily. "Tigerstar, my warriors are not yours to command. They will attack when I tell them, and not before."

Tigerstar stared at the rogue in disbelief. His eyes flashed with hatred.

Hope flickered in Leopardstar's chest. Was Tigerstar's ally deserting him? She stiffened as Firestar stepped between them. Didn't he realize how dangerous these cats were?

Graystripe darted among the ThunderClan warriors. "Firestar, be careful!"

But Firestar was staring at Scourge. "I am Firestar," he mewed. "Leader of ThunderClan. I wish I could say you were welcome in the forest. But you would not believe me if I did, and I have no wish to lie to you. Unlike your supposed ally here, I am a cat of honor. If you've believed any of the promises he made to you, then you are mistaken."

It's true! Leopardstar wanted to call out. Tigerstar had lied to her too.

"Tigerstar told me he had enemies in the forest," Scourge mewed. "Why should I believe you instead of him?"

Firestar held the kittypet's gaze. Leopardstar found herself willing him on.

"Cats of all Clans," he mewed. "Especially BloodClan. You have no need to believe or disbelieve me. Tigerstar's crimes speak for themselves. When he was still a warrior of Thunder-Clan, he murdered our deputy, Redtail, hoping to be made deputy himself."

Leopardstar blinked. Hadn't Oakheart killed Redtail in the battle for Sunningrocks? She pricked her ears as Firestar went on.

"First Lionheart was chosen as deputy, but when that noble warrior died in a fight with ShadowClan, Tigerstar achieved his ambition at last."

He paused, and grim silence gripped the clearing, broken only by Tigerstar.

"Mew away, kittypet. It won't change anything."

Firestar ignored him. "Being deputy wasn't enough," he went on. "Tigerstar wanted to be leader of the Clan. He set a trap for Bluestar by the Thunderpath, but my own apprentice strayed into it instead. That's how Cinderpelt came to have a crippled leg."

Leopardstar's eyes widened. Tigerstar's crimes stretched back for moons.

"Then Tigerstar conspired with Brokentail," Firestar went on. "The former leader of ShadowClan was ThunderClan's prisoner. He brought a pack of rogues into ThunderClan's camp, and Tigerstar tried to murder Bluestar with his own claws. I stopped him, and when ThunderClan had beaten off the attack, we drove him into exile."

At last, Leopardstar knew why the dark warrior had left ThunderClan. If only she'd known that his ambition had been murderous. Why hadn't Bluestar warned the other Clans? She flexed her claws. All this might have been avoided if Thunder-Clan had shared the truth about Tigerstar's crimes earlier.

Firestar went on. "As a rogue, he slaughtered yet another of our warriors, Runningwind. Then before we knew what he was up to, he had made himself leader of ShadowClan. But Tigerstar still wanted revenge on ThunderClan. Three moons ago, a pack of dogs got loose in the forest. Tigerstar caught prey for them, then led a trail of dead rabbits between the dogs' lair and the ThunderClan camp to lead them to us. He murdered one of our queens, Brindleface, and left her near the camp to give the dogs a taste for cat blood. If we hadn't found out in time to escape, the whole of ThunderClan would have been torn to pieces."

"Good riddance," Tigerstar growled.

Leopardstar looked at him. Would he one day be so dismissive of RiverClan's destruction?

"As it was," Firestar went on, "our leader, Bluestar, died the bravest death of any cat, saving me and all our Clan from the pack."

Fear was spreading icy claws beneath Leopardstar's pelt. She knew Tigerstar was evil, but she'd never guessed the full extent of his violence and cruelty.

"This is Tigerstar's history." Firestar had turned back to Scourge. "It all shows one thing—that he'll do anything for power. If he promised you a share of the forest, don't believe him. He won't give up one paw print. Not to you, or any cat."

Scourge's eyes had narrowed. Leopardstar held her breath. Was the vicious rogue going to abandon his ally? Had Firestar persuaded him? She tried to press back the hope surging in her chest. If Scourge left, she could carry on with her plan to support ThunderClan and WindClan. She could get rid of Tigerstar once and for all.

Scourge turned his gaze toward the TigerClan leader. "Tigerstar told me what he was planning to do with the dogs when he visited me two moons ago."

Why didn't I know any of this? Leopardstar swallowed back a growl, angry at having been used. Tigerstar had only ever shared what had been useful to manipulate her.

"He didn't tell me his plan had failed," Scourge went on.

"None of this matters." Tigerstar whisked his tail. "We have an agreement, Scourge. Fight beside me now and you'll have all I offered you."

"My Clan and I fight when I choose," Scourge mewed. To Firestar, he added. "I will think about what you have said. There will be no battle today."

Thank StarClan! Relief washed Leopardstar's pelt. But Tigerstar was bristling with rage.

He lashed his tail, his muscles bunching as he dropped into a crouch. "Traitor!" He leaped at Scourge, claws outstretched.

Leopardstar tensed. Scourge was no match for the powerful tabby! He was half his size. But he was fast. He whipped to one side, avoiding Tigerstar as he landed, and when the dark warrior spun to face him, he lashed out with his front paws.

Leopardstar's eyes widened as she saw the sun glint unnaturally on the tips of each claw. The other warriors saw it too. Shocked murmurs rippled through the patrols. Scourge's claws were reinforced with long, sharpened dogs' teeth.

One blow to his shoulder unbalanced Tigerstar. He fell on his side, exposing his belly, and Scourge's vicious claws sank into his throat. Blood pulsed from the wound as the kittypet ripped him down to the tail with a single slash.

Tigerstar screeched with fury, but his wail choked into a groan as his body convulsed, limbs jerking and tail thrashing. Leopardstar watched, sickened, and yet hope sparked afresh in her chest as Tigerstar fell still. Was he dead? What about his nine lives? She supposed it was possible that StarClan had refused to reward a cat this cruel with the true mark of Clan leadership. . . . But then the wounded tom convulsed again, yowling with rage, and then fell still, all the time the blood flowing from his wounds like water. He jerked again, and Leopardstar realized, with a sense of dread, that he was losing life after life. She watched as another spasm seized the dark warrior's body. His claws tore up clumps of grass in his agony as his screeches turned from fury to terror.

She grimaced. No cat should die like this. And yet Tigerstar's death would mean RiverClan was free. Leopardstar wanted it to happen. She glanced at the sky. *Forgive me, StarClan.* Tigerstar's warriors were breaking ranks now, some of them turning to flee the hollow. Even WindClan's warriors had started to back away; Tallstar had to order them to hold the line.

Leopardstar glanced at her own warriors. Blackclaw looked stiff with shock. Vixenleap and Voleclaw were trembling, while Sedgecreek and Reedtail had moved in front of the apprentices, trying to block their view of the grisly scene. She wouldn't blame them for running. She'd proved over and over that she could not protect them. But none tried to leave. They were staying with her. Her heart ached with gratitude.

Tigerstar was panting now, the fight for his life draining his last drop of energy. And yet hatred still blazed in his eyes, sparking there until his body gave one last jerk and lay still.

He was dead. Grief unwound like twisted moss in Leopardstar's chest, filling it until she could hardly breathe. Not just for Tigerstar's death, but for all the lives he'd destroyed in his short time in the forest. Why had StarClan ever let him be born?

Scourge was still facing Firestar, and, behind him, the cats of BloodClan moved forward as if they were about to attack. Leopardstar flexed her claws. Which side would her warriors fight on now? Who was the greatest threat?

Scourge had hardly looked at Tigerstar as he'd died. His eyes were cold now as he looked at Firestar. "You see what happens to cats who defy BloodClan?" he warned calmly. "Your friend here"—he gave a contemptuous flick of his tail toward Tigerstar's body—"thought he could control us. He was wrong."

"We don't want to control you," Firestar mewed. "All we want is to lead our lives in peace. We're sorry that Tigerstar brought you here with lies. Please feel free to hunt before you go home."

Leopardstar blinked at Firestar. Was he really so naive? Scourge had seen what the forest and river had to offer. And he'd killed the most powerful warrior in the forest with a single blow. Did Firestar really think Scourge would walk away? Had watching Tigerstar's hunger for power taught the ThunderClan leader nothing?

"Go home?" Scourge's words didn't surprise her, and yet they still filled her with dread. The kittypet's eyes were filled with scorn. "We're not going anywhere, forest fool. In the town where we come from, there are many, many cats, and live prey is scarce. Here in the forest, we won't need to depend on Twoleg rubbish for our food." He looked around at the warriors still left in the clearing. "We're taking over this territory now," he mewed. "I shall rule the forest as well as the town.

But I understand that you may need some time to reflect on this. You have three days to leave—or meet my Clan in battle. I shall wait for your decision at dawn on the fourth day."

In the days that followed, Leopardstar focused on feeding her Clan. The ShadowClan cats who hadn't fled after Scourge had killed Tigerstar had followed her home like lost kits. Boulder had come too, and Darkstripe. Even Blackfoot dipped his head to her now. She only wished that Mistyfoot, Stormpaw, and Featherpaw might return home, but they had chosen to remain with ThunderClan ever since Firestar had helped to free them from Tigerstar's prison. She didn't trust the former ShadowClan cats enough to let them stay in the RiverClan camp with the elders and apprentices. And there was no way she was letting a ShadowClan cat sleep anywhere near the nursery. Instead, she'd left warriors to guard the island, with Mudfur to take care of Skyheart, and brought the rest of RiverClan with the ShadowClan warriors to the Bone-hill clearing. They could make camp there until she'd decided what to do next.

The river, at least, had thawed. It was a blessing from StarClan now that she had ShadowClan as well as RiverClan mouths to feed and was wary of sending patrols to the pine forest in case they ran into Scourge's cats. But she wasn't sure what to do. There was still a day to go until Scourge would demand a response to his ultimatum. She barely slept, and it was hard to swallow prey. She'd brought her Clan to this; now she must decide whether they should stay and face Scourge or leave and look for a new home beyond Highstones. Would Scourge ever allow them to stay peacefully by the river? She wanted to believe so, but she knew it was probably expecting too much from the violent rogue.

Now, as dawn lit the sky, Leopardstar lay beside the Bonehill. She'd grown used to the stench of it. She should dismantle it, but why bother if they were going to leave? Stonefur should be organizing the patrols for the day. But Stonefur wasn't here. He'd never be here again. Blackfoot moved behind her, picking bones from the pile and dropping them into the river to be swept away.

Darkstripe was watching him, scorn glittering in his eyes. "Why get rid of them when it took so long to collect them?" he scoffed.

Blackfoot eyed him resentfully. "What true warrior would collect crow-food?"

Loudbelly crossed the clearing and dipped his head as he neared Leopardstar. "Should I take Pikepaw out for training?"

She blinked at him. "I guess," she mewed.

"He should practice fighting skills," Loudbelly mewed. "All the apprentices should."

She met his gaze, fear moving in her belly. "Why? Do you think they'd stand a chance against BloodClan? They'd be ripped to pieces."

"They should be allowed a chance to try." Loudbelly's tail swished slowly behind him.

His courage touched her, but was he really willing to sacrifice his apprentice?

But why argue? "Train them all," she told him. They might as well stay busy.

As he turned away, she saw Mudfur. Her father was crossing the clearing, his eyes dark with worry. Had something else happened?

She sat up. It took every shred of her energy, as though the air were made of water. "Is Skyheart okay?" Her kits were due any day.

"She's fine."

Leopardstar was relieved. But the relief didn't last long. Anxiety flooded back as Mudfur looked at her expectantly.

"Have you decided?" he asked.

"There's nothing for me to decide," she answered. "Scourge gave his ultimatum to Firestar and Tallstar."

"And you think it doesn't affect us?" Mudfur looked unconvinced.

"We were Tigerstar's allies," she mewed. "Scourge might leave the river to us. He might just want the forest and moor."

"Do you believe that?" Mudfur stared at her.

Her shoulders drooped. "No, not really. But I don't know what else to do. We can't defeat him. We can't leave." How could RiverClan travel with a queen so close to kitting?

"So we sit here and wait for him to drive us out?" Mudfur pressed.

She stared at him, not knowing what to say.

"You're going to save the Clans," he mewed.

He must be bee-brained. "How many times do I have to fail before you stop believing that?" she mewed bitterly.

"I don't know why you don't believe it anymore." Mudfur's gaze grew urgent. "It's still true." .

"Look around you." She swept her tail around the clearing. ShadowClan cats sat hopelessly around the edge while River-Clan's warriors wove new nests they'd probably never sleep in.

He thrust his muzzle closer. "The Clans have never needed saving more."

"And you think I'm the cat to do it." She snorted. "Go talk to Firestar. He's the one you should be pinning your hopes on. He's a *true* warrior. You saw him face Tigerstar and Scourge. Nothing scares him. Let him save the Clans."

"He can't do it without you," Mudfur mewed. "*You* should be talking to him, not me."

"Why would he listen to me?" Leopardstar growled. "I'm Tigerstar's ally, remember? As far as he's concerned, I'm the traitor to the Clans, not their savior."

"He needs you," Mudfur mewed. "He needs all the help he can get. Look!" He nodded toward Blackfoot. "You have more warriors now than ever. Use them. Tell them to fight. They'll listen to you."

"They're fools if they do," she grunted.

Anger flared suddenly in Mudfur's eyes. "You are a good leader," he growled. "No cat has worked harder than you to make RiverClan strong."

"I've destroyed it."

"You've made mistakes," he conceded. "But it was Tigerstar who hurt us, not you. You only ever tried to protect your Clanmates."

"I didn't protect Stonefur."

Frustration flashed in his gaze. "Stop feeling sorry for yourself and do something!" he spat. "You can't change the past. But you can change the future. You can save the Clans, and you *will*. You're strong and smart, and these cats decided to follow you, even after everything that's happened. They're looking to you to protect them. You can't let them down, not after everything they've been through. You owe them one last fight."

Leopardstar looked at him. *One last fight*. Was he right? Her heart seemed to quicken for the first time in days. She gazed across the clearing. Heavystep had moved scattered bones away from a patch of grass and was demonstrating a battle crouch to Dawnpaw. Ottersplash, her pelt still wet from the river, was carrying a trout toward Shadepelt. Vixenleap was plucking reeds for Mosspelt to weave into a nest. While she was lying here, despairing, her Clanmates were getting on with the duties they'd carried out for moons, trusting that RiverClan would go on and that, whatever happened, they would still be warriors. She straightened. "Do you really think I can save the Clans?" she asked Mudfur.

"You will make the difference between Firestar winning the battle with BloodClan or losing it."

"Is it worth the risk?"

"What do you think?"

Her heart ached at the thought of Primrosepaw or any of the other apprentices facing a BloodClan rogue. But did she have the right to stop her—to stop any of her Clanmates—from living as true warriors? "I think it's dangerous." As she spoke, she saw a familiar orange pelt. She lifted her muzzle. Firestar was crossing the clearing, heading toward her. "But," she mewed to Mudfur, getting to her paws, "I think we have to fight."

CHAPTER 34

Sunningrocks shone in the weak leaf-bare sun. Leopardstar waited at the edge. The conversation with Firestar had gone well. She'd agreed to become part of LionClan and fight BloodClan. And Firestar had given her permission to be here. She looked at the puddles now, pooling in the dips on the wide stretch of stone. Would RiverClan ever own this stretch of territory again? Would they even own the river after the battle tomorrow?

Leopardstar lifted her chin. She had to believe they would, or why risk her warriors?

The brambles—no more than a tangle of bare branches—rattled. Leopardstar got to her paws as she saw a familiar blue-gray pelt slide between them. The cat's gaze, so much like Stonefur's, made guilt open like a wound in her chest.

Mistyfoot padded across the stone.

Leopardstar dipped her head as she neared. "Thank you for coming," she mewed. She pressed her paws against the stone. She must accept whatever Mistyfoot had to say, no matter how harsh.

Mistyfoot's eyes shimmered, but there was no reproach their icy-blue depths. "Firestar says you're going to fight with us."

Us. Did Mistyfoot see herself as part of ThunderClan now? Leopardstar pushed away regret. She couldn't blame the gray warrior for her choice.

"RiverClan will face BloodClan beside ThunderClan and WindClan," she mewed.

"Tigerstar would never have agreed to support Firestar," Mistyfoot mewed.

"Tigerstar's dead." Leopardstar swished her tail.

"Are you leader of TigerClan now?"

"There is no TigerClan," she mewed.

"But ShadowClan warriors are still on RiverClan land."

"I'm giving them shelter. While Scourge is in the forest, they have nowhere else to go." Leopardstar wondered when she'd stopped thinking of the ShadowClan cats as Clanmates and started thinking of them as refugees. Perhaps she'd never truly thought of them as Clanmates. "I have a responsibility to them. They were victims of Tigerstar, just as I was."

"Victims?" Mistyfoot's gaze hardened. "You didn't seem much like a victim while we were being held captive."

Leopardstar looked at her paws. "How are Featherpaw and Stormpaw?" she mewed quietly.

"They're well," Mistyfoot mewed. "ThunderClan is taking care of them. They have new mentors."

The words felt like claws in Leopardstar's belly. They had *ThunderClan* mentors. "Does that mean they're never coming home?"

"Are you surprised?"

"They're RiverClan."

"I wished you'd believed that a quarter moon ago." There was bitterness in Mistyfoot's mew.

"I believe it now."

Mistyfoot gazed at her, sadness rounding her eyes. Was she thinking about Stonefur? Leopardstar's change of heart had come too late for him.

"I'm sorry." Leopardstar lifted her muzzle and met Mistyfoot's gaze. "I was wrong to make RiverClan part of TigerClan. I should have seen that Tigerstar was greedy only for power. As soon as I saw he was a threat, I should have stood up to him. I should have protected you." Her mew cracked, but Mistyfoot only stared back at her sadly. "It's my fault Stonefur died." Leopardstar forced herself to go on. "I will never forgive myself. I don't know now how I could have doubted him. I don't know how I doubted any of my Clanmates, no matter their blood. None of you ever showed disloyalty. You loved RiverClan as much as I did. But I changed RiverClan into something no warrior could love." She stretched her muzzle forward. "Now I'm going to change it back. I'm going to rebuild it."

Mistyfoot looked away. "What does that mean to me, or to Stonefur, or to Featherpaw and Stormpaw? We have a new Clan now. ThunderClan has accepted us completely. They don't care about our blood. They care only that we are willing to hunt and fight for our Clanmates."

"I understand." Leopardstar fluffed out her fur. "But I still have to ask this. . . ." She took a breath. "If we survive the battle tomorrow, I would like you to come home and help me rebuild."

Mistyfoot's eyes betrayed nothing.

"I want you to be my deputy." Leopardstar looked at her earnestly. "I can't think of a better cat to help me make River-Clan what it was always meant to be."

Mistyfoot frowned. "Would you listen to me?"

"Yes."

"You ignored Stonefur's warnings."

"I was wrong. I've learned from it. I've learned from everything that's happened. I will let you advise me. You can be my conscience when I am uncertain."

Mistyfoot didn't move. Leopardstar held her breath as, behind her, starlings gossiped and the river gurgled below.

At last, Mistyfoot's tail twitched. "I can't give you an answer now."

"Take all the time you need." Leopardstar blinked at her hopefully. She couldn't imagine RiverClan without Mistyfoot, Featherpaw, and Stormpaw, and she knew that the wounds she'd inflicted on her Clanmates would never fully heal unless their lost Clanmates returned.

"I should go." Mistyfoot turned away.

"I hope, one day, you'll be able to forgive me," Leopardstar mewed after her. She watched the gray she-cat pad toward the trees, her heart aching for all she had lost.

As she padded to the edge of Sunningrocks, preparing to scramble down to the riverbank, a mew called from behind. "Leopardstar!"

Her heart quickened. "Mistyfoot?" Why was the gray she-cat calling her back? Was there something she'd forgotten to say?

Leopardstar turned back toward the trees and met Misty-foot hurrying toward her.

"I'll do it." Mistyfoot's eyes were shining. "I love my Clan, in spite of it all. I'll help you rebuild RiverClan."

"You'll join us again?" A rush of joy surged through Leopardstar's chest.

"Yes, as deputy." Mistyfoot's tail was quivering. "I'll never be a ThunderClan cat, not truly. If we survive the battle, I'll come home."

"We'll make RiverClan the Clan it always should have been," Leopardstar mewed. Hope was fizzing through every hair on her pelt.

Mistyfoot's eyes darkened. "But first we must win the battle against BloodClan."

CHAPTER 35

Leopardstar paused at the edge of the river and watched the Shadow-Clan warriors cross, making sure they were safe. They were still not strong swimmers, but this was the quickest way to the meeting place where Firestar and ThunderClan would be waiting. This would be the last time ShadowClan and River-Clan would fight together. If the battle was won, Blackfoot would take his warriors back to the pine forest. If it was lost, there would be no more battles to fight.

Her RiverClan warriors were already pacing the shore like shadows in the half-light, their pelts dripping. The first pale streaks of dawn were coloring the sky, painting it red and gold beyond the forest.

Blackfoot waded out of the water, Runningnose, Little-cloud, and Russetfur at his heels. Boulder followed close behind. The ShadowClan medicine cat was carrying a large leaf wrap between his jaws, stuffed with herbs and cobwebs he might need to treat the wounded. Mudfur was already on the shore, his leaf wrap open as he checked that none of his supplies had been washed away.

As the last of ShadowClan climbed onto the shore, Leopardstar surveyed the battle patrol. They were sleek and well-fed. She knew that whatever happened today, they would fight with their last drop of energy. And they would obey her orders without question. During the last-minute training, hunting, and preparations for battle, no cat had second-guessed her or hesitated to follow her command. Part of her felt that she did not deserve the respect they showed her, but she was determined to earn it now and forever, over and over, every day she was leader of RiverClan.

"You will stand with me today as the courageous warriors you have always been," she yowled. Their gazes lifted toward her, and she saw fear there. Every cat knew that this battle would be harder than any they'd ever fought. She puffed out her chest. "We have traveled a difficult path together. Tigerstar persuaded us to do things no warrior should ever do. I'm sorry I didn't protect you from him. I believed he would make our Clans stronger. I believed he would make every Clan in the forest stronger. But he only ever used your loyalty and your courage and your pride to make himself more powerful."

Blackclaw whisked his tail. Loudbelly's pelt rippled along his spine as she went on.

"It is not your fault. I should have stood up to him. I should have realized what he was doing. I should have tried to stop him. I'm sorry that I didn't. I let you all down, and that knowledge will stay with me, even in StarClan."

She steadied her breath. "But my failure has made me stronger. Never again will I believe that cruelty is the path to strength, or that fear can lead to any change worth having. If our Clans are to be better Clans, they must be good and kind and fair. That is the only true strength, and I promise I will never again forget it."

She met Blackfoot's gaze. "ShadowClan will be strong again," she mewed. "And so will RiverClan. We will rebuild our Clans and be proud once again to belong to them. They will become stronger Clans, and smarter and more just than ever before. Clans that will never be beaten by rogues like BloodClan." She lifted her tail. "Today we show Scourge what true warriors are capable of. Today we drive cruelty and viciousness from our borders. Today . . ." She looked around the ranks of hopeful faces. "Today we will *win!*"

Satisfaction washed over her pelt as her warriors cheered, their tails lashing with determination.

If our Clans are to be better Clans, they must be good and kind and fair. She stiffened as she realized that the Clan she'd described—the Clan she dreamed of—had existed once already. It was the RiverClan of her kithood: the Clan that had raised her. She'd tried so hard to reshape it into something stronger and better, only to discover that it was already perfect. She'd never had to save RiverClan after all. She'd only had to learn its true value.

Mudfur glanced up the slope, his gaze sharpening. What had he seen? Leopardstar jerked her muzzle around. Firestar was standing at the top of the slope. He was waiting for them. In the dawn sunshine, his orange pelt looked like flame against the forest green.

She looked around at her warriors, her heart pounding. "Ready?"

"Ready!"

"Ready!"

Their mews rose above the swishing of the river and the chattering of the birds. Leopardstar's pelt bristled with determination as she turned and led her warriors up the slope, the bushes sweeping her flank.

At the top, Firestar dipped his head. His warriors were waiting behind him. Mistyfoot hurried from among them to greet Shadepelt and Vixenleap as Leopardstar's patrol fell in beside them.

Firestar met Leopardstar's gaze. "Shall we do this?"

She nodded. "Yes."

As she turned toward Fourtrees, Mudfur called after her. "This is your destiny, Leopardstar." His mew rang in her ears. "Go save RiverClan."

She glanced over her shoulder, her heart aching with love for him and for her Clan. "I will," she promised.

When she'd been a naive kit, she had believed she would save her Clan easily, because of the potential her father had seen in her. Now she realized that she might "save" her Clan only after nearly destroying it. She had been foolish and greedy; she had aligned herself with an evil cat who'd told her only what she wanted to hear. She had caused her Clanmates great pain and even lost some of them forever. But now she recognized what was most important to her: not making RiverClan all-powerful, but ensuring that the Clan she'd been born into would live on forever. That was how she would save RiverClan.

And, as she rushed into battle alongside her Clanmates, she was certain they would succeed.

READ ON FOR AN EXCLUSIVE **WARRIORS** COMIC . . .

CREATED BY
ERIN HUNTER

WRITTEN BY
DAN JOLLEY

ART BY
JAMES L. BARRY

THE PROPHECIES BEGIN
- Into the Wild
- Fire and Ice
- Forest of Secrets
- Rising Storm
- A Dangerous Path
- The Darkest Hour

THE NEW PROPHECY
- Midnight
- Moonrise
- Dawn
- Starlight
- Twilight
- Sunset

POWER OF THREE
- The Sight
- Dark River
- Outcast
- Eclipse
- Long Shadows
- Sunrise

OMEN OF THE STARS
- The Fourth Apprentice
- Fading Echoes
- Night Whispers
- Sign of the Moon
- The Forgotten Warrior
- The Last Hope

DAWN OF THE CLANS
- The Sun Trail
- Thunder Rising
- The First Battle
- The Blazing Star
- A Forest Divided
- Path of Stars

A VISION OF SHADOWS
- The Apprentice's Quest
- Thunder and Shadow
- Shattered Sky
- Darkest Night
- River of Fire
- The Raging Storm

HARPER
An Imprint of HarperCollinsPublishers

warriorcats.com